Duel in the Dark

Blood on the Stars I

D1569418

Jay Allan

system 7
publishing

Also By Jay Allan

Marines (Crimson Worlds I)
The Cost of Victory (Crimson Worlds II)
A Little Rebellion (Crimson Worlds III)
The First Imperium (Crimson Worlds IV)
The Line Must Hold (Crimson Worlds V)
To Hell's Heart (Crimson Worlds VI)
The Shadow Legions(Crimson Worlds VII)
Even Legends Die (Crimson Worlds VIII)
The Fall (Crimson Worlds IX)
War Stories (Crimson World Prequels)
MERCS (Successors I)
The Prisoner of Eldaron (Successors II)
Into the Darkness (Refugees I)
Shadows of the Gods (Refugees II)
Revenge of the Ancients (Refugees III)
Winds of Vengeance (Refugees IV)
Shadow of Empire (Far Stars I)
Enemy in the Dark (Far Stars II)
Funeral Games (Far Stars III)
Blackhawk (Far Stars Legends I)
The Dragon's Banner
Gehenna Dawn (Portal Wars I)
The Ten Thousand (Portal Wars II)
Homefront (Portal Wars III)

www.jayallanbooks.com
www.bloodonthestars.com
www.wolfsclaw.com
www.crimsonworlds.com

Duel in the Dark

Duel in the Dark is a work of fiction. All names, characters, incidents, and locations are fictitious. Any resemblance to actual persons, living or dead, events or places is entirely coincidental.

ISBN: 978-0692803417

Chapter One

Excerpt from Kimball's The Rise and Fall of Civilization

The Cataclysm wasn't a single event, and it didn't take place all at once. Wars, corruption, rogue politicians, complacent populations...all played their part in the final catastrophe. But when the end came, it came quickly. The inner worlds—those closest to Earth, the oldest and richest—fell the farthest and the fastest. Most of them are lifeless ruins today, surrounding the haunted remains of mankind's birthplace.

It was out on the fringes that some semblance of civilization survived, and it was there that mankind began to rebuild. The first century AC was dominated by the growth of individual worlds that had preserved at least some level of the earlier technology. These planets were able to grow quickly into interstellar nations, using their science to entice—or coerce—their neighbors to join them.

The rising nations grew along the surviving Schwerin transit lines. Where the transwarp links still existed, communications, trade—and war—could move from system to system. Little is known of the worlds whose transwarp lines were destroyed in the Cataclysm, save for the occasional radio signal attesting that some people survive there, outside the functional transport system. How many of those planets have slid fully into barbarism, or extinction, and how many continue to rebuild, to grow, trapped in their solar systems, remains a mystery.

Mankind's rise from the Cataclysm has been as violent and warlike as his slide into destruction. There are a few bright spots, like the Confederation, which offers some level of freedom to its inhabitants. But most humans who survive in the centuries after the Cataclysm live under despots and oligarchies, and few know any level of liberty. And everywhere, the nascent nations are at war, struggling for worlds, power, tech...pushing ever closer back to the brink.

AS Vindictus
Approaching Heliopolis, Steggus II
Alliance Year 58 (307 AC)

Vindictus shook hard, the bridge lights flickering for an instant.

Katrine Rigellus stared straight ahead, paying no mind to the beating her ship was taking. At least none that her crew could see.

Another hit, a bad one this time...

She could imagine the impact on her ship's hull, the massive heat from the deadly blast, *Vindictus's* armor melting, buckling, space ripping into the compromised compartments below. Men and women dying, incinerated by the heat of the plasmas or sucked out into space through great rents in the hull.

The Helian primary batteries were focused plasma beams, highly advanced weapons, well beyond standard Alliance technology. Gaining access to the enemy's science would be as great a spoil as adding a new highly industrialized world to the Alliance. It was enough reason alone to fight this war. But before the fruits of victory could be gathered, the Alliance's warriors would have to run the gauntlet, drive straight into the teeth of the enemy's deadly weapons and win the victory.

Kat's body was tense. She could feel the effects of the stimulant she'd taken before the fighting began, the edginess, the increased awareness. She'd been in battle before, many times, and it was always the same. The almost electric feeling as her mind raced, analyzing each bit of information, constantly moving and reprioritizing her focus.

There was something else there too, a feeling that lurked below the surface, nagging at her but never taking control. It was one she pushed back against, fought. It had always been there, but it had grown stronger over the years, intensifying with each promotion, each new mission. Was it fear? Alliance officers weren't supposed to feel fear. Or at least they weren't supposed to admit it, even to themselves. But if it was fear, it was of failure, not of danger. Kat was ready to die in battle if her time came—it was the way of things—but the thought of failure, of returning home in disgrace, was too terrible to imagine.

The battle had been fierce, the resistance far stronger than the intel reports had suggested. That was no surprise to Kat. She tended to have little regard for intelligence officers, less even than was common among the Alliance military in general. She suspected the image of fearless operatives risking their lives on missions to gain priceless information was almost a complete fabrication, an illusion designed to add nobility to a bunch of deck jockeys who spent their time paying off informants and analyzing communications intercepts, while Palatian men and women like Kat were on the front lines, fighting like honest warriors. The Alliance was a martial society through and through, and the Palatians considered themselves the greatest fighters in the galaxy. As far as Kat was concerned, skulking around in the shadows was beneath the dignity of a true warrior.

Vindictus was in the vanguard of the invasion, tasked along with her fellow lead vessels with smashing the Helian orbital defenses and securing the way for the troopships to land on the planet. It was a position of honor, one she knew she should regard that way. But she had seventeen dead on *Vindictus* already. She did her duty, always—and she would give her life in the service if that was her fate—but as she'd grown older and advanced in rank she'd found herself struggling more with watching the men and women under her command die. She kept her feelings to herself, of course. Such thoughts would be deemed signs of weakness, perhaps enough to derail a career that had, to date, been exemplary and unspotted. Death in battle was the highest honor a Palatian could achieve, and there was no place in the service for differing points of view.

"Engineering reports significant damage to the outer compartments, Commander, but our major systems remain fully-functional. Several overloads, but all disabled systems have been rerouted."

Katrine snapped her head toward her tactical operations officer. Tylian Wentus was *Vindictus's* third-in-command, and Kat's main link to what was happening on her ship. Alliance protocols were heavily based on the chain of command, and it was considered beneath a ship commander to issue orders directly, except in the direst emergencies. She tended to think such practices were pure idiocy, but she was a creature of duty, and it wasn't her place to question things.

"Very well, Optiomagis. Maintain course and thrust."

"Yes, Commander." Wentus's tone was as sharp and crisp as her own.

Kat turned back toward the main display. She knew her officer well. Very well. They'd even engaged in a brief fling during their Academy days. It had been little more than recreation, and certainly nothing she'd consider resuming now that he was under her command. Alliance society tended to frown on romantic relationships and attachments, viewing them as distractions from duty, and instead encouraged casual affairs. Sex had its place for relaxation and stress relief between campaigns—and, of course, for reproduction with genetically-compatible partners—but it had little place on a ship at war. And petty sentiments had none. Not on a warship. Not anywhere in Alliance society.

Wentus's service had been exemplary since he'd been assigned to *Vindictus* half a year before, but Kat still wondered if her tactical officer harbored any resentments. They'd graduated in the same class, but Wentus came from normal Citizen stock, while her family was Patrician. Kat's father had been a hero, killed heroically in battle, while Wentus's parents had been journeyman officers who had served well but achieved little distinction. The divergence in their career trajectories had been entirely predictable, and while Kat knew she had earned every promotion and decoration she had received, she questioned how her old lover saw it from his lower position on the chain of command.

Those thoughts were all secondary, drifting through the back of her mind. Her focus on the battle was unbroken, her eyes staring right at the main display when the icon representing *Draco* winked out of existence.

Commander Ellus…his entire crew…

Her eyes were locked on the display. *Draco* had been one of the lead ships, about fifty thousand kilometers ahead of *Vindictus*. It had been hit several times on the approach, and the records showed it had sustained moderate damage in the long-range missile exchanges, but Kat was stunned the big capital ship had been destroyed already. Her fingers moved over her controls, pulling up the last data transmitted from the stricken vessel. It confirmed her suspicions. Something powerful had hit the battleship. Something unexpected, a weapon strong enough to destroy a capital ship with one shot.

So much for the intelligence services…

The Helians were well known for their advanced technology. Perhaps they had a new weapon, something they'd kept secret. If so, the entire Alliance fleet was in danger.

"Get me Optiomagis Hyllus." Hyllus was her fighter commander. He and his four squadrons had launched ten minutes earlier, and they were deployed around *Vindictus* in a standard defensive formation. She knew she probably should have passed the order through Wentus, but she had a bad feeling about what was going on, and she intended to stay on top of it.

"Optiomagis Hyllus on your com line, Commander."

"Optio, I want you to move your squadrons forward. Scout out the far side of the second moon, and report back immediately."

"All squadrons, Commander?"

"Yes, Optio, all squadrons. Now."

"Yes, Commander." Hyllus's response was hard, disciplined, but she caught a hint of surprise too. Kat knew the chance she was taking. Without her fighters, or at least a few squadrons on defensive patrol, her ship would be vulnerable to enemy sorties. The Helians hadn't shown so much as a single interceptor yet, but she knew that was only a matter of time. The intelligence reports suggested there were more than three hundred fighters in the orbital forts, and Kat suspected the true number was close to double that.

But there's something beyond that moon…

"Get me Commander Quellus." Her orders to her fighter groups had come close to exceeding her authority, an act of instinct and not of procedure. That fact hadn't stopped her, and it didn't compel her to cancel the orders. But she had to report it to the commander of the advance guard.

"Commander-Altum Quellus on your com."

"Sir, I believe we have detected something behind…"

She twisted to the side and pulled off her headset as a loud screeching sound blared through the speakers. Her eyes darted up to the main display, but in her gut she knew what had happened.

She stared at the screen, at the empty spot where Quellus's flagship had been. She paused, just for an instant. Then she sprang into action, instinct taking over.

"All fighter squadrons, full thrust. Move around the moon, and engage any enemy vessels or installations." She snapped the order toward Wentus, and before he'd even acknowledged, she was crouched over her small workstation, running a calculation.

She looked up a few seconds later. "Engine room, full thrust now, course 134-67 mark 3.6." Her eyes darted back to the operations officer, catching a slight, surprised hesitation. "Now!" she snapped. "Get us around the far side of that moon!"

She reached down, grabbing her restraints and clicking them into place. The rest of the bridge officers were doing the same. Full thrust meant a rough ride, heavy g-forces, especially with the radical course change. But Kat knew she had to get around the moon, and she had to do it from the far side. Before the rest of the fleet advanced into a deathtrap.

I just hope we're in time…

*   *   *

"*Julianus* is gone too, Commander." Wentus was having trouble hiding the concern in his voice. *Julianus* was the fourth Alliance battleship destroyed. There was definitely some kind of weapon behind the moon.

No, a superweapon…

Vindictus's fighters had whipped around a few minutes before, but they were cut off from direct communications. She'd had a passing hope that Hyllus would send one of his birds back with a report, but she knew it wasn't possible. The squadrons had been moving fast, and it would take at least five minutes for one to reverse course and reach clear line of sight to make a transmission—especially since *Vindictus* was blasting full toward the other side. Kat wouldn't know what she was facing until her ship came around the other side of the moon. In three minutes.

She sucked in a deep breath, a struggle at the high g's her ship was pulling. She'd had years of training and experience, but she'd never quite gotten used to being squashed as her ship raced to battle.

"Bring us into orbit, Optio. Snap us around with a gravity assist. I want as much velocity as we can get as we come to bear."

"Yes, Commander. Adjusting course and thrust."

Kat nodded, staring ahead, trying to ignore the knot in her gut. This wasn't her first time leading *Vindictus* into battle, certainly, but for the first time she had a feeling the result of the entire battle rested on her actions.

She knew she was acting on her own, without authorization, without even coordinating with the other ships of the advance guard. But there was no choice, no time to waste. There were almost a dozen battleships ahead of *Vindictus*, and they were heading directly into the enemy kill zone, their velocities too high to allow a course change in time. If she didn't succeed, the Helians would hand the Alliance the worst defeat in its sixty-year history.

"Ninety seconds, Commander."

Kat sat still, waiting. She could see the moon on the scanner, close now, *Vindictus* swinging around barely five hundred kilometers from the surface. The grav assist was a difficult maneuver, especially when it took a ship this close, but she was confident her people could handle it.

"All weapons, prepare to fire as soon as we come around…" She didn't have a target yet, but she was confident there would be one. And whatever it was, it had to be destroyed.

"All primary batteries charged and ready to fire, Commander. Torpedo tubes loaded and armed."

Her eyes darted back to the main screen. The icons representing the fleet were still there, but they had hazy circles around them, the computer's way of indicating the information displayed was historical, that no new scanning data was coming in. The moon was between *Vindictus* and her fellow Alliance vessels. She and her people were on their own.

"One minute."

The bridge was silent. Kat knew her people knew what to do. They were veterans, most of them at least. And the few newbs on board were still trained Alliance warriors, raised since birth to serve and graduates of the harshest training program ever devised. They would do whatever was necessary. She was sure of that.

"Thirty seconds."

Kat took a deep breath, centering herself. She pushed the emotions aside, banishing fear, worry, regret, to the depths of her mind. A familiar coldness flooded through her, her focus intensifying. She was ready. Ready to face whatever was waiting for her ship behind the moon.

"Coming around now, Commander."

Her eyes were already on the screen. There was a delay, no more than a few seconds, while new scanner data came in, and the computer updated the display. And when it did, she almost gasped.

What the hell is that?

It was a construct of some kind, over four kilometers in length, hovering in high orbit around the moon. Even looking at the sanitized icons displayed on the screen, she could feel the menace of it. And around it, standing like a pair of sentinels, floated two of the biggest orbital fortresses she had ever seen.

Fighters were pouring out of the fortresses, engaging her own squadrons. Her people were fighting hard, but they were outnumbered four or five to one.

Retreat...it's the only choice...

Vindictus couldn't defeat the heavily-armed platforms. It would take half the fleet to destroy those fortresses. And her fighters could only hold so long against the massive cloud of enemy interceptors.

Then she saw the energy spike, the strange construct firing again, a massive burst of laser light, stronger than any she'd encountered before. Any she'd heard of before. It could only be one thing.

Bomb-pumped lasers.

The Alliance had been pursuing the technology for years, the use of controlled nuclear detonations to power extremely strong laser blasts, but it had never managed to get the system to work. Apparently, the Helians had...

She felt the tension in her body. Every military doctrine she knew, all her training told her *Vindictus* couldn't face the two giant fortresses, not without help. She had to pull back, warn the fleet.

No...you can't wait.

The Alliance fleet had blundered into a trap. Alliance arms had enjoyed half a century of unparalleled success, and with victory had come arrogance. They had viewed the Helians as a lesser foe, one they could easily overwhelm.

And now half the fleet is headed into a deathtrap...

"Increase reactor to one hundred ten percent. All power to thrusters."

"Commander?" Wentus sounded confused.

"We're going in, Optiomagis. We're going straight for that space-cursed thing, and we're going to blow it to scrap."

"What about the fortresses?"

"Damned the fortresses! Forward...full power!"

Her eyes darted to the sides, to the two red circles on the screen, the orbital platforms that were going to blow her ship to scrap.

Let them do their worst…but we're going to destroy that blasted gun.

Chapter Two

Lecture to First Year Cadets, Confederation Naval Academy, 286 AC

The War of Shame. Remember that name, all of you. Your texts will refer to it as the First Confederation-Union War, but that sterile designation is wholly inadequate, stripped of the true meaning, the grim reality. For it is only by the grace of fortune that we are here today, that our Confederation survived that disastrous conflict...and that we were afforded a chance at redemption, at an opportunity to regain our honor.

It is to that terrible struggle that we owe the navy you are privileged to serve, for from the ashes of defeat rose a new resolve, and a military force dedicated to one ideal, without question and above all others. Never again. Never again would we accept defeat, see our fellow citizens conquered, enslaved, by an enemy.

We will review the campaigns of the Second Confederation-Union War later in the semester, the glorious campaigns of Admiral Rance Barron and his colleagues, the victories that gave us back our pride. But we start now with ignominy, with defeat, so that you may understand what you truly fight for, and never forget that the Confederation exists only as long as we have the strength to defend it.

CFS Dauntless
340 Million Kilometers from Sentinel Three
Confederation-Union Border
307 AC

Tyler Barron stared at the three-dimensional display in the center of *Dauntless's* control room. The complex holographic system, colloquially called the "tank," was an expensive luxury. The Union—and most of the other interstellar nations that had formed in the centuries since the Cataclysm—got along fine with two-dimensional screens that simply used small numerals to show the Z coordinate. But the Confederation was the richest of the powers, with a per capita income three times that of the Union, and its politicians vastly preferred bringing home contracts for sophisticated holographic displays than orders for normal screens costing one fiftieth as much. So *Dauntless* and her sister ships in the fleet were equipped with the sophisticated tanks.

Barron felt an uncomfortable sensation, one that had dogged him for weeks now, a feeling of eerie silence. Space, of course, was always soundless, but what troubled him was more than literal quiet. It was the crew, their demeanor, the lack of conversation, even in the wardrooms. The reduced amount of recreation, the somber, hushed conversation in the corridors. His people were tense, and it was showing in all kinds of ways a watchful captain could see. He knew that was normal, to a point. But he also realized that at some point, the tension would affect *Dauntless's* readiness.

Dauntless had been on patrol for almost nine months now, and the pressure had built steadily, wearing hard on his crew. He'd tried to keep formal alerts to a minimum, an effort to control the stress levels as much as anything else, to keep his people as rested as possible. But it was a losing fight. They all knew why they were there, and for all their training and courage, they were afraid. Even without the yellow or red warning lamps lit, they all knew the call to battlestations could come at any moment.

War was coming. They'd all heard about it for years now. Vague warnings at first, then firmer ones, reports from the intelligence services of Union buildups, force movements. Finally, the Code Black alert had gone out, a designation that had one meaning. Invasion imminent.

But the invasion *hadn't* been imminent. It had been almost a year, and the frontier had been quiet. The intel reports were still coming hard and fast, manifests showing fleets of new Union warships pouring from shipyards, moving toward forward bases behind the border. But they hadn't attacked. Not yet.

Barron looked around *Dauntless's* bridge, feeling a twinge of guilt as he watched his officers at work. They were here to patrol the frontier, and to report if—when—the enemy came streaming across the border. It was a dangerous job, suicidal, many would say. The primary mission was to send off a warning, along with as much data on the invasion force as possible. Survival was decidedly a secondary prospect, and an unlikely one at that. And that weighed heavily on Barron, for reasons that went far beyond personal fear.

His people were here because of him, because he had rebelled at the preferential treatment he'd experienced his whole life, the assignments to rear areas, the efforts by the admiralty to keep him safe even as he served in the fleet. He'd practically demanded the frontier posting, going so far as to threaten to resign his commission if his request was denied.

And now, more than nine hundred officers and spacers face desperate danger because you wanted to prove you're more than just Rance Barron's grandson…

Barron shifted slightly in his chair, expending a bit of nervous energy as much as anything else. *Dauntless* had been his for almost a year, and she had spent most of that time on the border, staring into the face of an invasion everyone knew would be massive when it came. He was the youngest captain in the fleet to command a capital ship, and he knew he owed at least some of that to his last name, the one he shared with his famous grandfather.

Barron's own service record had been exemplary. He'd graduated first in his class at the Academy, and his postings as a junior officer had earned him commendations from every commander he had served. But he knew deserving had little to do with his command of *Dauntless*. If his name had been Garibaldi or Elione or Jacarde, respected naval families all, he'd still be a first officer somewhere. There wasn't a doubt in his mind about that. But his name was Barron, and the Barrons were like royalty in the Confederation navy.

"Sentinel Three transmitting security protocols, Captain." Lieutenant Vin Darrow manned *Dauntless*'s communications station.

"Authenticate." Barron was sure the codes would be verified, but the command procedures were clear, and there were no exceptions. Barron agreed with the regs on this one. This close to the enemy on the eve of war, it didn't make sense to take chances.

Darrow paused a few seconds. "Confirmed, sir."

Barron moved his hand toward his own comm unit, flipping up a small cover and punching a series of numbers into the hexadecimal keypad. "Barron, Captain, CFS Dauntless. Transmit priority identification codes now." He pressed his finger against a tiny scanner. It looked like a fingerprint reader, but it was much more. The device also analyzed DNA from a microscopic skin sample it harvested, making it as close to foolproof as Confederation science could manage.

"Identity confirmed, Captain Barron. Transmitting now." The AI's voice sounded almost human, though Barron could pick up on the difference. The tell was the almost overpowering calm of the tone. Barron had confidence in his people and their courage, but no one human sounded *that* relaxed waiting for an invasion.

The fleet was already on wartime protocols, and that meant using the priority codes to confirm the identification of any vessels or installations. It tended toward the cumbersome, but it was worthwhile. In the unlikely event the crew of Sentinel Three were clustered in their control room under the guns of Union commandoes, he needed to know…just as they had to be sure his ship was really *Dauntless*, and that she hadn't fallen under enemy control herself.

The Sentinel stations were the extreme forward vanguard of Confederation defense, positioned mostly in the empty systems between the inhabited space of the two powers. Their primary purpose was to keep an eye on the border and to warn the forces positioned farther back of any incursions. The stations were armed, but no one expected any of them to survive more than a few seconds in battle against a serious invasion fleet.

"Sentinel Three reports all codes confirmed, sir. Beginning data dump now."

"Acknowledged. Relay to my screen after decryption."

Barron glanced over at the lieutenant. Darrow was a good young officer, but he'd had the misfortune of serving under the only Confederation captain ever convicted of treason. Clive Toland's name had become synonymous with treachery when he was caught selling secrets to the Union, and while Darrow had been completely exonerated of any involvement in his commanding officer's betrayal, that kind of mud splattered widely. The gifted comm officer had struggled to find a posting after that, rejected by half a dozen captains before Tyler pulled out the Barron name and threw its protective aura around the grateful lieutenant. Tyler had been angry at the injustice of the whole thing, but there was a more manipulative angle at play as well. He had learned many things from his illustrious grandfather, and how to cultivate loyalty among men and women had been at the top of the list. Vin Darrow did his job as well as any officer in the fleet…but now, he'd jump into the reactor core as well, if Tyler Barron ordered it.

"Sending data stream now."

Barron nodded in the direction of the comm officer. Then his eyes dropped to his own screen.

Dauntless had been in stealth mode, Barron setting his own course as his vessel patrolled the border. There were no orders detailing its route, no records that could be stolen or fall into enemy hands. And without accurate locational data, there was no way for the high command to communicate with its battleship until it showed up at one of the stations. Communiqués intended for Barron, and the members of his crew, were sent in code to the Sentinel outposts, and transmitted when *Dauntless* checked in.

He watched as the batches of data continued to move down the screen, folder after folder of routine dispatches, supply manifests, news updates…and mail. Terabytes and terabytes of mail, the best possible therapy for his crew's strained morale.

"It looks like the enemy will have to wait. It's going to take two weeks just to get through the mail."

A few tentative chuckles broke the bridge's silence. Barron had recently been making an effort to loosen up a little. With limited success. He knew he looked a little like a martinet, a hardcore "by the books" type with a puffed out chest and a raging ego, ready to bust a subordinate for the slightest infraction. But his crew knew him better than that after ten months' service together, and for all Barron was aware they considered him a little stiff in his mannerisms, he knew he had their loyalty…and their true affection too. They had been through a lot together, endured the tension of patrolling the front line.

They should live a week in my shoes, feel what it's like to be the grandson of the great Rance Barron. "Ironheart" Barron, the man who saved the Confederation…

Tyler's grandfather had been more than a hero…to the people of the Confederation he was *the* hero. Tyler had loved the old man for as long as he could remember, and he'd grown up as awed by the great admiral as everyone else. But he had other memories too, fonder ones. Fishing trips and long walks through the woods, days the two had spent together with not a word spoken of battles fought and glorious victories won.

Still, the legend of Admiral Barron had proven to be inescapable, and the family reputation had dogged him from his first day at the Academy, enough to induce him to go by his middle name instead of being the family's fourth Rance to serve the fleet. He couldn't remember a time when he wasn't being rated against the older Barron or when he'd last received praise that didn't compare him in some way, favorable or otherwise, to his grandfather.

Tyler had endured such comparisons since childhood, but they had only become worse after the old man died in the last war, and he passed from living hero to deceased legend. Compliments like, "that was how your grandfather would have done it," had come to grate on him, like an unpleasant squeak. And the worst part was, the frustration seeped into his memories, dulling fond images of a grandfather he'd loved dearly and creating resentments he regretted but felt nevertheless.

Tyler had mourned his grandfather's death even as he endured the increased attention it brought upon him…and he did his best to live up to the pressure to follow in the great man's footsteps. He carried the weight all the more for the loss of the father he had hardly known. Rance III died in a reactor accident years before, when he was still a junior officer, leaving the heavy expectations of an adoring and demanding Confederation on the shoulders of his three-year old son.

It had been a heavy burden for a young child, and for the cadet he became…and it remained so even for a seasoned captain. Ironheart Barron was a tough act to follow, and with war imminent, things had only become more intense.

"Lieutenant Darrow, you may distribute the mail and personal communications to their recipients. And forward housekeeping communication to the appropriate department heads." Barron was a hands on captain, but he didn't feel the need to poke his nose into updated equipment specs and reactor cooling rod process modifications. Rank had its privileges, and one of them was delegating at least some of the boring nonsense to someone else.

"Yes, Captain."

Barron's eyes focused on one of the items addressed to him. Orders.

He moved his hand over the screen, opening the file. He read it carefully, getting about a third of the way down before his eyes darted up with surprise, and he started again, checking a second time to be sure he'd read it correctly.

Dauntless was to proceed to the fleet base on Archellia for rest and refit. After ten months of sneaking around, of waiting for war, his people were being relieved.

But Archellia? That's clear across the Confederation…

He realized then just how mobilized the fleet was, how ready for a war it considered imminent. If Archellia was the nearest base with available capacity to refit a battleship like *Dauntless*, everything the Confederation had that could fly must be clogging the facilities nearer the Union border.

He nodded to himself. Archellia was a few weeks' extra travel, but the trip would be like a vacation itself, without the crushing stress of watching the frontier. And there wasn't a quieter place for his frazzled crew to take their shore leave and prepare for the struggle everyone knew was still coming.

He leaned back and sighed softly. The constant stress had worn him down as much as his people, and his refusal to acknowledge that, to himself or anyone else, made it no less true. It was time. He had demanded a dangerous posting, and he and his people had completed it with distinction. Now they were going home.

He looked around the bridge, his face expressionless for a few seconds as his eyes moved from station to station. Then he decided *Dauntless's* discipline could withstand a smile from her captain, and he grinned widely.

"We're going home," he said, feeling of rush of satisfaction. "We're going to Archellia for refit…and for shore leave."

He held his smile as the bridge officers met his announcement with a round of applause. It wasn't strictly by the book, but Barron didn't care. Not one bit.

Archellia…I can't think of a quieter, more relaxing spot…

Chapter Three

From the Last Testament of Stantus Allius
First Imperator of the Alliance

I leave these words to my peers and countrymen, and to all who have followed me. I, who was born into servitude, who knew the sting of the lash on my bare back, and yet rose to the leadership of my people, lay this sacred burden on all Palatians... to pay forward the debt they owe for freedom, and to secure it for generations to come.

Go forth then, and be always the strongest. Attack before you are attacked. Defeat those who would be your masters. Reduce them to the servants they would make of you. Bring fear to all who would be your enemies. Remember always the mantra, the grim verdict of the universe, that we now adopt as the central tenet of our own Alliance. Vae victis. Woe to the defeated.

Victorum, Alliance Capital City
Astara II, Palatia
Alliance Year 58 (307 AC)

The streets of Victorum were festive, the massive, blocky buildings of the city draped with banners and flags, their broad marble columns and facades polished to blinding white and shiny midnight black. The air was alive, strident chords rising from a seemingly endless procession of marching bands. All the martial brilliance of the Alliance was moving down the Via Magna, to the delight, real or feigned, of the hundreds of thousands present along the line of march.

The day was a special one. Indeed, its like had not been seen for many years. Life in the Alliance was generally a Spartan affair, its culture and economy focused almost entirely on feeding the endless needs of the military machine that formed the centerpiece of its society. Armed strength was almost a religious imperative in the Alliance, and frivolous pursuits were usually sacrificed to the call of war. But the arms being celebrated had just won another great victory, perhaps the most momentous in their history, conquering more neighboring systems, rich prizes that would bolster the strength and power of the Alliance, and launch it once and for all into the ranks of the great powers. That was a cause for celebration, one of the few events worthy of an official holiday, of a break from the endless toil and discipline of daily life in the Alliance. There were speeches and parades, fairs and festivals in every town on Palatia's three continents. And with the fall of night, fireworks and glittering balls would follow the day's reveries.

Commander-Princeps Katrine Rigellus sat quietly and watched the procession go by, rank after rank of stormtroopers clad in their crisp black uniforms, marching perfectly in unison, each step a model of precision.

Just like they were taught to do. Born to do.

The troopers were mostly Probs, natives of Palatia and probationary-citizens of the Alliance. The Probationary-Aspirants who served thirty years—and survived—would retire as full Citizens, their children guaranteed enrollment in their old units, perpetuating a system so successful it had allowed a single planet to field an enormous and extremely effective military, one that had known nearly sixty years of uninterrupted victory. One that had subjugated thirty systems and more than fifteen billion people in just over half a century.

The processions were spectacular, the best ever staged, many were saying, and those in the multitude whispered with joy and pride. The celebration had been going on for hours, since dawn, the parade route lined with cheering Citizens and, behind them, the throngs of Probs, even louder and more excited, making sure to broadcast their enthusiasm and patriotism to any who might sponsor their citizenship one day. The life of a Probationary-Aspirant was an ongoing audition for promotion to the upper ranks of society.

The masses of Plebs were gathered the farthest back, screaming as loudly and with as much fervor as their betters in the forward positions, though Katrine suspected there was more fear than sincerity in their cheers. The Plebs were the workers, the men and women who toiled in the mines and factories and shipyards. For the most part, they were not native Palatians, but rather populations drawn from the conquered worlds, relocated—often forcibly—to do the work that freed the Probs for service in the army and navy.

The Plebs weren't slaves, not quite, but they weren't free either, and most of them were barred from military service and assigned on the basis of aptitude tests to lives working in one industry or another. An intelligent and capable Pleb might be educated and rise to become an engineer or a computer programmer, positions that would allow a moderately comfortable standard of living…and some hope of moving into the Prob class. Those with less aptitude were relegated to the fields, the mines, and the massive factories that produced an unending flow of munitions. Plebs whose ability or effort were below par tended to find themselves treated as expendable resources, with accordingly short life expectancies.

A few Plebs had burst out of their lesser stature, gained access to the military and worked their way to positions of power and influence—and even full Citizenship—but not many. Those who achieved success often did so at the sides of notable Patricians and Citizens, enjoying the benefits bestowed by their powerful masters after long periods of faithful service. Most others worked twelve hours a day, and except for those at the very top, lived joyless lives devoted to maintaining the vaunted Alliance military machine and enjoying few of the spoils of victory.

The system had not always been that way. Building ships and arms had been regarded as a sacred duty in the earliest days of the Alliance, as important even as the service of the soldiers and spacers on the front lines. There were images in the Archives of cheering groups of Prob workers standing outside arms factories or inside the orbital shipyards, watching as the warships they'd built fired up their engines and moved off on maiden voyages. But conquests and access to subject populations had gradually changed that perception, and military service had become virtually the only path to full citizenship for a Prob. A taint of cowardice now clung to any who chose a different route.

"Long live the Alliance!"

The shout rose from across the way, no doubt the over-enthusiastic efforts of a particularly ambitious Prob. But it was a challenge to the others standing nearby, and they joined in, repeating the cry, shouting it again and again until thousands were chanting.

Kat sighed. She hated parades. Indeed, she despised most public spectacles. She acknowledged the utility of such events, and she recognized the current one as the largest and most magnificent she'd ever witnessed, but even as she watched she hardly saw the precision marching or the endlessly rehearsed bands. It was all false, empty symbolism and a pale image of the heroism and effort it purported to represent.

Instead, faces floated before her, men, women, comrades... friends. The dead of the last campaign, hundreds from her own vessel, spacers who had served her loyally, carrying out her every command with the last of their strength. And thousands more. Indeed, many more than *Vindictus's* dead had fallen taking Heliopolis. The crews of the battleships destroyed by the enemy pulsar, the dead on twenty other damaged vessels, the stormtroopers who pacified the surface after a bitter fight. The price of the glory on display here had been paid by thousands of loyal Palatians, men and women who would never see home again. What did a marching band have to do with such devotion, such sacrifice? The dead were feted as heroes, but what did that do for them?

She was watching from an unfamiliar place, the central grandstand, the province of officers of exalted rank, men and women who commanded armies and fleets, and those who sat on the Council itself. She glanced across the broad avenue, acutely aware of her own discomfort, looking toward the platform holding the other ship commanders and their first officers. Theirs was an honored place as well, if slightly less stratospheric than her present perch. It was also where she belonged, save for one fact. She was one of the heroes of this war—indeed, *the* hero of the final campaign—and that very morning she had received a decoration from the hand of the Imperatrix herself, with all Palatia watching the transmission.

Katrine was a celebrity now, a symbol of the might and the warlike ethos of the Alliance, her success in battle being spun into the legends that would encourage the next generation. Even the parade below was working its magic in that regard. The grand procession included rows of trucks, displaying the broken wreckage of enemy ships...vessels the Alliance fleet had destroyed in battle. And next in line, carried with solemn respect, a series of great trailers hauling more debris, twisted metal...much of what remained of *Vindictus*.

Her ship had done its duty, given its all in pursuit of victory. She could still remember those deadly moments, her battleship pressing forward despite all the firepower the two massive fortresses poured into her. She hadn't returned fire, hadn't so much as targeted either of the great orbital platforms. *Vindictus* had pressed on toward its primary target. Its only target. The enemy laser cannon.

Vindictus had somehow made it to point blank range and, even more miraculously, her main guns had still been operational. Kat closed her eyes for a few seconds, remembering the moment she'd given the order to fire, the feeling she'd had as she saw the great pulsar cannon split down the middle, her laser batteries tearing into it. Success. Victory. Though earned at the ultimate cost. *Vindictus* sat under the guns of the forts after the destruction of the pulsar cannon, its weapons silenced, its engines torn to scrap, and Kat had known her ship was doomed, that her people would all die. Then it happened.

The ships, the vanguard of the Alliance fleet, the great battleships her impulsive maneuver had saved…they came whipping around the other side of the moon, and as each vessel moved into the clear, it opened fire, targeting the fortresses, blasting them to atoms.

Kat remembered sitting in her chair, waiting for death. She'd known her position was hopeless, that the cost of saving the fleet had been the loss of her ship and crew. But *Vindictus* held, somehow it stood firm despite all the enemy forts could throw at it. Her vessel had been blasted almost to bits, its reactors shut down, its weapons gone. But the twisted hull of the great warship still stood, hanging on just long enough, providing emergency life support to the half of her crew who had survived to that point.

She savored the images…watching the fortresses die. One first, and then, seconds later, the other. They died under the relentless assault of the fleet. They died as the Alliance warriors pressed forward, fighting with all they had, struggling to rescue *Vindictus* and the great heroes aboard who had saved them all. And *Vindictus* and those left in her crew had indeed been spared. Kat's ship had been as good as lost, blasted far beyond repair, but in the end it was saved from final destruction, and half its people survived. Though it would never fight again, *Vindictus's* name had entered the Honoreum, the hallowed records of the Alliance military.

Now she was back on Palatia, paraded around, hailed, shaking hands and being put forth as the ideal Alliance warrior. She detested the addition of role model to the list of her duties, but she knew her place, and her obligation was to serve however she could. Kat questioned things quietly sometimes, but she was a Palatian Patrician, and obedience and devotion were bred into the very cells of her body. It was in her to question herself, but never to rebel against what she was.

She'd endured an almost unending series of congratulations and interviews, days of them, and then the excruciating few moments when the Imperatrix placed the gleaming platinum decoration over her head and turned to the crowd calling for acclimation. The shouts had been deafening as she received an honor every young officer in Alliance service craved beyond all others. But Katrine simply endured, as she had been taught to do, though more than anything she wanted to slip away, to escape from the fawning elites and the endless noise and shouts of the crowd.

That was impossible, of course. It would have been so even if she'd been across the avenue, attending the festivities as an ordinary ship commander, but it was unthinkable for her to leave the exalted company she found around her now, the great and mighty of the Alliance. She had no choice, save to stay and play the role of hero of the state.

The recent battles had won the Alliance six of the Unaligned Systems, worlds that had now surrendered, taken their place among the other conquered planets that formed the Alliance. They brought their industry with them, and millions of their former citizens, new Plebs to feed the endless war machine. It was the Alliance's way, to conquer or die. And it was the lot of the subjugated to become part of that apparatus, to spend their lives hard at work in the mines and factories, producing ships and weapons under the watchful eyes of their masters. The Alliance's flag was emblazoned with its mantra, *Vae Victis*. Woe to the defeated. And the Patricians and Citizens of the Alliance—and the Probationary-Aspirants who served under them—took it to heart.

It was a hard way, a life dedicated to duty, to strength...but it had seen the Alliance grow from the seed of a single world, poor and subjugated by offworld conquerors, to a proud interstellar nation of thirty systems in less than sixty years. There were Alliance citizens still alive with living memory of servitude, and as a people they had sworn a collective oath. Never again.

These are your people, she thought, trying to encourage herself but realizing how uncertain she felt about that realization. She was descended from ancestors who had been heroes of the Rising that had freed Palatia—and of the brutal Cleansing that had followed. Her grandmother had risen from the slavery and servitude of pre-Rising Palatia…and gone on to lead fleets to victory in the early wars of the Alliance's expansion. Kat was heir to a great tradition, a benefit that had aided her rise…and a burden too, a constant pressure to excel, to achieve ever more and to live up to her family's reputation.

A load that became heavier the day my father died…

"Commander Rigellus, allow me to congratulate you on your victory in the recent campaign. It is officers like you who will lead the Alliance into the future."

Katrine turned at the sound of the voice, shaking herself quickly from her thoughts. Her eyes fixed on the speaker, a man, old, his hair completely white. He leaned hard on a cane, and the dress uniform he wore was rumpled and ill-fitting, as if it hadn't been out of his closet in many years. A flickering of familiarity stirred. He was a fleet commander, retired now of course. It took a few seconds for a name to surface…Commander-Altum Bacchallus. A man who had somehow managed to rise to a position of considerable power and prestige, despite an almost total lack of identifiable accomplishments. He was accompanied by a young woman, quite attractive, and at least forty years his junior.

A Prob, no doubt—or even a Pleb—seeking a path to citizenship in an old man's bed…

Katrine held back a sigh and forced a smile to her face. "Commander-Altum, what a pleasure to see you, sir. Thank you for your kind words. You are most gracious."

She nodded slightly, hoping the brief exchange of pleasantries would suffice. But, alas, it was not to be. The aged officer beamed back at her and launched into a retelling of one of his old campaigns, one she was sure was wildly embellished.

She listened quietly, politely. Her mind, so attuned to tactics, to maneuvers to get herself out of tough spots, failed her utterly. There was nothing to do but listen, and feign interest. She'd dealt with her share of "I remember whens" and "I knew your father back in the days," but Bacchallus had a reputation for droning on endlessly.

And Kat knew she was going to get a good idea of how well

that reputation was deserved…

Chapter Four

"Archellia Control, this is the Confederation Fleet Ship *Dauntless*, requesting permission to approach." Darrow spoke slowly and clearly into the comm system.

It took about eight seconds for his signal to reach the planet and the response to arrive. "Acknowledged, *Dauntless*. Please hold at the outer marker until we have completed our scan."

Tyler Barron sat in the command chair of *Dauntless's* bridge, listening to the exchange. He wanted to be surprised at the formality of the procedure, but he wasn't. Archellia was a long way from the disputed border, and such precautions hardly seemed necessary. But war with the Union was imminent, and however far from Archellia the battlelines were likely to be, Confederation forces were on alert everywhere. No officer wanted to end up defending lax security procedures if something went wrong.

Not even in a backwater like Archellia. Not now.

The specter of war still hung like a shadow, but Barron's crew was in good spirits, bound for well-deserved shore leave and a break from the grind of duty. He knew it would be a relatively short break, with danger lurking on the other side, but he'd been in the service long enough to realize just how much

28

spacers lived in the now.

Tomorrow we may face destiny, we may fight and die and fall to the fires of perdition, but tonight is ours, and we drink and make merry.

It was an old quote, from pre-Cataclysmic times, but whatever centuries-dead spacer had first spoken it, Barron realized he had known his brethren well. Barron tended to be a bit over-serious himself, the inevitable result of growing up as he had, feeling the crushing expectations from the moment he was old enough to understand. But he knew there was logic in the simple spacer's view. His crew couldn't do anything to affect what was coming, and if war indeed erupted, there was little doubt many of them would die in the fighting.

They might as well savor the time they have…

He knew he was different from his crew, even from his officers. But he was devoted to them all, and his first thought was always to provide them the best leadership he could manage. He never let himself forget that every command he uttered had consequences, that his mistakes could get his people hurt. Or killed.

The first few months of his command had been difficult ones, as such things usually were, especially since he'd had to overcome the usual resentments, the impression that the Barron name had more to do with the insignia on his collar than his skills and service. But he and his people had gotten past it all and become a solid team, and Barron would have put *Dauntless* against any other ship in the fleet, despite the fact that she was neither the newest nor the largest.

"*Dauntless*, all scans check out. Please transmit alpha codes for final authorization."

Barron leaned forward slightly and flipped open the small panel on the armrest of his chair, revealing the keypad below. His fingers punched out a code, one only he and his first officer knew. It was another wartime procedure, a failsafe designed to prevent an enemy from using a captured vessel to approach a Confederation world. Its implementation before the outbreak of hostilities, and on a world so far from the prospective battle zone, attested to just how worried the Confederation's leaders were of an impending attack, and the fifth column tactics the Union would almost certainly employ if hostilities broke out.

He felt himself snapping back to his rigid posture, staring straight ahead as he waited for the confirmation. No one on the planet had *Dauntless*'s code—at least, no one living. Only the base's AI. And security protocols prevented any direct contact between the core data systems and unconfirmed ships, for fear of viruses and cyber attacks. That meant the base crew would have to manually input *Dauntless*'s code to check its validity.

"*Dauntless*, you are cleared to dock at bay three. Welcome to Archellia." The voice on the speaker was crisp, professional... but there was something else there too, something besides the provincial accent. A touch of excitement perhaps. Archellia was far from the core worlds or the disputed frontier, a quiet frontier capital overseeing a cluster of fringe systems and mining colonies on the far edge of Confederation space. The planet was home to a sizable naval base, but the frontier it guarded was a quiet one, facing mostly independent and militarily weak systems, and its naval complement was one of small patrol vessels and scoutships, designed to counter piracy, not to face invasions. A visit by a frontline warship was a quite a rarity.

"Understood, Archellia Control." Barron's hand moved toward the com controls, but then he paused and added, "Thank you, Archellia. It is good to be here." He tapped the sensor pad, closing the connection. He could have allowed the comm officer to conclude the transmission, but he had a lot of nervous energy, and he disliked the idea of an aloof commander, acting as if pressing a button or reading a report himself was too much of an effort.

"Commander Travis, you have the con." He stood up slowly, taking a step from his chair. "Bring us in..." He turned and looked around the bridge. "...and authorize shore leave for all off-duty personnel as soon as base operations have secured *Dauntless*." He fought back a smile as he heard the not-so-quiet rumble. It wasn't exactly a cheer, but it left little doubt as to how much his overworked bridge crew was looking forward to a break. He imagined the areas of the ship farther removed from the exalted presence of the captain would experience a rather more…enthusiastic…celebration when Travis passed on the command.

"Yes, Captain." Atara Travis's voice was sharp, crisp. Travis was a tough officer, one whose relentless intensity left no doubt how far she would go to keep *Dauntless* functioning at maximum efficiency. She'd come with Barron, transferred from *Excalibur*, where they had been first officer and tactical officer, respectively.

Barron remembered the first time he'd met her, three years before. He'd been struck by her beauty at first, but it was quickly followed by respect. Travis was smart…more than smart, brilliant. And she was hard as nails.

Travis hadn't come from a naval family. She had fought her way up from the streets of Hepheseus, the most notorious world in the Iron Belt, an industrialized hell whose ruling Oligarchs lived in orbital refuges to escape the sludgy waterways and dark gray haze that hung heavy in the sky. She'd never spoken of how she'd gotten the money to book passage off her native world, nor the means by which she had obtained the education to pass the Academy's fearsome entrance examinations. And Tyler had never asked. Travis had become like a sister to him, and a best friend too…and they were a solid captain-exec team now, the best in the fleet, many said.

He'd had a passing impulse to pursue more than friendship and professional respect when they'd first met. He wasn't above using the Barron name to supplement his own charms when sufficiently motivated, but it had never gone beyond a passing thought with Travis. Discipline had won out. Tyler Barron had a bit of a reputation in the bases and ports of the Confederation, one he had to admit was at least partially deserved, but he never let any of that come aboard his ship or interfere with duty. That had been his policy as a first officer, and he only redoubled his conviction as captain.

And it worked out for the best in the end.

That relationship was more important to him than any dalliance. Even one with a woman as striking as Travis.

He walked toward the hatch leading to the lift. "I will be in my quarters if you need me, Commander."

"Yes, sir."

He walked through the doors, taking a deep breath as they slid shut.

"Deck three," he said softly.

He leaned back against the wall and let out a long, hard sigh. *Dauntless* had come back from her dangerous posting, and at least for now, his people were safe. His demand for a dangerous posting, his need to prove—to himself as well as anyone else—that he was as capable of facing danger as his renowned grandfather, hadn't cost him any of his crew. War still loomed, and he wasn't naïve enough to expect that his people would come through such a conflict unscathed. But at least none of them paid the ultimate price solely because their commander had felt the need to prove himself. Only now did he truly think about how he would have carried that guilt. He was thankful he didn't have to.

Now, maybe he could actually get some rest himself.

Maybe.

* * *

"It was nice of the high command to send us clear across the Confederation so you could be home in time." Lieutenant Walt Billings looked down from a narrow catwalk, five meters above *Dauntless's* main engineering deck. He had a burnt system control rod in one hand, and a fresh one in the other, but his attention had been diverted from the power flow regulator to the conversation taking place on the main deck below. "We didn't know we had such a big shot down here in engineering."

Sam Carson looked up and smiled at his comrade. "Yeah, Walt, well you know the fleet admiral and I are like this." He held up his hand, his thumb and forefinger almost touching. "So, I just asked him if a hundred extra lightyears added to the trip was such a big deal…"

The two men laughed, and in a few seconds it spread to the others working in the engineering space. *Dauntless's* crew was tightly knit, but its engineering teams were even more so. They'd only had minor repairs to contend with until now, but they all knew if—when—it came to open war, the survival of the ship would rest on them as much as, possibly more than, anyone else. The gunners took credit for blasting enemy ships, and the fighter pilots notched their throttles with each kill, but when it came to getting a damaged laser cannon back on line in time to fire, or giving the captain maximum thrust when he needed it, it was the engineers who would get the job done.

They tended to relish their roles as the unheralded and unappreciated branch of the service, but *Dauntless's* team knew that didn't apply to them. Captain Barron had made it clear from day one he thought they were the living, breathing heart of the ship, and for almost a year now he had been true to his word, even making frequent visits to the engineering spaces. The captain had picked up a set of tools more than once, and joined his engineers in whatever task they were completing, though it was an open question as to whether his efforts had been of any help. Barron's lack of engineering skill had become the joke of the section, but the men and women there had come to love their captain.

They had all been surprised when they got the word *Dauntless* was headed to Archellia, but none more than Lieutenant Sam Carson, engineer and native Archellian. Carson had only been with *Dauntless* for five months, but he liked to think he'd made many friends among the rest of the crew. He'd been the victim of a few practical jokes when he'd first arrived, a fate his earnestness had made inevitable. But he'd taken it well, and within a few weeks he was knit into the fabric of Dauntless' engineering team as though he'd been there for years.

The news of *Dauntless's* destination had been doubly opportune for him. Carson was not only going home…his wife was pregnant with the couple's first child. He hadn't known about it when he'd shipped out to join *Dauntless's* crew. Indeed, with the difficulty of communications along the border, he'd only found out a few weeks before *Dauntless* was ordered off the line. And now the ship was arriving in plenty of time for him to be there for the birth.

"It's such an honor to serve with someone so important, isn't it, guys?" Billings grinned at the half dozen engineers and technicians working alongside Carson. "You'd think having a good pal of the fleet admiral on board would be worth something. Better rations, at least."

The group turned and looked over at Carson, spitting out a wave of affirmative responses.

"I'm going to miss you all, I really am." Carson smiled broadly, though there was a touch of sadness behind it.

Dauntless would be on Archellia for a month, perhaps five weeks, depending on how quickly the base's maintenance team could complete the battleship's refit. Then she would be on her way, presumably back toward the front, to join one of the battle fleets massing behind the border. But Carson wouldn't be with her.

Carson had considered asking for a transfer when he got the news about his wife's pregnancy, but he'd hesitated, not wanting to desert his new shipmates on the eve of war. But Captain Barron himself had gotten the news and intervened. He'd called Carson to his quarters, told him he was one of the most promising young officers he had ever seen. Then he'd told him there was a posting available at the fleet base on Archellia. He'd offered it to Carson then and there, and Carson had accepted, though not without some sadness about leaving his new comrades so soon.

"It looks like everyone's having a grand old time here. Isn't that nice. Can I assume today's maintenance roster is complete already?" It was a low-pitched growl, one that would have been gender-indeterminate if everyone on *Dauntless* didn't know the roar of the ship's chief engineer by heart.

Anya Fritz walked into the center of the main deck, her eyes moving from one of her people to the next, cutting through them like a high-powered laser. Fritz was an engineer, but as far as her people could tell she was nothing less than a sorceress, wielding some kind of black magic to pull shattered systems back from the brink, to coax a few more megawatts from a dying reactor. Her skills were renowned across the fleet, and most of her team suspected it was the Barron mojo that had secured her transfer along with the captain.

They were glad to have her skills aboard, but that didn't change the fact that she scared the shit out of them all. The captain called her Fritzie, but none of her officers and techs would dare do the same. The very thought was enough to evoke night terrors in a veteran spacer.

"Sorry, Commander. We...ah..." Billings was staring down from the catwalk, his cockiness gone, struggling for words.

"I'm sorry, Commander." Carson flashed a glance up at Billings and then back toward Fritz. "We were talking about my transfer. It won't happen again. We're actually in good shape on the repair manifests. We'll be done before the ship docks."

Fritz sighed, her eyes focused on Carson. Then she shocked them all. She smiled. "Don't worry about it." She glanced around the room, throwing a quick frown up toward Billings. "Just finish up...and then we can give Lieutenant Carson here the sendoff he deserves. And I've got a bottle of twenty-year old bourbon to get us started."

She turned and took a few steps toward the exit. Then she stopped and looked back. "I'm going to miss you, Sam. Just like everybody else."

Chapter Five

"Commander-Maximus, you sent for me?" Kat stood at the open door, peering into the palatial office.

"Kat! Come in. Please, have a seat." The officer sitting behind the massive desk stood up as he spoke. He was a large man, tall and muscular, and his face was scarred and hard-looking. But now he smiled, and his voice was almost soft, affectionate. "And, please, none of this Commander-Maximus nonsense. Not when it's just the two of us. I remember when you used to sit on my lap and call me Uncle Taks."

Commander-Maximus Tarkus Vennius was a man to be reckoned with, one few ship commanders would dare to address with anything but the gravest formality. But Katrine was the daughter of Lucius Rigellus...and Lucius Rigellus had been Vennius's best friend since childhood. The two boys, later men, had been virtual brothers, through decades of life, war, struggle. They had completed the coming of age Ordeal together, and they had served side by side as they rose through the ranks. Vennius had practically adopted Katrine after her father's death in battle.

Kat smiled. "That was only because Tarkus was too much of a mouthful for me back then. A breach of protocol, perhaps, but I *was* only three." She walked up toward the desk, a tentative smile slipping onto her lips. "Still, it's a bit unseemly for a lowly ship commander to address a Commander-Maximus in such a familiar way, wouldn't you say, Uncle Taks?"

Kat had been troubled since she had returned from the front lines, but her spirits lightened now, at least temporarily. The Commander-Maximus was widely feared by the officers under his command, especially those who had seen him on one of his tirades, but she had long thought of Tarkus as a second father. She loved the gruff old man, and she knew he loved her.

Vennius gestured toward one of the guest chairs. "Sit, Kat. Be comfortable…and humor an old man who has far too few joys in life." He paused until she had taken the seat, then he dropped back into his own chair. "And I wouldn't call you a *lowly* ship commander, certainly not after your exploits in the last war. I can't walk down the Via Magnus without seeing your image hanging from a building in ten meters of Gybilian silk."

The recent battles had won the Alliance six of the Unaligned Systems, worlds that had now surrendered, taken their place among the other conquered planets that formed the Alliance. They brought their industry with them, and millions of their former citizens, new Plebs to feed the endless war machine. It was the Alliance's way, to conquer or die. And it was the lot of the subjugated to become part of that apparatus, to spend their lives hard at work in the mines and factories, producing ships and weapons under the watchful eyes of their masters. Indeed, the Alliance's flag was emblazoned with its mantra, Vae Victis. Woe to the defeated. And the Patricians and Citizens of the Alliance—and the Probationary-Aspirants who served under them—took it to heart.

It was a hard way, a life dedicated to duty, to strength…but it had seen the Alliance grow from the seed of a single world, poor and subjugated by offworld conquerors, to a proud interstellar nation of thirty systems in less than sixty years. There were Alliance citizens still alive with living memory of servitude, and as a people they had sworn a collective oath. Never again.

Katrine nodded slightly, but the smile died from her lips.

The recent war had been as successful as any of those that pre-ceded it, perhaps more so. The losses had been terrible, espe-cially among the fleet and ground units that had fought the final campaign to take Heliopolis. The planet had been the strongest of the Unaligned Systems fighting the Alliance, and the most technologically advanced. The captured technology would be as valuable as the planet's considerable resources and industry, though much of value—including the secrets of the great pul-sar weapon—had been destroyed in the conquest. The weapon's inventor had been onboard his creation, and Kat's people had blown him to atoms along with the gun itself.

At least the fall of Heliopolis had broken the will of the other worlds, ending the war in one bloody stroke.

"There were many heroes in the campaign, Uncle. I fear my contributions have been overstated."

Vennius smiled. "Overstated? Nonsense. If anything, you deserve more accolades, though I fear we've run out of honors to bestow. I have no doubt, Kat, my dearest…one day they'll add Magnus to your name. I only hope an old man lives long enough to see it."

Only three commanders had been granted the appellation Magnus in the sixty years since Alliance forces had burst forth from their homeworld. It was an honor beyond honors, and even the imperatrix would bow before one who held it.

Kat shook her head. "You're far too kind, Uncle. I do only as duty demands."

"So do all, at least they pretend to do so. Yet few have achieved what you have, despite duty and effort." A hint of sad-ness slipped into his voice. "Your father would have been proud of you, Kat. Proud to bursting."

"It is kind of you to say so, Uncle…and yet I find that as time presses on, I remember less and less of father. Indeed, most of what I know of him is from retellings, not from time I spent with him. In that regard, all I have are vague recollections. There is a lake on the estate, inland from the coast, up in the mountains, pure, cold. We used to go there when he was home on leave. I remember swimming in the early mornings, the sun just rising over the western peaks, the water so cold it nearly took my breath away. It is a pleasant memory, but it seems all too little when so much else is gone."

"I have many memories of your father as well, Katrine. There has been no one I called brother with more sincerity than your father, though we shared neither mother nor father. To this day I'm grateful to have had such a friend for much of my life."

"You miss him terribly, don't you, Uncle? Even after so many years?"

"Our way is hard, Kat. Yet, it is the way. But you're right... not a day goes by I don't think of Lucius, or remember some adventure we shared." Vennius stared down at his desk for a few seconds, silent.

"I sense more than sadness about the past in your words, Uncle." Kat lowered her head, drew the commander's eyes up with her own.

"I've never been able to hide anything from you, my dear Kat."

"What is it, Uncle? Are you unwell?"

Vennius laughed softly. "Long life runs in my family, and the multitude of enemies I've faced have failed to put me down. I fear that my destiny is to survive to dotage."

"Then what?" Kat's voice was soft, her concern evident.

"I have orders for you, Kat."

She sat unmoving, holding his gaze. "Orders you disagree with?" A pause. "Dangerous orders?"

"Both, though it's dangerous to say so. This assignment comes directly from the Council, and it's signed by the imperatrix herself."

Kat could feel the tension building inside her. It wasn't the exalted source of the assignment as much as the discomfort she could see in Vennius's expression. She sat silently, waiting for him to continue.

"As you're no doubt aware, intelligence reports suggest that the Confederation and the Union are on the verge of war." He hesitated. "I can now confirm that both powers have mobilized their fleets to their respective borders."

"The history of the two powers left little doubt there would be a rematch, Uncle. But such a war will be far from the Alliance. Does it involve us in some way?"

Kat couldn't imagine what a Confederation-Union war had to do with the Alliance, at least not in the short term. The Confederation and Alliance didn't share a border. The remaining independent Unaligned Systems lay generally between the two powers. And the Union was clear on the other side of the Confederation.

"The Council has decided that it does." He paused. "I can't over-emphasize the sensitivity of the information I am about to share."

Kat nodded. "You needn't have told me that, Uncle."

"We've received a proposal from the government of the Federal Union, one that calls upon us to join them in their attack the Confederation."

Kat felt herself shaking her head, an involuntary response she stopped as soon as she realized she was doing it. "But Uncle, our losses…they were considerable. I fear no enemy, but we need time to rebuild, to refit."

The Alliance had always been aggressive, but not foolhardy. And taking on an enemy like the Confederation while half the ships in the fleet were still being repaired…

"I can assure you the Council has considered those facts. It's been decided the chance to gain a significant chunk of Confederation space is an opportunity that cannot be easily disregarded." He sighed. "But it's more than simply that, and in this part I must also agree. The Confederation will be hard-pressed in this coming war, and if the Union is allowed to win the victory without us, to absorb all of Confederation space, there can be little doubt we would be next."

"So we're to strike pre-emptively, to secure as much of the Confederation as possible ourselves to keep it from them?" There was doubt in her tone.

"The Council doesn't believe we can sit by and passively watch events unfold. They feel that the Confeds are too weak, morally if not in arms, and that they will inevitably fall to the

Union when war begins. The Union is already vastly larger than we are…to sit by and allow them to swallow up the Confederation, and all its industry as well, would be disastrous." He paused. "No, if the Confederation is to be conquered, as much of it as possible must fall to us, and quickly. Before the Union invades and wins without us. Then it will be too late."

She shook her head. "Can we even mount such an invasion now? Half the fleet is still on garrison in the conquered systems. Getting them back to base for refit will take…"

"The Council believes it can be done in six months." Vennius's tone suggested he had a rather different opinion than the Council.

"So, am I to be given a command in the invasion force? A new vessel?"

"No, Kat…at least, no, you won't be with the invasion force. At least not initially."

She looked back at him, not entirely hiding her confusion.

"However, you *are* getting a new command. The greatest ship ever constructed by Alliance industry. *Invictus*."

It was an honor, one of momentous proportions. *Invictus* had been under construction for three years, the greatest battleship in Alliance history. And the command of the strongest ship in the fleet would be a direct stepping stone to the high command.

"I'm honored, Uncle. To be Commander-Primus in the fleet…" Her words drifted off as she saw Vennius's face.

"You deserve *Invictus*, Kat, more than any officer I have ever known. In fact, your elevation to fleet command is all but assured. But…"

"But?" She was beginning to realize just how uncomfortable Vennius was. "What am I to do, Uncle?"

"The Council hasn't abandoned all caution, Kat. An invasion of the Confederation, one launched in coordination with a Union assault, will likely encounter limited resistance. Most of the Confederation fleet is posted to the Union border. But even if our forces face only token garrisons, the logistical challenges of mounting and maintaining an invasion are considerable. If we're unable to supply our forces adequately, our fleets could bog down. We could even find ourselves exposed to Union treachery if our respective fleets meet when they're well-supplied and we're overextended."

"I agree, Uncle, certainly. But what can I do to change that?"

"The Council has decided to dispatch *Invictus* on a preliminary mission, one with two primary goals. As you know, there's only one reliable route to Confederation space that doesn't pass through one or more of the remaining Unaligned Systems."

"The Dragon's Tail."

"Yes, exactly."

"But that course runs through eight systems. We would need..." She suddenly understood.

"Yes, and that's the first purpose of your mission. You are to take *Invictus* down the Dragon's Tail and into Confederation space. You are to probe, to confirm that there are no capital ships deployed to the border. You will destroy their frontier outposts, and occupy the planet Santis. It has a refueling station the fleet can use to support the invasion, and its defenses are minimal. It is essential to our purposes."

"I understand, Uncle." She paused. "You said there were two primary purposes. What's the other?"

"To test the Confeds, to confirm that they are indeed weak in the sectors we would attack. As I said, the Council has not given up all prudence. They believe the Confeds are soft, that the way is open to invade, to slice deeply into their underbelly. And they want you to prove it. Your success will be the catalyst, the signal for war. If you secure Santis, if you defeat anything they are able to throw at you, the fleet will be dispatched."

Vennius looked down at his desk, pulling his eyes from hers. "I wouldn't have chosen you for this mission, Kat." His voice was soft, grim. "I do you a dishonor, perhaps, to say this, but I would have you spared from this danger. The Council views the Confederation as weak, the second-line forces you are likely to encounter as no real threat." He paused again, his discomfort clear.

"But you feel differently?" There was no recrimination in her voice, no offense at Vennius's words.

"I don't know, Kat. I fear we may be underestimating the strength of the Confeds. We assume the Union, larger and stronger, will conquer them in the coming war, yet there have been three such conflicts before, and the Confederation stands, stronger perhaps than ever before. I wonder if we wouldn't be better served seeking alliance with the Confeds and not conquest."

Kat sat silently for a few seconds, pondering the older man's words. They were bold, and they tread close to challenging Alliance orthodoxy. Conquest was the way, the only way. So it had been since the first days when the former slaves of Palatia burst forth to take their revenge for a century of subjugation and despair. War was the only policy the Alliance knew, military strength the unquestioned priority of its ruling class. Katrine had been brought up in that culture, and she had lived and breathed its disciplines. She understood it all...yet she respected Vennius's intelligence, and she saw the logic in his words.

"But sir, the Confeds *are* far less aggressive than the Union. They're paralyzed by their republican government, pulled one way by corrupt politicians and another by a soft and spoiled populace. Perhaps the Council is correct. If we're able to seize half their territory, the relative size difference between the Union and us would swing in our favor. And if they're forced to face the bulk of the Confederation's strength, their own forces will be badly attrited by the end of the conflict. They will be weak in victory, even as we will be strong."

"That's the Council's rationale. But I fear we'll discover they are less easily defeated than we expect. They have weaknesses, no doubt, but their navy is strong, their Marines a force to be reckoned with. They're different than us, their priorities strange to our way of thinking. We've paid little attention to their history, but I've read several accounts of the past wars they fought with the Union. They were outnumbered in all of them, yet they've survived the Union threat longer than the Alliance has existed. I believe they'll fight to the end, and that it will be far more difficult to conquer them than the Council anticipates. And I suspect the Union knows as much. Why else would they seek our aid, offer to share the spoils?"

"Perhaps you're correct, Uncle…and yet it doesn't matter—orders are orders. They are to be obeyed, not questioned."

"You speak the truth. Which is why you're here, why I'm giving you these orders." His tone made it clear if he'd had any other option, he would have taken it.

Kat nodded. "Very well, Commander-Maximus." It seemed to her the acceptance of such orders should be done formally, even by one who used to call the issuing officer Uncle Taks. "I will do all I can to see these orders successfully executed." She frowned a little. Vennius's words were still going through her mind…and she was seeing the sense in them. And the success of her mission would bring the Alliance another war, the biggest one in its history. More dead comrades.

"The Santis system is crucial, Kat. You must take the refueling station there before the fleet can commit to a full scale invasion. You'll have three full strike forces of stormtroopers on *Invictus*. That should be a sufficient force to defeat the Confederation Marines deployed there and effectively garrison the planet until the fleet arrives."

"Understood." There was something else, something the older man was reluctant to tell her. She almost asked, but she held back, waited.

"There is one more provision in your orders, Kat." She could tell instantly how much Vennius didn't like it, whatever it was.

"*Invictus* will be considered a rogue ship during your mission, Kat, not an Alliance naval vessel. The Council was adamant about this, just in case the Confeds' defenses are stronger than we expect. It is imperative that none of your people are captured, or that any physical proof links you to Palatia in any way. You cannot retreat in any way that would allow the enemy to follow you back to Alliance space. You must succeed, or…" Vennius paused, his voice strained, cracking. He didn't finish the sentence…he didn't have to. Both he and Kat knew what he was telling her. Alliance ships didn't surrender. And they both knew if *Invictus* was challenged by a superior force, retreat wouldn't be an option either. That only left one alternative to victory.

Vennius didn't say anything further, but the sadness in his

eyes was unmistakable.

Kat sat still for a moment, digesting what she had just been told. "I understand, sir." She could feel how much it was hurting Vennius to send her on such a dangerous mission. She tried to think of something to say, any words from her that would ease the old man's mind. But there was nothing. Finally, she just asked, "What about a crew?"

"All of your survivors from *Vindictus* have already been transferred. And I've taken the liberty of selecting the rest for you."

"Thank you, sir." She felt a wave of relief. If Vennius had chosen the new members of her crew, she could be sure of every one of them.

Vennius looked down at the desk for a few seconds, silent, sad. Then he reached into a small drawer, pulling out a data chip. "I was able to extract one thing from the Council, Kat. It won't make the mission any easier—or less dangerous—but it is well deserved." He slid the chip across the table. "Your promotion to Commander-Altum, effective immediately on your return. If the war comes, you will not command a ship, Kat. You will lead a fleet into battle."

Kat felt a rush of surprise. She was young to be a Commander-Princeps, but a Commander-Altum? It was almost without precedent. She would be the youngest she could recall, perhaps the youngest ever.

"Thank you, Uncle." The words seemed inadequate, but she didn't know what else to say. So, she decided to throw all protocol and decorum to the wind. She stood up and walked around the desk, and then she leaned down and planted a kiss on the old man's cheek.

Chapter Six

Confederation Intelligence Report
Highest Classification

As per previous directives, we have increased analysis of recent Alliance activities, notably the apparent success they appear to have had in recent wars with a number of the Unaligned Systems. It is now confirmed that six previously independent planets have been conquered, including Heliopolis, which has a considerably higher general technology level than the Alliance itself. This increases the number of confirmed Alliance systems to thirty. It is recommended that additional intelligence assets be assigned to monitor the Alliance and that diplomatic efforts be initiated to neutralize any potential threat of future conflict.

During our operations, we uncovered circumstantial evidence of Union communication with the Alliance. Previously, our operating assumption had been there was no contact between the powers. There is little concrete information on what types of communications may have taken place or how long the two powers have been in contact. However, we consider this a situation of the direst import. All customs and transit authorities have been instructed to increase security procedures to discover any Union personnel traveling through Confederation space en route to the Alliance. Further, we have activated a level one operative on the Union capital to attempt to obtain more information of any Union-Alliance communications.

CFS Dauntless
In Space Dock
Archellia, Cassiopolis III
307 AC

The Confederation had fought the Union three times before.

Barron knew that well, and he was convinced the secrets to victory in the looming fourth conflict lay in the lessons to be learned from the first three. He had plenty of work to do in the present, even with *Dauntless* in port for repairs, but he was distracted. The past had always called to him, promising answers to current problems if he was clever enough to decipher them.

He glanced down at the screen on the side of the desk. He'd been trying to catch up on some work, but his mind had wandered, and he'd ended up flipping back and forth between the boring supply requisitions and the history text he'd been reading.

Barron was a bit of an amateur historian, and he indulged his hobby whenever possible. He tended to spend his free time prowling the data systems of planets he visited, searching for rare histories and memoirs he'd never seen before...like the one on the screen now. He'd downloaded the massive file before *Dauntless* had deployed to the Union border, intending to read it during the deployment. But it was a heavy, academic work, not an easy read, and he'd found himself too on edge to make much progress. He'd had trouble concentrating on the thick wording and massive lists of statistics, at least with the threat of Union attack weighing on him every moment.

That is something I plan to correct here on Archellia. I should have plenty of time to polish this off here.

The text was yet another account of the Confederation-Union conflicts, but it had some perspectives he'd never seen in any other work, and he found it thought-provoking, at least from what little he'd read. He wasn't sure he'd agree with the author on many of his conclusions, but he was certain they'd be worth analyzing.

Our lives, at least as we know them, depend on finding a way to defeat the Union. If the Confederation is conquered by the Union, a hundred worlds and billions of free people—more or less free, at least—will fall into slavery...

Barron had his criticisms of the Confederation government, with the corruption and the deceit of its politicians. But he had seen the intel reports from the Union, and they had awakened him to how much of a nightmare government could become. The standard of living in the Union was appalling, at least by Confederation standards, and most of the people lived at bare sustenance levels, in constant fear of the authorities, while the masters, the ministers and commissars and party officials, lived lives of obscene luxury. He knew the Confederation had lost millions of people in the wars with the Union, but he was sure of one thing. None of them had died in vain. The Confederation was a spark of light in the post-Cataclysm universe, and even if that illumination sometimes appeared dim and faltering, it was vastly preferable to any of the alternatives.

The first conflict between the powers was still called the War of Shame, and it had cost the Confederation ten border systems, a swath of planets still called the Lost Worlds...and all still claimed by the Confederation, despite three generations of inhabitants born under Union rule.

The story of the second war was the tale of his grandfather. The Union was larger and stronger, and the second war began as the first one had ended, with defeat before the superior arms of the enemy. Until Rance Barron led a phalanx of young officers to the forefront, casting aside the fossilized high command and revolutionizing the Confederation navy. In a series of running battles, this new guard fought the Union to a standstill. The elder Barron hadn't been able to liberate the Lost Worlds, but he had saved the Confederation from total conquest, and he'd become a national hero in the process.

Rance Barron's exploits were taught in every school in the Confederation. But Tyler had memories of his grandfather the others didn't...fishing trips to the cold rivers north of the family estate on Corellia, late night games of chess in front of a roaring fire. Rance Barron wasn't just a great warrior to him, he was much, much more, and Tyler resented how the constant pressure and repeated comparisons so often pushed those pleasant thoughts from his mind.

The Third War had picked up where the second ended…at least until the Union managed to obtain intel on the location of Admiral Barron's ship. The resulting attack cost the Confederation its greatest hero and threatened to turn the tide yet again. But the Union First died shortly after, and a massive power struggle erupted, crippling the enemy's ability to wage the war.

Admiral Barron's protégés had been quick to take advantage of the situation, but their victories were limited. The Union sued for peace, and the civilian government opened talks almost immediately. The military commanders begged for the authority to continue their attacks, but the Confederation was a republic, and its people and politicians were sick of war. The warnings of the generals and admirals, that once the Union restored internal order the threat would reappear, were largely ignored, and the war ended with the Confederation regaining two of the Lost Worlds, but leaving the remaining eight to enter their third generation in captivity.

Barron leaned back in his chair, putting his hand to his forehead. He wondered what his grandfather would have said, if his influence would have been enough to gain the support he would have needed to push the last war to a more definitive conclusion. But that was immaterial. The past was set, and now his own generation would have to finish what the previous one had left undone. The Union was determined to subjugate the Confederation. The better part of a century of warfare had proven that beyond doubt. If the Confederation was ever to have true peace, Barron realized, it had to do more than beat back another Union attack. It had to destroy its enemy…or at least inflict enough pain to make another attack unthinkable.

A small buzzer sounded, pulling him from his thoughts.

"Yes?"

"Captain, Commander Travis is at the door."

"Open," Barron snapped to the AI. The door slid aside, and *Dauntless's* tactical officer walked in.

"I saw you were still aboard, Captain."

"Tyler will do, Atara. I strongly suspect we are the only two members of the crew still on the ship. Or onboard again, should I say? I thought you left yesterday."

"I did, Tyler. But then I got a comm from maintenance command. I'm afraid the fact that *Dauntless's* captain is still lurking in his quarters is rattling the maintenance teams."

"So they sent you to ease me out?" He laughed softly. "Very well, tell them you were successful. I'll be out within the hour. Have they arranged quarters for me at the base?"

"Better than that, mon capitaine. The locals have invited you to stay at the finest hotel in Archa City. In the Starburst Suite, no less. I'm told it's quite plush."

Barron sighed. "Now you know why I try to hide onboard, especially this far out in the provinces."

"They are honored to have you here, Tyler. It does no harm. Enjoy it."

"I'd never be disingenuous enough to argue there weren't advantages to being his grandson, Atara…but trust me, there are burdens too. Dinner with the local functionaries is a given wherever we put into dock, but we're going to be here a month, so who knows what they'll cook up. I wouldn't put a parade out of the question."

"It's your lot in life, my friend. Your birthright. Take the bad with the good—after all, your grandfather was the greatest hero in Confederation history."

"And he died when I was thirteen. I loved him, Atara, I truly did. But to me he wasn't the great admiral, the hero. He was the man who taught me how to fish, who helped me restore an old speeder. We used to go out on these amazing camping trips for days and days. And then he went to war…and he was gone. I'm not him, as much as I loved him. I have to be my own man, and it's wearying when all they want to see is some vestige of the great hero reborn."

Travis walked up to Barron, put her hand on his shoulder. "You *are* your own man, Tyler. To me, to the rest of the crew. Everyone who works with you, fights alongside you…they know the real you. I know it's hard sometimes, especially in places like this. People love your grandfather, they believe he saved the Confederation. But never forget that the people who truly know you value you for your own achievements."

Barron forced a smile. "I do know that, Atara. But thank you for saying it."

The two stood for a moment, silent. Then Barron looked right at his first officer. "Okay, Atara…you can go and tell them you got me off the ship. The coast is clear."

Travis nodded. "Okay, Captain, consider it done." She snapped off a crisp salute.

Barron smiled again and returned the salute. "Carry on, Commander…" He stood where he was, watching Travis turn and walk through the door. Then he reached over to a shelf against the wall, grabbing a small duffel bag and sighing.

Time to go see what the Starfire Suite has in store for me…

* * *

"You look like you're feeling better." Lise Varov walked through the door, her uniform showing the hasty tailoring that accommodated her advanced pregnancy.

Sam Carson smiled as his wife entered the room. He'd slept late…Lise had been hours gone by the time he'd stirred, halfway through her duty shift. He'd felt like death warmed over when he'd first dragged himself from bed, but a long—very long and very hot—shower, and a handful of analgesics had gone a long way to convincing him he would survive. A fresh uniform and a few pieces of dry toast had gone even farther, and he now felt almost downright human.

"I was in bad shape last night, wasn't I?" Carson still couldn't remember exactly what had happened. He wasn't much of a drinker, but he'd taken a glass to toast his comrades. The next thing he knew, they'd dropped him off at his quarters…and he was pretty sure someone had carried him down the last stretch of hallway.

Lise laughed as she dropped a small bag on the table. "We've had our share of sendoffs in the chem lab too, but I think your mates from *Dauntless* put us to shame. I know combat units party harder than career lab rats, but you must've made a big impression in such a short posting."

Sam nodded, a somber look slipping onto his face. "She's a good ship…with a good crew. And Captain Barron is…"

"You really liked him, didn't you? I asked around after you got posted there, and I heard some good things."

"He's a first class officer, Lise. He didn't have to approve my transfer here, especially not with war looming. But he actually insisted."

"I'll have to thank him one day. It will be nice to have you here when it's time."

Customs surrounding reproduction and childbirth varied around the Confederation. Cloning was illegal on all but a few of the Iron Belt worlds, but controlled artificial insemination with genetic scans and scheduled induced births was common in the inner worlds. On most provincial planets—and the true frontier outposts like Archellia—things tended to be done the old-fashioned way. Sam and Lise knew their child was a son and, based on the prenatal scans, healthy, but that was all.

"Yes, I'm glad things worked out too." Sam worked his face into a smile.

"You're really going to miss *Dauntless*, aren't you?" Lise paused. "Or is it duty with the battle fleet?"

Sam hesitated. "Lise, you know I'm happy to be with you, and to be here when our son is born. But *Dauntless* is a good ship. I've been battle fleet since I graduated from the Academy. Leaving them when war is about to break out seems…"

"You'll still be Combat here, Sam. Not Support like me. Archellia base is…"

"We just got back from the Union border, Lise. Where the war will be. I know I'll still be Combat, technically at least, but it's hard to imagine being farther away from the actual war."

Lise shook her head. "I understand what's bothering you, but I'm not going to pretend I'm not happy you'll be safer. That you'll be here with me…and with your son."

"I'm happy about that too, Lise." He took a few steps and put his arms around her. "I really am. But I still feel like I'm deserting my comrades. They'll have a month of shore leave like me…and then they'll go back to the front and wait for war to come. I'll be here, safe with my family, far from danger." He paused. "It's just hard."

"I know, Sam." Lise stepped back from his embrace, and she put her hand on his face. "But I'm still glad you're home."

Sam smiled. "So am I." He put his hand on hers. "So am I."

Chapter Seven

Letter from Lucius Rigellus to his Daughter

Kat, I am leaving this letter because one day I may not return from one of my missions. If you are reading this, I am gone, likely killed in battle.

I have written several versions of this over the years, revising it as you have grown. When you were younger, my words were briefer, simpler. I told you I loved you, that I would always be part of you, even when I wasn't there anymore. Those sentiments are as strong today as they ever were. My love for you has grown every day since you were born.

But you're older now...old enough to understand what it means to be a Palatian. *The way is the way.* You have recited it since you could speak, as all Palatians do. But now it is time for you to understand the true meaning behind it. And also what it means to be one of the Regulli.

We are a proud family, Katrine, and our traditions are rooted in adherence to duty. Palatia's history is one of shame, of subjugation and servitude. Never again, we have sworn, shall we be the victims...always the conquerors. This is the way. Remember it well, never forget...for it will demand much from you.

Begin your adherence to the way, my daughter, now, by not mourning me. If my life has been lost in service to our Alliance, have only joyous thoughts, for death in battle is honorable, a fitting way for one of the Regulli to die.

Grow, my child, revel in the joys of life at Litora Montis. Run, hike, feel the sun on your face. And when, in time, you reach

adulthood, know that my pride follows your every achievement. I
know you will bring only glory and honor to our great house.

Litora Montis, Rigellus Family Estate
Astara II, Palatia
Year 58 (307 AC)

Katrine fought off the wave of sadness. It was unbecoming
to someone of her station.

It was disappointing perhaps, that she couldn't see her children for a longer time before she embarked. It had been over
a year since she had last been home, and she felt a longing to
spend more time with them, hold them close. But duty was first.
Always. It was the way. And it fell to her to teach them that
lesson, by example. Her natural instincts to shower them with
affection would only make them weak.

The way is the way…

She owed even the two days she'd had with them to Vennius,
who had dispatched his private flyer to take her home. Kat had
been ready to cancel her trip back to the estate after the Commander-Maximus had given her the orders to take command of
Invictus, but the old man had insisted she return, that she visit her
children, even for a few hours.

She smiled thinking of the old man. Palatians weren't supposed to mourn parents lost in battle. They were supposed
to proudly wear their status as war orphans. But she was still
grateful she'd had a second chance to enjoy a father's love and
support.

She'd wondered if the children had been as anxious to see
her as she had been to see them. She remembered her own
childhood, her mother killed in action when she was only three,
her life among the stewards and tutors of the family manor.
Her father had been on campaign much of the time, of course,
a ship commander first and then a fleet exec. She had seen him
perhaps once a year on average, generally for no more than a
few weeks, though she recalled one stretch of almost three years

he'd been gone during the Eucallus War.

And then the last time.

She remembered the day she'd seen him off on that final mission like it was yesterday. It had seemed no different from the other partings. She was older, perhaps, than she had been before, but still a child. She had been first in her class, and the elder Rigellus had told his daughter of the pride he felt in her achievements as they had walked the grounds of the family estate. Neither had known that would be the last time they would speak…and Katrine held that memory close to her, feeling gratitude that her parting from her father had been a good one.

It had been a bleak day when she'd gotten the news that he'd been killed, the heavy clouds and fog rolling in off the sea echoing her mood. The pain, the urge to cry…and then the discipline, the Alliance's hard teachings slamming into place. To cry would be to dishonor her father. There was no place for tears, and certainly not for a warrior who had died heroically, bringing victory to his people.

She looked out over the same rocky ridges she knew from childhood, the wall of stone that rose above the crashing waves. Litora Montis had been in the Rigellus family since the founding of the Alliance, when her grandmother had taken it from the offworlders who had ruled over it before the Rising. Kat had heard the story told many times, at her grandmother's knee when she was younger, before the old woman died, and later from her father, and even the senior retainers on the estate. It was treasured family lore, the type of tale that most Patrician families had in one version or another.

The elder Katrine Rigellus, Kat's namesake, had been, by all accounts, an extraordinarily beautiful woman when she was young…and that beauty had brought unwanted attention on occupied Palatia. Kat suspected the old woman had never been entirely truthful about the abuse she had suffered, but she'd lived to take her vengeance, leading the other enslaved Palatians on the estate against their former masters, and by all accounts, letting not a single one escape. Kat suspected the outworlders' deaths had not been pleasant, and save for those who fell in battle, not quick either.

Gran was born into slavery, and she lived to see her world freed, her family established among the leaders of a strong and growing Alliance. She was a strong woman, and the matriarch of the Regulli. She could have done far, far worse…

Her eyes moved across the vista, watching the roiling waves of the sea. There was a storm coming. She could see the wall of clouds rolling in. It was part of life on the northern coast, especially in autumn, when the two moons crossed each other's orbits, shaking up the tides and the weather. Kat had loved the storms as a child, sitting in the great hall in front of a roaring fire as the massive rains and wind beat against the house. The storms were deadly for the estates a bit farther south, lower lying and subject to catastrophic flooding. But the lands of the Regulli lay high up on a rocky plateau, above a wall of great cliffs that seemed almost to laugh at the sea's attempts to challenge it.

Kay breathed deeply, savoring the cool morning air. She was accustomed by now to the recycled air and water on a spaceship, but she knew wherever duty took her, she would always miss the crisp autumn breezes of home.

It was early, predawn, only the faintest rays of morning glow illuminating the sky. She had risen hours before—indeed, she'd hardly slept. She knew how she was supposed to feel, but it was difficult looking into the children's eyes, seeing the love they felt, but the unfamiliarity too. She was proud to be a Palatian, but it was a heavy load at times.

Perhaps they are better seeing me less often. It will ease the burden on them if I fall. Doting on them would only make them weak. And they must not be weak, for they will inherit great obligations as well as high station…

She knew Alliance customs had purpose. Children had to become strong, self-sufficient…or they would make poor warriors. And then they would die. They would die in defeat…and those who followed would again know servitude. The way was hard, but it was the only choice.

They will still have their fathers if I fall…

Katrine knew many of the other human societies were built

around one version or another of pair bonding and subsequent reproduction, but the Alliance had rejected such inefficiencies. Kat had borne children because it was her duty to do so. Her station had placed her in control of the process, and she had selected each partner carefully, paying far more attention to such factors as genetics and social standing than to emotional nonsense.

That wasn't to say she hadn't enjoyed the process—though it had been far more satisfying with one partner than the other. But such distinctions were unimportant. Attraction and pleasure had their place in recreational sex, and trust and affection certainly played their role in the selection of friends and confidantes. But she had chosen her mates for their DNA, and nothing more.

It was the way, at least among Citizens and Patricians. The Alliance frowned on cloning and artificial insemination, and reproduction was done the natural way. It was another duty, to preserve and enhance the family's gene pool, to breed ever stronger and more capable heirs.

She'd had the higher social standing in both pairings, which meant the children had been raised as Regulli, the fathers assuming the roles of junior parents. Even if she died, the children would remain on the estate, raised by the family retainers to assume their places as the next generation of Regulli.

A dark thought pushed into her mind, and she wondered if she had more to offer the children dead than alive. She'd mourned her own mother, then in due course, her father. Yet the losses had hardened her, strengthened her to face the challenges of war, of leadership. She wondered how much of what she was now had been born in that pain. The children were Patricians, and as much as she loved them, she knew duty would rule their lives, as it had hers.

She turned and looked back at the house, a great manor, expanded massively, first by her grandmother and then her father. Perhaps when she returned, she would take a more extended leave, add her own mark to the property. The family was wealthy, indeed it had bled so much on the Alliance's battlefields it had accrued massive spoils of war, though few of its sons and daughters had survived to spend the treasure they had fought to amass. She wouldn't dote over the children, even if she was able to spend more time with them. She promised herself that. It was not the Alliance's way, and the last thing she wanted was to strip away their strength, to send them one day to war as weaklings.

But perhaps it wouldn't be so bad for them to actually know their mother…

Katrine sighed softly. The ways of the Alliance were indeed hard. But they were as they had to be. The alternative to strength was slavery…the Palatians knew that from bitter experience.

Her eyes caught the sun rising, dawn in all its brilliance.

Sunrise at Litora Montis, one of nature's great spectacles…

And time to leave as well…

She sighed, taking one last look at the sky, at the sun shining through a gap in the gathering clouds. Then she walked slowly around the side of the house, to the small landing strip where the flyer waited. She had kissed her children before she'd left the house, standing for a long time watching as each of them slept. She'd almost awakened them, but she decided it was easier to just slip away. The evening before had been pleasant, and she'd told them stories of her youth, and of their grandfather and great-grandmother as they sat in front of the fire, hours past their normal retirement hour. Those were better memories, she decided, than tearful pre-dawn farewells.

She walked toward the flyer. The retainers had already loaded her bags, and they were standing in two parallel lines, waiting to bid farewell to the mistress of the estate. She walked slowly, nodding to each of them. There were a few new faces, but most of them she remembered from years past, even a few from the days of her own childhood.

"Goodbye, Yuricus." She smiled at the old majordomo. The ancient man had run the household staff for longer than Kat had been alive. She remembered her father telling her stories about Yuricus teaching him to fish when he was a boy. As he had done for Kat as well.

"Goodbye, Mistress. May the fates protect you and bring you

back. I will see to the children while you are gone, as always." There was sadness in his eyes, but his voice was firm. Even the servants of a great house were expected to act as true Palatians.

"Thank you, Yuricus. Be well, my old friend." She nodded briefly, and then she climbed up the steps and slipped through the hatch into the flyer. She sat down, turning to look out the window, a last glance at her home. She had no idea how long she would be gone this time, whether she would return after her mission or whether a new war would begin. She could be years on the front before she again saw the craggy shores of her family's estate.

She sighed softly. Kat had known her share of glory—she was the most celebrated officer of her generation, and it was widely expected she would advance in due course to the highest ranks. Some of her comrades and allies even spoke in hushed tones of her eventual ascension to the Council, as if it was already a given. But she knew the cold mathematics she faced, that all of her peers did. Fewer than half of Palatian Patricians survived to the age of fifty. The constant combat took its toll, and thousands fell in battle. War cut deeply with its scythe, and those it carried away were often the best and most honorable of their generations.

She sat back in the plush chair, leaning her head to the side and looking forward to the cockpit, toward Commander-Maximus Vennius's pilot.

"You may take off when ready, Lieutenant."

*   *   *

"For those of you who have served with me before, veterans from *Vindictus*, welcome back. You are warriors and heroes all, and it fills me with satisfaction to have you all with me again as we serve mother Palatia. You are men and women of honor, of courage, and you do pride to your families, and to the Alliance you serve." Kat felt a little discomfort as she addressed her old crew. She had been hailed a hero, but she was also the commander who had gotten half of them killed. Not a man or woman from *Vindictus* didn't carry the memories of friends dying in those fateful moments around Heliopolis, dying because they had followed their commander's orders.

There was something else too. She had been decorated, hailed as a hero for her actions. Her crew had also been feted, but she knew most of the credit had accrued to her. It was the way of things, that junior officers and common spacers bled to feed the advance of their commanders. But now, addressing the warriors she had commanded before, she felt a strange discomfort about it.

"For those who are new to my command, welcome. It is your honor, as it is mine, to serve upon the Alliance's greatest instrument of war. This vessel is a triumph of Alliance engineering, and the great fist of our peoples' power and might. I call upon each of you to rise to meet this honor, to serve your new ship with all the courage and ability you have brought to your previous postings, and more, to exceed even that lofty level, for we set off now into the unknown, alone, our mission one of the gravest importance. To you, I promise all a commander can give…focus, tenacity, dedication. And *from* you I demand nothing less. Let us serve together, and bring honor upon this ship, and upon the Alliance we serve."

Kat felt a bit overwhelmed at the size and power of her new command. She had known about *Invictus*, at least in a general way. Most senior Alliance officers had been aware that a new flagship was under construction. But she'd almost gasped out loud as her shuttle approached the giant vessel. It was almost twice the size of her old ship, and its hulking form had filled the viewscreen. She'd arrived early, wanting a few days to familiarize herself with the new ship before the crew reported in, but now her complement was complete, one thousand one hundred twelve men and women…engineers, technicians, gunners, stewards, computer specialists, fighter pilots, mechanics. Everything the Alliance's largest battleship needed to begin its maiden voyage.

Kat moved her hand, her finger sliding over the small controls, shutting down the com unit. It was time for *Invictus* to leave.

She turned toward Tylian Wentus. The tactical operations officer had assumed the same post on *Invictus* that he'd had on *Vindictus*, tactical operations officer and second-in-command. She was glad to have him back, relieved to see him fit for duty. She could still remember him on *Vindictus* in the closing moments of the terrible battle at Heliopolis, his face, his uniform, every millimeter of him it had seemed, covered in blood. His wounds, it turned out, had looked worse than they actually were, but she had still been a bit surprised when she'd gotten the word he was cleared for action and assigned to *Invictus*.

"Optiomagis Wentus, take us out. One percent power until we clear the space dock."

"Yes, Commander." Wentus moved his hands over his controls. "Thrust at one percent."

Kat stared straight ahead, her eyes fixed on the main screen, watching as the massive orbital platform slowly receded into the distance. *Invictus* was underway. Another mission.

And if we succeed, another war…

Kat tried to push the doubts from her mind, but she couldn't forget Vennius's words, his concerns about the true strength of the Confederation. The Alliance prided itself on its martial success, but apart from the initial wars following the Rising, it had tended to face smaller adversaries. The Confederation was more than three times the size of the Alliance, and the Union more than six. This was a different game, one with far greater stakes.

Fear had no place in Alliance thinking, nor did intimidation. She had seen the price of weakness, of subjugation…she had seen it as a child, the dead coldness in her grandmother's eyes when she thought no one was looking, the price her sufferings as a young woman still extracted from her years later, after she had taken her vengeance, established a great house. The pain Kat knew had gone to the old woman's grave with her.

But how much is enough? How much war? How many dead?

She shook her head gently. Those questions weren't for her to consider.

"Take us to the jump point, Optiomagis. All stations prepare for translight operations."

It was time to do her duty.

Chapter Eight

Pronouncement from the Presidium

Despite the greatest and most profound efforts by our esteemed diplomats, the Confederation has continued to build up its military forces on our border. Though we seek only peace and mutual cooperation, we will do everything necessary to defend ourselves against this aggression.

The Presidium has today ordered our military forces to the highest alert status, ready to repel any invasion. We are saddened by the prospect of war, but we are unbowed, and we hail our brave military forces as they prepare to defend our beloved Fatherland.

The Federal Union is one, united, and we all stand together to face this grave threat. The need to support our forces as they prepare for war requires further austerity and sacrifices from all. Effective immediately, all weekly family rations will be reduced 7.5 percent. Residential electrical power to level three and level four sectors will be reduced from eighteen hours a day to fourteen.

We call upon all citizens to remain strong. We will never yield to Confederation aggression. No invader shall ever seize our worlds, conquer our sacred Union.

The Union forever.

Sector Nine Headquarters
Liberte City
Planet Montmirail, Ghassara IV,
Union Year 211 (307 AC)

"Greetings, Gaston. It's good to see you, my old friend. It's been a long time."

Gaston Villieneuve had been standing at the entrance to the plush office, but now he walked inside, closing the door behind him.

"My way has been difficult. It's a quite a distance to the Alliance, a path winding through the Confederation and then a backwater of independent systems you wouldn't believe. And the Confeds are so worried about war, they've got their pathetic security ramped up to something effective. They almost caught me twice."

The man behind the desk rose, walking over to the side of the room, where a small bar sat against the wall. Ricard Lille was clad in a civilian suit, clearly expensive and perfectly tailored. He turned toward his companion as he reached out and picked up a crystal decanter. "Wine? It's from the last case of the 167 vintage. It's really not to be missed, and we'll not see its like again."

Villieneuve nodded, walking across the floor, his heels clicking loudly on the polished wood floor, at least until he reached the area rug under the desk and the two chairs in front of it.

"By the Gods, yes, Ricard. Please. I thought Confederation wines were bad, but the Alliance? I swear they believe that if it tastes like cow piss it makes you stronger to drink it." His eyes dropped to the rug. "This is new, isn't it? Very nice. Must have cost you a fortune."

"Yes, I quite like it too. But no, it wasn't expensive at all… actually it was free." Lille turned and walked back toward the desk, stopping and holding a glass out to this companion. "We've been cracking down in anticipation of war, and we arrested several Ministers on suspicion of sharing information with Confederation agents. There was very little actual evidence, but with hostilities looming, we decided better safe than sorry. Even the innocent can serve as examples if handled correctly." He glanced down at the rug. "I had to have a few bloodstains removed...I'm afraid the previous owner wasn't too keen on ending up in Level Zero, and he'd gotten enough warning to barricade himself in with an assault rifle and a crate of ammunition. He managed to kill three agents before they took him down."

"Still, the state is more secure...and you got a fine addition for your office. I call that a win-win." Villieneuve raised the goblet to his lips and took a drink. "Wonderful," he said, holding the glass up and looking at the crimson liquid before taking another sip. "There's nothing remotely like *this* in the Alliance, I can assure you of that."

"Please, sit, relax." Lille waved for his guest to take one of the chairs, and he followed suit, plopping down behind his desk. "So, tell me. Was your mission a success? I read the reports, but I want to hear it from you. Did the Alliance take the bait? Will they attack?"

Villieneuve sighed. "I think so, Ricard." He hesitated. "At least I believe they'll do *something*. It's difficult to get a read on these Alliance officials, and I'm not sure we can trust what they promise."

"All previous accounts suggest that honor is a significant factor in their culture. Lying is frowned upon, except in matters of extreme national security. Do you disagree with that assessment?"

"No..." Villieneuve paused, shaking his head. "Not exactly. But I felt as if they believe destroying the Confederation would be a stepping stone for them to defeat us. They believe their destiny is to conquer...and I don't think they fear anyone."

Lille laughed. "Ambition is to be applauded, I suppose, even when it borders on insanity."

"Yes, but they don't behave in an insane manner, Ricard. There is a relentlessness to them, a firmness. I don't believe it's bravado. I think they truly feel that they can defeat us, or at least that there is a path to that result."

"What they believe in that regard is of no consequence, Gaston. If the Confederation falls, they will be next. And if they suffer losses while drawing Confederation strength away from our forces, their end will come that much sooner."

"Much rests on how they proceed. They have promised action, but they have been frustratingly vague as to specifics. And while they're warlike in the extreme, they aren't reckless. If they attack the Confederation, they'll do it methodically, and only if they believe they can win."

Lille leaned back in his chair, staring across the desk at his friend. "Let us hope that your long trip was not in vain. Though perhaps it's of little consequence. We outnumber the Confederation two to one in hulls, and three to one in ground forces. Even bearing the burdens of the invader, our projections suggest we have the advantage, even *without* Alliance involvement, by a significant margin. If the Alliance commits in strength, the Confederation is doomed to a rapid defeat."

"Perhaps." Villieneuve almost said more, but he stopped himself. He and Lille had been friends for twenty years, and he trusted the Minister as much as he dared trust anyone, but those who had reached a position of power in the Union and held it for any amount of time knew better than to be careless with words. Betrayal was simply too effective a route to high position, and relying on friendship was a very dangerous game. In a society where accusation was often regarded as tantamount to guilt, turning in associates—even friends—had aided the path of more than one aspiring Minister.

His eyes dropped to the floor. The rug's origin reminded him how quickly one could go from a powerful position to a pile of goo on the floor of an interrogation cell on Level Zero.

Lille just sat still for a moment. Villieneuve knew his superior was as aware of the dangers of loose talk as he was, that he would be just as cautious. It always paid to be careful, even with people you trusted. Especially with those you trusted... they were often the ones who could hurt you the most.

"There's no doubt. The fleet is strong, ready to face the Confederation." Lille's tone was guarded. It was clear he was choosing his words with care. "But the slightest distraction to the Confeds will have an exaggerated effect on their ability to meet our forces. The diversion of even ten percent of their active strength would create large gaps in their defenses. Our forces would be spared much hard fighting, and our losses and costs would be correspondingly smaller."

"Agreed." Villieneuve knew what they were truly discussing. Both of them were concerned about the Confederation's defenses, about how quickly their forces could win the victory. They would have the numbers in the initial assault, but though neither would admit it, they both knew the Confeds could outlast them. If the war turned into a grinding stalemate, the advantage would shift to the Confederation. The enemy was morally weak, their democracy mired down in intolerable chaos…but their economic strength was undeniable. The Union had to win the war in the first two years. If they didn't…

But there was nothing to be done. Villieneuve knew that his friend agreed with him, that they both felt the Union should wait, continue its build up. The Confederation was a republic, weak, subject to the whims of its undisciplined people. Given time their vigilance would fail. It was a strong argument, but one they dared not make. The rest of the Presidium had been overwhelmingly in favor of attacking now, and neither man was prepared to take the risk of disagreeing with their comrades. The power struggle that had ended the Third Confederation War was still fresh in everyone's minds. The Union had almost torn itself apart, and the amount of blood spilled—among its highest level politicians as much as its military forces—had been enormous. No one wanted to risk a return to that kind of infighting, and the prevailing attitude made it even more dangerous to oppose the majority view.

The two men sat, silent for a few moments. Villieneuve suspected Lille's thoughts were similar to his own, but he knew his friend would be no less disciplined than he. Paranoia was an essential trait for a Union politician, at least one who wanted to survive for the long term. Finally, he simply said, "Although I would not want to make a specific prediction, I am optimistic the Alliance will take some action…and virtually anything they do is likely to be helpful."

Lille nodded. "Let us hope so." A pause. "So tell me about Palatia, and about the Palatians. Are they as strange as rumors suggest?"

"Indeed they are, Ricard. I have never seen anything like it."

"I have heard their culture is austere."

"Austere? I wouldn't be surprised if they beat themselves with leather straps each morning. Their Patricians do live in considerable luxury…in a way. But I'd swear they manage to not enjoy any of it. However, their focus on military endeavors makes them perfect for our needs. They're small, with ambitions that exceed their capabilities. They can hit the Confederation hard if they choose to, but they're not fools. They'll move slowly at first, probe the border."

"Anything they do is a help, Gaston." Lille looked down at his desk, at the piles of reports stacked neatly to the side. "Planning an invasion is so much work, even for those in a supporting role like us. But I wager it can wait until morning…and I'd further bet you haven't had a decent meal in months. Dine with me tonight? I would look forward to hearing more about the Alliance and its strange ways."

Villieneuve smiled and nodded. "I would consider that a mercy, Ricard. The leavings from your pantry would make a feast in the Alliance."

* * *

Tom Warren ducked into a small alley, and dropped down behind a garbage bin.

He was scared. He was scared shitless.

He knew they were after him, but he couldn't run any more, not without resting for a few minutes. It was summer in Liberte City, and the alley reeked, so much he had to force back a retch. But it was a place to hide, at least for a little while.

He'd been an agent all his adult life, and he'd been in tough spots before. But all of that paled before running like a rat through the back streets of the Union's capital city with a pack of Sector Nine agents on his tail. He'd thought he'd been afraid before, but now he knew what terror *really* felt like.

He'd been in Liberte City for three months, sent there to investigate rumors that the Union was working to secure an ally in the war everyone knew was coming. He'd come with a few contacts, and massive amounts of cash for bribes, expecting it to go far with the deprived Union masses. But he'd never seen a population so effectively terrorized by its government, one that they would choose squalor and despair over any prospect of reward. He'd been there weeks before he'd managed to get anyone to talk to him, and even then the information he'd paid dearly for had been sparse, non-conclusive.

He'd kept at it, but even as he did, he'd found his own courage failing. He knew the Union's government was a totalitarian oligarchy, that the vast majority of its people had long been cowed into submission, but then he began hearing stories. Of Sector Nine. Of Level Zero, the maximum security section of their headquarters. Stories of small rooms with stone floors… and drains for the blood.

He'd powered through the fear, and he'd finally gotten the evidence he needed. The Union had reached out to the Alliance, sought to bring them into the war.

Warren had been surprised at first. He knew of the Alliance, of course, but they were far away, beyond the Unaligned Systems. And they were small, a growing power, no doubt, but not one that had registered on the Confederation's list of plausible threats. Not until now. With everything mobilized against the Union, any other threat was deadly serious.

His head snapped around, looking toward the street. He thought he heard footsteps. It was late, well past curfew, and that meant anyone out there was trouble. He froze, listening carefully, but there was nothing but silence.

He felt a tiny wave of relief, and he took a deep breath. Then he heard it again. There was no doubt. Someone was out there.

He looked down the alley. It was dark, just a single light hanging from the side of one of the buildings. He couldn't see the end. Did it offer an escape route? Or was it a dead end?

He heard the sound again, closer this time. There was no choice. He had to take his chances.

He stood up, slowly, quietly, and he took one last look toward the street. He was about to turn around when he saw movement—someone was coming around the corner.

The time for caution was over. He lunged forward, running down the alley, leaping over piles of garbage, broken crates. He passed by the light, and as he moved forward it got darker. He stared intently ahead as he ran, doing his best to avoid obstacles, but it was too dark now. He caught his foot on something, a broken piece of a chair, he thought. He tumbled to the ground, putting his arms out in front of him and feeling the pain shoot up to his shoulders as he landed hard on the pavement.

"Fuck," he muttered to himself, as he struggled to get up. He had to run, it was his only chance.

No, you have no chance…

He could hear the sounds behind him now. Footsteps, more than one pair.

He reached inside his jacket as he stumbled forward, ignoring the pain that wracked his entire body. His hand closed around the cool plastic of the gun, pulling it out. It was a pistol, short ranged, underpowered. Its primary utility was its ability to foil detection devices.

He thought about the firefight that was coming, and he knew immediately it was hopeless. There were at least half a dozen agents on his tail, and it was a dead level certainty they were armed better than him. If he fought, he might be wounded, and captured. And he knew what that meant.

Level Zero…

No, there was no point to fighting. But the gun could still be useful. It couldn't get him out of this, nothing could. But it could keep him out of Level Zero. He knew he was going to die. There was nothing he could do to stop that now. But he could still decide *how* he died.

He heard voices now, the agents yelling at him to surrender. They weren't shooting. That meant they wanted to take him alive. And he shuddered at the thought.

He took a deep, ragged breath, slowly raising the gun as he did.

How does one do this? How do you make yourself pull the trigger?

He heard movement, his pursuers getting closer. He wanted to delay, to buy even an extra minute of life, but he knew he was out of time. If they hit him with a stunner or a tranq, his death would be slow, agonizing. He had to do it now.

He put the barrel of the gun against his head, and he tightened his finger, slowly, struggling to finish it. His mind reeled as images filled his consciousness, old memories, strange thoughts he hadn't had in years. He wasn't ready to die. But ready had nothing to do with it.

He closed his eyes, focused on his finger. He could feel tears streaming down his face, and he was trembling. But then one last thought moved through his mind, and a small smile slipped onto his lips. The enemy had caught him, tracked him down... and now they would force him to take his own life. But they hadn't stopped him. He had succeeded. He'd sent his messenger two days before. The Confederation would get its warning. He had accomplished his mission.

His finger tightened all the way, and he heard a loud crack. Then darkness.

Chapter Nine

From the Log of Commander-Princeps Katrine Rigellus

We're about to enter Confederation space. I know little concrete information about the Confeds, but I find myself on edge, for reasons I can't entirely quantify. The mission is dangerous, certainly, but that's of no account. Still, its success is my duty. I must pay heed to my instincts, my experience. I must not ignore even intuition. I must be ready for whatever lies ahead.

Those who command have decided on war with the Confederation. My purpose is to obey. The invasion hinges on my mission. The fleet awaits our success. I've been granted an honor, the forward position in the next struggle. I was born to serve my homeland.

AS Invictus
Ishelar System
Alliance Year 58 (307 AC)

"Launch a spread of probes. Full stealth protocols." Kat was taking every possible precaution. *Invictus* had come through seven systems, and the next jump would take the battleship into Confederation space.

And that will be an act of war...

"Yes, Commander. Passive scans are still negative."

Invictus's commander felt the urge to use her active scanners.

The new vessel's suite had more than twice the power of *Vindictus's*, enough to pull in data from half the system. But it was also like shining a bright light in the darkness…it would alert any ships that might be lurking out there to *Invictus's* presence. And one transit from Confederation space, that wasn't a chance she was willing to take.

The systems she had passed through so far had been mostly empty, valueless save for the presence of still-functioning transwarp lines. The technology that had allowed man to create the faster than light links between worlds had been lost during the steady decline of human civilization leading up to the Cataclysm. The amazing portals between systems seemed almost like magic now, even, she suspected, to technologically advanced powers like the Confederation. The ancient lines dominated the strategic layout of human-occupied space, and the political entities and nations were largely based on links to other systems rather than actual locations in physical space.

Kat leaned back in the command chair, still surprised after two weeks at how comfortable it was. Alliance culture tended to be hard, and excessive luxuries were usually frowned upon. But whoever had been in charge of *Invictus's* final specs had ignored that tradition. The chair was upholstered in jet black Dhurallian leather, and it was plush and overstuffed. And the luxury went far beyond the bridge. The commander had a full office just off the control center, also luxuriously outfitted, and her quarters were downright palatial for a spaceship, four full rooms, richly-appointed.

Kat had to admit, on some level she enjoyed the comfort, but on another it bothered her. Her family was enormously wealthy, but she'd been raised to be tough, to be a warrior. When she'd gone on camping trips, first with her father, and after that with Yuricus, they had hunted or fished for their own food, and if they'd come up empty, they went hungry. They'd slept under the stars, on the hard, cold ground, not in tents erected by servants. It was normal for wealthy children of the Alliance to be pushed in this way, and though it was often hard, it was the way. Soft chairs and plush, luxurious quarters seemed wrong…and the fact that someone involved in the design process believed otherwise suggested an erosion of Alliance values that made her uncomfortable.

If Alliance discipline waned, if those who followed her failed to meet the demands of the way, her people would fall again, the shame of the past repeated. She imagined her children, grown but not warriors, soft instead, enslaved, tormented, as the people of Palatia had been. Her son, crucified, nailed to a large tree as an example to the other workers of the cost of rebelliousness. And her daughter, beautiful, but the fire in her sparkling eyes extinguished by the servitude and brutality of that was her life.

She didn't like the mission, not at all. She hated the idea of war with the Confederation, and the thought of allying with the Union, even for a short time, turned her stomach. But the way didn't require her to like her duty, it only required her to do it.

"Commander, we're getting probe data. No contacts yet."

"Very well, Optiomagis. Continue probe sweeps and passive scanners. And prepare to initiate thrust at twenty percent."

"Probes continuing into the system, Commander." A short pause. "Engine room reports ready for thrust on your command."

She stared at the main display for a few seconds. She didn't really expect to find anything in this system. The primary was a massive blue star, an O type, she recalled from the mandatory astrophysics training she gotten in the Academy. Ishelar was a stellar curiosity, a rare hypergiant, but that was the extent of its utility. A young star, it was doomed to an early death as its enormous mass and high core temperatures caused it to exhaust its nuclear fuel at a rapid rate. There were three planets orbiting the star, Kat didn't need her probes to tell her that...the system had been charted centuries, even millennia before. But none of the hot, rocky worlds had ever been deemed suitable for colonization or mining, and so Ishelar remained a system whose only utility was the ancient transwarp lines ran through it.

"Initiate thrust at twenty percent, Optiomagis. Let us be cautious until the probe data is more complete."

"Yes, Commander."

Kat stared straight ahead, trying to ignore the knot in her gut. She wasn't thinking about the Ishelar system and the vast emptiness she knew she'd find there. She was worried about the next jump…and whatever awaited *Invictus* beyond the border, in Confederation space.

*   *   *

"I'm definitely getting a reading from the transwarp gate, sir. Looks like a ship coming through." Stan Poole paused, staring at his instruments. There was surprise in his voice, and on his face as he turned toward the ship's commander. "And from the readings, I'd say it's a big sucker."

Lieutenant Higgins shook his head, surprise pushing away the boredom he'd felt a few seconds earlier. "Check the schedule. Did we miss a freight shipment due from the Rim? Look ahead a few days. Maybe we've got one running early or something." Higgins snapped out the questions because he couldn't think of anything else to say, but he knew damned well there was no scheduled traffic, and certainly nothing as big as the ship that seemed to be coming.

He'd been *Stingray's* skipper for over a year now, patrolling the Rim border and monitoring incoming ships, what few there were. The Confederation maintained a trickle of trade with several of the Unaligned Worlds, but traffic was always slow, usually no more than one or two ships a month. And mostly free traders, small operator-owned vessels that risked the deep space journey to bring back exotic luxuries from the systems beyond the Rim. Certainly nothing that would qualify as "big."

"Okay, let's get moving toward the gate and get a closer look. Three g's. Active scanners on full." Higgins held back a sigh. He'd managed to get himself assigned to the remotest corner of the Confederation, as far as possible from the looming war. Dealing with things like unknown ships was exactly what he'd hoped to avoid when he'd taken the posting.

It's nothing. Just a some kind of mix up.

After all, what else could it be out here on the edge of nowhere?

Still, there was no reason to be careless. Or to ignore procedure. "Send a flash com to *Condor*. Give them an update, and inform Lieutenant Childress we are moving to investigate." Higgins wasn't the bravest spacer in the Confederation fleet, he knew that much about himself. He hadn't been above trying to find a quiet posting before the start of a war everyone knew was likely to be a holocaust. But he wasn't a coward either, nor was he incompetent. And whatever was coming through the transwarp link, he knew it was his duty to check it out.

He didn't really think the ship would be a problem, more than likely just a foul up in the shipping schedules, or at worst someone trying to smuggle some embargoed shipment from one Rim system or another. But he understood the safeguards border protocols demanded too.

"Yes, sir. Sending flash com now."

The bridge was silent, save for the faint sounds of the engines in the background. There were only three crew members present, and only eighteen on all of *Stingray*. Higgins's ship was technically navy, but he knew his customs boat was far from a true warship. If it *was* something hostile coming through...

"Approaching the transwarp portal, sir. Ship exiting now..."

Higgins sat quietly, trying to ignore the fear building in his gut, despite all his self-assurances about what was coming.

"Lieutenant, it's through. Scanning now." Then: "Lieutenant, it's..."

Poole's voice told Higgins all he need to know. Trouble.

"It's huge, sir. Scanners are still chewing on it, but I'd estimate four klicks in length at least. And the power readings... they're massive." Poole turned and stared over at Higgins. "It's got to be a warship, sir. A damned big one too."

Higgins froze for a few seconds.

A warship? But whose?

Then he snapped out of his shock. It didn't matter whose ship it was. It was here...and he was the Confederation commander on the scene. "Reverse thrust, Ensign Poole. Full power away from the contact."

"Yes, sir. Full thrust."

"Flash com to *Condor*…tell them we have an unidentified vessel coming through the transwarp portal. Include all scanner data. Com status Omega-Two."

"Yes, sir. Omega-Two protocols."

Omega-Two was the Confederation's signal for a possible invasion. Higgins knew Lieutenant Childress would pass the warning through the transwarp com system.

Higgins slumped in his chair, struggling to maintain his calm as panic began to creep over him.

I didn't put all that effort into this transfer to the Rim to end up staring down some mysterious battleship. Or to get blasted to atoms before a shot is fired on the real battle front.

He shook his head, staring at the small, locked control panel on his workstation, the one that activated the Omega-One call.

He moved his fingers over the smooth metal. He unlocked the small door, flipping it open. There was a button below, not red or yellow or any other color that spoke of war and strife and danger. It was black, the same as every other control on the bridge. But this one was special. If he pressed it, *Stingray's* com system would send out a communications blast, one that had a single meaning.

Omega-One. War.

* * *

"Contact confirmed, Commander. Small vessel, roughly five thousand tons, on a direct course toward us…no, scratch that. They appear to be decelerating. My guess is they're trying to reverse their vector and run."

"I want their com jammed, Optiomagis. Now!" Kat stared at the display. The data was still coming in, but she was going on the assumption it was a Confederation patrol ship. It was no real threat to *Invictus*, at least not in a fight. But it could cause trouble with its com units. She had hoped to get much deeper into Confederation space before the incursion was detected. Running into a patrol as her ship transited was just bad luck. "Engage active scanners—I want to know what else is in this system. Full thrust as soon as possible. I don't want them getting away to send any warning."

"Yes, Commander. Jamming on full power." A few seconds later. "Engines ready." Another short pause. Then: "Commander, I think they might have sent some kind of communique before the jammers engaged."

"An alert?"

"I don't think it was a strong enough signal to reach the transwarp relays. It seemed like a normal flash com. It must have been to…another ship…"

Another ship…one outside jamming range…

"Full thrust…establish direct approach vector and close." Kat stared at the system plot on the main display. It was a lot of space, far more than even her active scanners could cover… and another ship could be anywhere out there. Anywhere at all. "Active scanners on full power. Duty patrol to the launch bays."

"Yes, Commander."

Kat felt the force of the thrusters as *Invictus*'s massive engines engaged. The Alliance's newest ship had enormous grav dampeners, more powerful ones by far than *Vindictus* had mounted, but she could still feel the g-forces pushing hard against her. She wondered if the Confeds endured such discomfort in battle, or if their technology afforded them an easier ride. She didn't hate the Confeds, but like most of her comrades, she considered them soft, weak. She didn't doubt they would waste resources and research making their ships more comfortable, even at the cost of more weapons and increased power…while the Alliance's priority was always combat effectiveness.

"We're closing, Commander. Range 550,000 kilometers. Active scanners on full. Optiomagis Junus reports patrol ready to launch."

"Continue full thrust, Optiomagis."

"Yes, Commander."

Kat stared at the display. The scanners had fully updated the contact's data. It was definitely some kind of patrol ship. Kat had hoped to get to Santis before she was forced to spill Confederation blood. But she had no choice now.

"Arm secondary batteries…prepare to fire."

"Gunnery stations report all secondaries ready, Commander. Project firing range in thirty seconds."

"Fighter patrol launch. They are to scan the system and find any other ships out there. Advise Optiomagis Junus he is to engage and destroy any contacts."

"Yes, Commander." A few seconds later: "Fighters launching now."

Kat felt the familiar vibration, the rumbling feeling of the magnetic catapults launching the fighters.

She stared straight ahead, watching as the range counted down. The patrol ship was trying to run now, but its vector was still moving it toward *Invictus*, its velocity too great to quickly reverse. And time was running out…

She had hoped to avoid any contacts this far out, but hope was a pointless emotion. Alliance warriors dealt in reality, in the tactical situation they faced.

"Optiomagis…" Kat looked straight forward, her body rigid, her tone cold, emotionless. "Open fire."

Chapter Ten

Base Tom Wills
Planet Santis, Krillus IV
307 AC

"Let's keep that sorry ass moving, Thoms. That goes for the rest of you too. You all look like shit warmed over and dumped on a plate." Clete Hargraves was running alongside the small column, taking delight in haranguing his Marines, just as any good platoon sergeant would do. "You're all soft…what are you gonna do if we get shipped up to the front when the balloon goes up? I'll tell you what. You're gonna get your fat asses shot off by those Union FRs, that's what."

"Sarge, we done ten klicks already, and it's gettin' cold. My balls are frozen." Joe Thoms looked the part of a Marine, a hulking kid who anyone would have guessed was at least twenty-five, although Hargraves knew damned well he was only twenty.

"Mine too," added Janet Blocker, somewhat less literally.

Hargraves turned around, running backwards—and making it look effortless, though it wasn't—as he faced his suffering group of Marines. "Yeah, try that with the Union FRs…maybe they won't blow those frozen fucking balls off if you ask nicely. Problem with that is, you ain't the only one who gets ganked. The rest of the Marines counting on your sorry ass get blasted too. So, let's cut the whining and show some hustle. It's just six klicks back to the barracks. If you pukes can keep up with me the rest of the way, I might even let you rest before chow."

There were a few scattered groans, but the twenty-odd Marines kept running, following the platoon sergeant and, for the most part, keeping up with him. Finally, the column snaked its way through a small town, nothing more than a single dirt road with a dozen buildings on each side, and then up to a large, low structure.

"I knew you could do it, kiddies. And I'm nothin' but a man of my word. So get a load off, rest those precious little bodies. You got an hour 'til chop."

Hargraves turned and walked down to the end of the building, listening to the sounds behind him, mostly exhausted grunts of one kind or another. He continued to the last door and knocked.

"Come."

He opened the door and stepped in, snapping to attention as soon as he was inside. "Sir!"

"At ease, Sergeant. And close the door…it's cold enough every day on this forsaken planet, but I'd swear it feels like deep space out there today."

Hargraves reached out, pushing the door shut. "I think first and second squads would agree with you, sir. They squalled like a bunch of baby birds, but they finished. They damned near even kept up with me…which goes to show just how much effort a Marine will make to get out of the cold."

Lieutenant Luke Plunkett turned and looked up from his desk, clearly trying to hold back a laugh. "You're a sick bastard, you know that?" Plunkett gestured toward an empty chair.

"Won't do them no favors goin' easy on them, Lieutenant. When they end up in the shit, every time I beat them to the ground gives them an extra chance to make it back home." Hargraves was the only real combat veteran in fourth platoon, and that included Plunkett. The career sergeant was forty-five, and he'd done service in the last war between the Union and the Confederation. He had stories of the Union ground forces that shook even the lieutenant.

"Tell me, Sarge. The FRs...they're really that tough?"

Hargraves sat down, letting out a deep breath as he did. He'd never have admitted it to his Marines, but he was pretty damned tired himself. "Well, sir...let's just say they ain't like nuthin' you ever saw before. Not better than us...not as good even, I'd say, not by a good chunk. But there's always more of 'em, Lieutenant, and the thing is, they're disciplined. Like nuthin' you ever saw. Every one of 'em would jump off a cliff if an officer ordered it."

The Foudre Rouge were the Union's ground forces, the counterparts of the Confederation Marines. The FRs were clones, genetically optimized for combat, and mentally conditioned for total obedience and a complete lack of fear. In theory they should have been the ultimate warriors, but it didn't work quite that way in the field, and the Confed Marines had held their own in the last war, at least wherever they weren't outnumbered two or three to one. The FRs were good fighters, highly effective against most enemies. But they met their match when they faced the Marines.

Confederation ethics frowned heavily on cloning for any purposes, and it was legal only on a few worlds. Breeding a customized class of slave-warriors and removing their will to resist, even to understand the idea of questioning an order, was extremely immoral to the Confederation way of thinking. Indeed, it was downright evil.

The two sat silently for a while. Then Hargraves said, "Do ya think we'll get redeployed when the war breaks out? I'm not sure I like the idea of sittin' out here in the middle of nowhere while Marines are fighting and dyin' trying to turn back the Union."

Plunkett shook his head. "I just don't know, Sarge. Normal procedure is to rotate after a year's deployment, especially on Santis. But I don't know. If the balloon goes up...I hope they don't forget us. It's not like one platoon's going to decide the war, but I don't like the idea of being stuck here for too long..."

Hargraves nodded. Santis looked like just about any world in the Confederation, but he knew it wasn't. The sergeant didn't have any pretensions as a physicist, but he was well aware of the planet's special characteristic, the one that made it valuable, but also the thing that had prevented extensive colonization and restricted the population to a hundred or so technicians and a platoon of Marines.

Santis's primary, Krillus, was a fairly normal sun, but it was part of a binary system, and the companion was a magnetized neutron star that bathed the system with hard x-rays in concentrations far above normal levels. That had two relevant effects on the planet. First, it caused a concentration of tritium in Santis's ocean over a hundred times the amount found on a more normal planet. Second, it made the planet a pretty damned unhealthy place to live, at least for any extended time.

The technicians, the ones who operated the massive refinery that extracted the precious tritium from the ocean, tended to stay for longer than they probably should. But they were making twenty times what they would have in a normal job, and there was no shortage of candidates willing to accept the health risk for *that* kind of money. But Marines just went where they were told to go, and the meager monthly pay of a sergeant—and even a lieutenant—was hardly compensation for waiting around as your DNA was slowly damaged and mutated by radiation. And the idea of sitting by and watching comrades fight a war that would determine if your people maintained their freedom was anathema to Marines.

"Sure as shit, the high command don't want my opinion, but I'd hate to sit here while the rest of the Marines are fighting to save the Confederation." Hargraves looked up at Plunkett. "I don't know big strategy or any of that stuff, Lieutenant, but I was there in the last war. I saw the enemy up close. They came to finish things, sir. No doubt about that. If their leader hadn't died, that woulda been a fight to the finish." He paused, looking down at the floor for a few seconds. "And now, they're gonna come again. This one's gonna be to the end, sir. I don't want to fight, not against those damned FRs, not again. But it ain't about what I want. We gotta fight, all of us. And if this is the big war, the final one…no Marine wants to sit here on the edge of nowhere getting eaten alive by rads while somebody else fights for the future."

Plunkett sighed. "Well, Sarge, I agree with you one hundred percent. But none of it is up to you. Or up to me, for that matter. I guess we'll just have to…"

The small com unit on the table buzzed. "Lieutenant Plunkett, it's Corporal Williams in the communications hut. Sorry to disturb you, sir, but I have Sergeant Jones on the com for you."

Plunkett shot a confused glance over at Hargraves. Jones was on the orbital platform with one of the platoon's squads. It was a regular rotation that put a quarter of his Marines up there at any time. But what the hell could Jones have to report? "Put him through, Corporal."

"Lieutenant, sir…it's Sergeant Jones. I…ah…there's something happening up here. The techs…their scanners show a ship coming through the transwarp, sir. They got nothing scheduled." There was a short pause, and Plunkett could hear voices in the background. Then: "Lieutenant, something's definitely wrong. Unless the scanners are going bonkers, that ship is over four klicks long. The techs say the energy readings are way too high for a tanker…which means…"

"All right, Sergeant…don't lose your shit. Let's take this one step at a time. Even if it *is* a warship, it could be one of ours… is probably one of ours. Maybe their com is down or something. Maybe…" Plunkett wanted to blurt out a whole series of maybes, as much to calm himself as his Marines. He had no idea what hostile ship could be there…it seemed impossible that a Union vessel could have gotten all the way across the Confederation undetected. But he knew the Confed fleet was massed to face the expected attack on the Union border…and it seemed unlikely a frontline battleship would be all the way out here. Not now.

"Yes, sir…" Jones didn't sound convinced. "What do you want me to do, sir?"

Plunkett hesitated. Hargraves could see the lieutenant had no idea what to do. If that was some kind of hostile battleship there wasn't much one platoon of Marines was going to do to stop it.

"Put your men on alert, Sergeant. Just to be safe. And ask Mr. Klyde if his people need any help manning the weapons stations up there."

The orbital platform was mostly a place for tankers to dock while the ground-to-orbit tenders ferried up refined tritium. It had a few guns manned by civilian techs who'd been given some extra training, a token planetary defense, but nothing that was going to make a four-kilometer long battleship stop and take notice. Still, he couldn't think of anything else.

"Yes, Lieutenant."

"And, Sergeant…keep me posted. If anything happens, anything at all, you let me know. And even if it doesn't I want hourly updates."

"Yes, sir. Understood. Jones out."

Plunkett turned toward his platoon sergeant. "So what do you think, Clete? Any ideas?"

"It's probably nothin' Lieutenant…"

"But?"

"Well, they ain't gonna much like this, but if I was you, I'd get the whole platoon—minus Jones's people, of course—and march 'em outta here. One blast from orbit, and the barracks is gone…and the armory too. The way I figure it, if that's a Confed ship, or somethin' else we ain't thought of, then no harm done. But if this is an attack, we ain't gotta chance sittin' here. There's caves all along the shoreline, and thick woods up north. Let's just say some kind of enemy lands here…even if we put up a fight, you figure we're beat in an hour. But if we're all spread out, dug in…that's a nightmare for an attacker. And if somebody does land here and occupy the place…we can do all sorts of hit and runs, keep 'em on edge. Might not be a way to win, but we can damned sure keep 'em on their toes."

Plunkett sat quietly for a moment. Then he looked right at Hargraves. "Alright, Clete…let's do it." He paused. "They're not going to like it…it's cold out there."

The veteran sergeant stared back, just the slightest hint of sadism in the crooked little smile on his lips. "They're Marines, Lieutenant. They'll complain about anything. But they'll damned well do what they're told!"

*   *   *

"Approaching firing range, Commander. Scanning data confirms our earlier conclusions. An orbital platform designed primarily for the loading of compressed tritium. It is armed, but minimally."

Kat leaned back in her chair, feeling another twinge of Patrician guilt for enjoying the comfort as much as she was. "Gold Dagger squadron to the launch bay. Advise Optiomagis Junus his people are to target the enemy weapon systems only. I need those guns knocked out, but I want damage to the rest of the platform kept to a minimum."

"Yes, Commander."

Invictus had passed through three Confederation systems since the initial contact at Ishelar. They had blasted the first enemy ship they'd encountered there to atoms with a single volley, but it had taken almost two days to find and destroy the second vessel. Her fighters had finally run the wily patrol ship down and destroyed its engines. After that, it was just a matter of a few strafing runs to finish the job.

Her forces had searched the rest of the Alaris system before moving on. It had been empty, save for half a dozen automated scanner stations, all of which she had destroyed. She was in Confederation space, but all hope of maintaining total secrecy had been lost. The second ship had almost certainly had time to send a report through the transwarp lines…and the automated stations as well. She doubted the Confeds would conclude they had an Alliance battleship on their doorstep. Most likely—hopefully, at least—they would assume they were dealing with some kind of pirate or renegade traffic. A problem for sure, but not one that called for immediate, desperate action. Time was the resource she needed, and the longer the Confeds waited, the greater her chance for success. With any luck, by the time a force of any substance was sent against her, it would find the entire Alliance fleet waiting.

There had been nothing of note between Alaris and the refueling station on Santis, just two small mining colonies, inhospitable worlds with a few hundred hardy souls digging out one sort of rare mineral or another, trying to get rich before their host planets killed them.

Kat had ordered their satellites and orbital facilities destroyed, but she'd left the ground settlements unmolested, a choice she knew had raised a few eyebrows among the crew. She had the authority to do as she deemed best for the mission, and her destruction of the orbital assets left the mining colonies cut off, unable to communicate or call for help. Still, she realized most Alliance commanders would have chosen to bombard the ground positions, slaughtering the miners and other civilians as an added security measure. Alliance doctrine wasn't genocidal by nature, but it placed first priority on the mission above all things, and enemy casualties, civilian or otherwise, were rarely considered.

Kat had felt the urge at first to do the same, but something had stopped her. Death in battle was one thing, the struggle to conquer or die rather than ever accept slavery again...she understood that. It was the nature of the universe. But slaughtering innocent civilians left her cold. She knew uncountable numbers had died on Heliopolis, and in her other campaigns. She hadn't really considered it until recently, but it had begun to trouble her. She would do whatever was necessary to execute her orders, but that was all.

"Gold Dagger Squadron reports ready to launch, Commander."

"Reverse thrust. Bring us to a halt five hundred thousand kilometers from the station." She had no idea of the range of the platform's weapons, but she was sure it was less than half a million kilometers.

"Reversing thrust."

"Launch fighters." The Gold Daggers were her elite squadron, under the direct leadership of her overall fighter commander. It was overkill launching a fighter strike, especially with her top pilots, but precision was important here, and the small craft could deliver that far more effectively than *Invictus's* massive batteries.

Santis was the primary goal of the mission, the refueling station the fleet needed to invade the Confederation. And if she blasted the orbital facilities to scrap, they'd have to be rebuilt before the fleet could move.

"Gold Dagger squadron launched, Commander."

Kat's eyes focused on the main display, watching the twelve tiny dots move forward, already traveling at three hundred kilometers per second, courtesy of *Invictus's* powerful magnetic catapults.

"Get me Praefectus Millius." Praefectus-Princeps Arn Millius commanded the three centuries of stormtroopers she had aboard *Invictus*. Millius was new to her service, but she'd reviewed his record and been quite impressed. He'd been at Heliopolis too, in the vanguard of the assault. He'd led a full cohort there, so his service aboard *Invictus* could be considered a step back, at least in terms of the numbers of troops under his command.

She saw the hand of Tarkus Vennius in Millius's assignment, and she suspected the old man had found a reliable ground commander for her. Millius's apparent lack of any resentment or concern at the nearly fifty percent reduction in forces under his command suggested that Vennius had promised him a promotion as a reward for completing the mission, much as he had with her.

I can see Uncle Taks's hand in almost everyone on this crew. Junus, Millius…he's really worried about this mission.

"Praefectus Millius, Commander." The infantry officer's voice was crisp, hard.

Kat turned toward the com. "Praefectus, we're going to knock out that station's offensive weapons, but I want to capture it intact. Prepare a boarding force…" She paused, her eyes drifting to the list of scanner results on her screen. The station was fairly large, but she suspected its crew was small…and that it had little in the way of a security force.

Still, no sense taking chances…

"I believe one century will be more than enough." It was also the most her four assault shuttles could carry in a single wave. Probably overkill, but better to have too much force than too little.

"Yes, Commander. We will be ready in ten minutes."

Kat hadn't intended to send Millius himself, but she respected the officer's intent to lead his people personally. Millius had a hard edge to him, and some of her other officers had found the Praefectus difficult, unpleasant. But Kat liked his directness. It seemed a match for her own.

"Very well, Praefectus. Remember, I want as little physical damage as possible. We need that station intact."

"Understood, Commander. Millius out."

She turned toward Wentus. "Optiomagis, prepare assault shuttles for launch."

"Yes, Commander."

Her eyes darted back to the main screen. Junus's fighters were almost to the station. The enemy batteries had opened up, and her suspicions were confirmed. They were light lasers, with effective ranges under one hundred thousand kilometers.

"Activate engines, Optiomagis. One-eighth thrust. Bring us to one hundred fifty thousand kilometers from the station."

"Yes, Commander."

"And maintain full jamming."

It was bad enough the border patrols got off some kind of warning...she didn't need to add a distress call from Santis. The intelligence reports maintained that the Confeds had no heavy ships based anywhere near the Rim, but Kat's opinion of the shadow services had not improved. She wasn't about to bet the lives of her people on the wild guesses of a pack of political appointees who considered themselves master spies.

It was bad enough she had to bet their lives on her own wild guesses...

Chapter Eleven

The Starfire Hotel
Archa City
Archellia, Cassiopolis III
307 AC

Barron sat on the plush sofa, staring out at the skyline of Archa City. At least that's what the locals called it, though the three dozen or so buildings that formed its downtown cluster topped out not much above one hundred meters. *Dauntless's* captain was from Corellia, one of the Confederation's seven core worlds. Corellia's soaring metropolises and kilometers-high towers made Archa seem like a quaint little village with a few farm stands and a general store by comparison. Barron knew that wasn't entirely fair, but he still thought the urban pretensions of the place were amusing.

He couldn't complain about the Starfire Suite, though he wasn't sure he had any use for the hulking grand piano or the three extra bedrooms. He wondered who rented the suite normally, what magnates or visiting dignitaries with money to burn ever found themselves on Archellia.

Most of the suite's comforts were wasted on him. Though his family was wealthy, he'd always had simple tastes. He'd hidden in the suite as much as possible trying to avoid the fawning of the locals, far preferring to sit and read rather than smile and carry the Barron flag through endless dinners and receptions. He hadn't been able to avoid them all, but he did what he could…and now he found himself about halfway through the history text he'd been reading.

When he'd been a junior officer, he'd always refused the offers of local communities to put him up in luxurious accommodations, but somewhere along the line, he'd realized they were just expressing their love and gratitude for his grandfather's heroism…and that as much as he had tried, there was no way to refuse without leaving a trail of hurt feelings behind. He'd never gotten comfortable with the celebrations and endless dinners with local dignitaries, but now he tried to strike a balance, humoring the locals enough to be gracious and hiding in his room enough to maintain his sanity.

He felt vibration in his pocket of his com unit buzzing. He pulled out the small device. It was usually clipped to his collar when he wore his uniform, but he'd been planning to go out for a run, and he was dressed in a pair of light sweats.

"Yes?"

"Captain, it's Atara. I just got a flash update from the base, sir." Travis took her duties seriously, and part of that meant being the information conduit between base command and the captain. Barron knew she took it upon herself to see that he wasn't disturbed unless it was absolutely necessary. He appreciated it, but he also regretted the added stress she took on herself.

"What is it, Atara? I know I wouldn't be hearing from you if there wasn't a problem."

"I don't know, sir. Admiral Lowery wants to see the two of us as soon as possible."

Barron didn't like the sound of that. Lowery was the base commander, the senior officer on all Archellia. Something *was* wrong. Had one of his people gotten into some kind of real trouble? Or had the refit crews found a major problem on *Dauntless?*

So much for a run…but I definitely need a shower and shave before reporting to the admiral. "Okay. I need about thirty minutes, and I'll meet you outside the command building."

"I'll be there. Atara out."

Barron sighed. He couldn't imagine a maintenance problem so bad it couldn't be discussed over the com. And, while he wouldn't be surprised if a few of his people—especially the pilots—ended up getting hauled in by base security, he couldn't imagine any of them had caused any *real* problems. Drunkenness and brawls were normal enough in any spaceport, nothing that should even get to the admiral's desk.

He walked toward the bathroom, pulling the tight sweatshirt over his head as he did.

So, what the hell is it?

The war? Has it started?

Barron shook his head. No, that couldn't be it. If that had happened, the whole base would be on alert. But what else?

What could it be, all the way out here?

* * *

Jake Stockton held the cards in his hand, folded up. He hadn't even looked at the one he'd just drawn. He just stared across the table, with the same non-committal look he'd worn on his face since he'd sat down two hours before.

The Siren's Call was a bar typical of the sort that lined the area around the naval base. It was large, and a little rougher looking than the average watering hole, the kind of place where half the tables and chairs had been patched together after being used as clubs in one brawl or another. It was also a place where a spacer or Marine on shore leave could find a poker game. Not just cards, but the kind of hard core game where real money exchanged hands.

Stockton had a huge pile of chips in front of him, at least ten times what he'd started with. The players around the table had changed, three of the originals busted and replaced by others, but the giant directly across from Stockton was still there. He'd been the big winner, at least before *Dauntless*'s resident shark had arrived, and he stared back at Stockton with undisguised rage.

"Aren't you gonna look at your cards?" The man's accent

was thick, a drawl Stockton figured came from someplace like Cavenaugh or Blackton, one of the coreward provincial worlds.

Stockton was a seasoned gambler, the only thing of value he'd inherited—or learned—from his father, and for all the bravado and cockiness he showed in the cockpit, he tended to keep as low a profile as possible at the poker table. But it didn't look like it was working this time. The big man was clearly getting hot. His uniform was filthy and stained with the local ale, but there was no mistaking the Marine grays. And Stockton had long ago learned to tread carefully around the Confederation's Marines. Especially big ones. Drunk big ones.

"No need, friend." Stockton's tone was cool, exuding confidence. He reached out and shoved a pile of chips toward the center of the table. "Five hundred." He held the Marine's stare, trying to push away the thoughts on just how easily the massive ground-pounder could snap him in half. Stockton was death personified in his fighter, but in a bar facing a Marine who outweighed him by at least fifty kilos, he suspected his prospects were less than rosy.

Play moved around the table, each player throwing in his cards. Until it got to the Marine. He stared back at Stockton as he pushed a stack of chips forward. "See your five hundred... and raise you another five hundred."

Stockton just nodded. His gut told him he had the big man. If the Marine had a strong hand, he'd have raised more aggressively earlier. He guessed it was more like a middling pair, perhaps two pair...something that felt too good to fold. His opponent was clearly a skilled player, but he was an emotional one too. Stockton had taken a fair amount of his money, and he knew the Marine wanted to win it back. That was a dangerous state of mind when facing a player like *Dauntless*'s ace pilot.

He hesitated a few more seconds, as much to increase his opponent's tension as anything else. Then he put both hands on the table and pushed forward. "I'm all in." His voice was stone cold, utterly without emotion. "That's eleven thousand, four hundred."

The Marine glared back. He was frustrated, and what control

he'd had was gone.

Stockton set his cards face down on the table, still not flashing so much as a glance at them. It was all part of the show, his efforts to unnerve his opponent. He didn't need to look. He knew what he had. Nothing. Absolutely nothing. His best card was a nine.

He returned the Marine's gaze, giving the big man nothing, not the slightest tell. He'd had good control over himself since his Academy days, but his years as a pilot had honed his cool. He'd never been in a full scale war, no one under the age of forty-five or so had, but he'd done duty against pirates, and in the badlands chasing down tech poachers. He knew what it felt like to sit in a tiny fighter, bearing down on ships a hundred times as large without flinching. The poker table was no different, except he wasn't risking his life playing cards.

His eyes focused on the size of the Marine across the table, the burning anger in his eyes.

At least I don't think I'm risking my life...

For an instant, he thought his adversary might just call his bluff. He'd been working the man for two hours, playing a tight game, only raising when he had the hand. His entire game had been a set up for this bluff. But there were no guarantees. Perhaps he'd gotten the Marine too unnerved...or maybe the big man had drawn three of a kind or some other hand that would tempt him to call. But then he saw it in opponent's eyes. Capitulation.

"I fold." The marine threw his cards down on the table in disgust.

Stockton mucked his cards, facedown.

"No...I want to see what you had..."

Stockton felt his adrenaline surge. They all knew the rules. He didn't have to show his opponent a thing. But the tone of voice suggested the Marine didn't care.

"Forget about it, friend." Stockton kept his voice even, though he allowed a little firmness to creep in. It didn't really matter what hand he'd thrown away...but he suspected his opponent would not react well to having been so thoroughly suckered and bluffed. Stockton had come to unwind, to win a little money. He didn't think much of the idea of spending his shore leave in the stockade.

Assuming this guy doesn't just break me in half.

"I said show me those cards." The Marine reached out, moving his hand toward Stockton's cards.

Stockton reached out and put his own hand down over the cards. "Let's move on." He held his ground, but he couldn't help but notice his hand was barely half the size of the giant Marine's.

"C'mon, J.T., we don't want any trouble." It was one of the busted players, who had hung around to watch the game. He was joined by two of the other players, all Marines and clearly friends of the big man, all urging their comrade to be calm.

"I want to see those cards!" he roared, standing up, completely ignoring his friends' efforts to calm him.

Stockton kept his hand over the cards. He knew the door was right behind him, but any quick escape meant leaving his chips—half a year's pay—behind. If he stayed, and the shit hit the fan, he was alone. The Siren's Call was mostly a Marine hangout. There were a few spacers, probably crews of Archellia's system patrol force, but no one he recognized from *Dauntless*. In a fight, he'd be on his own…

"Friend, come on…"

"There you are. We've been looking all over for you." Kyle Jamison walked through the door, flanked by two of *Dauntless's* other pilots. Jamison was the ship's strike force commander, Stockton's superior officer…and his best friend. "You're supposed to have your com unit with you, even on shore leave. I *know* you know that."

"You're right, Commander. My fault." Stockton stood up and reached across the table, pulling the chips toward himself and gathering them together as he did.

"Come on, we've got to get back to *Dauntless*. We got a recall notice."

"But we're on shore leave, Commander."

"Not any more, Lieutenant. All leaves are canceled."

The Marine stood up and glared across the table. He was

clearly still angry, but the appearance of a superior officer and more pilots had taken him by surprise.

Jamison looked at Stockton then at the enraged Marine. He fought back a smile. "Sergeant," he said to the Marine, "I'm afraid we have to break up your game."

The big man stared back, but then he just nodded, clearly not willing to risk a brawl with a superior officer.

Jamison looked back at Stockton. "Let's move it, Lieutenant. Orders." He turned and walked toward the door.

Stockton pulled up his shirt to hold his chips, and then he followed behind, hurrying to catch up. Once they were outside, he hustled up alongside Jamison. "What's going on, Kyle? What's the alert about?"

"I don't know, Jake...but its priority one, so it must be something big."

Stockton frowned. "Somebody's probably lost a dog." A few second later, he added: "We're not leaving Archellia, are we?" He looked down at the makeshift pouch in front of him. "I have to cash in all these chips..."

*   *   *

"But you're not even part of the crew anymore. You already had your sendoff." Lise Varov was upset. It wasn't anger, and certainly not directed at Sam. But damned if that wide-eyed dedication of his wasn't infuriating at times...

"Lise, you know it doesn't work that way. I'm still on *Dauntless*'s crew roster, officially. My transfer doesn't take effect until my leave is over."

"That's a technicality. You know Captain Barron will excuse you from duty if you ask. After all, he helped you get the assignment here in the first place."

Sam looked at her, a pained expression on his face. She knew just how he thought. Damned if it wasn't one of the reasons she loved him so much. But it was inconvenient now, to say the least.

"I can't do that, Lise. You know that. They were supposed to have a month of maintenance. My replacement isn't even here.

If I don't go, they'll be shorthanded."

"*Dauntless* has a crew of over nine hundred men and women, Sam. One can't make a difference."

He shook his head. "Are you saying my job isn't important?"

She winced. That hadn't been what she had meant at all. She knew he was one of the best at his job. "No, of course not. But you're not the only engineer. I just meant they could do without you, that one empty roster slot isn't going to hurt them."

"Lise, those nine hundred people are gunners, bridge officers, ship's services, and an entire fighter wing with all its associated staff. A ship like *Dauntless* is incredibly complex machine... and everybody has a place within it. In a fight, at battlestations... everybody has a job to do."

"A fight? Do you really think there will be a fight? Out here?" It was the core of her own fears. She didn't relish the idea of Sam leaving for an indeterminate period, possibly missing the birth. But it was the idea of him going into some unknown battle that scared her to death. She'd just spent almost five months worried sick about him deployed on the Union border, waiting every day for word that *Dauntless* had been lost with all hands. She'd just gotten him back. She knew she was being selfish, but it just wasn't fair...

"I don't know what is going to happen, Lise...but they didn't cancel *Dauntless*'s refit, or call nine hundred spacers back from an overdue shore leave, for nothing. There must be something out there, and the ship has to face it alone. There are no other deep space capable fleet units here. Everything is on the Union border. I can't let them go without me, with my spot unfilled. Any deficiency could be the difference between victory and defeat...even my empty slot." He paused, moving over and putting his hands on her shoulders. "I'm sorry, Lise. I would stay here with you, you know that. I just can't."

She stood silently for a moment. Part of her wanted to argue, to fight with him...to throw everything she could at him in an effort to get him to stay. But she'd known the kind of man he was when she'd married him, and she couldn't blame him now for being what he'd always been. And she knew he might still go, despite her begging him to stay, and that was something she didn't want to face.

She leaned forward and wrapped her arms around him. She took a deep breath, struggling to hold back her tears. "You be careful…promise me."

"I promise." His answer was quick, almost robotic. She knew he was telling her what she wanted to hear. She tried to believe him, to convince herself everything would be okay. But she had a bad feeling, one that had resisted her attempts to push it aside.

He hugged her tightly, and he leaned in and kissed her. Then he took a step back. "I have to go."

She could see the sadness in his eyes, and she realized he was doing what he had to do, not what he wanted. At least not what he wanted most.

"I know," she said softly. "Remember…be careful."

"I will." He smiled at her for a few seconds. Then he reached over and grabbed a duffel bag he'd laid on the small couch. He threw it over his shoulder and walked toward the door…and then out into the hall.

Lise stood watching, waiting. Then, when the door was closed, she let the tears come.

Chapter Twelve

Base Tom Wills
Planet Santis, Krillus IV
307 AC

"For the love of the Spacer's Ghost, move your asses!" Clete Hargraves stood in the middle of the snow-covered field in front of the barracks shouting at his Marines as they loaded up the platoon's four transports. Lieutenant Plunkett had been clear as a bell. They were to take everything they could cram onto one of the all-terrain trucks, and then destroy the rest. They still had no idea who was coming, but there was no longer the slightest doubt. They were under attack. And the last thing they were going to do was let an invader use their own weapons and equipment against them.

They'd listened to the battle on the station, the fighters attacking, destroying the platform's weapons. Then the landings, and the ten Marines stationed there putting up a desperate battle against boarders. Sergeant Jones and his Marines had armed and organized the station's technicians, but the attackers still outnumbered them five to one. They'd put up a good defense, but when the com line was finally broken they were on the run, half their number dead, the rest trying to organize a last-ditch attempt to hold.

An attempt Hargraves knew was hopeless. He was sure the

fight was over by now. He knew the Marines would have fought hard, that few, if any, of Jones's people would have surrendered.

If this enemy would even accept a surrender. We still got no idea who we're fighting...

He turned away from the area where the transports were lined up, and he zipped the heavy parka all the way up to his neck. It was cold. No, beyond cold. It was damned freezing. But the last thing Platoon Sergeant Clete Hargraves was going to do was give any of his Marines the satisfaction of seeing that he was cold.

He was hard on his Marines, but he was proud of them too. They were a good platoon, and for all their grumblings, he had no doubt they would fight hard. But he was the oldest by far, and the most experienced. He knew what lay ahead. Running, hiding in the wilderness. Huddling together in the frigid night, enduring every painful moment while longing for the meager relief of morning sunlight. There would be no fires, no heaters. That would be as good as sending up a flare marking their location. And as bad as it would be in the beginning...it would get worse after a few fights.

He'd seen wounded men and women before, on the front lines, far from aid stations and doctors. He'd watched comrades bleed to death, die of injuries that could have been easily treated in any hospital. But here it would be worse, he knew, and the Marines would likely watch their wounded brethren freeze to death, shivering uncontrollably until they finally succumbed.

They were facing a nightmare, and he knew it was a good thing none of them realized the full extent of what was coming. Even the lieutenant. Hargraves respected Plunkett, and he liked him too. But he wondered if the officer had what it would take to hold his command together.

"We're loaded up, Sarge. At least, these things ain't gonna hold nothing more." Joe Thoms stood in front of the lead transport, staring right at Hargraves.

"All right, Private. You know what to do." Hargraves had already given the orders. The village was to be destroyed. All of it. Completely.

Lieutenant Plunkett had given the civilians a choice. Retreat with the Marines, move into the hills and caves and join the resistance. Or stay and surrender when the enemy landed. But either way, he had declared, the buildings of the village had to go. He wasn't about to leave warm quarters behind for an invader to use, and that meant the civilians were screwed. They'd split into two roughly equal groups, one of them lining up to follow the Marines, and the other staying behind, ready to give themselves up.

Hargraves knew the group staying behind were as likely to be shot on sight as anything else, but he held his tongue. His own people were better off without them. The civilians they already had were going to be enough of an impediment, and a drain on the limited food supplies as well.

Hargraves watched as his people moved around the village, preparing the explosives. The civilians stood in the center of what passed for the village's 'street,' watching morosely as the Marines worked to destroy their homes, their workplaces. He sympathized, to a point. But he knew Plunkett was right. Anything they left behind for the enemy only worked against whatever miserable chances they had of getting through this alive.

"Sergeant?"

Hargraves turned around. It was one of the civilians, a manager of some kind by the looks of his clothing.

"I'm sorry, sir, but we don't have any choice. We gotta destroy all this so the enemy don't…"

"I understand that, Sergeant. But the tritium tanks…"

"The what?"

"The tank farm with all the tritium. We've got a hundred megaliters of refined tritium sitting in those tanks." The civilian paused. "Fuel, Sergeant. Spaceship fuel. If an enemy is attacking Santis, that is why. They want the tritium. And the production facilities."

Hargraves held up a hand. "Wait," he said, grabbing the com unit clipped to the outside of his parka. He fumbled with it for a few seconds, before he sighed hard and pulled the bulky glove off his hand.

"Lieutenant, I've got…" He turned toward the civilian.

"Avery, Sergeant. Darren Avery. I'm the senior engineer."

"I've got one of the civilians here. Darren Avery. He's the top engineer. He says we gotta do somethin' about the tritium, sir."

"It's too late, Sergeant." Plunkett was trying to sound calm, but it was clear he was rattled. We've got assault shuttles inbound. We're out of time. Get ready to bug out. Now!"

Hargraves turned toward Avery. "Sorry, Mr. Avery…but the enemy is on the way. It's time to get the hell out of here."

* * *

Arn Millius sat against the hard metal of the lander's inner hull. The craft had gyrated wildly on the way down to the surface, partially the result of the speed of insertion, but mostly from the evasive maneuvers that were standard, even when the defenders were unlikely to possess any real surface to air interception capability.

Santis had a thick atmosphere, and that only made things worse. Millius remembered his earliest days in the legion, and his first combat drops. He'd been prone to space sickness…and his first hard ride down to a planet's surface had threatened to turn him inside out. At least he'd been a line trooper then. The sight of a Praefectus vomiting all over his comrades would be unseemly to say the least.

The fight for the station had never been in question, but a doubt tugged at him from the back of his mind. There had only been ten of the Confederation Marines on the platform, and they had fought ferociously. His forces had outnumbered them ten to one, five to one even counting the civilians they had armed. Still, the battle had gone on for over an hour, and in the end, a dozen of his troopers were killed and as many wounded before the enemy had been wiped out. It was a far higher toll than he'd expected, and he wondered if it was a fluke…or if the Confed marines were simply that good.

It didn't matter, he told himself. Alliance stormtroopers did what they were ordered to do, they prevailed, whatever the cost. Based on the size of the enemy settlement, he expected his forces would have a large numerical advantage once they got to the ground. Still, he'd requested that the second cohort follow up the first wave immediately, and Commander Rigellus had approved without question.

"Six kilometers." The voice of the lander's AI was loud in his headset.

He could hardly move, strapped into the thick harness, clad in body armor and loaded down with his weapons. Alliance stormtroopers went into action ready for battle, even the senior officers, and he carried everything his troopers did.

The ship banked hard to the right, angling down directly toward the LZ. The enemy's records on the station confirmed the scanning reports. There was only a single settlement on the surface, situated right next to the massive coastal refinery that separated the precious tritium from seawater.

That will make things easier. One place to assault, one group of Confeds to...

Millius had seen Commander Rigellus spare the miners on the outer Confed colonies. But he knew his people would face a different situation on Santis. They weren't passing through. This wasn't a raid. They were here to take the planet...and hold it. When the fleet arrived, its ships would need to refuel. And his people had to make sure the tritium they would need was waiting for them.

And I don't have enough strength to worry about prisoners...

Commander Rigellus hadn't given him any orders about how to handle ops on the ground. The decision was his. And while he was no more inherently bloodthirsty than *Invictus*'s commander, he already knew what he had to do. The mission came first, whatever was required. It was the way.

"Three kilometers."

"Alright, troopers...double check all weapons. We're going to hit the ground in two minutes."

He glanced down at the heavy assault rifle laying across his legs, and punched a finger at the small control on the side to activate the self-diagnostic routine. The Gallius-VII assault rifle was the leading edge of Alliance weaponry. The AI-assisted gun incorporated considerable technology of subjugated planets, and in its superior capabilities, it manifested the Alliance's mantra of strength through conquest.

Millius was still starting down when the small light turned green. Check.

"One kilometer."

Millius closed his eyes for a moment, centering himself. He'd been in battle before, many times, and it was the same with each drop. He knew the slogans…Alliance warriors weren't supposed to feel fear. He also knew that was nonsense. They didn't admit fear, didn't discuss it, didn't allow it to dictate their actions. But he would have bet anything that every Alliance stormtrooper and spacer felt it.

He breathed deeply, in through his nose, out through his mouth. Five times. Like he did every time. He had no idea what was waiting for them, but he knew a civilian's lucky shot could kill him as dead as a sniper's bullet to the head. There was no room for carelessness in battle. None.

"Landing in ten seconds…"

"Okay, troopers…it's time." He gritted his teeth, prepared himself for the landing. A few seconds later, the craft hit the ground with a jarring thud. Then the harnesses popped open and the back hatch dropped, controlled by the ship's AI.

Millius watched as his troopers poured out, in perfect order, the first few running out about ten meters and crouching down, forming a defensive perimeter in case of an enemy counterattack. The others followed, pushing farther forward, repeating the same tactic until the lander was empty.

Millius looked north and south. The other three landing craft were down too, the troops onboard repeating the same procedure. They were ready for a resistance, prepared for a fight. But there was none. There was nothing. No enemy soldiers, no hastily fortified positions. Just columns of smoke ahead, and the pungent residue of explosives in the frigid air.

"Scouting parties, forward."

Millius was nervous. He knew many considered the Confeds weak, but he'd expected at least some kind of fight, an effort to defend their world before they tried to surrender.

What did they do? Run? Hide in the wilderness?

He pulled the collar of his coat tightly around his neck. It was damned cold.

They've got to know we can track any fires or heat sources. What do they think they'll achieve making us hunt them down? Where could they even go?

He looked all around. He was edgy, worried about some kind of trap. But there was nothing. The LZ had been carefully selected. The enemy settlement was just on the far side of a large rise, blocking the use of any line of sight weapons the defenders might have. But the plumes of smoke pouring into the air left little doubt that the Confeds had destroyed their own town.

An odd thought—unwelcome, disturbing—went through his mind. Destroying one's home, denying its use to an enemy. It seemed like an action worthy of Alliance citizens and warriors. But the Confeds were supposed to be soft. Weren't they?

Destroying everything and pulling off into the hills...was it just unfocused fear? Or do they intend to carry on the fight from there?

He was just about to turn and organize scouting parties to send out into the hills when his eyes caught movement at the top of the rise. It was a group, moving up over the crest and toward his troopers. They appeared unarmed, disorganized. And they had their hands up in the air.

The Confederation sign of surrender...

Millius felt the tension in his body. Perhaps the Confeds were giving up after all. But he was wary of treachery. Was this a ploy, a way to trick his soldiers into letting down their guard?

"Centurion Tinnius," he snapped into his com. "Take a party forward. Surround and secure that group of Confeds."

"Yes, sir." Tinnius was the commander of the first century, the troops currently on the ground.

Millius turned back, taking a few steps toward the lander and looking toward the pilot standing alongside the craft. "Optiominus, you may lift off and return to retrieve the second century."

The spacer nodded. "Yes, sir." He turned and climbed back inside the landing craft. A few seconds later, the hatch closed, and Millius could hear the sounds of the engines powering up for launch.

He looked around. Nothing but the forty or so civilians—apparent civilians—on the hillside. No resistance, no fire… nothing. Still, he decided he'd be happier when he had his other two centuries on the planet. He had no intel, no idea what size force the Confeds had. It was nothing but a guessing game. And Millius hated guessing.

His eyes fixed on Tinnius's troops, moving behind the disorganized mass, shouting, directing them into a rough line. The civilians—prisoners now—seemed to be obeying.

Perhaps they are just sheep, as the propagandists would have us believe. No Alliance civilians would surrender without a shot fired, march willingly into captivity…

But something still nagged at him, a worry he couldn't quite zero in on. The ragged band yielding so meekly to his troopers didn't seem like the type who would burn their homes, condemn themselves to living outside, enduring the freezing cold just to deny shelter to an enemy. That was an act worthy of Alliance Citizens.

He would find out. These prisoners didn't look like the kind of men and women who would resist questioning for long… and when he had gotten everything out of them he could, he knew what he would have to do. He'd had his doubts, but watching them march up with their hands in the air had sickened him. They were weak, and the Alliance had no use for weakness, no respect for those who lacked the courage to fight for themselves.

Disposing of this lot would be like taking out the trash…

Chapter Thirteen

CFS Dauntless
Wheel Nebula
Two Transits from Archellia
307 AC

Tyler sat on *Dauntless's* bridge, staring into the 3D display as though if he gazed intently enough, all the answers he sought would appear in the flickering holographic light. It had been a week since he and his people had left Archellia after what had turned into a crazed race to get his ship ready for action.

Dauntless had already been in spacedock when the alert came, and the crews had to hastily reassemble every system that had been torn open for refurbishment. Then the battleship had to be fully re-equipped and re-provisioned. Food, water, medical supplies, reaction mass...and weapons. *Dauntless* was heading out to investigate a distress call...and that meant all the ordnance—laser cores, plasma torpedoes, missiles, fusion mines, fighter payloads—that had been painstakingly removed to allow for the refit had to be reloaded.

Somehow, it had all gotten done, and forty-two hours after Barron had gotten the first alert, his ship was blasting out toward the transwarp link. After almost a year patrolling the threatened border, *Dauntless* was on her way toward the far frontier, the last place anyone had expected trouble.

Barron felt a burning in his gut, a tension he knew was caused by the unknown. He'd been fully aware of the danger his people had faced on the Union border, but now he had no idea what lay ahead. The distress call had been vague...and the patrol ship sending it had not been heard from since. Barron was enough of a realist to know what that likely meant. But what hostile force was out there? Was it some kind of Union trick? That was his first suspicion, of course, but he had no idea how Union warships could possibly have reached the Rim. The entire Confederation lay between the two.

But what else could it be? Some kind of criminal traffic? He hoped that was it. Whatever pilots and smugglers were out on the frontier plying their trades, he was sure none could stand up to a front line battleship like *Dauntless*. But he didn't believe he'd been sent to chase pirates, not for a second. And that meant it was a foreign power...one or more of the Unaligned Worlds. Or the Alliance...

He didn't know much about the Alliance. The Confederation had no direct links to the shadowy power. A trickle of trade flowed back and forth through intermediaries in the Unaligned Worlds, along with a few nuggets of information, likely mixed at least 50/50 with rumor.

It has to be the Alliance. None of the Unaligned Worlds would dare to attack the Confederation...but then neither would the Alliance...

Or would they? If *Dauntless* hadn't been sent to Archellia to refit, there wouldn't have been a warship worth the name within ten systems. What little he'd heard of the Alliance suggested it was extremely aggressive, that it had long preyed on its neighbors. The Confederation had sent aid packages to some of the Unaligned Worlds, to systems ravaged by war.

But they're far from the border, more than half a dozen systems. Too far to mount a real invasion. At least without...

Barron leaned down over his workstation, his hands darting to his keyboard, as vague recollection flooded into his mind. He punched at the keys, bringing up a map of the sector.

Wheel Nebula...Harah...Jankau...Santis...

Santis...

He moved his fingers over toward the small sphere representing the star Krillus. The screen displayed a close-up of the system…and its only inhabited planet. Santis.

His eyes narrowed, focused on the text to the side of the planetary display.

Tritium…

The planet was a major tritium production center. It was almost uninhabited, just a handful of technicians working the mostly-automated tritium refinery. And a single platoon of Marines as garrison.

Could it be? Could the Alliance be moving against us? Making a move toward Santis? Control of a refueling site might—just *might*—make an invasion feasible.

You're making assumptions on wild guesses now…

But he couldn't get the thought out of his head. And if a power like the Alliance had designs on Confederation space, there would never be a better time to make a move, with the entire fleet massed against the Union.

He tapped his hand on the com unit, toggling Commander Fritz's line.

"Fritzie…"

"Yes, Captain." The reply was sharp, but he could hear a commotion in the background. *Dauntless* had left so quickly, they'd only had time to do the bare minimum before getting underway, and that left a lot of work for the ship's engineers.

"What's the status down there, Fritzie?" He paused then added, "The truth Fritzie."

"Those base techs tore apart half my systems, Captain. And they put it back together like shit. I've got to rip half of it out and redo it all. If I work my teams hard, I can have everything fully operational in two days…maybe three."

Barron sighed. He had some idea of what Fritzie meant by working the crews hard, and he felt a fleeting moment of sympathy for her engineers. But he might not have more than three days.

Assuming you even have three days. If you're facing an invader at Santis, you've got the time. If they're still heading this way, maybe not…

"Fritzie…" He lowered his voice, regretting that he hadn't gone to his office before calling his engineer. "…I'm concerned we might have a nasty fight ahead of us. I don't know for sure, and maybe it will be nothing. But if we do run into something tough…"

"Understood, Captain. I'll get everything at one hundred percent. Two days." She sounded determined, but there was still the slightest hint of doubt in her voice. "Two days, sir…I'll get it done somehow."

"Thanks, Fritzie." Barron cut the line, and returned his gaze to the main display.

Two days…we'll be ready in two days.
But ready for what?

* * *

"So, he's looking at me across the table, trying to stare me down. The guy's huge, two meters tall if he's a centimeter. And a nasty son of a bitch…even for a Marine. So I stare right back at him, and I shove all my chips into the center of the table…"

"Are you telling that story again, Raptor?" Kyle Jamison stepped into the wardroom, a shit-eating grin on his face as he walked up behind Stockton. "I'm surprised you found anybody who hasn't heard it. Or at least hasn't heard it enough times to run for it the minute you open your mouth."

"Sir!" A ragged chorus went around the table. About half the pilots present were new enough, raw enough, to suspect that normal military protocols were in place. But the pilot's wardroom was behind Bulkhead Eight, deep in the fighter wing's territory, and the unique culture of the Alliance's attack squadrons was in full effect, including what looked like a disturbing lack of propriety when it came to senior officers.

"C'mon, Thunder, give me a break…" It was common behind Bulkhead Eight to refer to pilots by their call signs. Stockton turned and looked back toward *Dauntless*'s strike force commander. The two were buddies, but they were pilots too, and friendship didn't prevent them from giving each other shit whenever possible.

Jamison smiled and moved his eyes over the pilots at the table. They were mostly from Green Squadron. "I guess you bored Blue Squadron to death already." Stockton was the Blues' commander.

Stockton frowned, but he didn't respond.

"Did he get to your people yet, Ice?" Jamison turned and looked across the room. Lieutenant Tillis "Ice" Krill was sitting—more accurately, he was lying—on a small couch, watching a vid.

"No way, Thunder. I'm not letting him anywhere near my Yellows."

Krill and Stockton were rivals in *Dauntless*'s fighter wing, and they were the two best pilots as well…though which was number one and which was number two was a contentious subject. It was a rivalry that had spread to their respective Blue and Yellow squadrons.

Jamison laughed. Then he walked over and sat in one of the empty chairs. "Seriously, guys…I'm a little worried about this run we're on. I don't know what's out there, but I do know *Dauntless* is the only warship worth the name within fifteen jumps. So, whatever we run into, we're going to be alone. I need your squadrons sharp, ready for anything."

"My Blues were born ready." Stockton's voice was cocky, but Jamison knew for all the pilot's wild behavior, he was one of the best squadron commanders in the fleet. If he said his people were ready, they were ready.

"Ice?"

"Yellow Squadron is in good shape. We got a lot of exercise time in while we were deployed on the border. Even the newer guys are looking good." A short pause. "Sharp enough to match Blue Squadron any day."

Stockton turned, but Jamison interrupted before he could respond. "Not today, guys. Let's put a hold on the back and forth."

"You're really worried, aren't you, Kyle?" Stockton's voice was earnest, all the arrogance gone.

"I just think we need to be ready for anything. I had a talk with the captain, and I could tell he was really on edge."

The door opened up, and a tall, slender woman with short, spiky brown hair walked in, her uniform spotless. "You wanted to see me, Commander?" Olya "Lynx" Federov commanded *Dauntless*'s Red Squadron.

"Yes, thank you…come in and have a seat." Jamison's eyes glanced over toward the other pilots in the room, mostly the ones who had been listening to Stockton's story. "If you all don't mind, I'd like to have a chat with the squadron commanders."

The pilots responded with a bunch of nods and a ragged series of, "Yes, sirs." Jamison watched silently as they filtered out of the room.

"I don't want to overreact," he said, just after the door slid shut. "I don't have any specific knowledge…and for that matter, I'm pretty sure the captain doesn't either. But he's worried…and that has me worried." He moved his eyes slowly from one of them to the other. "I want all of you to do everything possible to make sure your people are ready. Maximum simulator time. I'd even like to try to turn routine patrols into training exercises. Try to assign less experienced pilots with some of your veterans… or better still, go out with them yourselves when you can."

"Certainly, Commander." Federov spoke first, her tone rigidly professional as always. There was a certain freewheeling culture in the fighter corps, but Federov was atypically formal in her bearing.

"Maybe we can run some extra patrols too." Stockton was businesslike now too, all hint of the undisciplined bad boy gone. "It would be some extra flight time, at least."

"We might be able to do that, Jake…though we're accelerating hard toward the transwarp link, so there may be limited opportunities." He paused. "I just want to be sure all your people are ready."

The three officers nodded.

Jamison knew their three formations weren't the problem. *Dauntless* carried four squadrons. The Blues were the best, though he suspected Ice would have argued that point. His Yellows were close behind. Federov's Red Squadron had a higher proportion of newer pilots, but he knew the gifted officer had forged her people into a capable unit.

Green squadron was the problem. The Greens had lost their commander a few months before, to a transfer thankfully and not in action. Lieutenant Hogan had gotten a promotion to lieutenant commander and an assignment to take over *Defiant's* fighter wing. The Greens had been the least experienced formation already, and Jamison hadn't considered any of its officers ready for a jump up to squadron leader. He'd held off naming anybody, and he'd filled the role himself. But even with his personal attention, he knew the Greens would have a hard time if they ended up facing veteran pilots.

"I know we just came off the border…and I know we were all under a lot of stress. I know you had your leaves ripped out from under you…but I need you all to be razor sharp now. As dangerous as it was waiting for the Union attack, at least we had the fleet behind us there. We're alone out here—weeks, even months, away from any possible help. Whatever's out here, it's *Dauntless's* problem. And that means it's our problem."

He sighed softly, watching as the three officers nodded. He knew his people would be there, that they would do whatever he needed them to do. He was proud of the job he'd done molding them into what he—and Captain Barron too—considered the finest fighter wing in the Confederation.

No, the problem won't be my people.

It will be whatever is out there waiting for us…

* * *

"Again, Rodrigues. Maybe I didn't mention it, but this isn't a fucking picnic. Now do it once like you give a shit!" Sergeant Ernesto Billos stood along the edge of the small gymnasium, scowling at the three men and one woman standing in front of him. "You all looked like crap, but congratulations, Rodrigues… you were the worst. I wouldn't even give a shit, but when you bring that piss poor effort into battle and get yourself scragged,

I gotta fill out the forms…and the captain's got to write the letter to your folks, so save us both the hassle and just pay fucking attention."

Billos was a Marine. Career. Every word that came out of his mouth, the way he stood, his bearing…it all screamed Marine. And he knew there was only one way to handle the men and women in his charge. Push them. Harder than last time.

The Confederation had been at peace for most of the last generation…and that meant the Marines had one job. Getting ready for the next war. The one that could come. The one that *would* come. And he wasn't about to let anybody coast…and especially not now, when *Dauntless* was racing out to the frontier to deal with some kind of crisis. If whatever was out there was on the ground then the Marines would earn their pay.

Billos was the senior non-com among *Dauntless's* Marines, and one of three who were old enough to remember the last war against the Union. Despite his caustic style, he was proud of the ship's Marines—most of them, at least. But he never forgot that for all their training, few of them had seen real combat. And just as bad, *Dauntless's* contingent was understrength. The ship had been designed to carry two full companies, but the deployment to the Union frontier had been an assignment unlikely to result in any kind of ground combat, so she'd shipped with a single company plus a few extra specialists. *Dauntless* had been scheduled to pick up a fresh batch of Marines to bring her complement to full strength, but they hadn't arrived yet, and with the concern over activity on the frontier, the Archellian command had declined to spare any of its own garrison to supplement the skeletal contingent.

"C'mon, Sarge…we've been at it for two hours now." The whole squad was staring back at the veteran platoon sergeant with various exhausted expressions, but Rodrigues was the only one with the guts to actually complain. Billos was going to hammer him for it…but he would also remember who'd had the balls to stand up to him, and who didn't.

"I'm thrilled to see you can count to two, Rodrigues. But what do you say we try something new? Let's pretend I've got the sergeant's marks on my shoulders, and you're a one-stripe puke barely out of boot camp."

Billos heard the door behind him slide open, and he could see from the way the Marines looking back toward him jumped to attention that one of the officers had come in. He turned, snapping to himself, with greater precision than any of the others.

"Captain Rogan." He saluted.

"At ease, Sergeant." Rogan looked across the room. "All of you."

The Marines started to relax, but then they saw a figure following Rogan, and they whipped back into rigid postures.

"Please…" Barron walked into the gym, gesturing with his hands for the Marines to relax. "I'm not here to interrupt your workout. I just stopped by to see Captain Rogan, and he invited me to come along for a chat."

Billos had to force himself to relax. Captain Barron was being informal with them, but he was the absolute master of *Dauntless*, and Billos knew damned well the officer didn't need an invitation to do anything he pleased on his battleship. Barron wasn't as aloof as some other ship commanders, but he didn't spend a lot of time down in Marine country either. *Dauntless's* ground forces were housed in the ship's lower aft, where there was room for their training facilities and armory. It was about as far from the bridge—and the ship's officers' quarters—as a place could get, outside of the reaction chambers and the launch bay.

"Sir," Billos said, realizing he probably looked comical trying to appear relaxed when he was anything but.

"I mean it, Sergeant—all of you—please relax. This is an informal visit, so at ease."

Barron stepped into the room. He turned toward Rogan then back to Billos. "Sergeant, the captain and I have been discussing our current mission." He paused, letting out a brief sigh. "The truth is, I have no idea what we may be facing…but I'm… concerned it might be something significant and dangerous."

Billos thought the captain almost said, "I'm afraid" instead of "I'm concerned." He wasn't sure, but it gave him a chill anyway. He'd never seen Barron look even rattled before.

"Yes, sir." Billos was focused on the captain, the other Marines standing around, watching, listening.

"I don't know if we'll have need of your particular talents on this operation, but I want you all to be ready just in case. I know you're understrength…" He paused. "…and that most of you have seen limited action. Not you, of course, Sergeant."

Barron hesitated again. "I just wanted all of you to know…" He looked over at the silent Marines standing around the workout equipment. "…I may ask a great deal of you before we return to Archellia. There are colonies out on the Rim. Small ones, mostly mining facilities, but they are home to Confederation citizens, and it is our duty to protect them. No matter what threatens them."

"I have assured the captain he has no cause for concern. The Marines will be ready to do whatever he requires." Rogan's tone almost dared one of the Marines to disagree.

Billos found himself nodding, almost involuntarily. Then he said, "Certainly, sir. Captain, I can assure you your Marines will be ready to do whatever you need." He paused for just an instant. "Whatever the cost, sir."

Billos understood the captain's visit now. The sergeant was junior to the contingent's three officers in rank, but he was the most experienced Marine aboard, and Barron wanted him to get the rank and file in line, ready to do whatever had to be done. Ready to die, if necessary.

He stared back at the ship's commander. Then he simply said, "You can count on me, sir. And on all the Marines. I will help the captain get them ready."

Barron nodded. He was about to answer when one of the Marines on the other end of the room spoke up.

"Yes, Captain…you can always count on the Marines." It was Rodrigues. "Whatever you need, sir, we'll be there for you."

Chapter Fourteen

Message from Unidentified Marine to his Mother
(Played for Each Class of New Marine Boots)

We're trapped, Mom, all of us. The Union forces are all around, and there are just too many. We'll fight...we'll fight like hell, but we ain't gonna make it. I don't know if this message will get to you, but if it does, just do one thing for me. Don't cry. I know you'll be sad, Mom, but remember I died as a Marine, with all my brothers and sisters. I died fighting for my country. I died with honor. And there are a lot worse ways to go...

Near the Ruins of Base Tom Wills
Planet Santis, Krillus IV
Alliance Year 58 (307 AC)

"I want the patrols doubled. Every millimeter is to be searched, out to a hundred kilometers from base. I want those Confeds found!"

"Yes, Praefectus. Immediately, sir!" The officer stood at attention, unmoving.

"That will be all, Optio. See to it at once."

The officer thumped his fist against his chest in the Alliance salute. Then he turned and walked swiftly to the door, opening it and stepping out into the swirling snow.

Millius sat at his makeshift desk, and he shivered as the door swung open. The small portable shelter wasn't what he would have called toasty, but it was a major improvement over the frigid conditions outside.

The commander of the Alliance ground forces had been reviewing the latest casualty reports. He'd landed with two hundred eighty-six stormtroopers, including himself, but not including the technicians assigned to take over tritium production and storage. Now, less than a week later, he had ten KIA, and sixteen wounded and in the field hospital. He was sure his people had drawn blood too, though he'd only been able to confirm two kills. Whatever other Confeds had gone down in the fighting—and he was sure at least some had—their fellows had dragged off the bodies.

He was surprised at the ferocity of the enemy, at their combat effectiveness. He'd never considered the Confeds to be the pushover some in the Alliance did, but he was shocked at the capabilities of the warriors he was facing. They were outnumbered nearly ten to one in actual combatants, at least if the data his people had extracted from the prisoners was accurate. And he was sure it was. His inquisitors had gotten the same information from multiple captives. Their methods had been harsh, and for the most part, the Confeds who had surrendered had broken quickly.

It didn't make sense. How could some of the enemy be so weak, and yet others could take to the hills, endure the brutal conditions…and fight his veteran troopers to a standstill?

What kind of society is this?

The Marines out there hadn't so much as lit a fire to ward off the frigid nights, nothing that could give their positions away.

Whatever the Confederation may be, these warriors are not to be underestimated…

Millius reached down and pulled his com unit from the small folding table.

"Optio," he snapped.

"Yes, sir!"

"Forget my order to double the patrols. I want them tripled."

"Yes, Praefectus."

"And all forces are to shoot on sight, regardless of position or numbers. I want those Marines eliminated…whatever the cost!"

* * *

"Quiet, all of you." Hargraves turned his head, looking at the thin column lined up behind him. He had ten Marines with him, and three civilians, techs who knew their way around the tritium tank farm.

He pulled the parka closed around his neck, a futile effort to ward off the cold. It had been freezing enough when they had bugged out of the base, but the weather had made itself their enemy ever since. A new cold front had moved in and stalled over the area, sending temperatures to levels that were low even for frigid Santis. He was proud of his Marines, but it was the civilians who shocked him the most, enduring the cold alongside his people, if with a few more complaints.

I've got the enemy to thank for that. Shooting the civvies who surrendered shocked the hell out of the rest…

Hargraves looked down at his feet, watching his step in the near total darkness. The ledge was twenty meters above the crashing sea below. It was narrow, wide enough only for a single file column, and if his people were discovered while still on the lip of rock they were finished—nowhere to run, no way to maneuver. But it was a hidden approach, five meters below the top of the cliff above, and it was the best way to get close enough to the enemy positions to complete the mission.

We'll be fine. As long as they stay quiet enough…

Hargraves and his people were here to finish what they'd been unable to do before they'd had to bug out. Destroy the tritium production and storage units, deprive the enemy of what they had almost certainly come for. The Marines had launched half a dozen raids over the last seven days, mostly smash and grab jobs to steal supplies and to keep the enemy on the defensive. There were close to three hundred enemy troopers on the ground now, at least by the best count Hargraves had managed to get, and Lieutenant Plunkett had agreed completely. If they didn't keep the enemy off balance, the invaders' patrols would find the hiding Marines and force a final battle at overwhelming odds. That would be the end.

It's the end anyway…The fleet, the Marines, everything is deployed against the Union. We might hold out a few more days, a week…even two or three. But no one's coming, not in that time. So, in the end all we can do is our duty. We may be lost…but I'll be damned if we're going to let these bastards have what they came for.

He took a step forward, stopping as he felt the rocks slip under his feet. The last thing he needed was to send a cascade of debris sliding noisily down the cliff…

Actually, the last *thing you need is to trip and go down with them…*

He moved slowly, cautiously, pushing the stones away from the precipice with his foot. He turned around again. "Loose rock up here," he whispered. His tone was soft, seemingly gentle…but there were unspoken threats there his Marines would understand, images of what he would do to anyone who barged forward carelessly.

He could see the tritium facility ahead. The refinery that pulled the precious substance from Santis's especially rich seawater glowed softly in the darkness. The facility was mostly automated, the small civilian population present mostly for maintenance and to handle any emergencies. As with Marines stationed on Santis, the civilian technicians were limited to relatively short terms of service exposed to the planet's unhealthy radiation levels. Unlike the Marines, the civilian technicians could become rich enough to retire after a two-year stint, and that mean there were always plenty of volunteers.

This group is paying for it, though…

"All right…we're here to take out the plant. We'd like to get the storage tanks too, but the first priority is the refinery." He looked down the line, his eyes landing on one of the civilians. "Tomas, here, is the ranking tech. He says the best way to scrag the whole plant is to take out the reactor that powers it. And the only way to do that without causing a two-gigaton explosion or blasting ourselves with enough radiation to kill us fifty times over is to destroy the cooling system. Right?"

Tomas Rivera was a short man, at least twelve centimeters shorter than Hargraves. He looked back at the imposing Marine and nodded. "Yes, Sergeant. That's right. If we blow the cooling lines, that should shut the whole system down. And there are no replacement parts on Santis. It's not a repair we expected to have to make. The cooling system is usually very reliable."

"It's reliable until we wire it with every piece of explosive we've got."

"Yes, Sergeant, that's true."

"Let's go. You guys with the explosives, you plant those things wherever Tomas tells you to…and you do it quickly. The rest of you, keep your eyes open…and keep it quiet. One guard walks by and the alarm will go out…and we'll be well and truly fucked."

The Marines in the line nodded silently. Hargraves had told them to shut up, and as tough as they were, none of them had what it took to defy the rugged veteran.

Hargraves struggled to suppress a shiver.

Damn, it's cold…

"Let's go." He moved forward a few feet and turned, grabbing onto a chunk of rock hanging out just above his head. He scrambled up the embankment, off the narrow ledge. His head popped up, and he scanned the area. Nothing.

He pulled himself the rest of the way up, and then he ducked down and waved for the others to follow.

I hope the civvies can manage the climb…

He pulled himself up on one knee, slipping his assault rifle from his back and extending it forward. He peered across the flat rocky ground at the top of the cliff. Still nothing.

Wait…

He saw movement, at least he thought he did. Then, for a second, he thought he was wrong.

But then they came. At least a dozen of the enemy. And an instant later he knew for sure. They had seen him.

"Let's go, Marines…move it! We've got a fight up here!"

He was already firing, his rifle blasting out toward the approaching enemy troopers.

Damn! We've got to get to that refinery…

* * *

Kat sat in her office, just off *Invictus'* bridge. It was a luxury, one she could only have dreamed about on *Vindictus*. Alliance officers were imperious, and they expected to be obeyed without question. But they generally adopted a Spartan lifestyle. The culture as a whole had shied away from opulence, from anything that might wear away at their resolve and toughness. Even a fleet commander considered himself or herself a warrior first and foremost. The intelligence services and propaganda bureaus had often had fun at the expense of the leaders of enemy nations, about how soft they were, how they lived in luxury while they sent their subordinates out to fight for them.

Kat felt uncomfortable with the plushness of the office, as any old school Alliance Patrician would, but she recognized the usefulness of the private space. She had even admitted to herself, she was enjoying it.

"Have you made any progress in suppressing the Confed fugitives, Praefectus?" Her voice was even, not accusatory in any way. She was surprised Millius had not pacified the surface yet, but she knew the infantry commander was a good officer, capable and dedicated to duty. If he was having difficulties, there was a reason. And it wasn't his lack of skill or effort.

"Negative, Commander. The terrain is very rough to the north of our position." There was a short pause. "I'm afraid the enemy has been able to engage in an effective hit and run campaign, striking suddenly and retreating before we can concentrate against them."

"Are there any indications there may be additional enemy forces on the planet?"

"No, Commander. I do not believe so. Our interrogation of the prisoners prior to their—liquidation—was extremely thorough. I do not believe they withheld any information from us.

The fault is mine, Commander. We have simply failed to hunt them down. But I assure you I will do everything necessary to complete the mission."

Kat nodded, a small smile slipping onto her lips. She appreciated Millius's honesty, his willingness to accept responsibility for the situation on the surface. It was the Alliance ideal, but it was one that was rarer than honorable Palatians liked to admit.

"You have my every confidence, Praefectus. If there is anything you require…additional satellites for surveillance, more supplies, ordnance…"

Though we don't have much more aboard to give you…

"No, Commander. Thank you, but I believe we are adequately supplied. We simply need to track down these Confed Marines and finish them."

"Very well. I leave it to you, Praefectus, but we must have the area around the tritium production and storage secured before the advance elements of the fleet arrive. I would offer orbital support, but without precise targeting data, I'm afraid we can't risk hitting your own people or destroying the storage tanks. Perhaps…"

She stopped suddenly as the sounds of muffled rumbles filled her earpiece.

"What is that, Praefec…"

"I'm sorry, Commander. We are under attack. I have to go."

She heard an abrupt click, and she reached up, pulling the headset off. She sat still for a moment, shaking her head. If Millius's interrogation data was correct, if he was having his much trouble with thirty Confederation Marines…what could she expect if she ran into any enemy vessels?

Her briefings had suggested that the entire Confederation fleet was deployed against the Union, that there was nothing more than a motley collections of aging patrol boats anywhere near Santis. But Kat wasn't about to bet the mission on the intelligence briefings.

She tapped her com unit, calling up Wentus's channel on the bridge.

"Yes, Commander?"

"Optiomagis, I want full defensive protocols in effect. This system is to be secured against attack. Directive Sigma-12."

"Yes, Commander. Initiating now."

"Advise me when shuttles are loaded and ready."

"Yes, Commander."

Kat slapped her hand down on the table, cutting the line. Hopefully, the spies were right for once, and all she had to do was sit here and wait for the fleet to arrive.

And if not…at least she'd be ready. For whatever.

Chapter Fifteen

Confederation Intelligence
Troyus City
Planet Megara, Olyus III
307 AC

"So, what's the emergency?" Gary Holsten walked through the door—stumbled was probably a more accurate description. He'd been out late, very late, and he rarely woke up *this* early. Being the sole heir to one of the Confederation's largest family fortunes was hard work, and the capital offered no end of parties and receptions craving his attendance...or breathtaking women seeking to accompany him. He generally found it hard to get to sleep much earlier than dawn, and it was barely an hour later than that right now. His hangover was industrial strength, the throbbing in his temples almost rhythmic. But his other, lesser known identity had called him to service. Megara's most eligible wealthy bachelor was also the head of its premier intelligence service.

"Coffee?" Michael Vonns gestured toward a side table holding a large pot. Holsten nodded earnestly as he made his way across the massive office, toward one of two large armchairs.

"You know I wouldn't disturb your revels or force you to kick last night's model out of your bed so early if it wasn't important." He filled a cup to the top with the steaming coffee. Then he paused and frowned. "We got a report from Tom Warren."

Vonns walked over toward the chair and handed the cup to Holsten, who reached up to grab it, taking an immediate sip then setting it down on a small table.

"I take it from your tone the news is not good."

"No, Gary…it's not. First, I'm pretty sure Warren is dead. Or worse, captured by Sector Nine."

Holsten winced. He knew only too well the reputation of the Union's feared intelligence bureau. He didn't often wish death on his agents, but if Warren had truly been blown and unable to escape…well, he hoped the man had gone down fighting, or he'd had the good sense to take his own life.

"How can you be sure?"

"I'm not sure…but I'd bet. His message had a Bright Light signal in it.

Holsten sighed. Bright Light was the code for agents who were blown and in immediate danger of capture or death. Tom Warren had gotten his message out, but it didn't seem like he was able to escape himself.

"Warren was—is—a good man." Holsten wasn't ready to give up on his agent until he was sure.

"Yes. He…is. And his mission was a success. He was able to confirm that the Union has been in contact with the Alliance. The report doesn't include extensive details, except that Gaston Villieneuve was in command. And that he has since returned to the Union."

Holsten had been about to take another sip from his coffee, but he paused with the cup halfway to his mouth. "Villieneuve? He's their top man. Whatever they were doing in the Alliance, it must have been serio…" He put the cup down on the table. The alert from Archellia…

"My thought exactly. If we were going to have any trouble with the Alliance, that's where it would be."

"If the Union was able to persuade the Alliance to attack us while we're heavily engaged with them…"

"It would be a disaster."

"Have you forwarded this to the Admiralty?"

"Not yet…I wanted to discuss it with you first, see what you wanted to do."

Holsten nodded. "You're right. Perhaps we should keep this under wraps for now." He knew the navy types would have gone ballistic if they'd heard him. They were constantly complaining that the intelligence service withheld data from them.

And there's no easy way to explain we do it for their own good…

"Didn't the Admiralty react to the alerts already?"

"Yes…coincidentally, they had a battleship at Archellia. Apparently it got routed there for routine refit because all the bases close to the Union were at capacity."

"Lucky break. What ship?"

"*Dauntless.*"

"Tyler Barron's ship?"

"Yes."

Holsten hesitated. He was all for sending a vessel to investigate, but Barron was the closest thing the Confederation had to royalty.

If he gets scragged out on the frontier, it's going to be bad for morale…

"Even if the Union convinced the Alliance to ally with them—and that is still a big if—I doubt the Alliance would move first. They aren't the most trusting people…and with their culture, they would despise the Union and its ways. That might not stop them from opportune cooperation, but they would never commit their fleets before the Union does. They would be too worried about treachery."

"I went through the same thought process. But something's going on out there, Gary. I saw the communiques myself. The Archellians think it's criminal traffic of some kind, smugglers or pirates. But with the information we have from Tom Warren, I'd say that looks like too much of a coincidence to me."

"I have to agree." Holsten sighed. He didn't believe in coincidence. "So, what can we do? War with the Alliance and the Union at the same time would be a disaster."

"The Alliance would face considerable logistical problems mounting a sustained invasion of Confederation space. Unlike the Union, they don't share a border with us. Their ships would have to travel a significant distance to even reach Confederation space. And more transits to get to any significant worlds."

Holsten nodded, but a frown slipped on his face. "Yes, but everything we know about the Alliance suggests they are a... stubborn...people. And since they won their latest war against the Unaligned Systems, they *do* have a route to the border that passes only through neutral space. So they'd have to deal with distance, but not with any hostile systems in the way."

"That's true, but sustaining an entire fleet so far from base? And they just fought half the Unaligned Systems. They won, but they took losses too. How could they possibly refit their forces and come at us so quickly? They need time to rest, to rebuild."

"That's the kind of logic you would use if you were analyzing *us*, Mike. You've read the reports. Their society is almost entirely military. Hell, they don't even have a society. They're just one massive armed force serviced by a bunch of conquered slaves. *We* would look at the distance and say it's not feasible. I'm not entirely sure *they* would come to the same conclusion."

"You may be right. But they still have to get their ships rearmed, repaired. They couldn't possibly have turned around a battered, exhausted fleet that quickly. Even if they can move faster than us, it has to take them *some* time to prepare."

Holsten took another sip of his coffee. "I have to agree with you on that point. I can't see how they could have launched a full scale attack so rapidly. They may be coming at us, but I don't see how they could actually do it, at least not for some months."

He laid the cup back on the table and turned toward Vonns. "But that brings us right back to where we were, Mike. I know the Rimworlders have a tendency to exaggerate things sometimes, but the base command at Archellia didn't panic about nothing. The patrol ships on the frontier encountered something...and if it really is some kind of criminal activity, that brings us right back to coincidence on the Alliance."

Vonns nodded, but he didn't reply. Holsten knew his friend didn't have anything to say. Neither one of them believed *Dauntless* was out chasing pirates. But none of the other possibilities made sense. Unless...

He leapt out of his chair. "Can you get a map of the border on that thing?" He pointed to the large screen that covered most of one of the office's walls.

"Yeah, sure." Vonns stood up and walked over next to Holsten. "Max, activate monitor. Display systems map of Rim Section One, from Archellia to the border."

Confederation science had experimented with artificial intelligence units that 'listened' to everything that was said in a room and determined through analysis when a command was being directed at them. The results had been somewhat mixed, but even a total success would likely have proven inadequate to convince the operatives at Confederation Intelligence that it was a good idea to have a computer analyzing everything they said. Much simpler to retain the naming convention, and program AIs to respond to a set designation and ignore everything else.

"Yes, Mr. Vonns."

The screen glowed to life, its background darkening to black, with a number of white circles connected by faint gray lines— stars and transwarp connections.

Holsten walked toward the screen, staring intently. The Rim was the very edge of Confederation space, and there was little of value there. A few mining colonies, but nothing of much importance. He started to turn back toward Vonns, but then he froze, his eyes locked on one of the glowing circles. Krillus.

Of course…Santis…

"Mike, you know our cultural profiles on the Alliance as well as anyone. Would you say they're prone to test enemies' reactions? To probe for weakness?"

Vonns hesitated for an instant, a confused look on his face. Then he said, "Yes, of course. Certainly. They respect strength. That doesn't mean they won't take on a capable adversary, but they will definitely go after anyone who shows them weakness. Like a predator."

"And we're the prey…"

"I'm sorry? What?"

"They could be testing us. The Union agents almost certainly tried to tempt them by arguing we cannot mount a defense on the Rim while we are facing a Union invasion. They're not ready for a full-scale attack, not yet. So they send something, a small force, even a single ship…and they see how we react."

"You mean if we don't meet them with strength, we're inviting war?"

"I mean if we don't destroy utterly whatever they sent, we are asking for war."

"But the logistics…they still face the same probl…"

"Santis."

Vonns stared right at his companion. He paused for a moment, and then he said, "Santis. Of course. The tritium facilities. If they capture them, they could use them to refuel an invasion fleet…"

"And having secured a source of reaction mass, they could probably come up with enough support vessels to carry minimal food and weapons and other supplies."

Vonns held Holsten's gaze. "We're speculating pretty wildly, Gary. Even with the reaction mass on Santis, we're talking about a logistical nightmare."

"Is it that wild? Can you think of anything else? Any reasonable scenario to explain the situation?"

There was a long silence. Then: "No."

"It makes perfect sense. A chance to probe our defenses, and a way to solve their logistical problem. If we don't respond—or if we come at them and lose—it is a sign of weakness, confirmation of the Union's promises that we can't spare forces to fight them. They'll invade as soon as they can get their fleets underway."

"But if we defeat whatever they sent…we might just dissuade them from coming at us, at least long enough to deal with the Union attack first."

Holsten was nodding. "But we don't know what they have out there. *Dauntless* is a good ship, but she's far from our biggest or newest. And Captain Barron is a good man, but he's young, relatively new to command." A pause. "What else can we get out there?"

"Now? Nothing."

"There must be some available forces."

"There aren't." Vonns' voice was hard with certainty. "Even the closest fleet units are a month away...and many of those are reserve ships still being refitted for action." He took a deep breath. "*Dauntless* is all we have out there, Gary...and we're lucky she's there."

Holsten turned and looked back at the screen. "So, Captain Barron is all we have...he and his ship are all that stands between us and a war with the Alliance?"

"If our assumptions are correct, that's probably true."

"And there's nothing we can do for him, no way to help him?"

"We can warn him, tell him he must prevail, whatever the odds, whatever the cost."

Holsten exhaled hard. "So we send the grandson of the Confederation's greatest hero into a possibly hopeless fight with no more help than to tell him to find a way to win?"

"I'm afraid so. Unless we count our best wishes as reinforcements..."

The head of Confederation Intelligence just stood and stared at the screen, his mind racing to find something, anything he'd forgotten. But there was nothing. A warning and best wishes were indeed all they had to send to Tyler Barron.

His hangover was gone at least, the alcohol-induced headache replaced by a new one, even worse.

"Godspeed, Tyler Barron..."

Chapter Sixteen

Near the Ruins of Base Tom Wills
Planet Santis, Krillus IV
307 AC

"Keep firing!" Hargraves was down on the ground, his rifle extended in front of him. He'd opened up on full auto, but now he was firing single shots. He didn't have enough ammo to be careless, and the enemy troopers had dropped to the ground too. He just didn't have a good enough target to waste more than a few rounds.

He'd taken one of the enemy down, maybe two…he wasn't sure if he'd hit the second trooper or if his target had just dived to the ground for cover. But now they were in a protracted fire-fight, and that was bad news. The enemy would be getting rein-forcements any minute now, and his Marines were on their own.

He stared out across the scrubby grass growing up and around the clusters of rocks. He was looking for movement, for any sign that he had a shot at an enemy. But it was clear they weren't facing poor quality troops. Whoever they were, they were as good as the Marines…almost. And that meant they weren't going to make any mistakes.

Hargraves was frustrated, angry. He had to get his people to the refinery, somehow. But he had no idea how that was possible now. He'd be lucky to get anyone out of here alive.

"Sergeant…" It was Tomas Rivera.

"Tomas, you need to get back. You and your techs need to stay…"

"There's another way to get to the refinery."

Hargraves was focused mostly on the soldiers to his front, the ones shooting at him. But Rivera's words got his attention.

"How? Where?" He reached out and grabbed Rivera, pulling him down closer to the ground as a series of bullets whizzed by overhead.

"Down along the sea. At the bottom of the cliff."

"There's a path down there? I thought the water came right against the cliff."

"No, not for most of the way, at least. There's a narrow spur of rock. There's only one stretch, maybe a hundred meters where we'd have to go through the water."

"Do you realize how cold that water is, Tomas?" Santis's sea was mostly ice this far north, and it was liquid here only because of the massive refinery and the immense heat it produced. That was enough to melt the ice, but barely. "You would freeze to death."

"Not if we can get across quickly enough, Sergeant."

"But you'll be soaking wet…it will freeze on you as soon as you get out. You'll die, Tomas."

"Not if we can get to the refinery. It's warm in there…we could heat up while we plant the bombs."

"How will you even get down there? It doesn't look like an easy climb."

"What's the alternative, Sergeant? Die here? At least this way we have a chance to accomplish something." The technician paused. "We both know none of us are getting off Santis, Sergeant."

Hargraves paused. He tended to look at civilians as soft, useless. But Rivera was showing him a side he rarely saw in those outside the Marines. Guts. Real hardassed, bloody guts.

"You sure, Tomas?"

"Yeah, Sarge. I'm sure. Give me two of your Marines with the explosives. My people and I will do our best."

"Okay…let's give it a try." He fumbled to get his com unit out from under him. "Wedge, Plinth…you're gonna grab the explosives and go with Tomas and the other techs. Do whatever he says, no bullshit. He knows what he's doing."

"Yes, Sarge." The responses came back almost immediately. They didn't sound enthusiastic about being placed under the command of a civilian, but Hargraves knew they would follow his orders no matter how they felt about them. They knew what would happen if they didn't.

"We'll hold here as long as we can, Tomas."

"Don't throw your lives away, Sergeant. Give us a ten-minute head start. Then bug the hell out of here. You won't be doing us any good after that."

"Ten minutes. You got it." The Marine paused for an instant. "Good luck, Tomas."

"And to you, Sergeant." The civilian hesitated for a few seconds. Then he turned and crawled back toward the cliff.

*　*　*

"Decurio, move your troopers forward now. I will send the rest of the century after." Millius's voice was a barely-controlled roar. He'd already been frustrated with the unexpected resistance on Santis, and now he'd been humiliated in front of Commander Rigellus. The matriarch of the Regulli was a stunningly successful officer, exactly the kind of commander who had coattails. But beyond that, Millius just respected her. She was the Alliance ideal, the Palatian Patrician born to duty. And he looked like a damned fool who couldn't round up a handful of Alliance Marines and civilians.

"Sir!" The junior officer snapped off a sharp, chest-thumping salute, and he turned and jogged toward his still-assembling unit.

Millius spun around. "First century, assemble. Anyone not in position in one minute will be digging latrines…if they're lucky." The troops were already lining up, rushing out of their make-shift shelters, pulling on bits of body armor and cold weather gear. His troopers had been grumbling about the weather, rushing into the semi-heated portable structures the instant they got off duty. He shook his head as he watched them hesitating for an instant as they opened the tent flaps and felt the frigid breeze.

Are we past our prime already? Is the heart of the Alliance rotten so quickly, even as our ancestors who made us are still warm in their graves… or, indeed, still alive?

He'd been brought up on tales of the idealized Alliance warrior, the iron man capable of enduring anything…pain, wounds, weather. Alliance warriors didn't stop, no matter what they faced. At least that was the mantra. Now he wondered if that had ever been true. Was it all propaganda, the heroic stories that had shaped who he'd become? Certainly, Alliance forces had conquered. But perhaps they weren't invincible after all. Maybe there were warriors out there who could match them.

Like these Marines…

He waved his arms, gesturing for the just-awakened stormtroopers to hurry. His people had a group of Marines cornered, trapped against the sea cliffs. And he wasn't going to let them escape, not one of them. No matter what it cost.

He walked over toward the troopers forming up. They looked a little ragged, but they were all armed and equipped. And they were Alliance stormtroopers. Perhaps they weren't the equals of their fathers and mothers, but Millius knew they were veteran soldiers.

"Prepare to move out," he shouted, staring out over the surprised group. He was Praefectus, commander of the entire ground force. But none of that mattered now. The image of Commander Rigellus, listening as the sounds of the enemy launching a raid blared through her com unit…it was too much. He wasn't going to leave this to anyone else. He was going to lead the attack himself.

"Forward…"

*   *   *

"Careful, sir." Tony Plinth was standing on the narrow strip of shoreline reaching up toward a man climbing down a rope. Plinth had scrambled down first, and now the civilians were coming…much more slowly than he had. But slow was better than falling, and even the Marine had to admit it wasn't easy scaling down a rope wearing a heavy parka.

"I'm fine, Corporal…just not as fast as you, I'm afraid." Tomas Rivera dropped down the last meter or so, grunting as he landed and stumbled on the slick wet rocks below his feet.

Plinth grabbed the technician, holding him up…though he figured the chances were about fifty-fifty the civilian would have managed to regain his balance without assistance. "You gotta watch this ground, sir. Not much of a beach, I'm afraid, just a bunch of rocks. And wet and slippery at that."

"Thank you, Corporal." Rivera leaned his head back and looked up, just as Plinth was doing. Joe Wedge was still up on the cliff, standing guard while the civilians made their way to the bottom. Plinth had come down first to check the area along the shoreline, make sure it was clear. He reached up again as the second tech lost his grip about two meters from the bottom. He dropped hard, but Plinth caught him. The two stumbled back together, but they managed to stay on their feet.

The Marine had known the civilians would have a hard time with the climb. Scrambling down a rope under near-combat conditions was tough enough, but even with the heavy gloves they all wore, the cold was biting through. Plinth's hands were half-numb, and he couldn't imagine any of the techs were in better shape.

The third civilian managed to make it all the way without incident. Plinth looked up to the top, seeing Wedge staring back down. He waved for his comrade to climb down, but even as he thrust up his arm, he saw Wedge spin around. Then he heard the sounds of fire, Wedge's gun first…then a higher-pitched sound. Enemy assault rifles.

"Go," he shouted, turning toward Rivera and the other two techs. The three men stood where they were, looking back with stunned expressions on their faces. "Go!" he repeated, gesturing wildly with his arms.

The three techs jogged down the narrow strip of rocky shoreline, moving as quickly as they could in the near-total darkness. Plinth spun around, looking up at the top of the cliff. He couldn't see Wedge, but he could hear continued gunfire. He wanted to throw his rifle over his shoulder and climb back up, but he knew his duty was to get the techs to the refinery.

He hesitated for a few more seconds, stepping backwards, trying to get a glimpse of his comrade. He was just about to give up and follow the techs when he saw movement...and then something falling. A body.

It crashed hard onto the rocks with a sickening thud. Plinth ran over, and in an instant he knew. It was Wedge. And he was dead. The fall alone probably would have done it, but the Marine had a dozen bloody holes in his midsection as well.

Plinth was staring at his friend's body as a blast of gunfire splashed in the nearby water. He snapped his head up, bringing his rifle around and firing at the top of the cliff. There were two—no, three—enemy troopers up there shooting down at him.

One of them dropped his gun and fell to his knees. His comrade reached out, trying to grab him, but he was too late. The soldier fell forward over the cliff and crashed down alongside Wedge's body. Plinth felt a rush, a small taste of revenge for his friend. But now there were at least four enemies at the top. They had position and numbers. It was a losing fight. And Plinth understood his duty.

He slammed hard against the rock wall, grabbing as much cover as he could from the enemy fire. He moved down the meter-wide slip of ground, back pressed against the sheer cliff. He couldn't see the techs...they were too far ahead and it was too dark. But there was only one way they could have gone, and he moved forward, stumbling over the loose rocks as he accelerated to a slow run.

* * *

Hargraves reached around, pulling a grenade from his belt.

It was his last one, and he knew he had to make it count. He was sure there were at least two enemy soldiers down behind the rock in front of him. He'd caught their movement several times as they'd worked their way forward, and now they were within twenty meters.

He knew what they would do, at least what two Marines would do. They'd come around different sides of the rock, force him to react in one direction or the other. He'd hoped his people could hold off their attackers indefinitely…at least while their ammo lasted. But these were skilled troops, far more capable than any he'd ever faced, and that included the Union FRs. They outnumbered his people too overwhelmingly. If he didn't order his survivors to bug out now, none of them would get away. Assuming it wasn't too late already.

He glanced at his chronometer. Nine and a half minutes. Close to ten. But it wasn't ten…and Marines kept their promises. His people would hold out another thirty seconds. Then they would get the hell out of here.

He tensed his legs, and then he sprang up, pulling his arm back and throwing the grenade. He felt the urge to watch, to see if his aim had been true. But his instincts took over, dropping him to the ground, hard, painfully, just before a stream of bullets zipped by overhead. A couple seconds later, he heard the blast of the grenade and, he thought, a muffled cry. He looked up, toward the rock. The sound had seemed spot on, just in the right place. But he knew he wouldn't know if he'd taken out his enemies until he made a break for it. He'd know he failed when the bullets slammed into his back.

His eyes dropped again to the timepiece. Ten minutes, ten seconds. It was time.

"Alright, Marines…let's get the hell out of here!"

He turned and threw himself up into a low crouch, moving as quickly as he could without straightening up. He scrambled over the rough ground, seeing his people do the same. There had been eight of them when he'd sent the techs away, but two of them had been hit in the firefight. He knew Lipton was dead, but he wasn't sure about Garavick. "Go," he shouted into the com unit. "Back to HQ!" But he didn't follow. He moved off to the side. He couldn't leave. Not without checking on Garavick.

He could see the shadowy image of the Marine, lying partially covered by the high tufts of grass. He scrambled forward, dropping to the ground next to unmoving figure. He let out a deep breath. It looked like Garavick was dead.

"Sarge…" The voice was weak, soft. But it told Hargraves all he needed to know. The Marine was still alive.

The sergeant turned his head, looking all around. He could hear the sounds of enemy soldiers moving forward, but none near him. The Marines had put up a fierce fight, and it seemed their attackers were moving cautiously.

"Alright, Rich, this is probably gonna hurt like fuck, but we ain't got no choice right now. Try not to scream, eh? You'll just lead them right to us."

He reached his arm under his comrade, pulling hard and pushing his head under Garavick's shoulder. He couldn't carry the Marine, not without standing up and making a perfect target of both of them. But he could help the wounded man crawl. If they could get a few hundred meters, the scrub became a lot taller and rougher…perhaps even enough to hide them.

He pulled hard, and Garavick winced, biting down, clearly struggling with the scream that wanted to burst from his lips.

"Hold it together, Rich. I know it hurts, buddy."

Hargraves staggered forward, his knees driving painfully into the rocky ground. Garavick wasn't the largest man in the platoon—*thank God!*—but he wasn't light either. It was all Hargraves could manage to move them both. He wanted to rest, to take a breath. But there wasn't time. It would be a miracle if they got away. If he stopped, whatever small chance they had would turn to zero.

He rasped in a deep breath, lurching forward again. Garavick let out a soft whimper, but he held back the cry of pain.

"Hang on, Rich…just hang on for me man."

Hargraves took another breath. Then he lurched ahead. Another half meter. That much closer to cover.

But he could hear the troopers behind him, closing.

He kept pushing, but he knew the hard truth. They weren't going to make it.

* * *

Tomas Rivera was scared. He was so profoundly fucking terrified it took all he had to keep himself from dropping to his knees and emptying his stomach. But he knew he had to keep moving. The refinery was just ahead, and he'd be damned if he'd let whoever the hell invaded Santis get what they had come for. He might not be a Marine, but he understood what an enemy was. And if all he had left was defiance and spite, then those would have to do.

"Let's go, guys. The sooner we plant these explosives, the quicker we're out of here." He was struggling to control the shivering. He and his companions were wet from the waist down, their soaked pants already starting to freeze around their legs. They'd only had to move a few dozen meters through the almost-frozen water, but Rivera couldn't remember anything so painful.

He didn't know if they would encounter any guards. He was taking his people to a secondary entrance, one deep in a fully automated area of the plant. It was likely—possible at least—that there would be no defenders in place.

He moved forward, looking all around as he did. They were slipping out of the total darkness, into the faint glow that surrounded the plant. The land widened out here too, the cliff dropping quickly down to sea level and opening into a wide plain. It was easier ground to traverse, but if there were any enemy soldiers in the area there was a far greater danger of being spotted.

Rivera moved forward, his legs feeling like sacks of wet sand, resisting every effort to push forward. The cold, the fear, the fatigue…he didn't know how he managed to take each step. But he did, and his companions did too. In a few moments, they were walking around the edge of the refinery. The walls were metal, rust-resistant, but still covered in a thick coating of slime and debris from the crashing waves. The main entry to the control center was around to the other side, higher up, farther from the sea's fury.

Rivera could hear the sound of the giant intake valves farther out, sucking in millions of liters of seawater. Santis's oceans had a far higher percentage of the precious hydrogen isotope than those on most occupied worlds, but it still took massive volumes to produce meaningful quantities of the nuclear fuel.

"The entrance should be just up here." Rivera had only been down in this area of the refinery once, and he'd only seen the door he was seeking from the inside. But he knew it wasn't far.

He was also aware that many of the lower levels of the refinery were highly radioactive despite the bots that frequently scrubbed the area down. It was unhealthy certainly, even more so than the planet itself was, and he suspected if they wandered into the wrong spot, they could get a lethal dose. But there was no choice, no other way.

He walked another twenty meters, turning as the building recessed inward…and he saw the door. He ran up, his eyes settling on the locking mechanism. He still had his passcard, but he didn't know if the enemy had reprogrammed the locking systems. That would be a considerable project, he knew, one they might not have completed yet. But if they did, his card would do little more than alert them to his presence. Still, it was a chance he had to take. The door was tough, and the only way they'd get in would be to blow it. And an explosion wasn't going to do anything to aid their stealth.

He paused, staring at his hand for a few seconds before he pulled off his glove. The cold was biting, and his fingers were quivering, almost uncontrollably. He managed to get the card from his pocket, and to finally swipe it through the small track.

He held his breath for what felt like ages, but he knew was less than a second. Then he heard a click, and the door slid open.

Warmth. Heat. The climate-controlled nirvana of the refinery's innards beckoned. He leapt inside, not looking, almost not caring what might be there. But there was nothing. Nothing but a smooth, sterile hallway…and a level of warmth he hadn't felt in more than a week.

His companions ran in, as drawn to the heat as he was. He just stood for a moment, and then he turned toward the entrance and pressed a small button. The door slid shut, and the last traces of the frigid cold were gone.

The three of them stood where they were, silent, savoring the precious warmth.

Chapter Seventeen

CFS Dauntless
At the Krillus Transwarp Link
307 AC

"We're coming through, Captain." Atara Travis stood on the bridge, her hands on the back of her chair, eyes focused on her workstation screen. "Passive scanners activated."

"Very well, Commander." Barron sat, staring at the main display, waiting for the scanner data to flow in. He almost gave the order to commence active scans, but that would give *Dauntless's* position away…and the more he'd thought about it, the more convinced he'd become that he would find the invader near the planet Santis.

The trip through the transwarp link had been interminable, almost three hours with nothing but the strange pale blue glow of the portal as *Dauntless* moved along at thousands of times lightspeed…and as its captain tried to decide what he expected to find.

"Passive scans negative, Captain. Nothing out of the ordinary." Travis's voice was hard, and Barron thought he heard skepticism there, even as she told him there was nothing. Barron was inclined to agree. He didn't necessarily expect the enemy to be waiting just beyond the transwarp line. But he did expect a fight somewhere in the system.

"Let's not take any chances. Yellow alert. Activate all primary and secondary batteries. Duty patrol to the launch bay."

"Initiating yellow alert, Captain. Duty patrol to…" Travis's voice changed to the stone cold tone she used in battle. "Energy readings, Captain. Straight ahead." She dropped down into her chair, her face buried in her console. "It could be scanner buoys, or…"

"Battlestations. Engines on full power, Commander. Bring us around immediately." Barron didn't know what was waiting ahead of his ship, but he had a bad feeling. And his instincts usually served him well.

"Battlestations," Travis repeated. The bridge was bathed in glowing red light from the battlestations lamps. "Full thrust, Captain." Travis activated the shipwide com. "All crew, strap in, prepare for high thrust maneuvers." She put a hand to her head-set for a second. Then she turned toward Barron. "Engineer Fritz reports we'll have full thrust in thirty seconds, sir."

"Tell her fifteen, Commander." Barron's bad feeling became an urgent foreboding. He slapped his hand on the com unit, connecting to his engineer even though he'd just ordered Travis to do it. "Fritzie, I need full thrust now…damn the risk."

A thought passed through his mind. He was being reckless, taking a real chance of overloading the reactor just to escape some unproven threat. Then *Dauntless* shook hard. The danger was no longer unproven.

"Incoming fire, Captain." Travis spoke calmly, though Barron knew his first officer was anything but. They'd been in the system less than five minutes, and they were under attack. Whatever battle they had come to fight…it had begun.

"Some kind of lasers, Captain. One hit, amidships. Damage report coming."

Dauntless shook again.

"Fritzie, I need that thrust. Now!" Barron hadn't seen all that much action in his career yet, but he could tell from the hardness of the shaking that the guns firing at his vessel were heavy ones.

"Active scanners, Commander. I need to know what's out there." Whatever enemy they were facing already knew they were there.

"Active scanners powering up, sir." A second later: "Full thrust engaging."

Barron felt the pressure as *Dauntless*'s massive engines blasted at maximum power, overwhelming the capacity of the dampeners to absorb the g-forces. He leaned back to offset the discomfort from feeling three times his normal weight, trying to get comfortable.

"Active scanners report a cluster of buoys ahead. Power readings are off the charts now, sir. Whatever they are, they're strong."

Barron cursed under his breath.

You damned fool. You knew there was an enemy here…and you blundered right into the system.

"Secondary batteries…fire at will. Target all platforms and destroy them." His weapons could clear the buoys; he was sure of that. But the trap—and that's exactly what he knew it was— would serve its purpose, at least partially. *Dauntless* would take considerable damage in a straight up fight with the laser platforms, leaving his vessel at a tremendous disadvantage later, when it faced whatever was waiting for them. And there was no longer any doubt something was waiting.

His orders to maneuver around the spread of weapons might just be enough…depending on how many there were. The mighty thrust was even now altering the battleship's vector, moving it out of the buoys' primary firing arc. *Dauntless* was still taking damage, but with a little luck she'd escape the worst of it.

"Secondary batteries firing, Captain."

Barron's eyes moved back to the main display. The ship's AI had projected yellow cubes representing the buoys. They were off to the side of the blue oval that depicted *Dauntless's* position. Barron could see his ship moving farther from the deadly weapons platforms. But the ship shook again, another hit. They weren't out of range yet.

He gripped the sides of his chair, keeping his composure, his eyes darting around the bridge, checking on his officers. Few of them had seen any real action before, but they were performing well, and there was no panic, no discernible fear.

"Commander Travis…" His eyes dropped to his screen, scanning the readout. Blue squadron was on duty. "…Blue squadron is to launch at once and assume a defensive position."

"Yes, sir," Travis snapped back. Then, a second later: "Blue squadron, you are ordered to launch at once and conduct combat space patrol operations."

"Blue squadron leader, here. Launch order acknowledged, Commander Travis." Jake Stockton's voice was hard, confident over the com. Stockton was a cocky sort, just the type to do well in the fighter corps. But Barron knew there was more to *Dauntless's* ace pilot than just bravado…and he was glad his elite squadron had pulled the duty shift.

A moment later, less even, Barron felt the familiar lurches of his ship. Not hits this time, but fighters launching. His mighty Blues. Fifteen pilots he'd put up against any in the Confederation…or the Alliance. He might be wasting time and fuel with the launch, but he'd already been caught careless once. He didn't intend to let it happen again.

"Blue squadron launched, Captain."

"Very well, Commander. Order Red squadron to the bays. Just in case."

His eyes dropped to the display. His gunners were earning their pay. Over two-thirds of the laser buoys were already gone, and *Dauntless* had moved out of the arc of those that remained. He stared at the screen, watching as his batteries cleared away the last of them.

"Scanners?"

"No further contacts, Captain."

"Report from Blue squadron."

"Blue squadron reports all clear, sir."

"Damage reports?" Barron caught the hint of an ozone smell coming from the air vents. Something was fried.

"We've lost hull integrity in three compartments, sir. None of them vital. But we took eleven casualties. Six dead, five on the way to sickbay."

Barron felt the reports of the crew losses like a thunderbolt. He had served in peacetime, not war. That didn't mean he'd never lost anyone, but it had always been an isolated accident involving one or two crew members. They hadn't been in the system for an hour yet, and six of his people were dead. He thought of his grandfather's battles, of the thousands killed, blown into space, incinerated in their dying spaceships.

How did you do it? How did you stay focused while people were dying all around you? People who followed you, men and women you were responsible for?

He pushed the thoughts aside. If he didn't keep his head clear, didn't do everything he could to bring *Dauntless* through this, he would lose a lot more than six of his spacers.

"Captain, Engineer Fritz reports a fifty percent power drain in C and D sections. She says one of the hits must have ruptured a conduit. She's got a team working on it, but she has no estimate on repair time yet."

Damn.

That meant half his primaries were out. At least.

"Advise her that is a priority affair, Commander. Meanwhile, cut thrust. I don't want to accelerate further until we get a better read on the system."

"Yes, Captain."

"And order Lieutenant Stockton to take Blue squadron into the system toward Santis. He is to advance as far as fuel status allows—or until he detects any enemy vessels."

"Yes, sir."

Barron leaned back and sighed softly to himself. He didn't know what kind of enemy he was facing, but whoever it was, he or she had taken him by surprise and won the first round. He had little now but guesses, but he was sure about one thing. The laser buoys at the transwarp link were the work of a methodical commander, a cautious one.

And probably a smart one.

Yes, he'd lost the first round. But he didn't intend to let that happen again.

* * *

"Laser buoys have engaged, Captain. Scanning reports coming in. One vessel, approximately forty million tons displacement, three point seven kilometers in length."

Kat shook her head slightly, the movement almost imperceptible. She forced the frown from her lips, but her thoughts were cold. She was sitting in the plush command chair, but this time she wasn't comfortable. She was worried. And she was mad.

Damned intelligence reports. Why do we even bother?

Her briefings had been clear on one point. All of the Confederation's capital ships were deployed against the Union, nowhere near the Rim. But unless it was a huge freighter or tanker coming through the link, forty million tons meant a battleship. One almost as big as *Invictus*.

"Readings from the buoys, Commander. The enemy vessel has fired upon them. Triple-mounted laser batteries, output somewhere in the four to seven hundred megawatt range."

No tanker or freighter would have guns like that...

"Put the ship on secondary alert, Optiomagis. All systems on battle footing." She knew the enemy ship was at least a day away, perhaps two or more, depending on its thrust capability. The Alliance's data on Confederation ships and capabilities was sketchy. They used particle accelerator cannons for their primary guns, highly effective weapons, especially at close range. The lasers would be their secondaries.

Seven hundred megawatts and triple turrets...that's strong for secondary batteries...

"Secondary alert in place, Commander."

Kat stared at the display. It was projecting the video feed from outside the ship, displaying the partially clouded surface Santis. Her stormtroopers were on the ground, by all accounts still fighting to assert total control. She couldn't pull them back now. Her orders about Santis were clear. She hated to leave the troops on their own, but she couldn't stay in orbit. If *Invictus* was facing a Confederation battleship, Kat knew she had a real fight on her hands. And floating in orbit, ceding the initiative to the enemy, made her vessel a sitting duck.

"Prepare to leave orbit, Optiomagis." She paused, thinking. "Plot a course to planet five...twenty percent thrust, full baffles. We'll hide there and wait. With any luck, the enemy will go into orbit here." The Confeds wouldn't have detected *Invictus* yet, at least not unless their scanning technology was vastly superior to anything the Alliance had seen. They knew they had an enemy, but not what it was. And that was an advantage.

"We'll leave orbit on the far side of the planet, and use its shadow to block the enemy's scanners."

"Course plotted and entered into the computer. Ready to initiate on your command."

Kat almost gave the order, but she paused, staring at the screen but seeing only the images in her mind. "How many laser buoys do we have left, Optiomagis?"

"Forty, Commander."

"I want them equipped with full stealth suites and launched into orbit before we leave. Program them to appear as communications satellites." She knew it was a long shot that the ruse would work. The enemy would know a world as undeveloped as Santis wouldn't have such an extensive satellite network. But even a few seconds of confusion, of uncertainty, could make a difference. The enemy would have trouble detecting the buoys until they got close. Very close. And if they were careless, if they went blindly into orbit, the buoys would get in some shots at point blank range. It wouldn't take too many hits from a few thousand kilometers to cripple even a battleship as large as the one she was facing.

"Preparing laser buoys now, Commander."

Will the enemy fall for this? Would I?

Kat was silent, her mind deep in thought.

No...I wouldn't. Not after what happened at the transwarp link. Too simple. Too obvious...

"Belay that last order. I want twenty laser buoys in orbit around the planet...and ten around each moon." It still might not work, but it increased the complexity of the trap. "Deploy two assault shuttles to ferry the buoys to the moons."

"Yes, Commander." A pause. "That will delay our departure from orbit."

"Yes," Kat replied, "but not by much. Calculate a course for the shuttles to swing around each moon and pick up a gravity assist to match our velocity. They can dock with us en route to planet five."

"Yes, Commander." Wentus was clearly trying to sound normal, but Kat could tell he was picking up on her edginess.

Good. Better he take this enemy seriously than succumb to arrogance and carelessness. Our propaganda could get us killed if it spawns overconfidence.

"I want a spread of probes launched as well, Optiomagis. Equal-spaced geosynchronous orbits." If her trap failed, at least she could get some information on what she was facing if the enemy came near the planet.

And if they don't, at least Millius's stormtroops will secure the planet without interference.

"Yes, Commander Rigellus."

Kat held her stare, her eyes locked on the screen even as her mind drifted.

Who are you out there? Are you soft, like everyone says of Confeds? Or are you something else? Your people held off the Union three times... there was more than softness in that. Are you cut from that cloth? Or are you a stuffed uniform, a blade dulled by two decades of peace?

Kat knew what the high command would say. What the intelligence operatives would tell her. But the feeling in her gut was something different. And it had proven more effective at sensing danger in the past than any other resource she possessed.

Chapter Eighteen

Near the Ruins of Base Tom Wills
Planet Santis, Krillus IV
307 AC

There was a loud pounding on the door. Rivera jumped, startled. He'd had his eyes closed, savoring the first warmth he'd felt in days and days. But now he reached around, pulling out the pistol the Marines had given him. He looked at the others one by one, trying to decide what to do. The gun felt strange in his hand, but if it was an enemy guard out there, he was going to need it.

He stared right at the door, holding his arm out, pistol aimed. "Go ahead," he said to his companions. "Open it."

The two other techs paused, looking uncertain, afraid.

"Open it…if that's one of the enemy, he'll call for help if we leave him out there. We've got to kill him."

The two men looked at each other, and then one stepped over and pushed the button on the control panel. The door slid open, and wave of frigid air blasted into the room.

Rivera aimed his gun, his finger tight against the trigger. He was about to pull it the rest of the way, but something stopped him. Recognition. The figure standing in the doorway wasn't one of the enemy. It was Plinth.

The Marine was soaking wet, half refrozen water covering

him to the waist as it had on all of them. Plinth's arm was red too, covered with blood from what looked like a gunshot wound.

Rivera's gun hand dropped to his side, and he ran forward toward the Marine. "Sergeant, you've been hit."

Plinth came the rest of the way through the door and leaned against the wall, sucking in a deep, labored breath. The tech by the door hit the button again, and the hatch slammed closed, cutting off the cold once more.

"I'm okay." Plinth's voice was hoarse, strained. He sounded anything but okay.

"Corporal...your arm..."

"I said I'm okay, Rivera. We've got work to do." Plinth pulled himself up off the wall. "Which way?"

"That way." The tech pointed down the corridor. "It's not far. We should be in and out in fifteen minutes." Rivera wasn't as confident as he tried to sound. The truth was, he'd only been down on this level two or three times, and there were kilometers of corridors and passageways. And if they were going to put the refinery out of service and wreck the tank farm, they had to plant the explosives in the right spots.

"Let's go then. We don't know how much time we've got." Plinth started off down the hallway.

Rivera could see the Marine was limping badly, but he held his tongue. He'd come to understand just how tough the Marines were over the past few days...and it didn't matter anyway. The mission was the mission, no matter how battered Plinth was. And, frankly, the warmth inside the refinery was worth the danger. They'd all been freezing their asses off for weeks without a break.

The group walked slowly down the corridor, Rivera stopping twice at intersections, trying to remember the right course. He was pretty sure they were on track, but doubts still nagged at him, making him second guess his choices.

Rivera was smart. He'd been offered jobs at a dozen research institutes, but he'd chosen to go to Santis. The mining combine always paid enormous salaries to technicians and engineers willing to do a two-year stint on the frozen radioactive hell. They'd absolutely thrown money at Rivera, enough to virtually set him up for life, giving him freedom to pursue the research of his choice. It had simply been too good to turn down.

And now I'm going to die here...

He didn't want to give up, but he was too smart to believe any of them had much of a chance.

"We're here." He'd stopped suddenly outside a large hatch as familiarity flooded into his mind. "This is it."

He pulled the ID card from his pocket and swiped it in the scanner at the side of the door. It clicked loudly and slid open, revealing a huge chamber beyond.

"Come on," he said, waving his arm. "The radiation is high down here. Techs who come down here wear rad suits."

"Well, we ain't got no rads suits." Plinth pushed forward, his eyes scanning the room, clearly looking for enemies. There were a dozen maintenance bots moving about, but no sign of anyone else. "So, let's get this done, eh? I'll watch the door and you guys get those bombs planted."

Rivera nodded, pulling a satchel from his back.

"You got it, Corporal."

*   *   *

"They're running, sir. I've got the whole century pursuing now. We'll get them, Praefectus."

Millius was standing in the middle of the high plateau, facing the sea cliff a hundred meters away. "What are those troopers doing over there?" He had listened to the optio's report, but his eyes had caught the activity along the top of the cliff.

The optio turned, looking now himself. "I don't know, sir," he admitted sheepishly. "I will find..."

"No...let's both find out." Millius walked quickly across the rocky field toward the cliff. "You soldiers," he shouted as he approached. "What's going on here?"

"Some of the enemy troopers climbed down the cliff." The report was matter-of-fact at first, but then the soldier recognized Millius. "Sir!" he added sharply.

"Did any of them escape?"

The soldier hesitated. Letting enemies get away was not something a stormtrooper wanted to admit to a Praefectus.

"Answer me, soldier." Millius's tone was ominous.

"I believe one escaped, sir. Or two." Another pause. "Perhaps three…"

Millius sighed.

I wish these troopers realized nothing angers an officer like this shit.

"Maybe they just ran here to escape, sir. Perhaps they couldn't catch up with their fellows."

Millius turned his head, looking the in the direction of the enemy retreat.

No, nonsense speculation angers an officer even more…

"No, Legionary, I don't think so. If you look at our lines of advance and their initial position, they could easily have withdrawn with their fellows. No…they went this way for a reason…" His voice trailed off as he looked over the cliff toward the eerie glow of the massive structure looming along the coast.

"The refinery…" He took two steps closer to the edge of the cliff. The refinery wasn't far, less than a kilometer.

Damn!

He spun around. "Optio…I want the refinery on full alert. Immediately."

"Yes, sir…" The junior officer sounded confused.

Millius looked in the direction the Marines had run. "And call off the pursuit." It galled him to let the bastards escape, but he had bigger problems than chasing down half a dozen enemy fugitives who had been nothing more than a diversion. "All forces are to move on the refinery at once."

Millius was angry with himself. He'd allowed arrogance to dictate his thoughts. He hadn't even imagined a few enemy troops would dare to move against the refinery.

And if you lose that production facility, you'll have singlehandedly blown the mission.

"Now, Optio. All forces converge on the refinery now!"

* * *

Hargraves felt like he couldn't take another step…but somehow he did. And another after that. His legs were screaming, the weight of the wounded Marine wearing him down.

He wanted to drop Garavick, to run for his own life. But thirty years of service made that unthinkable. It was base fear that made him even think such a thing, and that was something Hargraves had never allowed to rule his actions. The part of him that was Marine through and through didn't want to live if he had to throw a comrade's life away to buy his own.

Besides, I wouldn't make it anyway…they're just too close…

He was surprised he was still up. He'd heard dozens of rounds zipping by, but his luck had held. Toughness, strength, skill, training, courage—they all had their place on the battlefield. But luck was the most powerful of all. He was a veteran, but that did little to make an enemy miss him while he ran. That was largely fortune's domain.

"Hang with me, Garavick. Don't you die on me, Marine." The private had been whimpering when Hargraves first picked him up, but now he'd gone silent. He was still breathing—Hargraves could feel the warm air from each exhale on his arm—but he was unconscious now. Or close to it.

Hargraves pushed, digging for everything he had, but he knew he was almost done. Even a Marine was subject to the physical laws, and he was out of juice. He needed to rest, even for a few minutes. But he didn't have time. The enemy was right behind.

Wait…are they?

The bullets were no longer whizzing by his head.

He stopped, dropping low, laying Garavick on the ground. He turned, pulling his rifle from his back as he did and looking back the way he had come. He could hear something rustling in the tall grass, but it was receding.

He stood stone still, not quite believing that the dozens of soldiers that had been at his heels were all gone. But a minute later there was still nothing. Then two minutes.

He took a deep breath. Even the short rest had done him some good. His arms and legs were still exhausted, but they weren't quite as dead numb as they had been.

He stared down at Garavick. The Marine looked bad. He was definitely unconscious, and he had lost a lot of blood.

And we don't have shit in terms of medical facilities…just a few aid kits and one box half full of drugs…

He put it out of his mind. There was nothing he could do. If he got Garavick back and the Marine died…well, that was war. But he wasn't about to leave him behind, not when there was any chance at all.

He reached his arm under his comrade and struggled to get up, lifting Garavick back over his shoulder. He felt waves of pain, soreness, exhaustion. But he trudged forward. It was a long way back to the refuge, but with no one chasing him down he was sure he could make it.

* * *

"Almost done, Corporal. Another five minutes, and we'll be ready to go." Rivera was hunched over, reaching down to affix explosives to one of the cooling pipes.

"The sooner the better. We've been lucky so far, but it ain't gonna last." Plinth was standing next to the door with his rifle in his hands, ready for anything. He'd already pulled off the wadded piece of cloth he'd shoved on his shoulder and cleaned the wound the best he could. He'd reflexively shuddered as he took his coat off, and then his shirt, but then the expected wave of cold hadn't come. The room was heated, indeed, in more normal times he'd have been uncomfortably hot. But now he savored every degree of warmth he could get.

"I'll try to make it three minutes. Is that good en…" Rivera's sentence cut off. There was noise in the hallway outside, and they'd all heard it.

"Get down behind something," Plinth said, his voice hushed. The Marine moved swiftly across the room, swinging around the edge of a small console. His had snapped around toward the techs. "Down, I said…now!"

The techs slipped behind the machinery near where they had been taping the explosives to the heavy lengths of pipe. The refinery's cooling system was vast, and they'd only managed to get half the bombs in place.

The main door opened. Then nothing happened. For at least ten seconds, Plinth crouched down, ready to open fire on anything that came through. But nothing did.

Then something flew through the air, tossed in from outside.

"Grenade!" the Marine shouted, ducking down lower under the console, and hoping the civilians had the good sense to do the same.

Then an explosion. Loud. Deafening. He felt a wave of shock, and he struggled to maintain his composure.

A flashbang. A stunner. That means…

He saw the shadowy images moving through the doorway, and he heard the sounds of their assault rifles firing.

…they're coming.

He swung to the side, bringing his rifle around the edge of the console. He flipped the switch to full auto, and his finger tightened.

He saw one of the figures drop. Then another. And then he pulled himself back as a blast of fire hit the front of the console.

He twisted himself around, moving toward the other end of the workstation. As he went, he reached behind his back—he was sure he had a grenade left, but his hand had trouble finding it. The pain in his shoulder was brutal, and despite his best attempts to ignore it, it slowed him down.

There…

His hand was on the grenade. It was no stunner, it was a frag. And if he put it in the right place…

He pulled the pin and hurled the thing over the console, not waiting for the explosion to dive to the far end and open fire.

There were at least a dozen soldiers in the room. His fire took down one, and the grenade hit three more. But the others returned fire. He felt the pain as a round hit his arm. It was a heavy slug, fired from a high-powered weapon, and it almost tore his arm off. The wound was grievous, a massive chunk of flesh torn away, exposing the gray-white bone below.

He rolled over on his back, howling in pain, his rifle falling to the floor, out of reach now. The agony was overwhelming, and it was all he could think about.

No...

He gritted his teeth, struggling to endure, to ignore the searing pain.

If I lie here, I'm dead. We're all dead. And the mission...

He heard gunfire behind him. Then a cry. It was one of the techs.

He fought to climb back up to his knees, letting his savaged arm hang to the side. His other hand reached to his belt, and he pulled out the pistol Hargraves had given him when they set out. He snapped his arm up, firing twice, just as an enemy trooper swung around the edge of the console.

More shooting from behind. And another scream. A familiar voice.

Tomas...

He turned his head, looking back. There were troops everywhere. And Tomas Rivera was down, surrounded by a pool of blood.

Plinth felt a wave of rage, a need to lash out, to kill as many of these soldiers as he could. But the Marine inside him clamped down. There was a mission. The techs had gotten some of the explosives in place. There was no hope of escape, of survival. Only a last chance to see the mission completed. At least partially.

Tomas has the detonator.

He lunged from his cover, almost without thinking, diving for Rivera's body.

Plinth felt pain, like a hammer slamming into his back. Then another, as a second bullet ripped into him. He felt his breath sucked from his body, and more pain. He knew he was done, but he kept pushing ahead, reaching for the small control unit clipped to Rivera's belt.

He hit the ground hard, grunting as he did, pain flaring everywhere in his tortured body. He extended his arm as far forward as he could, but he was almost a meter short.

He could hear the sounds of enemy troopers moving, shouting to each other. Then more pain, his leg this time. He could feel his awareness slipping away, the heaviness growing in his limbs. But he crawled, clawing forward with his remaining hand. The he lunged one last time…and he felt the hard metal of the unit. He closed his hand on it, his fingers feeling around for the button.

He wanted to pause…one last thought of home, of his mother and father. And his sister. She was only fourteen, but they had always been close. She would be inconsolable, he knew, when she found out. She would cry her eyes out.

No, Cyn, don't cry…just be happy…live your life, for both of us…

His finger pressed down, just as his enemies moved over him and began riddling his body with bullets. But amid the agony, he felt the click under his finger, and he smiled back at his killers. And then, for an almost imperceptible instant, he heard the sound, the explosion that ripped through the massive chamber. Then silence, darkness.

Chapter Nineteen

From the Commentaries of Rance Barron

War is hell. Death, suffering, despair. Yet there is glory too, a shimmering reward that looks best from afar, when the costs it extracts are unseen. Still, for all the blood and suffering it demands, glory itself is intoxicating—unless you resist. I have been given decorations, awards...I have ridden at the head of parades and stood before cheering throngs. And each time, amid the adoration and the chanting of my name, I have tried to remember those who served with me, the legions of brave men and women ignored by glory, whose only legacy for combat and struggle is pain and death.

Glory is fickle, selecting some as its children and disregarding others. The victorious fleet commander becomes a national hero. The captain of a vessel collects combat awards, medals. The gunners who target enemy ships are cheered for their steady eyes and hands. Yet, in the bowels of the ship, braving radiation and heat and deadly dangers, are the engineers. It is they who keep the gunners' batteries working through damage and the stress of battle. It is they who give the captain the engine power he needs. Who ensure the admiral's fleet is ready to do as he commands.

So let me share the glory that I have received in far greater share than I deserve, and join me in a silent thanks to those too often unheralded men and women in the engine rooms and snaking access tubes...as much as any who serve, the true arbiters of victory.

CFS Dauntless
Approaching Planet Santis, Krillus IV
307 AC

"I'm pretty sure I got it, Commander Fritz. It was hiding deep in the aft cooling complex, but I finally tracked it down." Sam Carson looked tired. His sleeves were rolled up, and his arms were covered with bruises. Crawling around in *Dauntless*'s bowels was hard work, and sometimes painful too. The deeply buried conduits of the reactor cooling system were not designed for human access—at least not easy access. But the maintenance bots hadn't been able to target the problem...and everyone in *Dauntless's* engineering team knew how vital if was to restore power. If the battleship was facing its equal—or something more powerful—Captain Barron was going to need every gun operational. And the freak damage to the cooling lines had effectively knocked out half of the battleship's primaries.

"I'm going to miss you, Sam, I really am. I'm glad we still have you for this mission." Anya Fritz was an engineer's engineer, the range of her thoughts rarely extending beyond the confines of the ship's guts and beating heart. But Carson could hear the tension even in her cautious tone. Everyone on *Dauntless* was on edge. They'd been apprehensive on the Union border during their long, lonely patrol there, but they'd known what they were facing then. As massive as a Union invasion was expected to be, it was a known quantity. Now they were facing a mystery, staring off into the darkness.

"I'll miss you too, Commander. I'll miss everyone on *Dauntless*."

Carson had served on a few ships in his career, and he'd always gotten along with his crewmates. But there'd been something special about his short time on *Dauntless*. The ship felt like home, and the thought of leaving was a painful one. He couldn't turn down the chance to transfer to Archellia, to be with Lise and his child—but part of him grieved at the thought of his new brothers and sisters going to war without him.

He was glad, at least, that he was with them now. Lise had

practically begged him not to go, and he carried the guilt of refusing her. But he couldn't stay behind, not now. He loved his wife, but he had to be able to face himself in the mirror…and the thought of allowing his crewmates to face whatever danger was out there alone made him sick to his stomach.

Besides, if this is a real danger, Archellia is the first major world in its path. Whatever we face out here, we have to win. If we don't…

As a sector capital, Archellia had its defenses—far stronger ones than a fringe world might be expected to possess—but it had weaknesses too. There was no fleet stationed there, nothing but a few aging patrol boats. The two thousand Marines garrisoning the base were a formidable force, but they were the remnant of what had been a five thousand strong brigade before the high command started transferring battalions to the expected front lines. They would put up a fierce fight, but they were too few to beat back a serious invasion.

If *Dauntless* was facing an Alliance force, Carson knew it was vital that she defeat whatever she encountered. The Alliance was mysterious in the Confederation, with little concrete information available, at least outside of the highest levels of state secrecy. What was known was more legend than fact, stories of a warrior culture where children were trained to fight from the day they could walk. The rumors Carson had heard all told of a brutal culture, one that abused and enslaved conquered populations. He couldn't let them get to Lise.

"Are you listening to me, Sam?" There was a touch of irritation in Fritz's voice.

"Ah…sorry, Commander. I…I was thinking about Archellia. About my wife." Carson had briefly considered making up a better story, one that sounded more military. But he didn't have it in him. For better or worse, he was a painfully honest man.

"Archellia will be fine, Sam." Fritz's tone was empathetic, something he'd rarely heard from the hard-charging engineer. "Captain Barron is the best in the fleet. Whatever is out there, he will deal with it."

"Thank you, Commander. Captain Barron has all my faith. It's…it's just hard."

"I know it is, Sam. But we're lucky to have you here. If you stay focused, you'll be a big part of us getting the job done."

Carson smiled weakly. "You are very kind, Commander. I can promise you everything I've got. *Dauntless* is my home, even if I am leaving soon." He paused, then repeated, "Everything I have, Commander."

"I know that, Sam. But first, get down to sickbay. There are all kinds of radiation spikes in those cooling tubes. Get yourself checked out and get a quick cleanse…before we end up in *real* action."

"I'm sure I'm okay, Commander. Besides, the aft torpedo loading system is running a little rough. I was going…"

"That wasn't a request, Lieutenant. Sickbay. Now. I'll see to the aft torpedo tubes."

"Yes, Commander." Carson stepped back and snapped off a salute. Then he turned and headed toward the main hall and the lift tubes. The smile on his face was gone, replaced by a twisted frown.

Carson hated doctors and hospitals.

* * *

"Maintain active scanning at full power, Commander. We will remain at general quarters. There is an enemy ship out here, at least one…even if we haven't found it." He knew the sustained alert status was hard on his crew, that each hour he kept his people at battlestations wore down their effectiveness. But it would be far worse if they were blindsided. That had already happened once, and Barron didn't intend to allow a repeat.

"Scanners at full, Captain."

Barron had already suspected that Santis and its tritium production facilities would be a target, and the trap at the transwarp link had only reinforced that notion. His scanners hadn't detected the enemy yet, but he *knew* they were out there. Somewhere close.

He twisted his head, trying to clear the knots from his neck. He'd been in his chair for over twenty hours without a break. He was going to have to order a round of stims for his people soon, that much was certain. But he knew such things only lasted so long, and he was going to need his people sharp when the battle he knew was coming actually began. He would wait, perhaps another few hours.

"Captain, Commander Fritz reports her people have fixed the reactor cooling system. All primary weapons are active and at full power."

Barron felt a wave of relief. He'd pressed on from the transwarp link, moving toward Santis as quickly as possible, disregarding the damage inflicted by the laser buoys. He suspected time was not his ally in this situation. But he didn't relish making contact, going into battle with half his heavy guns out of action. The particle accelerators were extremely powerful weapons, but they were greedy of energy, requiring almost all of the output of *Dauntless's* massive reactors to fire. And he was glad to have them all back online.

"Give Commander Fritz my compliments."

"Yes, Captain."

Barron stared ahead at the 3D display. Santis was projected in the center of the tank, a fuzzy-looking gray-white sphere. The planet had two moons, Lyra and Assul, represented by smaller globes, currently at opposite edges of the tank. Barron had reviewed the data banks. Lyra was a dead rock, lifeless and airless, but Assul was as different from its frigid parent world as possible. Heated by massive volcanic activity, it was warm— too warm for humans to endure for more than a short period without survival gear. The large moon was covered with dense jungles, teeming with carnivorous plants.

"Approaching Santis, sir. Should I plot a course into orbit?"

Barron sat silently for a few seconds. Finally, he said, "No, Commander…not yet. All engines are to decelerate. Bring us to a stop half a million kilometers out." Barron's gaze was focused on the tank, his eyes boring into holographic light depicting Santis.

"Yes, Captain. Decelerating now."

"Red squadron is to prepare to launch."

"Sir?"

"I want every millimeter around this planet and both moons searched, Commander. And I have no intention of entering orbit until I know exactly what is there. In orbit or hiding behind one of the moons. I want full power to active scanners. Concentrate on the planetary and both lunar orbits."

"Yes, sir. Scanning now." A moment later. "Yellow squadron reports ready to launch, sir."

"Launch. Advise Red leader to break her people up into teams of three. I want the far sides of the planet and both moons scouted."

"Yes, Captain." Travis relayed the order, and a moment later the ship shook softly as fifteen fighters shot down its magnetic catapults in rapid sequence and out into space. "Red squadron launched, Captain."

"Order Yellow Squadron to alert stations, replacing Red." He knew it was Green's turn in the duty rotation, but most of the squadron's pilots were raw, fresh out of the Academy. He didn't know what his people were up against, or what they might encounter. But he knew damned well he wanted his experienced pilots out there.

"Yes, sir. Yellow squadron to alert stations."

Barron listened to Travis's voice, steady, firm. He trusted her completely, and the two worked together seamlessly. He'd have sworn she could almost read his mind somehow, and there was no one he'd rather have on the bridge…or in command if anything happened to him.

"Very well, Commander."

Barron stood up, holding back the wince that wanted to escape as every muscle in his body rebelled. He had to get up and move around, at least for a while. "I'll be in my office. Contact me immediately with any reports."

"Yes, sir."

He walked across the bridge toward a large hatch. "Open," he said softly, pausing as the door slid to the side. He stepped through and said, "Close," pausing as the hatch shut.

Then he let out a deep sigh. He really wanted to go to his

quarters, to lie down, even for a few moments. But he couldn't. He wouldn't. Not while he had his people at battlestations.

His recollections of his grandfather were those of a young boy, and most of their conversations had been about fishing, the family estate, or the exotic worlds the admiral had seen. But the old man had imparted some of his experience to his grandson, and Barron knew that a captain who shared his crew's pain and struggles would gain a level of loyalty well beyond the norm. Rance Barron had won his victories as much due to the extraordinary effort and sacrifice of his crews as to his own tactical wizardry. And Tyler knew his grandfather had gained that respect and devotion by sharing every hardship and danger with those who followed him. He'd always been at the forefront, in the thick of the fighting, at the center of the combat.

Barron resolved he would do the same. He would be everywhere with his people, through whatever danger he led them to. And one thing he damned sure would never do was sneak off for a nap while his spacers struggled to stay focused at their stations.

He walked across the room, limping slightly from the numbness in his leg, and he sat behind his desk. It was a relief to have a few moments of privacy at least, if not rest. His crew could display their uncertainty, their apprehension, at least to a point. But not him, not the ship's captain. He knew they all looked to him, and the slightest sign that he was not in control, that he had his doubts, would crush morale in an instant. And Tyler Barron's mind was flooded with doubts at the moment.

He stared down at the screen on the side of the desk, reviewing the meager scanning data. He didn't have much beyond gut instinct to tell him what he was facing. The laser buoys suggested a fairly large ship, or perhaps a number of small ones.

Or even a freighter…

It seemed clear, however, that there was no massive invasion fleet, at least not yet. If there were that many ships out there, he would have detected something. Residual ion trails or some kinds of energy readings. Besides, a fleet would have attacked *Dauntless* immediately, not played a cat and mouse game trying to gain advantage.

No, whatever we're facing, they're respectful of us, wary. That's the only reason we haven't been attacked with anything else yet.

Barron rested his head in his hands, closing his eyes for just a few seconds.

Who are you out there? And what are you doing now? What trap are you laying for us?

Chapter Twenty

"They're just sitting there, Commander. They may be launching fighters. It's hard to be sure with just passive scans."

Kat listened to her exec's report with disappointment, if not surprise. She'd set another trap for her Confed counterpart, but it didn't look like he was going to fall into it.

"Maintain position and continue minimal energy output."

"Yes, Commander." There was something in Wentus's voice—a touch of discomfort perhaps?

Kat understood. Her exec was a gifted officer, but he was as indoctrinated in Alliance thinking as anyone else in the service. Kat knew she was too, at least to an extent, but she saw other things as well, realities, dangers. She knew where the enemy was, and standard doctrine called up on her to finish things, to advance and engage—and destroy—the enemy. Immediately. But her instincts were calling out to her as well, screaming for caution. The Confeds weren't supposed to have substantial military assets deployed to the Rim...yet here she was, facing what could only be a frontline battleship. That was a colossal failure, at least as far as information gathering was concerned. A four-million-ton battleship was a big thing to miss.

169

She was confident she could defeat the enemy. Even with her belief that the Confederation wasn't as weak as many in the Alliance believed, she couldn't imagine the Alliance's flagship with its handpicked crew couldn't defeat a similarly-sized enemy vessel. But she was also aware that *Invictus* was the only ship in the area, the sole Alliance force tasked with holding Santis. She not only had to defeat this Confederation battleship, but she had to come out of the fight with her own vessel in reasonable condition, strong enough to hold out until the fleet arrived.

She'd almost issued the order to swing around Krillus V, to set a course for the enemy ship and begin the final battle at once. But she'd held her tongue. She had an edge now. She was getting real data on the enemy…and she suspected they had nothing at all on her own ship. It was an advantage she intended to press to its fullest effect. Whoever was on that ship, they weren't like her hardened Alliance spacers. They were vulnerable to fear, to psychological warfare. And she was going to make the most of it. If she could win with finesse, with maneuver—and avoid a toe to toe slugging match—she could minimize her own damage. Keeping her vessel operable was worth spending some extra time waiting.

Hiding, as Wentus and the others probably consider it…

Invictus was on the far side of the fifth planet, the bulk of the gas giant hiding her from even the most intensive scans initiated by any ship near Santis. She'd positioned two small satellites on opposite ends of the planet, her communications link with the probes in orbit around Santis and its moons. She'd kept the probes on passive mode…but whoever was commanding this Confederation vessel, he was no fool. He'd stopped short of the planet, clearly fearing a trap. Now it looked like he had launched fighters.

Of course…he's going to have his squadrons scan the planet rather than risk his ship. This one knows what he is doing. He fell into one trap, but now he's wary. He won't be easily fooled again…

"Switch probes to active scan mode." There was no point in maintaining stealth. If the Confed ship was launching fighters, they would detect the probes soon enough, even operating in passive mode. Better to get as much data as possible while she could.

"Switching to active scan mode."

"Issue a launch alert to Gold Dagger, Red Banner, and Dark-wind squadrons. They are to be equipped for anti-fighter operations. And Black Fist and Hydra squadrons are to be armed for anti-ship strikes."

"Yes, Commander." Kat could hear the animation in her exec's voice, the satisfaction at her hints of an impending attack.

She sat still, not responding, just looking ahead at the screen.

Maybe the enemy will move closer…maybe the fighters will miss the platforms orbiting the moons…

There was at least some chance a few of the laser buoys would score hits. She didn't expect to cripple the enemy ship… it was clear her rival was too smart to be lured into a killing zone. But even a few shots could make the difference, especially when her fighters would be coming in hard, right behind the laser attacks. It was a risk, committing five of her six squadrons to the attack. But *Invictus* was out of range, well-protected for the moment. It was time for an aggressive move, time to strike a deadly blow.

"Optiomagis…you may launch all squadrons as soon as they are ready."

*   *   *

Optiomagis Ellian Junus sat at the controls of his fighter, breathing deeply through the mask that covered the lower half of his face. The pressurized oxygen flow helped force the breaths into his lungs, partially counteracting the high g-forces pressing down on him. The Talon-class fighters were new, the latest generation of Alliance attack craft, and they included technology gleaned from a dozen conquered worlds. The range of the new craft was nearly double that of the old Ripper class, and they carried a larger payload as well. *Invictus* was the first ship to be equipped with the fighters, all six of her squadrons replacing their old birds with the sleek new ones.

Junus was a Patrician and an experienced pilot, the veteran of a dozen battles. He'd been hand-picked by Commander Vennius to lead *Invictus's* six squadrons. He'd been a typical pilot of the fighter forces in his youth, all aggression and arrogance with a constant need to prove himself fearless. But he'd seen enough death around him—and almost died himself several times—and now he was cooler, wiser, his thoughts more tactical, less emotional. He suspected that was one reason Vennius had chosen him for the post. The relationship between the Commander-Maximus and Commander Rigellus was well known, and Vennius had spared no effort to ensure that his informal daughter had the best the Alliance had to offer.

Junus didn't resent his assignment, though. He liked Commander Rigellus. He'd long been an admirer of her career from afar, and her daring assault on the enemy pulsar cannon at Heliopolis had only increased his esteem. He'd jumped at the opportunity to serve on her new command, though he'd had mixed feelings about the mission itself. The fighter pilot in him, the cockiness and senseless courage that still remained, was thrilled to be on the vanguard of a new invasion. But the commander, the man who'd lost so many pilots in the Alliance's constant wars…that part of him was apprehensive, both about the mission itself, and the war that success would surely bring.

None of that mattered, though. It wasn't his place to pass judgment on the high command's orders. Duty came first. It was the way, and he was no more able to meaningfully question his orders than Kat Rigellus was herself. Junus knew officers such as the two of them could nurse their doubts, even their disagreements with the directives they were given. But neither could ever—would ever—speak of such thoughts, nor allow them to influence their decisions. And they certainly would never let their subordinates to see anything but total confidence in their demeanors.

He twisted his body, trying to get comfortable. The Talons were a bit larger than the old Rippers, but little of that extra space ended up in the cockpit. He'd never noticed how cramped the space was when he was a young pilot, but now his legs ached, half a dozen old wounds taking their toll on an aging warrior.

He lurched to the side, taking some of the weight off his aching left leg. Then he glanced down at the small display on the console. The array of neatly aligned dots told him what he needed to know. His squadrons were formed up perfectly, a testament to the Alliance's high standards of training…and perhaps to the fact that Commander Vennius had scoured the fleet for veteran pilots to transfer to *Invictus*'s squadrons. Junus had never seen so many ace pilots assigned to one ship before. There wasn't a man or woman in his force that hadn't seen at least two or three battles, and many could match his own dozen. The elite of the Alliance's fighter corps was here, and he was determined to see them live up to their reputation.

He looked down at the throttle, unused for now as he allowed the AI to pilot his bird. There were notches on the side, carved roughly into the otherwise smooth steel. Twenty-three of them, one for each enemy fighter he had destroyed, and enough to rank him in the Alliance's top tier of aces. It was a vanity, he realized, to mark his kills like that, and even a greater one to transfer the notches to his new ship. But he'd done it anyway, as he suspected most of his people had. You could sometimes teach a pilot wisdom and patience, but you could never completely take the bravado away.

And if you could, you'd take his soul with it. And then he would be useless…

He stared down at his com unit. It was utterly silent. No chatter, no status reports. The orders were clear. Total radio silence until he was sure the enemy had detected his fighters.

Which will be soon anyway…

He glanced down at the positional display. His squadrons were almost halfway to Santis, close enough for the enemy's active scanners to pick them up. It was only a matter of time.

What would happen then was the real question. His birds were moving at high velocity. They'd been accelerating steadily since *Invictus*'s catapults had launched them, and now they were moving at roughly one point five percent of lightspeed. He had a decision to make—Commander Rigellus had given him two options. Hit the enemy at high speed, making one blindingly-quick strafing run, or decelerate as his birds approached, slowing down to engage and destroy any fighters the enemy launched, followed by a sustained attack against the enemy vessel.

Junus wouldn't make that decision, though, he knew. Not really. The Confeds would. If they were slow to respond—as all the intel reports suggested they would be—he would sustain his velocity and try to reach the enemy battleship before it could deploy its defensive fighters. A strike like that could be devastating, even though his squadrons would get only a single pass.

If, however, the enemy was able to get its full complement of fighters into space, he would slow his fighters on the final approach. He would begin a protracted dogfight, one in which his people would destroy or drive way the enemy fighters. He didn't expect the Confeds to be a pushover, as the high command did, but neither did he think they could stand up to his veteran squadrons. And once he'd stripped the battleship of its fighters, his second wave, equipped for an anti-ship strike, would go in and pound the giant vessel. He knew his people didn't have to destroy the enemy; his purpose was to damage the vessel, weaken it so *Invictus* could finish the job. Still, he couldn't help but think of the glory of the kill, to hold out some prospect of his birds winning the victory on their own.

He heard an alarm bell going off, the warning that enemy launches had been detected. His eyes dropped to the display, waiting, watching as the AI assimilated incoming scanner data and updated the screen. It looked like one squadron launching, in addition to the one the Confeds had already sent into planetary orbit.

His hands moved to the com unit, his fingers moving lightly over the headset. The enemy launch could mean they had detected his strike force. But only one squadron? He hesitated, trying to decide if it was time to break the silence.

No, wait. More than one squadron. Two, at least. Possibly a third.

There was little doubt. The Confeds had located his fighters.

"Attention all squadrons, initiate active scanners. Close to attack formations."

His eyes were locked on the screen, watching the Confed fighters shake out into battle array. They moved smartly, crisply. Indeed, they reminded him of his own squadrons. They were heading right toward his force, moving slowly, positioning themselves to intercept his attack.

This is not what we were told to expect...

He watched, waiting for signs of disorder, for a ragged formation. But the Confed fighters were positioned perfectly, far enough from their mother ship to engage the assault force before it entered range, but moving slowly enough to quickly change course, to fight a protracted battle. Exactly how he would have formed up in their position.

He hesitated for a few more seconds. Then he sighed softly. He couldn't blow past these fighters—he had to destroy them. They were too good, too much of a danger if they were allowed to operate freely.

He reached down, grabbed the headset and pulled it on. He pressed the button for the main channel. "All fighters are to cut acceleration on my mark and begin full deceleration." He paused for a few seconds, and then he added simply, "Mark."

He flipped off the AI piloting system, and he punched at the nav controls, cutting engine thrust. He felt the crushing weight lifted, replaced by the relief of free fall. Then he grabbed the throttle, turning it hard to the right, engaging the positioning jets to re-angle his ship. He punched at the thrust controls again and the oppressive force returned. It felt the same as it had, but his ship's engines were now blasting along the opposite vector, slowing his velocity as they did. A glance at the display and a quick calculation told him what he already knew. His birds would be almost at a dead stop when they engaged the enemy, ready to maneuver and fight it out.

He closed his eyes, his lips moving slowly, almost silently, repeating the words of an old Palatian proverb. It was his good luck charm, one he recited every time he went into battle. Most fighter pilots had a superstition or a good luck charm of some kind. It all defied logic, and yet it made sense too. Anything that put his mind at rest, created confidence—even if it was baseless—was worthwhile. An unfocused, distracted pilot was a dead pilot.

"All squadrons, perform final checks and arm all weapons. Gold Dagger, Red Banner, and Darkwind, you are in the lead. Once we engage, you are to stay on those enemy fighters. Black Fist and Hydra, you are to form up behind the leading squadrons and prepare to execute strikes against the enemy battleship."

He took a deep breath, feeling the pressurized mask force oxygen into his aching lungs. It was time.

"For the Alliance," he said into the com unit, his voice firm, hard. "To victory."

Chapter Twenty-One

Excerpt from "A Pilot of the Late War," by Kevin "Striker" Grierson

Death is my wingman. He is always nearby, following me, shadowing my every move. I cannot shake him, and no evasive maneuver will break his lock on me. I cannot defeat him, no pilot can, so I have befriended him. I do not try to escape from him anymore. He will come for me in his own time...and until then, I will blast every enemy with the guts to show himself in front of me.

Interplanetary Space
Between Krillus IV and Krillus V
307 AC

"Alright, Blue squadron, you know what we're here for. You've trained for this day, you've flown millions of kilometers...all to bring you to this moment. These are invaders, enemies. If we let them get through us, they will attack *Dauntless*, they will bring death and destruction to our mothership and our comrades. And they will do it because we *let* them do it. I say never! They shall not pass." Jake Stockton was strapped in his fighter, his hand gripped tightly around the throttle. He could see the mass of fighters on his scanner's display, coming on in two waves. The first was less than five hundred thousand kilometers from the Confederation forces…almost engaged.

Blue Squadron was on the left, with Yellow on the right and the inexperienced pilots of Green squadron in the center, their flanks covered by their more experienced comrades. Stockton had a reputation as one of the best pilots in the service, but he suspected the Alliance forces—if they were indeed from the Alliance—had more combat experience. He wasn't going to let that make a difference, no matter what he had to do. But it was still on his mind.

"Raptor, Thunder here. I want your people to accelerate. Try to get around the flank of the enemy formation." Stockton nodded as he listened to Kyle Jamison's orders. *Dauntless*'s strike force commander went by his call sign in combat, as all Confederation fighter jocks did. It was tradition mostly, but it also ensured that the enemy wasn't given easy information about ranks and command structures. If they were going to pick off the commanders, they would have to find them some other way than listening in on comm frequencies for mentions of rank.

"Thunder, roger that." He moved his hand to the com unit, his finger hesitating over the channel selector. "And good fortune to you, Thunder. Happy hunting!"

"And to you, Raptor. Thunder out."

Stockton moved his finger, switching the com over to the Blue squadron line. "All birds, prepare to engage thrusters, one quarter power. We're heading for the enemy's flank. And wingmen, remember to stay tight with your leaders. These aren't pirates or renegades out there. We're facing veteran pilots, sure as hell, and if you let your guards down, they'll blow you to atoms."

He grabbed the throttle and moved it slowly, angling his fighter and then blasting the engines. He felt the pressure, but at one-quarter thrust, the dampeners quickly adjusted. He looked down at the display, watching the Blues move with him, their formation almost as perfect as it had been. He was proud, and he felt a wave of satisfaction. But there was another thought there as well, a darker one. The realization that he was, in all likelihood, about to lose some of his pilots.

Blue squadron had become like a family, and the thought of watching his brothers and sisters die suddenly hit him. Stockton was the epitome of the apparently fearless pilot, but he'd found that his ability to seemingly ignore the danger of his own death didn't transfer to those under his command.

This is war. It's one thing to think about it, to prepare for it…but quite another to face it.

He reached down, his fingers flipping a series of levers, arming his weapons.

This is it. Your entire life has led you to this moment…

* * *

"Gold Dagger, Red Banner…engage. Darkwind in support."

Junus nudged his throttle, pressing on the thruster control as he angled his bird toward the enemy. Regulations stated that the force commander should be positioned behind the attacking squadrons, but that was one of the few rules widely ignored in Alliance service. No officer who'd come up in the fighter force could obey such a covenant, not without disgrace. And Ellian Junus, for all his accumulated wisdom and experience, was still a fighter pilot at heart, still subject to the same callings.

He stared straight ahead. There were two enemy fighters moving toward his ship. He put his finger on the top of the three firing buttons on his throttle. His weapons were all armed and ready, and he watched as the enemy closed.

His threat detectors whined, the high-pitched signal telling him one of the enemy fighters had launched a missile at him. He waited, counting softly under his breath, eyes on the range readings. Then he pressed the small stud, and he felt his fighter buck as his own missile launched.

Then he pulled the throttle back hard, angling it to the side, gasping for oxygen as his dampeners struggled to partially negate the crushing g-forces. He'd launched his weapon…now his attention was completely focused on getting away from the missile coming at him.

He angled the controls again...then again, changing his vector and velocity wildly, almost randomly, in an effort to shake the enemy weapon.

He could feel the sweat on the back of his neck, the stress of battle, tight throughout his body. He'd been in combat many times, but he'd rarely had so much trouble evading an enemy's missile. The fighter that had launched it had managed to get in close, its velocity higher than his own, adding to the missile's acceleration.

That's a good pilot...I hope they're not all this capable...

He moved the throttle again, hard. He could see the enemy missile closing. It was still on his tail. He looked at the chronometer. Two minutes, thirty seconds. Alliance missiles had less than three minutes of fuel at maximum acceleration, but he realized he had no idea about the Confed weapons. If they were similar, he would escape from its lock. But if the Confeds somehow managed to pack more fuel into their missiles...

A tingling raced through his body, every nerve, every cell alive. He felt the adrenaline flowing through his blood, bringing a rush beyond even that of the stim he'd taken before engaging. His hand angled one way and then the next on the throttle, his mind racing. But nothing he did shook the deadly weapon on his tail, and the warhead continued to close.

Three minutes...and it's still accelerating...

He'd have escaped an Alliance missile by now. Once the weapon ran out of fuel, its velocity and vector would be set... and all he'd have to do is move out of its path. But the Confed weapon was still coming, matching his every directional change.

He felt the sweat pouring down his neck now, his back, the slick wetness under the skintight pressure suit. He sucked the pressurized air from his mask, hungrily, greedily. He could feel his heart beating in his chest, a drumbeat growing more rapid with each passing second.

His mind filled with recollections, maneuvers and tactics he was taught during his days at the Academy so many years before. And newer memories too, battles he'd fought, tricks he'd invented on the fly, the moves that had saved his life more times than he could easily recount…and had sent twenty-three of his enemies to hell.

He pulled back hard on the throttle, spinning his small craft, drastically changing the angle of his thrust. It was a bold maneuver, but its effect on his overall vector would be slowed by his existing velocity. Still, it was an unexpected move, as random a turn as he could throw at the missile's AI. The weapon's guidance system would adjust, there was no question of that. But if he confused it enough, he could gain a few seconds, and seconds would be the difference between life and death.

It was a game…a deadly game about time. If he could outlast the missile's fuel supply, he would escape. But he was at three minutes, thirty seconds, and the weapon was still blasting at full, still reacting to his every attempt to escape. He glanced down at the screen, looking for other bogies. There was nothing. His flight from the missile had pulled him from the main battle area. That was good news, at least. The missile was enough to worry about. The last thing he needed was another enemy fighter on his tail.

He swung the throttle hard again, spinning the tiny craft in an almost random direction. His eyes were locked on the missile's icon on the display. It overshot, took perhaps three seconds to match his maneuver. It didn't seem like much, but he'd just bought himself more time.

Four minutes. Fuck…these missiles have one hell of a range…

He thought of his squadrons, imagining the losses they would suffer facing the superior Confederation weapons. All of their maneuvers and training were based on evading missiles for three minutes. But hitting that mark wouldn't save them here.

Four minutes, thirty…

The missile was gaining. It wouldn't be long now. Junus figured he could last another thirty seconds, maybe forty-five. If the missile's fuel lasted longer than that, he was a dead man. He'd imagined this moment before, many times. But now he realized he'd never *really* thought about it, never believed the day would come. His pilot's bravado had always been there, but now he felt it slipping away, pouring off like water from a melting block of ice.

Five minutes…

The missile was right on his tail, barely five hundred kilometers back.

His hand was sweatsoaked, slipping around on the throttle. He could feel death coming, like a shadow looming over him, blocking the light. He had seconds left to live. He felt an urge to yield, to surrender to the inevitable. But veteran Alliance pilots did not yield. Defiance filled him. He might be defeated, but he would never surrender. He would fight to the last.

He jerked the throttle hard again, a move so abrupt, the force dampeners couldn't respond quickly enough. Twenty g's of force slammed into him, and he felt a sharp pain in his chest as one of his ribs snapped from the pressure.

He gasped painfully for oxygen, even the pressurized feed inadequate to force the flow of air into his tortured lungs. And with each rasping, desperate breath, the broken rib hurt like fire. But it didn't matter. In a few seconds it would all be over.

Wait…

His eyes snapped down to the display. The missile hadn't matched his last maneuver. It was continuing on its previous course.

Out of fuel!

He released the throttle, and the thrust vanished, the crushing pressure replaced by the relief of free fall. He breathed hard, deep, ignoring the agony in his chest.

He was in pain, his heart still pounding. But he was alive. And there was a battle raging. His people needed him. His eyes were focused on the display, and he gasped softly. Two-thirds of the enemy force had engaged, and a massive dogfight was underway. He was shocked at what he saw. His people were hard-pressed, ten fighters already destroyed. It looked like the enemy had suffered similar casualties, but that parity came to him as a terrible shock. He'd expected the Confeds to be better than the intelligence reports made them out to be, but even his most pessimistic projections had assumed a considerable advantage to his squadrons in losses inflicted versus losses sustained.

He couldn't afford a bloody stalemate…his force had to defeat the enemy fighters, especially since two more of his squadrons were fitted for anti-ship attacks, waiting. They would be sitting ducks if the interceptors failed to turn back the enemy.

But things were even worse than that. A third of the enemy force had moved off, and now they were maneuvering around his flank.

"Stupid fool," he spat to himself. "You move too far forward and get yourself in trouble…then you take your eyes off the battle." He flipped on his com unit. "Darkwind leader, this is Force Leader. Deploy your squadron to the right of the formation, intercept enemy forces moving against the flank."

"Force Leader, this is Darkwind Leader. Acknowledged. We're on our way. Out."

Junus stared down at the display. The fight was raging, and his people were hard pressed in multiple areas. The fighters on both sides were moving at very low velocities, which allowed rapid course changes, placing an emphasis on pilot skill. That should have given Junus's people the edge, but his eyes were telling him otherwise. It was a true dogfight, with both forces locked together, fighters slashing in and out of enemy formations, firing their missiles and then diving in for attack runs with lasers.

Junus had seen many battles, but he'd never encountered an enemy as effective as the Confeds were proving to be. Their fighters were better, faster, and he suspected longer-ranged as well. He'd discovered the superiority of their missiles firsthand. Alliance forces weren't supposed to allow technical differences to interfere their tactics or their pursuit of victory. They were a warrior race, and no enemy gadgets could overcome their invincible fury. So went the mantra.

But these Confed pilots are good…

He stopped short of thinking, "as good as we are." That would be a hard thing for an Alliance officer to accept, almost a sacrilege. But there was no arguing that his force had lost more birds than the enemy so far.

Except in the center…

The Confeds were pressing forward against his forces every-where…everywhere except in the center of their formation. Their fighters there had suffered badly, and the survivors were being forced back.

That is the place to press. Darkwind will secure the flank. But the enemy center is the route to victory.

He pulled the throttle to the side, bringing his fighter around, facing toward the very midpoint of the battle. Then he took a deep breath, and he pulled back hard, feeling the g-forces slam into him as his engines fired at full power. There was pain, his chest felt on fire, but he ignored it. He'd seen the route to vic-tory, and there was no place for anything else. Not now.

*   *   *

Olya "Lynx" Federov sat in the cockpit of her fighter. The Lightning-class attack craft that formed the mainstay of the Con-federation's fighter corps were sleek and powerful. The pilots of the fleet almost universally loved the design, save for one factor. The cockpits were too small, too cramped. But Federov didn't care. She was slight in build, barely forty-five kilograms, and not much taller than a meter and a half. Her body was lithe, flexible. She'd wanted to be a dancer when she was younger, until she'd seen a squadron of fighters putting on a show on the vid. Flight had captured her imagination that day, and her life became a relentless pursuit of a slot at the Academy, one which saw suc-cess three days after her nineteenth birthday, when she received her billet in the following year's class.

That had been almost twelve years earlier, and Federov had long since given up her cadet's circlets, first for an ensign's insig-nia and then for lieutenant's bars. She'd served six years as a second lieutenant, and then she'd gotten her promotion to first grade…and the command of a squadron on *Dauntless*, arriving on the same shuttle as the battleship's new commander. She and Captain Barron had spent the trip in conversation, and by the time they had docked, Federov hoped she had given the famous officer reason for confidence in his new squadron leader. She was certain she'd developed that trust herself in *Dauntless*'s captain. Tyler Barron wasn't boastful, but there was something about the simple, calm confidence he exuded that created almost instant trust.

Federov was a dedicated officer on her own account, but she felt an added burden on *Dauntless*, the need to never let Captain Barron down. And since the probes around Santis and its moons started banging away with their active scanners, her instincts were on fire. There was more here than orbiting sensors. She was sure of that.

"Red nine and Red ten…begin your orbit and report."

"Red leader, this is Red nine. We are approaching the planet. We should enter in…" There was a pause, one that made Federov's stomach twist into a tight knot. "Red leader, we're getting other contacts. It looks like some kind of satellites…wait, we're getting an energy spike…"

"Get out of there, Red nine. Now!"

"More laser buoys, Red leader. We're…" His voice was replaced by static.

"Red nine, report."

Damn.

"Red nine…report."

"Red ten here, Leader. The laser buoys have opened fire on us. They got Red nine, Lieutenant."

Federov felt her hands balling into fists. "Get out of there, Red ten. Now." She wasn't going to lose another pilot, not needlessly. The laser buoys were primarily anti-ship weapons, but that didn't mean they couldn't target fighters, at least at very short range. As Red nine had just proven.

"Yes, Leader. I'm on my way."

"How the hell did we not detect those farther out?"

"I don't know, Leader. They're fuzzy on my display…they must have some kind of stealth capability."

Federov toggled her com unit, switching to the squadron-wide frequency. "Red two, Red three…Red six, Red seven, exert extreme caution. We have found active laser buoys in orbit around Santis." She had no idea if there were more weapons orbiting the moons, but she was gaining respect for whoever they were facing in this struggle. She'd pretty much assumed it was the Alliance, just as almost everyone else had, though she knew little about that mysterious power. The fuzzy information she had suggested an almost totally militarized society. That was bad enough, but now she was thinking about the officer in charge, about the series of traps they had encountered. She had great confidence in Captain Barron…but now she was also beginning to wonder if he was facing his equal in this contest.

"Red leader, this is Red two. Active mode probes confirmed around moon number one." A pause. "Detecting energy readings now." Another second, perhaps two, passed. "Laser buoys confirmed, Lieutenant. Executing evasive maneuvers now."

Federov shook her head. The planet and a moon. Both moons, she realized. She hadn't gotten the report yet, but she had no doubt there were weapons in orbit around *both* Lyra and Assul.

She flipped the com again. "Red leader to *Dauntless*. Red leader to *Dauntless*. I need to speak with Captain Barron immediately." She was half a million kilometers from the mother ship. It took nearly two seconds for her signal to reach *Dauntless*, and as long for any reply to travel back to her. It wasn't a long time, not by any reasonable measure, but sitting in her cockpit staring out at Santis, it seemed like forever.

"What is it, Lieutenant?" Federov could tell as soon as she heard Barron's voice that something else was going on.

"Sir, we've encountered laser buoys in orbit around Santis and both moons. Also, a string of probes in all three locations running active scans. Request permission to engage and destroy."

"Negative, Lieutenant. Leave the buoys for now. All other squadrons are currently engaged with enemy fighters. Return to base at once to refuel and rearm." A short pause. "And hurry."

Federov felt like she'd been punched in the gut. Here she was with her people, out scouting when the rest of *Dauntless*'s fighters were in battle.

"Yes, Captain. At once." She flipped back to the main frequency. "Attention, Red squadron. We have been ordered to abort the current mission and return to base as quickly as possible. Form up on me in thirty seconds, and prepare for maximum thrust."

She reached out to her console, flipping a row of switches, sending maximum power to her engines. She looked down at symbols the on the display, watching her fighters maneuvering into formation. Her eyes froze for a moment, fixed on the empty spot. Red nine's position.

No time for that now...

She waited, watching the numbers count down on the chronometer. Ten seconds. Five.

Her hand tightened around the throttle...and then she pulled back, blasting forward at full thrust. Back to *Dauntless*. Back to join the fight.

Chapter Twenty-Two

Interplanetary Space
Between Krillus IV and Krillus V
307 AC

"All right!" Stockton's finger was still on the firing stud, his lasers blasting away. But the enemy was gone, nothing left but a cloud of expanding plasma. "That's three!"

Somewhere below the surface, "Raptor" Stockton was as scared as anyone in battle facing the prospect of death. But three kills later, his blood was up, his cockiness and bravado fully in charge. Stockton was the stylized ideal of a fighter pilot, skilled, deadly, relentless…and for all practicality, fearless. But he was also an officer, a squadron commander, and he was responsible for fourteen other pilots.

Twelve, he thought, grim reality forcing its way through his aura of invincibility. Two of his birds were gone. One of the pilots might have had time to eject. Blue four had been crippled before the final shot came in and vaporized the fighter. But Hendricks was dead for sure. Blue seven had strayed too far from his wingman, and he'd gotten in a nasty head to head fight, alone and too far from any support. Hendricks had been a good pilot, and he'd handled his fighter well…his enemy had simply been better. The shot that wrecked his ship had obliterated the cockpit. Stockton doubted his pilot had even had time to realize

188

what was happening. He certainly hadn't been able to eject.

"Keep up the pressure, Blues. The Greens are hurting bad. We've got to hit these bastards hard in the flank before they wipe out our center."

Stockton had never seen—never even heard of—a fighter battle as intense and sustained as this one. Typically, squadrons came at each other at high velocities, launching missiles and conducting passing strafing runs at each other before overshooting and decelerating to reform for another run. But *Dauntless's* fighters and the enemy were locked in a death struggle, and neither side showed any signs of backing down. Exhausted fuel supplies and dwindling power cells would eventually force one or both sides to withdraw.

Assuming there's anyone left by then…

"Blue three, Blue four…on me. We're driving through." His eyes darted down to the screen, to the cluster of dots sitting motionless behind the main battle area.

"Acknowledged, Lieutenant."

"With you, Lieutenant."

Those birds are armed for anti-ship strikes. Have to be…or they would have committed them by now…

"Blue Ten, Eleven, Fourteen…with us. The rest of you, hold off that reserve squadron."

The enemy had sent a dozen birds against Blue squadron, and they were almost in position. Stockton knew he was being aggressive, even reckless. But if he could get to those anti-ship squadrons…they'd be almost defenseless, cumbersome and loaded down with plasma ordnance intended for *Dauntless*.

Still, splitting the squadron was a wild gamble. The fighters left behind would be outnumbered two to one by the enemy reserves. And the six ships making a run for the rear enemy squadrons had a long way to go, past a lot of opposing fighters. He was also betting the lives of Green squadron's survivors. The enemy might react to the danger posed to its anti-ship squadrons, pulling back its forces in the center to chase his own birds. But if they didn't, the Greens were as good as dead, outnumbered and outclassed, with no help coming. At least none soon enough.

Kyle…

Kyle "Thunder" Jamison was more than just *Dauntless*'s strike force commander, and Stockton's immediate superior officer. He was Stockton's closest friend, even a brother. And his maneuver would leave Jamison alone with half a dozen raw pilots facing the brunt of the enemy attack.

He felt the temptation to cancel his orders, to come around and head toward the center, to come to Green squadron's rescue. But he pushed it aside. The twenty-four fighters to the enemy rear could inflict enormous damage on *Dauntless*. And if there was one bit of training, of mantra, driven into every pilot's head, it was that the mothership comes first. If he pressed on, maybe—just maybe—he could hurt the enemy force before it had a chance to hit *Dauntless*.

Thunder can take care of himself…

He wanted to believe it, he tried to make himself believe it. But he was plagued with doubts. The only thing that drove him on was the sound of Jamison's voice, urging him to do his duty, to focus on what had to be done. No matter what the cost.

He pulled the throttle, feeling the impact as he blasted forward at full acceleration. He was burning half his fuel, he knew that. But the sight of those laden-down fighters was impossible to ignore.

Lined up like just so many sheep…

* * *

"Optiomagis, we've pushed through the center. We've knocked out seven fighters from the central squadron, and the rest are scattered."

"Very well, Optiominus. Continue to engage. Do not allow the enemy to reform."

"Yes, sir."

Junus knew his orders fell squarely into the category, "easier said than done." It seemed clear the Confeds had positioned their weakest pilots in the center, but now that they had broken, chasing them down would obliterate his own formation.

And that squadron on the flank is good. Too good…

He cursed himself for not outfitting more of his birds for anti-fighter operations. Commander Rigellus would have listened to him, he was sure, if he'd urged a pure interception strike…or the commitment of *Invictus*'s sixth and last squadron. But arrogance had reared its ugly head. He'd been sure he could defeat anything the Confeds threw at him with three squadrons, but now doubts were eating away at his certainty. And even if he could prevail, the losses were going to be…

He thought about ordering a withdrawal, but every bit of his training rebelled against the idea. Alliance forces did not run.

But they do retreat when it makes tactical sense…or at least they can.

He knew few Alliance commanders were willing to risk the dishonor of fleeing from an enemy, no matter how much it was tactically the right thing to do.

No, we've shed too much blood to come away with nothing. It's time. The best time we're going to get, at least.

"Black Fist and Hydra Squadrons…full thrust now. Vector directly toward enemy capital ship. All other squadrons, protect the flanks of the attack force. Keep the enemy fighters from breaking off and pursuing. At all costs."

Losses had been heavier than he'd expected, and now he was doubling down. It was all or nothing. If Black Fist and Hydra could do enough damage to the enemy vessel, the casualties wouldn't matter. *Invictus* would finish things. And the Confeds were losing as many birds as he was. Two crippled strike forces canceled each other out.

Still, his mind drifted back to *Invictus*'s sixth squadron. He'd left the Gleaming Shields behind, committed to combat space patrol duties. It was standard procedure, but now he wondered if he'd made a grave error, if those twelve fighters would have been the weight that shifted things to total victory.

There was no point in debating such things now. The Gleaming Shields were too far away to intervene, even if Commander Rigellus would be willing to release them. He had what he had… and he'd just doubled down.

Once thing he knew for sure. He needed every fighter in the mix. Every fighter.

He gripped his ship's controls, angling the vessel toward the center of the melee. Then he pulled back, fired his engines at full thrust. It was time to finish this.

One way or another.

*   *   *

"Green squadron reports heavy losses, sir. Casualties in excess of fifty percent."

Barron heard the words, but his mind blunted the true meaning. There was no point in beating himself up over the deaths of so many pilots. Not now. There would be time for that later, when the battle was won. And if it was lost, Barron would likely join them in death. The only reward for such a disastrous outcome would be to escape the doubts and recriminations.

He'd almost held the raw Greens back, but there had just been too many enemy fighters inbound, and he'd needed their numbers…especially with the Reds all the way over at Santis, too far away to intervene in time.

If we had Federov's people here…

"Very well, Commander." Barron almost didn't answer at all. He probably wouldn't have if it had been anyone else but Commander Travis. But he knew she was mourning the lost pilots as much as he was.

"Commander Jamison reports the remainder of Green squadron is hopelessly scattered. Two enemy squadrons equipped for anti-ship strikes are moving through the gap."

Barron just sat in his chair, staring across the bridge at *Dauntless*'s exec. He felt the urge to answer, to react to the report, somehow. But the crew was already at battlestations, all weapons manned and ready. There was nothing to do but wait.

Finally, he said, "Put estimated time to combat range on the display, Commander." Then, a few seconds later, "All crew are to take a course of stims five minutes before contact."

"Yes, Captain." Travis' hands moved over her workstation.

"Forty-one minutes until fighter strike enters firing range."

"Time until Red squadron arrives?"

"Twenty-nine minutes, sir."

Barron sighed, trying to keep it as silent as he could manage. *That's twelve minutes to refuel and relaunch...not enough.*

He looked over at the display. The data was old, he knew, and somewhat of an estimation. But he saw the situation clearly enough. The enemy force was heading directly for *Dauntless*. There was a cluster of his fighters hot on their tail, but he couldn't tell if they would reach the strike force before it was able to launch.

And if they get in range intact, we'll never shoot that many birds down quickly enough. They'll get through the defenses, and...

He remembered his grandfather's tales, stories of massive fighter strikes devastating capital ships. He'd taken a grave risk leaving *Dauntless* with no combat space patrol. That had paid off in terms of the fighter battle still raging. But now the cost of having numbers in the dogfight was coming due.

He slapped his hand down on the com unit. "Fritzie, I want you to send a team of your best people down to the launch bay alpha immediately. They are to help Chief Evans refit Red squadron."

"Captain...yes, sir." Fritz sounded like she might argue, some version of "my people are engineers, not fighter support techs." But Barron suspected the seriousness in his voice had deflected any argument.

"And Fritzie...we need to get the Reds refit and back in the launch bays in about ten minutes, or your people are going to have a shit ton of damage to deal with. I need everything you can spare. I realize that will leave damage control understaffed, at least for a while...but there's no alternative."

"Understood, sir. I'm on it now. Fritz out."

*   *   *

"Shit."

Stockton was cursing to himself. It was pointless, he knew,

but he did it anyway.

"Shit."

He stared straight at his display, watching the cloud of dots in front of him heading directly toward *Dauntless*. He'd taken a gamble, left half his squadron to withstand double their number so he could move against the enemy's reserve squadrons, the two dozen craft outfitted for attack runs against *Dauntless*. But the enemy blasted forward before he could engage, escaping from his attack and heading straight through the gap where Green squadron had been. He and four of his pilots were in hot pursuit, straining their engines to the breaking point, trying to catch up before the enemy ships were able to launch their torpedo salvoes.

His eyes caught movement on the short-ranged display, three small dots, moving toward his small group of fighters.

His com crackled to life. "Raptor…Thunder here…form up on me. We've got to hit those bombers."

Stockton allowed himself a little smile, and he felt a small wave of relief. Commander Jamison was alive…and he had two Green squadron pilots with him. Stockton hadn't been sure any of the inexperienced pilots had survived.

"Thunder…damn, it's good to hear your voice."

"And yours, Raptor." Stockton could hear the strain in Jamison's tone, the exhaustion. And he knew his own rasp couldn't sound much better. The two were experienced, capable pilots, among the best in the service. But neither had ever been involved in anything like the battle they'd been fighting for the last couple hours…

"We've got to catch those ships, Raptor. I don't care if we burn our engines to cinders…we've got to get there."

"I'm with you, Thunder." Still, Stockton felt strange, wrong somehow. He stared at the screen, at the still-raging battle he and *Dauntless's* strike force commander were exiting at full thrust. They were doing their duty, trying to catch the enemy force ahead…but it still felt like running. He hated abandoning the rest of *Dauntless's* pilots—including half of his own Blue squadron—but the first rule of the fighter tactics was clear. Protecting the mothership was always the priority. Always. And that was just what they were doing.

"Thunder, if we force-power our reactors we might be able to catch those birds before they launch."

A few seconds of silence passed. Then: "That's against regs, Raptor. You know that."

"Regs? Who cares about regs? We're out here on the edge of nowhere, on the way to losing half our people. And that tin can is our ticket back home. We've got to take out those fighters, at least some of them. It doesn't matter how good we are if we can't catch them in time."

Stockton could hear his friend's breathing on the line, but there was no response, not right away. Finally, Jamison said, "Okay, let's do it, Raptor. All fighters…full force power procedures now."

"You'll have to disable your AIs," Stockton added, "or the failsafes will stop you."

"Yes, Raptor is right. Shut down AI safeties."

Stockton took a deep breath. He punched in his override code, disabling the ship's AI. Then he flipped a pair of switches on the side of his throttle, committing his reserve fuel, and force pumping it into the reactor. It was dangerous, something regulations expressly prohibited, an overload that could easily scrag the reactor…or worse. But it was also good for a ten percent bump in acceleration.

Fuck regulations. We have to get to those fighters…

He looked at the display, watched as the AI updated the projections, taking into account the fleeting burst in acceleration. It was going to be close, really close. But they just might get an attack in before the fighters launched. And every bird his people took down was one that couldn't plant a plasma torpedo into *Dauntless's* guts.

Chapter Twenty-Three

AS Invictus
In Orbit, Krillus V
Alliance Year 58 (307 AC)

"The strike force is approaching the enemy battleship, Commander. They are being pursued by a small number of Confederation fighters. The rest of our squadrons are still engaged with the enemy. The battle is…apparently even, the end result still in doubt." *Invictus*'s executive officer was clearly trying to hide the surprise in his voice, with limited success.

Kat heard Wentus's words, and she understood his disbelief. The forces engaged in the dogfight were roughly equal in numbers. And Alliance forces didn't fight to draws, not when they matched their enemies in strength. They had a sixty-year tradition of victory, an imperative to win at all costs. Yet, every report from the battle still in progress suggested a stalemate. At best.

Her thoughts were elsewhere when Wentus made his report. She had a choice to make, whether to press forward, gamble and take some risks, or stay where she was, exert caution, and wait.

There was no question what Alliance orthodoxy demanded. She knew where the enemy was, and she had the advantage. It was time to advance, time to go in for the kill. The enemy's fighters and her own were locked in a struggle to the death, and soon all the engaged forces would have to break off to refuel and rearm. She still had two squadrons moving in against the enemy vessel, and unless that battleship had more fighters in reserve, there was no chance *Invictus* would face the same kind of attack. Not if she engaged now, before the surviving enemy fighters could land and rearm for anti-ship strikes.

The way was the way, and its demands were clear. She knew what she had to do. But there were doubts as well. She was beginning to truly respect this enemy commander, seeing in his actions a mirror image of herself. She tried to imagine his responses to her actions. What would he do if *Invictus* moved forward, closed to firing range? Would he stand and engage? Accelerate and seek to whip by her ship, limiting the immediate combat to a single pass? Or would he withdraw, run?

And what would her fighter strike accomplish? She wanted to wait, to be sure her squadrons caused enough damage to give her a clear edge in the fight to come. But if she waited, she might allow a wounded enemy to pull back...or to recover and refit its surviving fighters, even launch a desperate attack against *Invictus* with its rearmed squadrons.

Kat had never had difficulty making bold decisions before, but now she was torn. She tried to tell herself she was overestimating her opponent, but the doubts remained, nagging at her, even as she made the only choice she could.

"Prepare for full thrust maneuvering. All personnel to battlestations."

"Yes, Commander." She could hear the enthusiasm in Wentus's voice, seemingly pushing aside the officer's earlier hesitancy. She wondered if it was sincere, or if it was nothing more than years of Alliance indoctrination. Ambitious officers did well to act as though they longed to be in battle, that facing and defeating an enemy was life's greatest pleasure. Kat had long lived that mantra, but now she wondered if there might be more satisfaction in bringing her people home alive, returning them to loved ones.

She wondered what she truly wanted. More glory, bought at whatever cost in blood? Or to walk the rocky shores of Litora

Montis, to hold her children close to her, to see them grow… and to know their mother as more than just a presence that passed in and out of their lives between campaigns. She understood such thoughts were dangerous. The way was the way, and that was all she needed to know, all any Alliance officer needed to know. She remembered her grandmother, the old woman's remembrances of servitude, the stories Kat had heard about the days before the Rising. Her people were warriors for a reason, because they refused ever to be slaves again. But still, she found herself having to push back against idyllic images of home more and more often.

She was in battle, and victory here would surely launch her into the lofty ranks of the Alliance's fleet commanders. Yet she couldn't push away the thoughts of her son's hugs, or the feel of her hand slipping through the soft silkiness of her daughter's blond hair.

The way is the way…

She slowly, methodically, forced herself to focus, to set aside the distracting thoughts. Alliance culture said there was no time for such things, but even if there was, it clearly wasn't now.

"All personnel at battlestations, Commander. Ready to execute full thrust operations."

She'd shaken herself from her brooding, and Wentus's words finished the job, cleared her mind.

"Execute," she said, her voice grim, controlled. The warrior was back in charge, ready to do what had to be done. "Course directly toward the enemy vessel."

"Yes, Commander. Interception course plotted. Engaging thrust now."

She took a deep breath, preparing for the force of the engine's thrust to hit her. It was a reflex by now, an unconscious act. The other thoughts were gone. Whatever questions she might have, or doubts, this was not the time. She was Katrine of the Rigelli, a Patrician, an Alliance warrior, and that was how she would behave. She carried the lives of her people on her every decision, even the future of her nation. And now she would do her duty. She would engage and destroy this Confederation battleship. Then she would hold Santis and its tritium production facilities until the fleet arrived.

Thus will be the spoils of my victory here. Another war, thousands more dead. Millions.

The way is the way...

*   *   *

"Captain, Red leader requests permission to land." Travis sounded edgy, with good reason. *Dauntless* was facing an imminent attack from the incoming fighters...and scanners had just picked up the mystery vessel, the enemy battleship they had all expected to find but that had been little more than a projection until a few minutes earlier. It was coming right at *Dauntless*, pushing to reach the Confederation vessel less than thirty minutes after the fighter strike.

"Permission granted. Advise Lieutenant Federov we are short on time. She is to get her people aboard as quickly as possible."

"Yes, sir."

Barron looked at his screen. Stats were coming in, updating...data on the ship heading directly toward his. It was big, the AI's best guess at this range was that the enemy vessel outmassed *Dauntless* by two or three hundred thousand tons. It wasn't a massive difference, not with four million ton ships. But any chance he was facing a lesser opponent had vaporized. The minimal intelligence he'd seen on the Alliance suggested they were somewhat behind the Confederation in technology, and that their ships were smaller, less powerful. But the vessel heading toward him looked like more than a match for *Dauntless*.

"Red squadron commencing landings, sir."

Barron just nodded. Then he tapped his own com unit. "Fritzie, are your people ready in the bay? I need those fighters turned around as quickly as possible." He paused, then added, "Seconds count."

"Yes, Captain. I'm down here myself. I've got a dozen people with me, and I've had a...chat...with Chief Evans about the chain of command." There was a twinge of residual anger in her voice.

Barron suppressed a smile. He knew Evans well. The chief was career, a long service veteran, one who'd seen action in the last war. He wasn't overly fond of officers, and Barron suspected the grizzled old spacer hadn't reacted well to Fritz showing up on his landing bay and taking charge. And he had no doubt, Anya Fritz had made it clear who was top dog the second she'd stepped through the door.

"Okay, Fritzie…carry on." He paused. "And try to take it easy on Chief Evans, okay?"

"Yes, sir." There was reluctance in her tone.

Evans must have really pissed her off…

"Out," he said, slapping at the com with his fingers. Then he turned back to the main display. He breathed deeply, staring down at his hands, making a conscious effort to hide his anxiety. He was the captain, the one all his people would look to for strength, for confidence. He was also a veteran of sorts, but like most of the officers in the Confederation navy, his experience had been limited to policing actions and minor fights with rene-gade forces. He had never stared down another battleship, never faced the prospect of a battle of equals, of two ships maneuver-ing, firing…a fight where only one vessel could prevail.

A duel…

He imagined two dandies from a lost era, swords in hand, fighting one on one. And like them, he realized, the cause of the dispute didn't matter, not now. The politicians and analysts would unwind what had caused an Alliance ship to be here, whether the Union had managed to gain an ally in the coming war…or if the Alliance was simply probing for weakness. The high command would decide how to respond to the longer term threat, what forces to deploy and where. None of that made any difference to Barron and his people, no more than the original insult that might have caused his imagined duelists to meet. No. Causes were irrelevant, right and wrong meaningless concepts. Now, there was only victory…or defeat, death.

He stared at the screen, imagining the space between the

enemy ship and *Dauntless*, the vast, frigid, black emptiness.

A duel in the dark...

"Commander..." His voice was softer than it had been, calmer. His people needed to see him totally in control, no matter how tense he truly was. "I want all gunnery stations to run full testing procedures."

"Yes, Captain. Implementing testing now."

He looked over at Travis's station. The officer was sitting straight, almost as if a metal rod had been affixed to her spine. He knew she had to be as edgy as he was, but if anything, she hid it better than he did. He was grateful to have her aboard, to know he had a first officer he could count on no matter what happened. Travis was capable...no, far beyond capable. If they made it through this battle, he knew he would lose her soon. It was only just. She deserved her own command. She rated it in every measurable way...and if she'd had any family influence at all, if she'd come to the service anything but a penniless refugee from a hellish world, she would already be wearing a captain's stars.

He promised himself, as much as he wanted to keep her with him as long as possible, when—if—they got back, he would throw the Barron name behind her, help her get her own ship. He felt a wave of regret he hadn't done that sooner...but it passed quickly, overwhelmed by the gratitude he felt at having her at his side for this crisis.

He looked back to the display, staring at the holographic depiction of the space around *Dauntless*. The cluster of incoming fighters was closer, almost in range. And right behind them, seven of his own birds.

"Launch a double spread of probes, Commander. Full active mode...let's get all the data we can on this enemy ship before we're engaged. It's not like anybody is hiding anymore."

"Yes, Captain." Travis punched at her workstation, leaning down over her com unit and relaying a series of commands. "Probes launched, sir. Feeding scanning data to your screen." A few seconds later she added, "Captain, launch control reports all Red squadron fighters safely landed. Refuel and refit operations are underway."

"Very well."

"Sir, Lieutenant Federov requests permission to launch fighters piecemeal, as they are ready."

Barron shook his head. He hated the idea of sending his people out one at a time, to stand in the way of two full enemy squadrons. But then he saw the seven dots in the display, less than half a squadron pursuing the incoming ships. He realized any fighter could be the one that prevented a critical hit to *Dauntless*.

"Granted," he said softly.

I'm sorry, Olya, but you're right. We need every bit of force we can get, no matter how much the risk to your people…

*   *   *

"Come on, baby…you know you can do it…" Stockton wasn't sure talking to his fighter was something his instructors at the Academy would have considered effective…or sane. But he was close, so close. And he knew the bombers were going to launch their weapons on *Dauntless* any second.

His eyes were fixed on the range display, the numbers counting down. He was closing. Another ten minutes would put him in optimum range. But he didn't *have* ten minutes.

He stared at the targeting display, his eyes locked on the closest fighter. It was long range, very long. The AI was showing the chances of scoring a hit at less than two percent, and below one percent of one causing enough damage to stop the enemy craft. But Stockton had never liked AIs.

Good pilots are born, not made. And they damned sure aren't programmed.

He opened his hand, stretching his fingers, closing them tightly around the throttle. He stared intently, his finger squeezing gradually as he focused on the target. His lasers would lose a lot of power at this range. A glancing blow wasn't going to do it. He needed an engine or cockpit hit. The shot had to be dead on.

His headset was quiet. He knew the others were doing the

same as he was, putting all they had into picking their targets, getting ready to fire. They would all wait, he was sure of that. They would hold their fire until the AIs said they were close enough. But not him…

Fuck the AIs…

Stockton's fingers tightened, the metal of the firing stud hard and cool against his fingers. His head was locked, immobile, his eyes fixed on the targeting display. The AI was feeding him data, but he ignored it.

If you don't think we can hit, shut the hell up. I'll do it myself…

His fingers tightened, slowly, steadily, even as he moved the controls slightly, correcting his firing angle. Silence…one second…two…

Then he heard the high-pitched whine, his dual turbo lasers firing. Once…then again. And again.

It was the third shot. He saw the dot on his screen, a small ring appearing around it, the designation for a hit. And then it vanished entirely.

"Oh yeah, baby!" His shout echoed in the cramped cockpit, and he thrust his arm up hard and screamed again.

The com unit crackled to life. "Nice shooting, Raptor!" It was Jamison. Thunder. And his voice was almost feral. "Raptor showed us how to do it, people. Now let's take these bastards down!"

Chapter Twenty-Four

Interplanetary Space
Between Krillus IV and Krillus V
307 AC

"They're breaking off, Lieutenant! They're running! Should we pursue?" The pilot's voice was excited, even giddy.

Tillis "Ice" Krill listened to the reports that continued to come in, half a dozen of them so far, all saying essentially the same thing. The surviving enemy fighters were pulling back. They were running.

Ice shook his head as he sat in his fighter's cockpit. He had managed to take down two of the enemy birds, and he was proud of the job his Yellow squadron pilots had done—proud of the entire strike force, actually. He was in command on the scene now, of the remaining Blues and even a few of the Greens that had made it through the fight, as well as his Yellows. Commander Jamison was chasing down the enemy bombers, and Raptor had gone with him. That left Krill in charge.

He was calm and cool now, as he was in battle and everywhere else, a trait that had long ago given him his call sign. But he felt the same anger as the rest of the pilots, rage at the losses they had suffered and the urge to chase the enemy down, to destroy every last one of them. But that wasn't possible.

"Negative, Lieutenant...all personnel, listen up. Fuel status says we head back now." He watched as the dots on his screen moved away, the enemy fighters returning to their own mothership. He wanted to believe *Dauntless*'s squadrons had won the fight, that the enemy was indeed fleeing, as his pilots were shouting. But he knew better. The Alliance fighters had come even farther than his own people had. They were breaking off to refuel and rearm, not because they were broken. They'd be back, Krill was sure of it. And his people had to be ready. Right now, they were low on fuel, out of missiles. No, there was no question of trying to continue the battle.

"Back to *Dauntless*, now. Form up on me."

He got a wave of acknowledgements, though the number of responses was small, especially considering he was in command of three squadrons right now. What was left of three squadrons.

He stared down at his screen, at the large blue oval that represented *Dauntless*. And the seven small dots following a cluster of enemy fighters, so close now, the icons were barely distinguishable on their own. The enemy strike force was almost in range…and no seven fighters ever made were going to stop it cold. *Dauntless* was going to endure a bombing run, and Krill knew his people might return to a mothership whose landing bays had been blown to oblivion.

"C'mon you guys…catch those bastards. Take some of them down." His words were barely a whisper.

Krill and Stockton were rivals, the two best pilots on *Dauntless*. They baited each other constantly, vied for the informal title of best on the ship. Though Krill would never admit it, he knew he was number two, and he considered Stockton the best natural pilot he'd ever known.

If anyone can catch and engage those bombers…

He smiled, his best wishes for his rival.

Get it done, Raptor. Get it done.

* * *

"Launch clearance granted. Transferring controls to your console. Good luck, Lieutenant."

Federov was strapped in, her hands on the throttle. "Acknowledged, control. And thanks."

She flipped the lever next to the throttle, activating the magnetic catapult. The force slammed into her like a hurricane, pushing her hard into her chair as her fighter raced down the launch tube and back out into space.

She angled the throttle, engaging her fighter's thrust, and adjusting her vector directly toward the approaching enemy ships. There had been twenty-two of them left when she'd climbed into her fighter. There were twenty now. The birds chasing the strike force had drawn blood, and each enemy bird they knocked out was one less to fire on *Dauntless*.

It's time for Red squadron to join the party...

She twisted around in her seat, trying to work out the kinks, the stiffness. Her people had been back from the mission to Santis no more than fifteen minutes before her bird had been cleared to relaunch. She hadn't even thought that kind of turnaround was possible, but the bay was swarming with ship's crew, including a dozen engineers sent down to help with fighter refit. And at the center of it all was Anya Fritz, *Dauntless*'s chief engineer, a taskmaster as unrelenting as Chief Evans, with a lieutenant commander's clusters to back it up.

The bay had seethed with tension. The normal staff were resentful of a bunch of engineer interlopers poking their noses where they didn't belong...and the engineers, considering themselves the masters, here to rescue the flight techs and get the job done. But the tension had created a weird sort of energy, a drive to get the job done, one that had pushed them all to do just that little bit extra.

She'd been so uncomfortable, she was grateful to be back out in space, but the strange partnership was working, she couldn't deny that. The fact that her fighter had launched so quickly was the only proof required.

"Red leader, this is Red Eleven...I've launched, and I'm following your vector."

"Acknowledged, Red Eleven. Let's go give these bastards a welcome they won't soon forget."

And now Red squadron had two fighters. Two ships to stand in the way of twenty.

She stared straight ahead, wishing she had missiles. The bay crews had refueled her ship and recharged her laser batteries. But there simply hadn't been time to reload the heavier ordnance.

She was moving directly toward the incoming enemy ships. No fancy flying. No finesse. There wasn't time.

She picked out the closest of the enemy craft, tapping her throttle, aligning her vector toward the target. She adjusted the guns slightly, a bit of intuition added to the AI's precise calculations. Then she fired. Her lasers blasted out, half a dozen shots in as many seconds. And then she watched her screen as the enemy ship winked out of existence.

She felt a wave of excitement, satisfaction…but it only lasted a second. She was staring at her screen when she saw it, all along the enemy frontage. Nineteen surviving craft, and coming from them, smaller dots.

Plasma torpedoes…

She slammed her fist against the fighter's console, swearing under her breath as she did. Nineteen was better than twenty-four, but it was still too many.

At least they had to fire at long range…

She sat for a few seconds, frozen, a passing moment of indecision. She felt helpless watching the torpedoes move toward *Dauntless*, but she realized there was nothing she could do. Then she heard a small ding, her scanners reporting another enemy ship destroyed. It was *Dauntless* this time, her anti-fighter turrets opening up, scoring a hit. Then another enemy ship disappeared…the work of the pursuing fighters this time.

She let out a hard sigh. There was nothing she could do about the barrage headed toward *Dauntless*. All she could do was make sure the enemy paid the price, that none of those ships escaped to rearm and return.

She glanced at the screen. She had four birds now. They were strung out, disordered. There was no chance to form up in any meaningful way. There was only one thing to do.

"Red squadron, attack at will. All ships…attack at will."

* * *

"All sections, brace for impact."

Barron reached down and grabbed the straps of his harness, pulling them across his chest and snapping the latches into place. Regs said all crew were to be strapped in during any red alert, but *Dauntless's* captain hated the damned bulky things, and they had hung down from the bottom of the chair, unused. Until now.

"All stations report ready, sir." Atara Travis was also strapped in, as was every other officer on the bridge.

Barron knew what had happening in the gunnery control sections. The anti-fighter turrets were targeting the incoming plasma torpedoes, firing as quickly as they could recharge. But the weapons were hard to intercept. They began their run as physical projectiles, but on the way to the target they triggered an internal reaction, converting the normal matter of the torpedo into a high energy plasma. It was a chess game between the gunners on the target ship and the AIs controlling the torpedoes. The warheads had small positioning engines, and they could adjust their vectors and correct targeting until they converted. After that, they were nothing but superheated plasma, traveling on a fixed vector and velocity, the AIs that controlled them vaporized by the conversion.

"Engine room, forward one-quarter thrust." Barron barked out the command, his eyes fixed on the display. Most of the torpedoes had already converted. That made his laser turrets obsolete, but it gave him a chance to evade, to move his hulking ship out of the path of the deadly weapons that could no longer adjust their own vectors.

"Forward one quarter." Travis echoed his command, and an instant later *Dauntless* lurched ahead, her engines blasting at one-fourth of capacity.

Barron's gaze remained set, his mind following each of the weapons heading for his ship. *Dauntless's* gunners had taken out five of the torpedoes before they converted. Now four more zipped by into the space where *Dauntless* had been. But there were ten more still coming.

"Bring us around, course 311-120-128…increase thrust to forty percent." Barron spoke rapidly, knowing his command was coming too late.

"Executing," Travis snapped back.

But Barron *had* been too late. *Dauntless* shook hard. Then again an instant later. The second hit sent a shower of sparks flying across the bridge as a power conduit overloaded. The lights flickered for an instant, and Barron could hear the distant rumbles of explosions.

He slapped at the com unit, his eyes still fixed on the display as he did. Two more torpedoes zipped by, but another slammed hard into *Dauntless*'s bow.

"Damage report." Barron reached down and grabbed his headset, pulling it roughly over his head. "Now, Fritzie. What's going on down there?"

"I don't have it all yet, sir."

Barron could hear the sounds of shouting in the background, urgent calls for teams to deal with one problem or another…and worse ones, cries that hit him in his stomach, those of wounded men and women. *His* men and women.

"How bad is it?"

"It's bad, sir. We've got power drains in multiple locations. At least half a dozen external compartments are compromised. I think the reactor's okay, but I'm worried about that jury-rigged repair to the cooling lines. I just got back to engineering from the launch bay, and I'm still trying to get on top of things. Give me another few minutes, sir, and I'll get back to you with better info."

"All right, Fritzie…just remember, we've got the enemy battleship heading right toward us. They'll be in range in…" He glanced down at the readout. "…twenty-nine minutes."

"Understood, sir. Fritz out."

Barron felt a chill. He'd never heard his chief engineer sound so rattled.

"Bring us around, Commander. Reverse thrust now."

"Yes, sir."

Barron watched another spread of plasmas move by on the display…and then two more, the last two, coming right at *Dauntless*. He knew there was nothing he could do. The weapons were too close, but he had to try.

"Increase thrust to flank, Comm…" The ship shook hard, and the bridge spun around, the grav control system giving out. Barron was thrown forward hard, his chest slamming into the harness. He felt the breath ripped from his lungs, pain in his shoulder, his sternum. The bridge was plunged into darkness for a few seconds, only the red glow of the battlestations lamps remaining to light the way.

Then the emergency lights snapped on, a soft glow replacing the brightness of the main lighting panels.

"Captain, Commander Jamison reports he has multiple fighters coming in, fuel status critical."

Baron stared down at his screen. He punched at the controls, pulling up schematics of *Dauntless*, each of them speckled with small, glowing dots…damaged areas. And both landing bays were lit up like holiday displays.

*   *   *

Sam Carson wiped his arm across his forehead, trying without much success to mop away the sweat that was pouring down into his eyes. He was crouched down, reaching inside one of the main panels, pulling out handfuls of fried circuitry. The plasma torpedoes had hit the outer sections hard, but internal explosions and burnouts spread the damage throughout the ship. There were radiation leaks in a dozen places, and burned out electronics in more spots than he could count.

"Sam, how does it look down there?" Commander Fritz sounded edgy. Carson couldn't even imagine the number of problems she was juggling right now.

"It's bad, Commander. I'm only on panel one, but I'd bet the whole system is fried."

"Damn…" Fritz cursed softly. Carson suspected he wasn't

supposed to hear it, so he pretended he hadn't. "All right, Sam… assign a squad of bots to replace it all. I need you up here. The primaries are down again, and we've got twenty-three minutes to get them back online."

"Yes, Commander. On my way."

He jumped up, wiping the black residue from his hands. He pulled the portable com from his belt, punching in the code for the engineering AI. "I need a squad of maintenance bots in sector F11. The entire central trunk needs replacement.

"Acknowledged. Dispatching bots now."

Carson nodded, a pointless gesture, he knew. Then he turned and moved out into the corridor, heading toward weapons control. He took a breath, and then he went into a coughing fit. There was smoke in the air, chemical residues.

We're going to have to deal with that too…

But the enemy battleship was coming…and that made the primary batteries the most important repair, even if half the crew was choking on toxic fumes.

Twenty minutes…

Carson was an engineer, not a tactical officer. But he knew how the ship would fare in the coming fight without its main guns. The Alliance battleship was fresh, undamaged. And *Dauntless* was already a patchwork of hurried repairs. Without the main guns…

He walked down to the end of the corridor, reaching up and grabbing a rung of a small ladder leading up. Half the turbo lifts were out, and he didn't have time to look for one that was functioning, or worse, to get stuck in one. Not now.

He climbed up, not even thinking about it for the first few levels, but by the time he'd scrambled past seven decks and was heading for the eighth, he was feeling it. And weapons control was another three levels from there.

He was breathing hard by the time he got there, his shirt half soaked through with sweat. Something felt off, like he was heavier than normal.

Probably the grav control system is out of whack…

That wasn't a priority. The main guns and the launch bays

were all that really mattered now.

At least the reactor seems to be at one hundred percent…or close to it.

He paused for a second at the top of the ladder, sucking in a deep breath. The air was better up here—there were still traces of noxious fumes, but they were far less concentrated than they'd been on the lower decks.

Carson moved quickly down the hall toward a large hatch. It was open, one side of the huge double door twisted and off its track. He stepped inside, nodding to the group of three technicians already there.

"So, what's the problem?" He moved toward the main console, staring down at it, his hands moving over the controls. "What is it? We're short on time, guys. So, what's the issue?" He was normally a patient man, but this wasn't the time for slowness and delay. If they didn't get these guns online in the next fifteen minutes…

"Sir, there's a power interruption of some kind. The guns themselves check out, we've run three diagnostics…there's no significant damage to the weapon units proper. And the reactor's operating at ninety-four percent, which should be more than enough. There's power getting through to the guns, but not enough. We're bleeding off energy somewhere in the system."

Carson exhaled softly. It was good news, sort of. A break in the power transmission system was probably the least serious damage that could affect the main guns. It was likely an easy fix, at least compared to repairing the guns themselves, or a damaged reactor…assuming they could find it in time.

"Okay, I want a dozen bots moving along those conduits, and let's get the AI working on an extended diagnostic. We're bleeding power somewhere, probably a lot of somewheres, and it shouldn't be that hard to find.

If we had the time…

"We're short on bots, sir. They're deployed all over the ship. We've only got four."

Damn…this is because Commander Fritz was in the landing bay. Everything is a mess here…

"Get those four working. I'll get more up here now."

He glanced at his chronometer, shaking his head slowly. Then he tapped the com unit on his collar. "Commander Fritz, I'm up in weapons control. I think we can get the main guns back online, but I need more maintenance bots up here. At least eight, preferably a dozen."

"Sam, those guns are our number one priority. I'm sending you twenty bots, and I'll be up there myself in five minutes."

Carson had never heard Fritz sound so frazzled. He'd come to view the chief engineer as a block of stone, unflappable. But she understood the same thing he did. For all their faith in Captain Barron, the outcome of the battle wasn't in his hands. It was in theirs…Fritz's, Carson's. The whole engineering team. Barron could only fight with what they gave him.

"Yes, Commander. Understood." He flipped off the com, and spun around. "All right, let's move it. All of you. Until the bots get up here we're going to climb down these tubes ourselves. We're going to find every break in the system, and we're going to get those guns online. Is that understood?"

Carson was usually mild-mannered, but he understood the importance of the repairs. The techs under his command jumped at his orders. Not one of them answered him in words, they did so by actions…and he was certain every one of them understood what was at stake.

Chapter Twenty-Five

Interplanetary Space
5,000,000 kilometers from Santis, Krillus IV
307 AC

"All right, Raptor, your fuel status is lowest. You go in first."
Jamison paused. "And be careful, it's gonna be a rough ride in."

"Roger that, Thunder." Stockton took a deep breath. "Don't
worry, boss...I've got this." Stockton's cockiness was part of
his demeanor. He sounded calm, completely relaxed, but it was
an illusion. His fighter was in rough shape. He'd destroyed six
enemy birds, an astonishing performance, and one that fully
met, if not exceeded, his peacetime reputation. But he'd taken
battle damage too, and his fighter was shimmying like crazy.
That would be bad enough on a clear landing bay...but from
what he'd been hearing, *Dauntless's* beta bay was a nightmare,
strewn with debris and scattered fires the damage parties were
still fighting to control. It only had one thing going for it as a
landing site: it was in better shape than alpha bay.

Stockton pulsed his thrusters, reducing his velocity. He
angled the throttle, fired his positioning jets, lining himself up
on the open hatch ahead of him. He could see flickering lights
inside.

Fires...

The outer bay was open to space, but inside the membrane

214

that closed off the pressurized deck from the vacuum, *Daunt-less*'s life support systems pumped oxygen-rich air through the ventilation systems. Most of the great battleship was built from metal and high density plastics, materials that wouldn't burn. But it took more than the basic structure to run a warship, and from fuel to weapons to all kinds of basic supplies, there was plenty that would burn. Internal fires were always a danger.

C'mon, sweetheart…you and me…after all we've been through, don't let me down now…

His fighter was handling like a pig. The sleek, deadly craft, almost an extension of his arm before, was now showing the wear and tear. He angled the controls, but the response was slow, sluggish. Even the braking thrusters were damaged, misaligned. He had to adjust each thruster pulse, struggling to stay lined up with the bay ahead. He was doing all he could, but he wasn't going to be able to cut his velocity completely.

"Raptor to Control, I'm coming in hot. You better clear the landing area…just in case…"

"Raptor, this is control. That's bullshit, Jake. You're just fine. You're the best pilot we've got. Now stop screwing around, and bring that thing in nice and smooth. Just like you've always told me you do it…"

"Roger that, Lieutenant. Nice and smooth." Stockton smiled, and he felt the stress—fear, if he'd been willing admit that's what it was—recede. Stara Sinclair was one of *Dauntless*'s launch control officers. She was also a woman who'd proven her ability to simultaneously resist and match Stockton's usually effective charms. He'd flirted with her incessantly for the past year, and she'd given it back to him in kind, but that's as far as it had gone.

His hand tightened on the controls as he focused on the bay ahead. He felt his hands moving, driven by instinct as much as conscious direction. He sucked in a deep breath and held it as his fighter slipped into the bay, decelerating at full thrust as he did. The normally open surface was littered with chunks of metal, and one large structural support that had collapsed and been only partially cleared. There were piles of debris on the edges of the massive room, but the larger chunks were still strewn about.

He twisted his arm one way, then the next, pulsing his positioning jets to avoid the debris, and then he braced himself as his fighter slammed into the bulkhead at the end of the bay.

His head snapped forward, a pain shooting down his neck. But otherwise, his harness had held him in place. He was covered in sweat, and his heart was pounding, but he was okay. He pulled the release, popping open the cockpit, and he climbed out of the ship…into a shower of flame retardant foam being sprayed by a damage control tech and two maintenance bots. He turned his head and closed his eyes, pausing for an instant before climbing down to the deck.

He paused and sucked in a deep breath, steadying himself, struggling to bring his usual unflappable demeanor back in place. Then he turned around…and fell back against his fighter as Stara slammed into him, throwing her arms around his neck and planting a kiss on his lips.

He was surprised, but he put his arms around her and pulled her close. Then he leaned back. "What was that for?"

"I'm so glad you're okay. I thought…"

"You thought I wasn't going to make it? Me? The best pilot we've got?"

"Well…that was…just…"

"Landing control officer bullshit?"

"Encouragement."

"And that kiss? Do you do that for every pilot who brings in a damaged bird?" He smiled, watching as her relief gave way to her normal discipline. "Or is that just for the best pilot we have?"

"You're an ass," she said, but she couldn't force the smile from her face. "But welcome aboard. It's good to have you back." She lunged forward and hugged him again.

*   *   *

"Enemy vessel entering range in four minutes."

Barron heard Travis's words, but he knew they were meaningless. The enemy ship would be in range of *Dauntless*'s primaries in four minutes, but the main guns were still down. And it would be at least another four minutes after that before the secondaries came into play.

The important question was, when would *Dauntless* come into range of the enemy's main weapons? And despite his analysis of every scrap of intel in the database, Barron realized that came down to a wild guess. Confederation intelligence's notes indicated that the Alliance didn't have anything that could match the particle accelerators on Confed battleships.

Maybe they're better off without the temperamental beasts...

The heavy guns required an enormous amount of power to charge, and they had a relatively low rate of fire. They were hard to keep online too, subject to all sorts of breakdowns.

Just the kind of issue it's easy to ignore in peacetime. But can the things stand up to battle conditions?

Barron realized his people would be the test case on that. The particle weapons were a relatively new development, one that had been introduced during the last war but had not seen significant action.

They'd better be effective...the whole fleet's committed to them now.

"Two minutes to range..."

Barron looked down at the com unit for about the fiftieth time. He hated commanders who badgered their crews, especially when the personnel had proven their reliability. He knew Fritz was doing everything possible to restore the operational status of the main guns. Nothing would be accomplished by nagging her. Nothing.

He tapped the com anyway, putting his hand on the headset strapped on his head. "Fritzie, I know you're doing all you can, but I need a status..."

"We're on it, sir," the engineer snapped back. It wasn't disrespect in her voice, but she was clearly distracted, her mind focused on what she was doing. "I'll let you know as soon as I know..."

"Very well, Fritzie. Barron out." He shook his head, cursing himself for wasting time, for doing the exact thing he so disliked. Then he turned toward his first officer's station.

"Commander, we may have to fight this battle with secondaries. I want them all firing at one hundred ten percent."

Travis paused for an instant. Then she replied, "Yes, sir."

Barron knew overloading the guns was a risk, and if he started losing secondary batteries along with the primaries…

Still, he didn't know what else he could do. He had to hit the enemy as hard as he could. He didn't like to gamble, he was a rational man by nature. But his analysis told him a stark truth. He wasn't going to win this fight, not without taking some risks. Some big risks.

"Captain, Lieutenant Federov reports the enemy ship has a single squadron deployed defensively. She requests permission to engage."

Barron paused, thinking. The fighters of Federov's Red squadron were the only ones he had left that were armed and functionally operational. Commander Jamison and the handful of pilots who had followed him against the enemy bombers had landed…but with the damage to the bays there was no time-table on getting them refit and launched again, especially with so many resources committed to getting the primaries back online. And the rest of *Dauntless's* squadrons were still on their way back from the dogfight. They wouldn't arrive before the battleships exchanged fire, and Barron was far from sure they'd have any place to land by the time they returned. But either way, they had neither the fuel nor the ordnance to engage the enemy before they were refit.

"Very well, Commander. Red squadron is authorized to engage the enemy fighters." He questioned the order as soon as it had come out of his mouth. Federov's ships weren't equipped to attack the enemy battleship, and the Alliance birds were in a similar situation. All that would result from allowing Federov to attack was more casualties, on both sides. Still, he stayed silent, allowed the order to stand. This was a fight to the finish, he knew that. And he might as well make peace with that now.

Barron closed his eyes, breathing deeply. It was his own habit, his way of calming himself, centering himself. He'd seen action, fought in some minor engagements…but he'd never experienced anything like he was about to. This was war, up close, deadly. The kind of wars his grandfather had fought.

What would you do? Would you have avoided the errors I blundered into?

Barron knew he was being unfair to himself. He'd been careless at the transwarp link, that was true. But the rest of the tactical advantage the enemy had enjoyed had more to do with being the defender. He'd had no choice but to move toward Santis… but his adversary had been warned by the scanners deployed at the link, and had time to hide, to prepare. From the very beginning of the engagement, Barron had been at a disadvantage in information, in position.

What do I do, Grandfather? Is there some secret, some kind of sight you had that I lack? I'm ready to fight, to strike at the enemy with all I have. But that seems so inadequate. There must be something else. What did you do? How did you win so many victories?

And how did you live with the dead whose lives purchased those triumphs?

*   *   *

"All fighters have landed, Commander."

"Very well, Optiomagis. Initiate refueling operations…and rearm all ships for anti-fighter operations." She wanted to order the squadrons armed for shipping strikes, to send them against the Confederation vessel again…but the math just didn't work. *Invictus* was moving at nearly 0.2c. That was *fast*. At that velocity, she would zip by the Confederation battleship, with barely enough time for a passing exchange of fire. She was already decelerating, but it would take hours to come to a halt, and more time to accelerate back the toward the Confed vessel. And fighters launched with an intrinsic velocity that high would have no chance of executing an attack run.

Even thinking about the fighters now was upsetting. The three squadrons that had engaged in the dogfight had been shattered, losing half their number. She knew some of her pilots might have managed to eject…but with *Invictus* ripping toward the enemy vessel at such high speeds, there was no chance of performing any rescue operations, or even scanning to locate lifepods. She told herself she could return after she destroyed the Confed ship, but she knew that was an empty thought. By the time she decelerated and returned to the site of the fighter battle, any of her people who'd survived the destruction of their craft would be dead, their life support exhausted.

"Firing range in four minutes, Commander."

"Very well. Charge all batteries. All crews, prepare to engage."

"Yes, Commander."

Her thoughts were still on the fighters. As badly as the dogfighting squadrons had suffered, the two that had engaged the enemy ship had almost been wiped out. The enemy had launched a fresh squadron, and it had torn into the strike force. Black Fist had lost eight out of twelve birds…and Hydra had fared even worse, losing ten ships. The few survivors were scattered, with far too little fuel to accelerate and match velocity so they could land.

They did their duty. Those who died—who are about to die—they will live on in the annals, as heroes of their people.

She'd been raised on affirmations like that, but she found that the more death she witnessed, the less effective they were on her.

"Two minutes to firing range."

Kat stared at the display, at the data streaming in from her scanners. She was still getting a feed from the probes in orbit around Santis, too. It all told her the same thing. The enemy ship had taken heavy damage from the fighter assault. She was proud of her people. They had executed the battle well, and now all that was left was to finish the job. Then the victory would be won.

Still, she felt nervous, an unsettled feeling she'd never had before. It was the enemy commander, something about the way he'd handled operations. He'd blundered into her trap at the transwarp link, but since then he'd handled everything the way she would have. He'd avoided her laser buoys at Santis, and he'd deployed his fighters with great skill. And the Confed squadrons had gone toe to toe with her own and proved themselves a match for the Alliance's best. Her enemy didn't seem like the sort to give up, to wither because he was at a disadvantage.

But what can he do?

What would I do?

"One minute…"

She took a deep breath, her mind still stuck on her adversary, on what would happen as *Invictus* entered her enemy's firing range. But there was no time for that now, no chance to guess. It was time.

She sat quietly for that last minute, calm, looking out on her bridge crew. The she said, simply, "Fire."

* * *

"Secondary batteries…ready…" Barron was leaning forward, staring at the display, at the range as it counted down." His people had gotten lucky, very lucky. If the enemy had weapons as long-ranged as *Dauntless*'s particle accelerators, his ship would have been torn to bits by now. But the Alliance vessel just kept coming, its batteries silent as it approached. In less than a minute, *Dauntless*'s own secondaries would open fire.

The enemy's velocity meant they would only be in range for a short time, perhaps two minutes. He knew his foe would do everything possible to make that count. And he had to do the same.

"All gunnery teams…prepare your targeting data. There's no room here for carelessness. We need to hit that ship with everything we've got." He switched the com to the shipwide channel. "All personnel, this is the captain. We're about to engage the enemy. We patrolled for a long time together, on another border where we expected to do battle. We're far from there now, facing a new and unexpected enemy, but none of that matters. We will meet them head on. I have never been prouder of a team before, and I have every confidence in each of your abilities. Fight with me, my spacers…my friends. And let us send the enemy to the blasted hells of Cagaria!"

The bridge crew erupted into applause and shouts of affirmation. If there was one thing his grandfather had taught him, it was that morale won battles. If his people stood to their posts an instant longer, focused more effectively through the fear and pain…they could pull victory from the gaping maw of defeat. And he needed everything he could get right now.

"Captain, I'm picking up energy spikes from…"

Dauntless lurched hard.

"Hit amidships, sir." Travis had her head buried in her scope, tracking the data as soon as it came in. "A laser of some sort, sir. Higher powered than our secondaries for sure, but if that's what they've got as primary weapons…"

"Before you get excited, Commander, remember we don't have any primaries now. So, whatever they have is just one more advantage to them, at least for the moment."

Fritzie…

Barron leaned back in his chair. He'd be able to return fire in just over a minute. But that could be a long time…

He was counting off the seconds, his eyes angled down toward the countdown clock. He knew the battle could be lost, even if his people were able to return fire. *Dauntless* was already wounded, and the Alliance ship didn't have a scratch. But he'd rather go down fighting than die helplessly, like some kind of prey.

Suddenly the ship shook uncontrollably, far harder than it had from any of the other hits. The bridge spun around, and Barron felt the gravity vector changing wildly. One instant he felt as though he was suspended off the ground, only his harness keeping him from falling into the ceiling. Then the ship felt like it was sideways. His body slammed one way and then the next, and each time the straps dug into him hard, exacerbating his injuries.

He gasped for breath, trying to hide the wince as he filled his tortured chest with air. There was no point in allowing anyone to see him in pain. Not now. He could have been bleeding from a dozen bullet wounds, and he wouldn't have left the bridge.

"They seem to have some kind of broadside, sir. It looks like ten batteries...from their port side. I think seven of them hit. It looks like we may have gotten lucky."

Barron sat, listening to his first officer, just glad for the moment that the grav stabilizers had kicked back in and returned the bridge to it normal orientation. Still, he might have suggested a word other than, "lucky."

"We took several hits near the storage holds, sir. There's heavy damage to outer compartments, but it looks like the reactor is still operating in excess of ninety percent, and I don't think they came anywhere near the primaries."

Barron nodded. That was good news. A bit more speculation than he liked to rely on, but he wasn't going to interrupt Fritz again for another update.

"Evasive maneuvers, Commander. Randomization plan Delta-four."

"Yes, sir. Delta-four."

Dauntless lurched forward, thrusting at ten percent or so for perhaps ten seconds. Then her thrust stopped abruptly as the positioning jets swung the ship around and engaged the engines along a completely different course.

The ship shook again, far more softly this time.

"Just two hits, sir. I think the maneuvers threw them."

Barron smiled. The enemy captain had proven to be a skillful adversary, one who had gained the upper hand early. But Tyler Barron wasn't out of tricks yet.

"Suspend evasive maneuvers...bring us around to firing position." His eyes watched the final seconds counting down.

The bridge was almost silent, just the normal hum of the reactor in the background. Travis's hands moved quickly over her workstation. Then she turned back toward Barron. "In position, sir. All batteries ready."

Barron watched the numbers changing. *Five...four...three... two...one...zero.*

"All batteries...open fire."

Chapter Twenty-Six

AS Invictus
5,000,000 kilometers from Santis, Krillus IV
Alliance Year 58 (307 AC)

"Laser batteries, Commander. Scanners suggest mostly triple turreted laser cannon. Not as strong as our primaries, but the area of effect appears to be larger, particularly if all three linked beams hit."

Kat took a deep breath. She'd kept the battle one-sided for as long as she could, used her tactical ability to inflict damage on the enemy while keeping *Invictus* untouched.

Well, untouched except for my ravaged fighter squadrons...

But now she had bigger concerns. The enemy had opened fire...and damage reports were flooding in from all decks. *This fight is going to be a slugfest now.*

Fighters existed to take risks, to keep the fight away from the mothership. That was cold math, but everyone who stepped into a cockpit knew they were accepting a level of expendability beyond that of their shipboard comrades. The long term survival rates for pilots were abysmal, and even in a military society like the Alliance, the service attracted a certain type of recruit. Brave, certainly, but also at least a little bit crazy.

She stared down at the screen, at the scanning data coming in. The enemy had fired six triple turrets and two doubles. That was twenty-two laser blasts. And seventeen of them had hit. That was outstanding shooting by any measure, a performance that would make any Alliance commander proud. But she'd never seen such efficiency in an enemy before now.

This enemy battleship was battling her tooth and nail, despite the fact that she had gained the early advantage. The enemy vessel could have run right back through the transwarp link, abandoning their tiny colony and its handful of ground troops. But instead, she'd watched as the Confederation fighter pilots fought her own veteran pilots to a bloody stalemate with nearly suicidal bravery.

Her stomach was crunched into a knot, and she could feel the tension in every muscle of her body. She didn't know what the enemy's courage and skills were like overall, but she'd made her decision about *this* captain and *this* ship. Her counterpart was dangerous, far more so than any opponent she'd yet faced in her unblemished career, and she suspected his crew was no less capable. They were not to be trifled with. She had to destroy them, before they did the same to her.

"Increase power flow to batteries, Commander. Twenty percent above maximum. And have damage control on standby to replace burnouts."

"Yes, Commander. Immediately."

"Secondary batteries are to open fire as soon as we enter range. Advise engineering we're going to need extra power from the reactor. I want all weapons firing full, and I hold engineering responsible for making sure there is enough power flow."

"Yes, Commander Rigellus."

Kat could hear the high-pitched whine in the background, *Invictus's* main lasers firing again. There was a variation in the sound, one few people would have noticed. But Kat was well aware what it was. One of her batteries was out, damaged by the enemy barrage.

She listened yet again as *Invictus* fired another broadside, the sounds changing once more, higher-pitched this time as her crews overloaded their lasers, pumping extra power into their ravening beams. It was a dangerous tactic, but *Invictus* was only going to be in firing range for less than six minutes…and she wanted to cripple the enemy in that time. She'd have to decelerate hard before she could bring her ship about for another attack, and that would give the enemy time to react. Unless she hurt them enough now.

"Commander, gunnery reports the batteries are heating up past regulation firing levels. They request permission to…"

"Maintain firing at one twenty on the power, Optiomagis. All batteries continue at maximum rate of fire.

"Yes, sir," Wentus replied, a hint of concern in his voice.

There would be plenty of time to repair burnouts when *Invictus* was decelerating, but now she intended to pour every watt of power she could into her enemy.

While she had the chance……

* * *

"Heavy damage to sections beta-four through gamma eleven. Multiple starboard hull ruptures. All compromised sections have been cut off, and…" Travis hesitated, her tone darkening. "Casualty estimates in excess of eighty, sir…including twenty-four missing in the ruptured sections." Another pause. "That figure does not include losses already suffered by the fighter wing…"

Barron nodded slowly. "Very well, Commander." He struggled to keep his voice stern, unaffected. He ached for the hundred plus dead among his crew and fighter squadrons, and for the dozens more wounded. But he had almost ten times that number alive, still fighting. He could save them, bring them through this battle. There was nothing he could do for the dead.

"Captain, the enemy vessel is entering point blank range."

Barron sucked in a deep breath. The enemy's lasers would really start to tear *Dauntless* apart at this distance. The hits suffered so far had been relatively weak, the power of the laser blasts severely attenuated by distance. But now every hit would rip through his vessel's hull, tearing apart vital systems, and killing more of his people.

He glared forward, a determined scowl onto his face. Everything he had just considered was true…and it worked both ways. His own shots would be deadlier as well. The enemy vessel had escaped any damage in the earlier stages of the engagement, but now his beams were ripping into its hull. He knew he was killing spacers there, as surely as his own people were dying. Barron wasn't a bloodthirsty man, but now anger drove him, hatred for this invader, attacking his ship, killing his crew. He felt the need to destroy them, whatever the cost. And though he wasn't proud of it, the thought of his enemies being blown to bits or sucked out of rents in their hull and into space put a small grin on his face. He'd never felt this way before, as though some dark aspect of himself, one he hadn't known existed, was emerging and taking control.

"Bring us around, Commander. I want the port-angled guns brought to bear."

"Yes, sir."

Dauntless's positioning thrusters were spinning the ship around, moving its battered starboard side from the enemy's fire arc…and bringing the previously unfired port guns to bear. Barron was protecting his wounded side, and committing fresh batteries while he cooled his superheated guns on the starboard.

He listened as the fresh guns opened fire, sending megawatt-powered beams of focused light toward the enemy. *Dauntless's* secondaries were powerful weapons, but he knew they wouldn't be enough.

If only I had the primaries…

The main enemy lasers were stronger still than *Dauntless's*, and now their fire was joined by that of their own secondaries. *Dauntless* shook as hit after hit slammed into her battered hull, each impact inflicting terrible damage and killing more of his people.

He stared at the screen, watching as the AI updated damage assessments from the enemy vessel. It was an imperfect list, just scanner data interpreted by a computer. There was no real way for him to know what was happening over there. But if the assessments were close to the mark, the deadly accuracy of his gunners had come at least fairly close to evening the score in the fight.

He didn't need estimates and assessments to know that the enemy's fire had weakened, that several of their batteries had been silenced. But *Dauntless* had been hit hard too. The immense battleship was riddled with great tears in her hull. His damage control crews had worked miracles keeping as many systems online as they had, but Barron knew it was only a matter of time before even miracles would be inadequate.

"All batteries, maintain maximum fire." He tried to keep the frustration from his voice, realizing his efforts had been woefully inadequate. He had nothing else to say, though, no words to offer but a renewed order for his people to keep shooting. He wracked his mind, trying to think of some tactic that might give him an edge, but at this range there was nothing for the combatants to do but pound away at each other, and hope to inflict more damage than they sustained. Somehow.

"Captain…" Fritz's voice came through his headset. The engineer's voice was hoarse, the tension and exhaustion clearly evident in each forced word. "We've got the primaries online, sir…but it won't last. Reactor A is on the verge of a meltdown, and B is even worse. I've got to cut to fifty percent power or we're going to lose both of them…and maybe the whole ship if I can't maintain containment. I can give you thirty seconds, sir, maybe forty-five. But you'll have to make it count."

"Fritzie, I'd give you a big wet kiss if you were up here."

He turned toward Travis. "We've got one shot with the primaries, Commander." It took a little over a minute to recharge *Dauntless's* main guns, so thirty seconds—or what was left of that now—was going to give him one chance to do some meaningful damage.

"That's good news." He could hear the relief in his exec's voice.

"I want you to handle the targeting." Travis had come up in gunnery, and she'd left an excellent record behind her when she'd advanced into the command track. Barron knew many of *Dauntless's* gunners were as good, but this was a vital shot. And

Travis was as unflappable a veteran as he'd ever seen.

"Yes, sir." Travis turned, leaning forward and pressing her face against the scope. "I'll target amidships, sir. Dead center. With any luck the primaries will…"

"Negative, Commander. I want you to target the engines."

Travis pulled her head off the scope for a moment. It looked like she was going to say something, but then she just leaned back down. "Yes, sir," she finally answered.

Barron looked across the bridge at his executive officer. She was right, of course. A shot from the primaries at this range could inflict devastating damage, and targeting the enemy ship dead center offered the greatest chance of scoring a critical hit. But combat wasn't a textbook exercise, and every situation was unique. Barron's ship was damaged, badly. The enemy was hurt too now, but they retained the edge. In a fight to the finish, they would win, barring some miracle. Barron needed time—to complete repairs, to regain some sort of parity with his enemy…and to prepare for the next round of the battle. He'd get some of that time, perhaps ten or twelve hours before his enemy could decelerate and reverse course to renew the battle. But if they could damage their enemy's engines, it would buy them more time.

"We need time, Commander, and if they can't decelerate…"

"Yes, sir." He could tell from her tone she understood completely now.

Targeting the engines was a tough shot, requiring pinpoint marksmanship. Which was another reason he wanted Travis on the controls.

"You can do this, Atara…" He realized he was staring at Travis, and he pulled his focus away, only to realize that every set of eyes on the bridge was fixed on *Dauntless's* first officer. He almost ordered them to pay attention to their own stations, but he stayed silent. Travis was as intensely focused an officer as he'd ever seen, and her face was planted against the firing screen. She could have had a thousand people staring at her, and she wouldn't have even noticed. Not right now.

Barron's eyes darted to the chronometer. Twenty-five seconds since Fritz's com.

That's cutting it close…

He watched Travis, counting the seconds off in his head, each one passing with excruciating slowness. Twenty-eight. Twenty-nine. Fritz had said maybe forty-five, but she'd only promised thirty. Perhaps that was only the way she'd said it, but his experience with the engineer suggested that she spoke in extremely precise terms.

He was tense. He felt the urge to order Travis to fire before it was too late. But he'd given her a precise target, and he trusted her.

Come on, Atara…

Thirty-two…thirty-three…

They were on borrowed time.

Then the bridge lights dimmed, as Barron knew they were doing throughout the ship. It took virtually all the power *Dauntless* could produce to fire the massive main guns. There was a loud noise, almost like the sound of metal twisting. The sound the primaries made was unique, like nothing he'd ever heard before. But it could have been music to him now, and he felt some of his tension fade. Travis had gotten the shot off. But it would be another few excruciating seconds before anyone on *Dauntless* knew if she'd scored any hits.

Indeed, he realized, the shot had already reached—or missed—the target. The primaries were usually fired at ranges of up to two light seconds, but the enemy was barely fifty thousand kilometers from *Dauntless*. It had taken less than a fifth of a second for the particle beam to cover that distance. The delay— if a few seconds could be called such—was the time required for scanners to analyze and report the results of the shot.

His eyes were fixed on the display, waiting…the same as everyone else on the bridge. Then he saw the images update, two small starburst icons. Hits.

The bridge erupted into applause, even as Barron was still processing what he saw.

She hit with both!

The display changed, a small image appearing to the side, a

blow up of the enemy ship...at least the best schematic the AI could guess at. And there were two glowing circles, both of the in the vessels' aft.

Right by the engines...

"Nice shooting, Atara." His head snapped around toward the communications station. "Lieutenant, any thrust readings from the enemy ship?"

Vin Darrow stared at his screens for a few seconds, turning away and snapping his head right back as if he felt compelled to check what he'd already seen. "No, sir. No thrust at all. Enemy moving away at previous velocity."

Dauntless shook again, a reminder that he might have damaged the enemy's engines, but their guns were still operative.

His com unit buzzed. He tapped the small control on his headset. "What is it, Fritzie?"

"The primaries are out again, sir. The reactors are at sixty and forty-five percent output. It will be hours before I can get the main guns up again...if I can do it at all this side of a space dock."

"You did what we needed, Fritzie. Just do what you can to keep us in this fight."

"Yes, sir." The com line clicked.

Barron looked over at Travis. "Secondaries, resume fire." He knew the order was premature—and unnecessary. The primaries had diverted almost all of *Dauntless*'s power, leaving her other weapons momentarily silent. His gunners would fire again as soon as they could power up their batteries, which would take longer with the reactors working at half-power.

"Yes, sir. We've got multiple power interruptions, Captain, and with the reduced output from the reactors, we've got..." She turned back to her workstation, staring down at her screen. "...four turrets still firing."

"Very well, Commander." He struggled to hold back a frown. *Down to four turrets...*

The ship shook again, and Barron could hear the sounds as *Dauntless*'s hull twisted and groaned under the incessant fire. Then he heard the secondaries firing. He'd turned his ship to protect the damaged starboard side, but now the port was in worse shape.

"Bring us back around, Commander. I want the starboard batteries brought to bear."

"Yes, sir."

Barron stared at the display. The enemy had been decelerating before *Dauntless's* primaries fired, but now there was no thrust at all. Did he dare to hope that Travis's shot had disabled the vessel's engines entirely? Any delay in the enemy slowing down would shorten the exchange now in progress, and it would give Fritz and her people more time to complete repairs.

Or it will give you time to withdraw…

Barron didn't like the idea of retreating, but he couldn't escape his own tactical analysis. His people had performed well, but they were still at a disadvantage. Assuming the enemy could repair their engines—and he had little doubt they could—there would be another fight here. As much as he wanted to believe *Dauntless* would win that battle, he knew he was still at a disadvantage. Perhaps it made sense to make a dash to the transwarp link, to get back to Archellia and rally the base's meager defenses. Santis was tactically important, but *Dauntless* was the only real force on the entire frontier. If he fought again and lost, there would be nothing between here and a dozen heavily-populated worlds.

The ship shuddered again, but the impacts were not as hard. The enemy was moving out of range. *Dauntless* had made it through the first exchange, though he wouldn't know the true extent of the damage until Fritz gave him an update.

I don't need Fritzie to tell me it's bad.

Damned bad…

The enemy would be working feverishly to get their engines back online. He wanted to stay, to finish what had begun here. But there was more at stake than his own wants. Hundreds of crew members, millions of citizens on Archellia…hundreds of millions on some of the worlds beyond.

"Sir, the enemy has moved out of range of our secondaries. They appear to have ceased fire."

Out of range. The first struggle is over, and we're both still here. But if we stay, if we fight again…

"Captain, Lieutenant Krill is on the com. He requests permission to begin landing operations."

Barron felt like he'd been punched in the gut. He'd been so focused on the battle, he wasn't even sure *Dauntless* had an operable landing bay.

He tapped his com again. "Fritzie, the rest of the fighters are back…"

"I've got alpha bay open now, sir…though God knows it shouldn't be. Just tell those hotshot pilots they're in for a rough ride. If one of them comes in too hard and wipes out, he'd going to trap the rest of them out there. Beta bay is depressurized wreck, we've got no hope of getting it functioning, not this side of base."

"Fritzie, you're a miracle worker."

"That's a good thing, sir…because we're going to need a few down here."

Barron cut the com and turned back toward Travis. "Bring the squadrons into alpha bay, Commander. Fuel status priority."

"Yes, sir."

Barron leaned back and wiped his hand over his face. He was exhausted, and he had a headache he'd have sworn should have killed him by now. But his people were still in the fight… and that was something.

Now he just had to decide what to do next.

Chapter Twenty-Seven

From the Journal of Commander-Princeps Katrine Rigellus

I leave these words here for you, my children. I am in a battle as I write this, and though I believe I can win, a warrior never knows when death is stalking her. I write this for you, as I have each time I go into action, because I would tell you some things before I leave you...because I always wished my father would have left me a final message.

We are Palatians, of a strong and noble house. Our wealth, our position...comes with responsibility, with duty. We have talked of this before, and if I should fall, the retainers and allies of the Regulli will teach you what is expected of you. That, at least, is well-handled. For this moment, I would write not as your matriarch, concerned with duty, but as your mother, who has loved you both since you were newborn.

I have ever placed duty first in my life, as you will both do, I am sure. It is the way. It demands much from us. Yet I would have you both know, had it been within my control, I would have spent more time with you. There is no greater joy in my recollections, even among my victories and the supplication of the Alliance's enemies, than autumn with the two of you at Litora Montis, and it is my great sadness that our times together are usually only a brief few days.

I would never ask you to shrink from your duties, nor do I believe it is within either of you to do so. But I urge you both: find the time to be there for each other, to appreciate each other...for when I am gone, you will be all that remains of the Regulli.

AS Invictus
7,800,000 kilometers from Santis, Krillus IV
Alliance Year 58 (307 AC)

"I need those engines back online now, Optiomagis." Kat had her hand on her earpiece as she spoke into the headset's microphone. Strictly speaking, she should have been issuing orders to Wentus and allowing her exec to pass them on to the more junior officers. But right now she didn't have the time or patience for it.

"We've got massive damage down here, Commander. Whatever that weapon was, it hit us hard." Raban Cinatus was *Invictus's* chief engineer, and Kat could hear the tension in his voice. Her ship had been badly battered, there was no question about that. But she was sure the enemy was in worse shape, and the sooner she could get *Invictus* turned around to finish the job the better. She was wary of the enemy commander, and the thought of giving him more time ate away at her confidence.

"It was a particle beam, Optiomagis," she said matter-of-factly. "Confed battleships have particle weapons as their primary batteries." Kat didn't place much stock in intelligence reports, but now she wondered if she was the only one who bothered to read them. Though short on details about effectiveness and power output, the reports had been pretty clear on the fact that the Confed navy had upgraded all its capital ships with the new weapon system. Still, she found herself surprised at how hard that shot had hit *Invictus*. There was no question, the enemy's primaries were superior to her own main lasers.

So, why did they wait so long to fire? Just to get in a point blank shot by surprise? Or were they having trouble keeping the guns online?

She'd seen schematics of the Alliance's own particle beam weapons, which unfortunately currently existed only as designs in progress. She remembered being struck at the size of the proposed weapons, and the complexity. She'd expressed a level of concern about durability, at least to the extent it was wise to question any project that had the Council's support.

"Commander, I have twenty engineers working on the engines, and half the maintenance units. I'm fairly certain we can restore some level of thrust, but it's going to take a while."

"Define a 'while,' Optiomagis. I'll remind you we are moving away from the enemy at greater than one percent of lightspeed."

"A day, Commander. It will take a day to restore thrust. At least. Perhaps two."

Kat felt a burst of something that felt like anger, but she realized almost immediately it was just frustration. Cinatus was a gifted engineer and an Alliance warrior though and through. She knew he wouldn't sleep, wouldn't rest, until the engines were back online. But that didn't change the fact that *Invictus* was racing away from Santis, and the enemy battleship, with no way to alter its vector.

That was no chance shot at our engines…he wanted time, and that's what he got for himself.

Her respect for her adversary grew, and her urgency to finish the battle as quickly as possible, while she still had the edge.

Before he gets the better of me and turns the tables…

"Eighteen hours, Optiomagis. You will get the engines back online within eighteen hours, no matter what you have to do."

"Commander…"

"Eighteen hours," she repeated, her voice like ice. "You may have any resources you require, but not a minute longer."

"Yes, Commander." He tried to sound confident, but Kat could see right through it. Cinatus was one of the best engineers in the Alliance service, but what was possible was possible, and what wasn't…wasn't. For all the sternness of her eighteen-hour command, she figured the odds Cinatus would meet the deadline were right around 50/50.

She looked out at the display, staring at the symbol representing the enemy vessel. She wanted to believe she had the advantage in terms of repairs and engineering…after all, she had the pick of the Alliance navy on *Invictus*. Surely her people would complete repairs more quickly than the enemy. Yet, something nagged at her. This was no ordinary captain she was facing. Could she afford to assume it was an ordinary crew?

*   *   *

"All right, we—I—have a decision to make, and I want your input." Barron sat at the head of the long table. *Dauntless's* conference room was right next to the bridge, and Barron had gathered his senior officers to assess the situation. All except Commander Fritz. Perhaps more than anyone—including the captain himself—she held their fates in her hands, and he wasn't about to pull her away from her repair efforts.

The conference room showed little sign of the damage he knew was all over his ship, but there was a sharp odor in the air, some kind of burning smell being spread by the life support systems. He didn't know exactly what was causing it, but the AI had classified it as insufficiently dangerous to warrant attention now. Barron had found that phrasing less than reassuring, but he had to agree that there were other priorities.

"We fight. What else can we do?" Commander Jamison sat at the opposite end of the table, providing just the sort of aggressive advice Barron expected from the leader of his fighter squadrons. What was left of his fighter squadrons.

"We can withdraw, pull back to Archellia and mass whatever forces we can gather to mount a defense." Part of Barron detested himself for even suggesting a retreat, but he had more responsibilities than his own honor, even than protecting the Barron name. *Dauntless* was the only defense to speak of for an entire sector.

"Captain…" Jamison's voice trailed off. "Yes, of course, sir."

"I don't like the idea any more than any of you. But we have to at least consider it." Barron paused. "We can't be guided by pride at the expense of reason. We're at least as badly damaged as the enemy, and very likely worse. If we fight…there's a good chance we will lose. And the sector will be completely unprotected."

"Captain?" It was Bryan Ragan, the commander of *Daunt-*

less's Marine company.

"Yes, Bryan?"

"Sir, whatever course of action you choose, I must respectfully request that you allow my Marines to land on Santis."

"Land?"

"Yes, sir. I have reviewed the scanning results from Red squadron's probe of the planet. They picked up signals, sir."

"Yes, I know. It seems clear the enemy landed a ground force and occupied the tritium production facilities."

"No, sir…I mean, yes sir. But I think some of the Marines down there are still holding out, fighting."

"There was only one platoon assigned to Santis, Bryan. We have no idea what kind of force the enemy landed, but…well, it's very unlikely the Marines managed to hold out this long."

"Sir, the signals. Mixed in with the enemy communications there was…well, it's an old Marine code. We don't use it anymore, but they still teach it at the Academy. It was a distress call, Captain. There are Marines down there still fighting…I'm sure of it."

Barron leaned back in his chair. He couldn't imagine how fewer than forty Marines could have held out this long, but Ragan was a gifted officer, and not one prone to follow hopeless causes.

"Okay, Bryan, if we stay, we will look into it."

"With all due respect, sir, I speak for the entire Marine contingent when I request that you allow us to land whether or not *Dauntless* will be staying."

"Bryan, we have no idea how many soldiers the enemy has down there. You have no idea what you'll be getting into. And if we leave, that enemy ship will be back. You'll be cut off on the surface, without reinforcements, with the enemy in total control of local space." He paused. "Your people will be wiped out, Bryan."

"We understand the risks, sir. As I said, every Marine on *Dauntless* has volunteered, knowing everything you just said."

Barron shook his head. He knew the Confederation Marines took their bond to each other deadly seriously. But how could he allow a hundred of his people throw their lives away if *Dauntless* retreated?

He was still thinking quietly when the com unit buzzed, and Darrow's voice came through the speaker. "Captain, we've just received a flash com update from the transwarp link."

"Yes, Lieutenant?" Barron was impatient, distracted. Flash updates were standard procedure, normally full of nothing more pressing that routine updates and crew mail. Nothing that justified interrupting a vital strategy session.

"There is a coded message for you, sir. Priority one designation."

Barron looked up at his assembled officers, trying to keep the surprise from his face. Priority one was the Confederation's highest level of urgency.

He stood up abruptly. "If you'll all excuse me for a moment." He turned toward the door, but then he stopped and looked back. "Commander Travis…" He gestured toward the door.

Travis got up with a nod. Then she walked around the table, following Barron out of the room.

* * *

"Well, that makes the decision for you, doesn't it?" Travis was sitting at one of the two chairs opposite Barron's desk. She was looking right at *Dauntless's* captain, her surprise at the content of the communique obvious on her face and in her tone. "There's no leaving now, no backing down."

Barron sighed hard. "Yes, I suppose it does. I thought the stakes were high enough when it was just life and death, but if they're right, we may be carrying the future of the Confederation in our hands, the difference between a chance at victory in the coming war…and total destruction."

The intelligence report had been clear, and exceedingly blunt. *Dauntless* was to engage the enemy and destroy them. Whatever it took. There could be no retreats, no stalemates. Only complete victory could avert war with the Alliance. And war with the Alliance and the Union at the same time would doom the

Confederation.

"Scanners report that the enemy ship is still progressing on its original vector. At least we have some time to prepare, and to get the crew some rest." A pause, then: "Targeting their engines was a brilliant idea, Tyler."

"Managing to hit dead on was pretty good too, Atara. Let's just say we'll share the credit. Assuming we survive to get out of this system."

"We'll survive, Tyler. I believe in you. The whole crew believes in you."

Barron nodded. "That means a lot, Atara…but this is no ordinary commander we're up against. If the Alliance sent one ship to test our defenses, it's likely they sent their best."

"Fortunately, we also have our best here." The words seemed like an empty boast, but her tone made it otherwise, as though she was only expressing what she really believed. "We can take them, Ty…you know we can."

Barron took a deep breath. "Maybe," he said softly. "A lot of this is on Fritzie's shoulders. And on how long it takes the enemy to repair their engines and get back here."

"Assuming we stay here…"

Barron's eyes widened. "What are you suggesting?"

"We have engines now, at least fifty percent strength. The enemy had the advantage when they positioned themselves behind planet five. Perhaps we can do something similar."

"Withdraw to the fifth planet?"

"No, I was thinking somewhere else." She looked down at the large screen on Barron's desk, and she reached out, pointing to a spot on the map displayed there.

Barron stared down, his eyes focusing on her finger. "Yes," he said. "That's perfect."

"We should have enough time to land the Marines, too."

Barron frowned. "You know as well as I do, we could be sending them into a death trap. Probably *would* be."

"It's their way, Ty. They *want* to go. They feel they *have* to go. As long as they believe their comrades are alive down there."

Barron exhaled hard. "Okay. Why not? We're all in a fight to the death here. There's no retreat for any of us, no way out save victory." He looked across the desk at his first officer. "We'll land the Marines. And then we'll move out, prepare ourselves for the final fight."

Travis nodded. "The final fight," she said, with a feral smile.

Chapter Twenty-Eight

CFS Dauntless
300,000 kilometers from Santis, Krillus IV
307 AC

"Fighters launched, Captain. Commander Jamison reports his pilots are en route and will be ready to begin in eight minutes." Vin Darrow's voice came as a surprise to Barron, even though he'd expected it. He'd tried to get Atara Travis to take a break and get some rest, but she'd fought him on it tooth and nail, refusing outright unless he also promised to take a nap. They'd finally compromised. He'd retreated to his office, where he hadn't exactly slept, but had certainly closed his eyes for a few minutes. She had run down to her quarters for a quick meal and a shower, after which she'd headed to the damaged gunnery sections to check on the repairs underway. Travis had been a gunner, a troubleshooter, and any number of other things as she'd risen in the service. Her hardscrabble rise to rank contrasted sharply with his own virtual inheritance of his position. They couldn't be more different in background, but they made an effective team. More than a team. Travis was like a sister to him now. He respected her ability to pull herself up from such difficult circumstances. And Travis had told him more than once, the first thing she'd noticed about him was that he wasn't a smug, self-entitled asshole, like most of the other scions of

242

navy families. It is of such stuff that great friendships are made.

"Very well, Lieutenant."

Barron was edgy. His fighter squadrons were already badly damaged, and now he was risking his best pilots, the commanders of all of his squadrons plus a picked force drawn from the rest of the survivors.

Alpha bay was operational, barely. Ideally, he'd have launched a full strike force to deal with the laser buoys in orbit around Santis and its moons, but with the bays virtually wrecked and a large number of personnel reassigned to damage control duties, his people had only managed to get ten fighters repaired and refit. And if ten pilots were going to clear the laser platforms, it had to be his ten best.

He was still unsure how he felt about landing the Marines. He understood their attitudes, that the Marine code required them to come to their comrades' aid. But he didn't like sending his men and women into a totally blind situation. He had no idea how many ground troops the enemy ship carried, or if they had all been landed. And *Dauntless*'s contingent was at half strength, just one company where two would have been normal.

He didn't have a choice, though. Not a real one. The fight his people were in would be decided in part by hardware, in part by the abilities of Fritzie and her crews to get as much of *Dauntless*'s weaponry and equipment back online in time. But he knew morale was just as important. The gunner who kept his shit together instead of panicking…and who scored that last vital hit. The pilot who ran down the enemy ship's throat and planted a torpedo right in its guts instead of firing from long range and then breaking off. He couldn't expect that kind of courage and effort from his people if he didn't respect them. And that included the Marines.

He shook his head. He was never going to be comfortable about it, but his decision was already made. He leaned forward, tapping the com unit.

"Prepare assault shuttles for launch."

"Shuttles report ready, Captain." The response was quick. Darrow had clearly known already that the Marines were ready to go.

Barron nodded gently. He was thankful, at least, that the shuttles didn't use the fighter bays. There was no way the bulkier ships could have managed their way through the debris and damage the agile fighters had struggled to avoid. The heavy landing craft docked directly against the ship's hull, and it was a miracle that, with all the damage *Dauntless* had taken, none of the shuttles had been damaged.

Barron sat silently for a few seconds. Then he hit the com again.

"Launch the shuttles."

* * *

Sam Carson was lying on his bunk, trying desperately to get to sleep. It seemed absurd, because he'd never been so tired in his life, but he had been there almost an hour, and he was still wide awake. He'd spied the same small scratch on the ceiling at least ten times.

It must be the stims. Your body is all strung out...

He'd been popping the stimulants like candy, along with the rest of *Dauntless*'s engineering team. The lull in the fight had given the battleship's crew a chance to get some real rest, all save those charged with repairing the enormous damage the ship had taken. Carson and his team had been at it for forty straight hours. And they'd still have been working if Commander Fritz hadn't expressly ordered them all to take a four hour sleep break.

Or, maybe you're just scared shitless...

Carson had been grateful to be too busy to seriously think about the situation. He was a combat officer, just like all the others on *Dauntless*, but he'd been a child the last time the Confederation fought a *real* war. Even the edginess of the duty along the Union border had been theoretical, the worry about what *might* happen. But the last few days...that had been combat, real and unfiltered. He'd watched comrades die, seen massive explosions rip through the ship's structure.

Now that a combat badge really means something...

He rolled over, slamming his fist into the pillow before putting his head back down. He thought about taking something to help him sleep, but the idea was so ridiculous it almost made him laugh. He had to be back on duty in just over three hours, and he'd probably need another hit of stims as it was. If he took a soporific now, he'd be a zombie when he woke up.

He sighed and sat up abruptly. He wasn't going to get to sleep, that much seemed clear. It was bad…a few hours of real sleep would have done him some good. But worse, now he had to sit here for three hours with nothing to do but think. And thinking wasn't something he wanted to do. Not right now.

His thoughts had a choice of methods to torture him right now. Fear of the enemy, of dying here in this forsaken place. Letting his comrades down, watching them die.

Lise…

Or he could think of his wife, of their last parting. She had sent him mail in the most recent com dump. It had been short, affectionate, but he still knew he'd hurt her when he'd left. He was glad they'd made up by the time he left, but even as he hugged her the last time, he knew she was still hurt. She'd tried to hide it, but he'd seen it in her eyes, heard it in her voice. To her, he had chosen *Dauntless* over her, his comrades of a few months' service over his pregnant wife.

But there had been more to his choice than that. Archellia was his home now, and it was right in the path of whatever was brewing out on the Rim. Carson, in his own way, was here for Lise, for his new child. To protect them, to stand in the way of whatever might threaten Archellia, and the rest of the Confederation.

He could have stayed behind, left that duty to others. But that wasn't who he was. He'd hated leaving her in tears, but he was far more terrified of the prospect of one day looking into her eyes and seeing that she was staring back at a stranger, a man utterly different from the one she'd fallen in love with. The man he'd have become if he'd been willing to turn his back on his own values.

He sighed softly. He'd done what he had to do, but he was

still troubled. He understood why he had made his decision, but he wasn't sure she did. And the thought of her believing he just didn't care enough to do as she asked cut at him deeply.

He got up and walked across the tiny room, leaning over and flipping on the workstation screen at his desk. The letter was still there, in all its generic warmth and caring. He could tell that she'd struggled to send him a pleasant message, to avoid burdening him with any bad feelings while he was in action. But he saw right through the canned affection, and he felt as if he was back in his quarters on Archellia, having the same fight they'd had before he left.

I'm sorry, Lise. I hope I can make you understand why I had to go, when I get back…

Carson looked over at the small clock next to his bunk. Two hours fifty-three minutes to go. Duty would be a relief, an escape from the thoughts haunting him in his dark quarters.

He sat down in the chair, landing hard. He reached out to the screen, scrolling pages, bringing up Lise's letter again. He read it, at least half of it, then he shook his head and flicked his finger, flipping back to the main screen. There was no point in brooding now, in stewing in guilt or sadness or whatever this was. He had a job to do, and for all the crushing fatigue bearing down on him, all he wanted was to be back at it.

He stood up, abruptly, and he walked toward the small closet, pulling out a clean uniform. Fritz had told him not to show his face for four hours, but he saw no reason to sit there, not sleeping, thinking about things he couldn't do anything about. There was damage to repair, systems to get back online. If the chief engineer pushed back, he'd be honest with her, tell her he just couldn't sleep, as incredible as that would sound.

He pulled on the uniform then he walked over to the table on the side of the room. He grabbed a small bottle, stims… and he dumped two into his palm. He paused for a moment, and then he shook the container, dropping a third pill into his hand. He picked up a bottle of water and threw the pills back, guzzling a deep drink to wash them down. Then he grabbed a large nutrition bar, and he walked toward the door…and then out into the hall.

Back to work. He felt better already.

* * *

"Raptor, ease up. I told you to be careful. These buoys aren't designed for anti-fighter ops, but that doesn't mean a lucky shot can't blow your reckless ass away."

Jamison's voice was sharp, with a hint of scolding. Stockton and Jamison were as close as two friends could get, at least until they stepped into their fighters. Then the commander sometimes turned into the parent, lecturing Stockton about his recklessness. It was annoying, but Stockton understood. He *was* reckless, or at least something close to it. But he was that good too. His skill and his daring went hand in hand. They made him the pilot he was.

"C'mon, Thunder. Something out there's got my number, I'm sure. But it isn't one of these giant laser buoys. They…" He was about to say, "they couldn't hit a gas giant," or something equally cocky. But then he remembered that the Reds had lost a pilot to the buoys. And Lynx was on the mission. Stockton knew he was prone to arrogance, but he didn't want to cause Fedorov pain. She was a good pilot and squadron leader, and he respected her abilities.

"I'll be okay, Thunder…I'll be careful." He angled his craft as he spoke, his finger pressing down on the firing stud and watching as the nearest buoy vanished from his screen. He smiled, to himself as much as anything. He felt he'd made his point.

The rest of the fighters were zipping down into orbit, targeting the weapons platforms. The buoys had begun to fire back, but the fighters were too close, too maneuverable. There were a couple of close shots, but in the end the fighters cleared their targets quickly, without loss.

"*Dauntless*, this is Thunder. Santis orbit is clear. Repeat, Santis orbit is clear. No casualties. We're heading toward the moons."

Stockton listened as his friend made the report. He knew the assault shuttles were coming up now, that *Dauntless*'s hundred

Marines would be landing within minutes. He saw faces in his mind, men and women he'd played cards with, and one or two he'd had altercations with. But now he wished them all well… even that snotty little corporal he was still sure had pulled that card from his sleeve…

"Okay, odds, follow me to Lyra. Raptor, you take the evens to Assul. Let's clear away the rest of these things and get back to the ship."

"Roger that, Thunder. Evens on me. Let's go finish the job."

*   *   *

"What the hell is that? Enemy reinforcements?" Joe Thoms was standing outside the cave staring up at the sky. It was almost dawn, and the dark still clung thick over the frozen hillsides. But the streaks in the sky were unmistakable, fiery trails that could only be one thing.

Clete Hargraves stepped out onto the ledge, holding a small foil bag in one hand. Wisps of steam escaped from the small package. The combat rations were heated through a small chemical reaction, one the Marines decided was too insignificant a heat source to be detected. After a month in the bone-chilling cold without so much as a campfire to keep warm, the eight survivors of Santis's garrison almost didn't care anymore. More than one Marine had broken down and tried to start a fire. But Hargraves had stood firm, preventing anyone from breaking discipline, with rousing words if they proved sufficient…and with iron fists if they didn't.

"Those are landers alright, but they're different from the ones the enemy used. I'd almost swear those are…"

"Sarge, we're getting a transmission on Marine priority channel one." Buck Miller came rushing out of the tent, a stunned look on his face. "We've got friendlies inbound, Sarge!"

Hargraves let out a deep breath, his eyes fixed on the glowing trails slashing across the sky. Could it be? After so long? It had been a rough time for the Marines, especially since the attack on the tritium facility. That raid had achieved some success, but nothing close to knocking the refinery offline. He had no question that production had been cut, but he was equally certain there was still tritium flowing into the almost full storage tanks. In the end, he doubted if the raid had been worth the lives it had cost. But that hadn't stopped them from trying again, with even less success and greater loss the second time.

The civilians were all gone now, as were more than two-thirds of the Marines, victims of combat, of the elements—and in two cases, of slipping on the ice and falling off the rocky coastal cliffs. Hargraves had been trying not to think about the fact that they would have run out of the rations he held in his hand days before if so many of their number hadn't died.

"Miller, get a fix on those ships. I want to know exactly where they land."

"Yes, Sergeant," the Marine said crisply.

Hargraves ran back into the cave, past the cluster of Marines in various stages of realization that something was going on. He turned a corner, moving into a small alcove beyond the main cavern. He stopped and dropped slowly to his knees, kneeling over a figure covered in a massive pile of blankets.

"Lieutenant?" Hargraves spoke slowly, softly, uncertain if the officer was awake.

"Sergeant?" Lieutenant Plunkett turned over slowly, looking up at Hargraves with unfocused eyes.

"Yes, sir." Hargraves reached out and pulled up a blanket that had slipped down off Plunkett's shoulder. "We have incoming landing craft, sir. I think they're ours."

Plunkett looked back, saying nothing for a moment. Then he rasped, "Ours?"

"Yes, sir. Corporal Miller's tracking them now, sir. I think we should go meet them."

"Are you...sure they're...ours?" Plunkett struggled to force the words out, then he twisted around and went into a coughing spasm. Hargraves could hear a rattling sound, worse than it had been a few hours before. Luke Plunkett was tough, especially for an officer, at least to Hargraves' way of thinking. But he knew the lieutenant was slipping away. Hargraves had treated the wound himself, after their medic had been killed, but the infection had already taken hold. Now, Plunkett's body was wracked by some native Santis bug, one that looked a lot like pneumonia. Hargraves was frustrated to the point of rage watching his commanding officer waste away, when a single injection might save his life. An injection the Marines on Santis didn't have.

"Can't be sure, sir." Hargraves paused. "But I'd bet on it."

"You need to go…" Plunkett spasmed again, his cough spraying speckles of blood onto the blankets. "…and you need to leave me, Sergeant."

"No, sir. We can't leave you. Marines don't…"

"Marines follow orders, Sergeant. And I'm ordering you to leave me." Plunkett coughed again, and then he lay back down, clearly too exhausted to hold himself up.

"Lieutenant…" Hargraves' tone was tentative. "We can't leave you…"

"You have to." Plunkett gasped for breath. "I'm done, Sergeant. You know that. I know that."

"You ain't done, sir. And I ain't leaving you behind." He turned and leaned backward, looking into the main cave. "Cole, Weir…get over here. We've got to rig up something to carry the lieutenant."

"Sergeant…no…"

"I've served since you were a boy, Lieutenant. Don't make me a mutineer, not now."

Plunkett looked back at Hargraves. "Okay, Sergeant…on one condition. If we run into trouble, you drop me and leave me behind. Whatever chance you guys have, I don't want it thrown away dragging my dying body around."

Hargraves took a deep breath. Then she said, "Okay, sir. Whatever you say."

"Your word, Sergeant."

"Yes, sir…my word."

Plunkett nodded. Then he laid his head back and struggled to take in a deep breath.

Hargraves turned away, partially to head back and get ready to head out…but mostly because he couldn't face the lieutenant, not after lying to his face.

Clete Hargraves had never broken his word before, but if it came to leaving Plunkett to die or forsaking a promise, he knew exactly what he would do.

Chapter Twenty-Nine

AS Invictus
30 light minutes from Santis, Krillus IV
Alliance Year 58 (307 AC)

"Open the power feeds…but slowly. No more than five percent at first." Raban Cinatus stood on the deck, looking up at the massive engines. The structures were immense, rising thirty meters from top to bottom, and almost seven hundred meters in length. And he felt as though his people had covered every centimeter of that vastness.

The Confederation weapons had torn huge gashes in the engines, and they'd shattered the hull, exposing most of the engine room to the vacuum of space. Thirty of *Invictus*'s crew had died almost instantly, most of them blown out of the rents in the hull. Another fifty, at least, had been wounded. And the engines themselves had shut down immediately, leaving *Invictus* tearing away from the battle at greater than one percent of lightspeed, with no way to decelerate.

Which it still was. Cinatus had deployed his crews immediately, and he'd worked them around the clock, pumping them full of stimulants and ruling over them with iron discipline. The gruff engineer had always believed loyalty and fear were a combination designed to squeeze the very best out of people, and he'd done his part to supply the fear as well as inspire the needed devotion.

Commander Rigellus had been clear. She needed those engines back online. Every day, every hour before *Invictus* could return and finish the battle, allowed the enemy to make more repairs, to prepare for the final engagement. At best, that meant more of *Invictus*'s crew would die in the final confrontation. At worst…

Cinatus stood behind a control panel, watching the indicators as his engineers fed power to the engines. In any other situation, he would have done days of testing before he'd dared to pump energy from the reactor into the engines. But there was no time, and the commander had been perfectly clear. Get the engines working, regardless of risk.

His team had patched hundreds of breaches, replaced millions of meters of conduit and wiring. They had fashioned metal patches to cover the largest of the tears in the great engines. But Cinatus knew the slightest hole, a loose connection, almost anything could cause a catastrophic failure, one that could set repairs back weeks or kill members of his team. A failure even threatened *Invictus* with massive damage from internal explosions. He'd done his best, focused on every detail to the point of driving himself close to insanity. Now he would see if that had been enough.

Ten percent…so far so good…

There were a dozen readouts, but he was mostly concerned with the pressure gauges. Too low meant the required energy density wasn't being achieved. Too high meant the control mechanisms weren't functioning properly. But so far the numbers were spot on, right in the middle of the expected range.

Twenty percent…

The floor under his feet began to vibrate. That was normal, at least unless it got too severe. It was the kind of thing no machine could measure properly…not as well as an experienced engineer's instincts. And his were telling him everything was still good.

Thirty percent…

Still good. And enough power to test the thrusters. He

tapped the com unit on his collar. "Commander, we've got thirty percent power flow and holding steady. We're ready to do a test burst now."

"Very well, Optiomagis…" Kat's voice was stony, determined. "Proceed."

Cinatus turned and waved to a group of technicians about thirty meters down the long room. Then he looked down at the console, and he extended his arm, his fingers resting on a series of levers. He paused a moment, taking a deep breath. Then he flipped each lever in turn, and he grabbed on to the sides of the workstation, holding tightly as he heard the roar of the engines…and then felt the g-forces pushing against him. There was thrust! The engines were working, pushing against *Invictus*'s vector, reducing the velocity that was carrying the battleship away from its adversary.

He glanced down at the controls. All committed power was going into generating thrust. *Invictus*'s engines were at thirty percent of capacity, which Cinatus knew was a miracle considering the hunk of junk they had been less than two days earlier.

"Congratulations, Optiomagis." Even Kat's iron voice showed signs of surprise. "You and your people are to be commended for a job well done…and I will see this is so when we return to Palatia."

"Thank you, Commander. I will pass your words to the rest of my team." Cinatus had been nervous communicating directly with the ship's commander. Standard procedure called for him to deal with the communications officer or exec. But Commander Rigellus had dispensed with all that, demanding constant direct updates from her engineer.

"How much thrust can we generate, Optiomagis?"

"We're at thirty percent now, Commander. I wouldn't go any higher yet. Give me a few hours to do some stress testing and review how the repairs are holding up under the pressure of actual operation. Then we can move up, to fifty, maybe even sixty." The engineer paused. "That's the best we'll be able to do, I'm afraid, Commander. The patches simply aren't strong enough to hold up at any higher thrust level. I'm afraid *Invictus* is going to need completely new engines when we get back home."

The com was silent for a few seconds, and Cinatus was tense, waiting for the commander's response. "Sixty," she said, finally. "Get me sixty percent, Raban...and not one watt less." There was no question in her tone, no sign of flexibility.

"Yes, Commander...sixty percent." Cinatus stood nervously, wondering if he'd just promised more than was possible. But he'd heard the commander's tone, and he knew he could throw all the laws of physics and the realities of engineering at her... and she would just stare at him calmly and repeat...sixty percent.

* * *

Damn.

Millius stood in the dark, filthy snow in the middle of the camp staring off to the north. It couldn't be. It just wasn't possible.

Millius had fought in many battles, worked his way up from the ranks, but he'd never encountered an enemy so frustratingly difficult to defeat. He'd interrogated the civilians who'd fallen into his hands, had his people pick through the burnt wreckage of the Confederation base...everything he could think of to find out what he was truly facing. But the answer he found never changed. There were about forty Marines assigned to Santis, and his people had wiped out ten of them on the space station.

He'd struggled to accept that his three centuries had been stymied trying to hunt down thirty Confederation Marines. Granted, they'd had some civilians bolstering their number, but his forces still outnumbered them five or six to one. Almost ten to one in trained fighters. And yet a month later they were still in arms, at least a stubborn remnant of them.

And now they're getting reinforcements...

There was no other explanation. *Invictus* was the only Alliance vessel within eight transits, and he already had every stormtrooper it carried down on the surface with him. The vessels he'd just watched land *had* to be Confeds.

He knew what he had to do. Hit them hard, pin them, and

fight it out to the end, before they could disperse to the hills and support the guerilla campaign he'd been struggling to stamp out. He didn't have a solid estimate on their numbers, but he'd only been able to confirm four landers. He had no idea how many each one held, but his best guess was he still had the numerical advantage, despite the sixty troopers he'd lost over the past month.

He had no idea how long that superiority would last, or even what was happening in the space above Santis. He'd lost communication when the commander had moved *Invictus* toward planet five, getting in position to face a Confed battleship that had entered the system. But that had been days ago, and he'd had no contact since. He'd even dared to consider the inconceivable…that the great Commander Rigellus and the Alliance's greatest and proudest flagship had been defeated. He found it hard to believe, but he'd spent hours staring at the com unit, waiting to hear something, anything. There had been nothing but silence.

It didn't matter, at least not in terms of his duty. He was here to hold the planet, and that mission stood, whether *Invictus* was somewhere finishing off the enemy vessel, or if the space above Santis was filled with Confed battleships.

He turned to Delv Tinnius, who had been standing right behind him watching the Confed landers come in. "Rally the troopers, Optio. All of them." He turned and looked back over the hill, toward where the enemy craft had landed. "We attack at once."

*   *   *

"Let's get to that ridge up there, fast!" Bryan Rogan was standing next to the assault shuttle, pointing toward a line of rocky heights about a kilometer to the north.

"You heard the Captain…move your asses." Ernesto Billos was standing next to Rogan, sounding exactly like the Marines expected a veteran senior sergeant to sound.

"See to it, Sergeant." Rogan had two lieutenants under him,

but they had the same lack of hardcore experience under fire he did. Billos had been in battle, fought the Union FRs. He'd even been wounded twice. And one thing Rogan was sure about…his people were about to go into battle.

"Yes, sir." Billos started moving toward the nearest group of Marines, but Rogan called him back.

"Sergeant…"

"Yes, Captain?"

"You saw the scanner data we collected. It's inexact, to put it mildly, but it seems pretty likely we're going to be outnumbered here. So, I want the men right at that ridge, and I want them to dig in. No complaints, no delays. We need the strongest position we can get. And I doubt we have much time. You agree with that, Sergeant?"

"Yes, sir. Completely."

"Carry on."

Rogan stood and watched as his Marines moved out, forming into something resembling a combat formation. Then he turned and walked back toward one of the landers, stopping in front of an officer wearing a flight suit. "Alright, Ensign, I think we're clear of your engines. You can lift off whenever you're ready…but I'd move it. I expect we're going to have company here soon.

"Yes, Captain. We'll launch at once."

"And, Ensign…do me a favor. Try to get a good scan in after you lift off. We could use a better idea of what's coming."

"Yes, sir…if they're deployed and on the way, we'll fly right over them. We might even manage a strafing run, maybe soften them up a little."

Rogan nodded. "Anything you can do would be a help, Ensign. And the Marines would owe you one."

* * *

"We've got twenty-six down, sir. At least half of those are dead."

Millius's face was twisted with rage. Alliance landers weren't armed. Invasion forces went in supported with special ground assault ships that pounded enemy positions. But these Confed landing craft had their own weapons, and the quad-autocannons had taken his people by surprise. One of his centuries had been caught in the open, moving toward the enemy positions. And they'd been hit hard.

"We've got to keep moving, Centurion. We can't afford any delays."

That's a diplomatic way of saying, leave the wounded behind to die...

"Yes, Praefectus." The officer nodded abruptly. Alliance forces were trained not to salute on the battlefield. There was no advantage in giving a gift to enemy snipers.

Millius watched the officer run back up toward his forward line. There hadn't been a hint of disapproval, nor even surprise at the command to leave his wounded behind. The way was the way.

No one ever said life as an Alliance warrior was easy...

Millius felt a pang of regret for those he was abandoning, but he understood the math of war, in a way few of the Alliance's enemies seemed to. He could pause, stop his advance, detach vital troops to tend to the wounded...but he'd just be trading one group of dying soldiers for another.

Besides, a wound is damned near a death sentence in this forsaken wasteland...

He moved forward, his legs pushing through the hip deep snow. It was exhausting, and the cold cut through him like a knife, despite his winter kit. But he wasn't about to stop. He'd spent a month chasing down Confederation troops who'd had the time to disperse, to hide in the hills. He wasn't going to let this new force do the same thing...and that meant bringing them to battle. Now.

He heard a crack, in the distance, to the front. Then another. His head snapped around, and he looked out over the slowly rising ground. There was a ridgeline up ahead, and his forward line had pushed beyond it. There was a valley beyond that high ground...he remembered it well. His people had pursued a band of Confeds right between the flanking ridges.

Another crack. Again. And then a whole series of shots.

Of course…they're on the far ridge.

He worked his memory, trying to picture the ground. It was rugged, with a rocky approach. It was a strong position… but he couldn't let that affect his judgment. He considered a flanking maneuver, but he didn't know how long the enemy line extended. And every hour he spent maneuvering was more time for the Confeds to disperse, to slip away and continue the guerilla war that had raged for a month.

But with five or ten times the strength.

No, he couldn't allow that to happen. Alliance stormtroopers were trained for actions like this. If they had to pay with blood for the victory then so be it.

He grabbed his com unit and flipped it on. "All forces…the enemy is on the ridge beyond the valley. We will attack at once. Prepare to advance…"

The way was the way.

Chapter Thirty

"I'm sorry, Captain. We've done everything we can, but I'm afraid getting any more batteries back online is going to take a month in spacedock."

"I understand, Fritzie. Your people have done an outstanding job. Please relay my thanks and my commendations." Barron was sitting as his desk, staring at the updated damage reports as he talked to his chief engineer.

"Yes, sir." A pause. "Thank you, Captain." Fritz's voice was somber. It was clear she wasn't used to admitting there was anything she couldn't fix.

"How about the primaries, Fritzie? Any chance?"

Barron could hear his engineer's exhale over the com. "Possible, sir. But I can't promise. The main accelerator tubes are intact, but the damned things are so fragile…and there's a lot of peripheral damage. Plus, we'd have to get the reactors back up a lot closer to one hundred percent, and that's an iffy proposition right now."

"Do what you can, Fritzie. It…" Barron paused. "Just do what you can. Barron out."

He tapped the com unit, and then he leaned back, closing his eyes. He'd almost told Fritz that getting the primaries back online—or even getting him one good shot from them—could be the difference between victory and defeat. Between life and death. But he'd held his tongue. She was the best engineer in the fleet, and the hardest worker he'd ever seen. She would do everything possible, he was sure of that. And the last thing she needed right now was more pressure.

"Commander Travis is at the door."

The AI's voice startled Barron. "Open," he said, turning his head and watching as his first officer walked into the room. He could see the bridge behind her, bustling at a somewhat lower intensity than it had been during the battle. The enemy ship was still at least two days away, and Barron had knocked back the status to yellow alert, sending half his people at a time to their cabins with orders to sleep. If they could.

Barron moved his neck around on his shoulders, trying to work out the knots and kinks. He hadn't slept, not in the nearly one week since *Dauntless* and the enemy ship had first engaged. He reached down to the desk, taking a pair of stimtabs in his hand and tossing them into his mouth.

"Sit," he said to Travis, as he grabbed a small cup of water off the desk and washed the pills down.

"How many is that for you?" There was concern in Travis's tone.

"I could ask you that too, Commander, couldn't I?"

"We're both going to need liver regens after this is over."

"If we make it back. At this point, growing a new liver doesn't seem like too high a price." He paused, and his face darkened. "Atara, we're in real trouble. Half the secondaries are out, blasted to scrap, with no chance of being repaired. With the primaries still offline, we're just too outgunned. Your shot hit their engines hard—I expect we'll have the edge on maneuver when we fight it out. But what does it do for us? We could make a run for it, get away…but that's not an option anymore. We've can't retreat…we've got to defeat them. Somehow. And I just don't know how we're going to engage and get the better of them. They've got too much operable firepower compared to us."

"This asteroid field will play havoc with their scanners. The concentration of radioactive elements is off the charts." She paused. "If we blast a few of the smaller ones before they get here, the debris field will be spread out. They'll have a hard time targeting through the background radiation until they're right on top of us."

"It'll be a gunfight at knife range...but they'll still win it. Your idea's a good one, but we need something more. We've got to find a way to inflict some damage beyond what our guns can manage. And some way to gain an edge with our advantage in thrust."

Travis stared down at the table, shaking her head. "Any way we can hurt them, we're in their range too, aren't we?"

"Unless..." Barron looked up. "We still have those U-111 units onboard, don't we?"

Travis nodded. "Yes, ninety-four of them, I believe. But..."

"They have stealth capability..."

"Yes, but it's old and outdated. I doubt it would work against the Alliance scanners."

"In the field? With the radioactive dust of dozens of pulverized asteroids floating around, degrading scanners?"

Travis's eyes widened. "That just might work...but we'd have to plan it perfectly. Ninety-four sounds like a lot, but space is a big place.

Barron smiled. "I know just how we're going to do it." He slapped his hand down on the desk, and jumped up to his feet. "C'mon, Atara...we've got a lot of work to do before that ship gets here."

* * *

"C'mon, Sam, show us!" Walt Billings dropped down from the shaft, stumbling slightly as he landed hard on the deck. "I saw you looking at it when we were up there."

"Yeah, Sam, come on."

"We want to see!"

Carson stood in the center of the engineering space, feeling the heat on his face, the redness coming on despite his best efforts to resist.

"We've got work to do, guys." He turned and walked toward the door, but Billings ran around and stood between him and the exit.

"The work can wait a few seconds. We could all use a short break, and something good in the middle of this shit. So, let's see!"

Carson opened his mouth to argue again, but then he closed it without saying anything. It was pointless. He knew his comrades well enough to realize they would never slack off, never tire of the chase.

"Fine," he said, pulling the small tablet from his pocket. He held it close to his face, swiping a few times, pushing the text aside. That was a letter from his wife, and it was none of anybody's business…no matter how much they hounded him. Lise's words hadn't really convinced him she wasn't still mad, but anything from her was a welcome respite from the hell of battle. She'd told him she regretted that they'd parted on uncomfortable terms, that she understood why he had to go. He believed she was sorry they had argued, less so that she understood his reasons for leaving. He was going to write her himself, as soon as he had a free moment, tell her he felt the same way. But that would have to wait until he'd worked himself through the still enormous list of repairs on the schedule.

He looked at his grinning comrades and turned the tablet around. There was a photo there, a newborn baby, all red with puffy cheeks. His son, the other news Lise's letter had delivered.

"He's cute, Sam…must have gotten most of his DNA from mom."

The engineers in the hold laughed, jockeying to get close and have a look.

"Congrats again, Sam." Billings was a wise ass, far more likely to give him a hard time than a serious emotion. But now his voice was sincere. "That's why we're working so hard…so we can get this tub fixed up and get the hell out of here. So you can give your son a kiss." The others nodded, and gave him a ragged round of applause.

"Thanks, guys. Really. I don't know what to say."

"Say about what? Why I have half a dozen engineers standing around like they're at some kind of picnic? Can I assume *Dauntless* is one hundred percent operational again?" Fritz stepped into the room, holding a section of heavy duty cable. Her uniform was covered in black dust, and it had a large tear down one side. She looked like she'd just been crawling around somewhere in *Dauntless*'s guts...which Carson knew was probably exactly what she had been doing.

"Sorry, Commander...we were just...ah..."

"Carson was showing us the kid, Commander." Billings looked a little startled still. "We kept at him until he gave in."

Fritz stepped forward, an ominous presence approaching like some dark shadow. "So, I can assume that all of you have work you should be doing, correct?" Her eyes focused on Billings.

"Yes, Commander...we're on it." Billings looked around at the others. Then they all started moving toward the exit.

"Not you, Sam."

Carson stopped, feeling like he was trapped in a spider web, watching as his comrades fled through the doorway and out into the corridor.

"Commander, I'm sorry. They kept asking me, and I finally..."

"I don't care about any of that, Sam."

Carson struggled to hold Fritz's terrifying gaze. "Yes, Commander."

"I don't want to hear about that pack of lazy dogs chasing you around, distracting you from your duty."

"No, Commander."

"No...what I care about is getting a look at that tablet myself. Congratulations, Sam, you've got the best reason of all of us to get through this...and back to Archellia."

Carson stared back, trying to hide his stunned surprise. Then he caught the smile on Fritz's face as the fearsome engineering chief walked over and held her hand out for the tablet.

* * *

"This is an important mission, more than any normal combat space patrol. I think we have a good chance to defeat the enemy ship, but half our systems are hanging by a thread." Barron's words were a bit more optimistic than his thoughts. He had a plan now, at least, which was better than just sitting and waiting. His people did have a chance…but he wasn't sure thought it was a *good* chance. "The asteroid field is going to reduce their effective range to less than fifty thousand kilometers. But if any of their fighters get through and launch a successful attack…well, that will probably be the battle. It won't take much to knock the reactors down or take more of our guns offline. I'm not even sure what's keeping the still-working ones functional."

Jamison turned toward Stockton, exchanging nods with his friend. Then he returned his gaze to Barron. "We'll see it done, sir. Whatever it takes."

Barron sat impassively. Jamison was his strike force commander, and he was downright dour by the standards of the fighter corps. But even he was prone to the bravado Barron knew was an essential part of what allowed a man or woman to crawl into the cramped cockpit of a fighter and launch into a battle.

"No bullshit, Kyle. I need those fighters kept away from *Dauntless*. Whatever it takes has to mean just that. *Whatever* it takes." Barron knew he was telling his officer that the mission was more important than any—all—of his pilots' lives. He hated it, but he meant it anyway.

Jamison's looked right into Barron's eyes. His look was cold, serious. "I understand, sir. Whatever it takes." He paused for a few seconds before turning back toward Stockton. "We'll have to go in waves…maybe three. We'll need birds positioned farther back to cut off any enemy fighters that try to run through our interceptors." Another pause. "That means we'll be outnumbered at the point of contact. Our lead forces could take losses. Bad losses."

"I'll take the lead, boss." Stockton's words were emotionless. The patina of arrogance that usually surrounded him was entirely gone, replaced by a grim determination. "Give me my Blues…and Ice and half his Yellows. You and Lynx can take the Reds and the rest of the Yellows and form two reserve lines."

He turned around and stared back toward his rival. "That good with you, Ice? You game to fly with me? I'd bet between us, we can do what has to be done."

Krill had been sitting quietly in the back of the small briefing room. He stared back for a moment, silent. Then he said, "I'll fly with you, Raptor." There was warmth in his normally frigid tone, and he even managed a rare smile. "And you bet your ass we'll do what has to be done."

"I'll take the second line." Olya Fedorov spoke up now. She had been standing along the back wall listening to the discussion. "I'll take most of my Reds." She looked at Jamison. "If you agree, sir, you can take the third line. The surviving Greens and the rest of Ice's Yellows…plus a few of my best Reds. You'll be the final defense, the last chance to take out anything that gets through us."

Jamison shook his head. "I'll fly with the lead group."

"No, Kyle…you can't do that." Stockton snapped at his friend in a tone that verged on insubordination. "I mean, you're the commander, sir. We don't know what's going to happen, how they'll come at us. We need you where you can see things happening and react. It's our place to be in the front lines, not yours."

Jamison looked as if he was going to argue, but Barron held up his hand. "I'm afraid Raptor is right. Your place is in the rear line…just as my place is here, and not in a fighter out there. I need your command abilities, Kyle, not senseless bravery that gets you killed. I need to know I can count on you, that you'll keep those fighters from getting through and launching any attacks on *Dauntless*."

The pilot sat for a few seconds, staring down at the floor. Then his head moved up and said, "Yes, sir. Understood."

Barron looked out at his four squadron leaders. "I can't express how fortunate I am to have such gifted and capable squadron commanders. I know what you went through in the first battle…" Barron hesitated. His fighter squadrons had lost half their strength already, and now he was sending them on another desperate mission. He knew the need to stop the bombers would put his people at a disadvantage against enemy ships fitted for dogfighting. And that meant more casualties, probably a lot more.

"We understand, sir," Jamison said. "We're ready to do our jobs, Captain, whatever it takes. You worry about *Dauntless*. We'll keep those bombers away."

Chapter Thirty-One

Planet Santis
Krillus IV
307 AC

"I'd say it's one company, Sarge. They're lined up on the ridgeline, and it looks like the enemy is moving to attack." Thoms was breathing hard as he forced out the words, each exhale turning into a cloud of white condensation in the frigid morning air.

"Enemy strength?" Hargraves was cold too, probably more even than Thoms, who'd run several klicks back from his scouting mission.

"Looks like two hundred or more to me, Sarge. I'd guess they want to pin down the reinforcements before they can get into the hills."

Hargraves nodded. "I'd wager we drove the bastards damned near crazy. The last thing they want is a hundred more Marines hidden in these hills." The sergeant was proud of what they had accomplished over the last month, the way they had held out against a much larger force. But his satisfaction was tempered by the losses they had suffered. All the civilians were dead... and so were three quarters of the Marines they'd started with. They'd been on the verge of annihilation when the reinforcements arrived out of the blue.

"We should get moving. We gotta go around those hills to link up with the…" Hargraves paused. "Wait…think, Thoms. Did the enemy have their whole force out there? All of them?"

The Marine looked right back at Hargraves. "It sure looked like it, Sarge. Had to be most of 'em if not all."

Hargraves turned and looked behind him, staring out over the rolling ground to the south.

"Whatcha thinking, Sarge?"

Hargraves didn't answer. He just stood still, looking off into the distance. Finally, he turned back toward Thoms. "Get everybody up and ready to go, Private."

"Yessir. We movin' around to link up with the Marines on the ridge?"

"No." Hargraves could see his answer was a surprise to the Marine.

Hell, it's a surprise to me too…

"Where we goin' then?"

"We're heading south. We're gonna see just how many troops they left behind in their camp…and we're gonna blow the place to hell. Their food, ammo…everything."

Hargraves knew it was a daring plan—some would say crazy—but if his people could pull it off they'd do a hell of a lot more for the cause than adding eight guns to the troops on the ridge. The fact that Confederation reinforcements, from wherever they'd come, had been able to land meant that the enemy no longer controlled Santis's orbit. And that meant the troops on the ground had no source of resupply.

"Shit, Sarge…even if they took almost everybody, there's no more than eight of us. You gotta figure they left more than that."

"Maybe so, Private. But they won't expect this. If we move fast enough…"

He didn't finish. He didn't have to. His people were Marines. All they needed was the order to go.

* * *

"Forward, all forces. The longer we wait, the more time they have to dig in." Millius was walking forward, watching his three centuries—what was left of them—shake out into an assault formation. Frontally charging an enemy on high ground wasn't an act of tactical brilliance, he knew that. It would be difficult and costly. But anything else took too much time, and after the last month he wasn't about to let another hundred of these cursed Confed Marines to break out loose into the countryside. He'd managed to keep the tritium production facility mostly operative, despite several attacks, but with so many fresh troops, he knew the Confeds would hit it again and again…and if they had enough chances they'd get lucky.

Casualties are bad enough, but if I let them destroy the production facility, I've singlehandedly blown the whole mission…

No, there was no time. It had to be a frontal assault, and whatever the cost in blood to crush the enemy, he was prepared to pay it.

The way is the way…

He watched as his forward units surged up the slope…and were cut down by the deadly fire. They pushed forward at first, ignoring their losses. He expected nothing less. They were Alliance stormtroopers, after all.

But the troops dug in on the heights were good too. That was no surprise. He'd spent a month trying to hunt down a single platoon, and whatever arrogance and sense of superiority he'd had when he landed was long gone. He didn't know what was happening in the space above Santis, but the arrival of enemy ground troops and the failure of Commander Rigellus to communicate in over a week weren't good signs. Had the intel been wrong? Had the Confederation been able to send a strong enough force to overwhelm and destroy *Invictus*? The intel reports had certainly failed to warn on the effectiveness of the enemy's ground troops.

He saw his lead elements, about halfway up the rise. They were slowing…in places they were stopping entirely. But they weren't running…he swore the day he saw an Alliance force rout would be the day he met his death in battle. They were firing back at the enemy, scrounging for the miserable few bits of cover available on that mostly open hillside.

No…

He knew he had to keep his forces moving. They couldn't win a firefight, not against a dug in enemy on higher ground. They had the numbers to win by sheer force of weight…but they had to keep going.

He grabbed his com, but then he clipped it back on his belt. Words weren't the answer, he decided. Deeds would win this fight. He reached around, grabbed the assault rifle strapped to his back. Then he started forward, a brisk walk at first, but then almost a run.

His forces would push those last few meters, take that position. And he would lead them there himself.

* * *

"Hold! Maintain fire." Rogan was bent low, keeping himself behind the ridge as he moved along the line. The enemy attack had shown signs of petering out, the enemy troopers stopping, looking for cover, firing back at his forces. He'd been worried the attackers would keep coming, heedless of the casualties his Marines were inflicting…and indeed they almost had. For a brief moment he'd considered ordering a retreat, but something had held him back. And the slackening of the enemy attack had put the thought out of his mind completely.

Then something changed. The enemy was moving again, rallied, driven forward. His best guess was his people had taken down seventy or eighty of the enemy. But his forces had taken losses too, and the enemy still outnumbered him close to two to one. They were right below the ridgeline now. If his fire didn't drive them back in the next few seconds, they would be up and over.

And then it will be hand to hand…

Numbers would tell in that kind of fight. Every enemy his Marines took down now was one less when it came to close quarters.

He hadn't known what to expect from the enemy, but he was wary about underestimating them. Their tactics were crude, wasteful of lives…but that didn't mean they wouldn't prevail. The troops were clearly well-trained and courageous, and that meant this was going to be a bloody day.

He glanced down and saw two of his Marines lying on the ground, both dead. His people had good cover, but the enemy fire was hot and heavy, and even behind the makeshift fortifications, more of his people were starting to fall.

He crouched low, going prone and bringing his own rifle to bear. There wasn't a single one of his people to spare, including himself. He stared out, keeping his head as low as he could. There was an enemy trooper approaching, less than thirty meters ahead, he guessed. He stared down the sight, taking aim. Then his finger tightened, and a single crack rang out. The enemy fell backward, shot dead center in the chest.

Rogan sucked in a deep breath, struggling to focus, to stay calm. He'd been in a few fights before, but this was the first time he'd commanded this many Marines in battle.

Just do what you were trained to do…

He scanned the field in front of him, searching for another target. Then he stared down the sights and fired again.

* * *

"Let's move it, Marines! Surprise is what we got!" Hargraves ran into the center of the enemy camp, his rifle grasped tightly in his hands as he looked back and forth for targets. His people had taken out six guards, and now it was time to finish the job. The camp had been lightly protected, the approaches not nearly as carefully watched as normal. He'd known the enemy had deployed most of their strength to attacking the newly-arrived reinforcements. But he was still shocked at how open they had left their camp.

They've underestimated us from day one…otherwise they'd have wiped us out weeks ago…

He jerked to the side, firing a three-shot burst as an enemy soldier ran out of one of the shelters. The man fell back the way he'd come, blood pouring from a trio of holes in his chest. Hargraves fired again...and again, whipping his weapon upward, firing over the dead man's shoulder and taking the trooper behind in the side of the head.

He ran toward the building, standing to the side of the door. He doubted the walls of the light, semi-inflatable shelter would provide much protection against bullets, but he was acting on training now, on instinct.

He swung around, moving through the door and into the shelter. It was some kind of storage facility. Food, he guessed, looking around at the stacks of crates, confirming that he was the only one left alive in the room.

We could sure use this food...

He shook his head. No...his people were there to destroy the enemy camp. His eight Marines couldn't hope to hold the place, or even carry off any of the supplies. They'd had enough trouble carrying the lieutenant with them. Hargraves' thoughts shifted to Plunkett for an instant. His people had left the sick and wounded officer about a kilometer from the camp, in the most sheltered spot they could find. He'd been nearly unconscious, and Hargraves wondered if Plunkett would still be alive when he got back.

You won't get back at all if you don't stay sharp here...

He reached around, pulling a small sack from his belt. It was the last of the explosives, enough to take out this building for sure. But finishing off the camp would require finding the invader's own weapons. He pulled the bomb up and looked down at it, his fingers flipping the timer to thirty seconds. Then he set it down on one of the crates and moved back out, looking in all directions before he lunged out into the makeshift street.

"Fire in the hole," he yelled as he jogged forward, away from the storage hut. He counted down to himself. He'd gotten to three when the explosion erupted, sending debris all across the camp.

My timing's off...

He was pelted with a few pieces of the shelter and the crates inside, enough to sting, but nothing that did any real damage.

"Sarge…"

Thoms was running down the street toward him, two of the others right behind.

"We found the main arsenal and rigged it to blow. We got maybe fifteen seconds…"

Hargraves turned, letting his three Marines move past him and then following them. The four of them ran hard, out of the small camp and over a small rise. Then Hargraves yelled, "Down…now!"

The Marines dove to the ground, covering the backs of their heads with their arms. A second later the explosion came. It was vastly louder than the one Hargraves had triggered, and the Marines felt the ground under them shaking.

Hargraves could feel the heat from behind him, and when he looked up he could see the plume of fire rising to the sky as the enemy arsenal consumed itself in a fiery spectacle.

The sergeant stood up slowly and looked back the way they had come. The camp was gone, nothing but fire and smoke. Their job was done.

"All right, Marines," he said as he scrambled to his feet. "Mission accomplished…let's get the hell outta here."

*   *   *

Millius froze where he was, snapping his head around for an instant. The plume of smoke rising up over the hills told him all he needed to know.

The arsenal…

He realized immediately what had happened. The remnants of the original Confederation garrison must have snuck around his main force, and hit the camp. But how? There were only a few of them left, he was sure about that. And he'd left more than a dozen guards behind.

Who are these soldiers?

The Confeds were good fighters, that much was clear. But his troopers were too. It was the enemy's tenacity, their stubbornness that had gotten the best of him. How had a battered force, frozen and exhausted, at twenty percent strength, pulled off an attack on his camp? Would Alliance stormtroopers have dared such an assault?

He turned to face forward. Whatever had happened to the camp, whatever the implications, it didn't matter now. He had to get his troopers forward, over the hill…and destroy the Confeds.

He threw his assault rifle to the ground. He'd used all his cartridges. His hand moved down to his waist, pulled his pistol from the holster. But even in the heat of battle, his mind was wandering, dark thoughts creeping up from within.

I am disgraced. Half my soldiers are gone…and the rest are in a fight to the finish, one few on either side will survive. I had numbers, support, every advantage. Yet the destruction of these Confed soldiers eluded me.

He waved his arms, held the pistol above his head. "Forward," he shouted. "Over the top, and destroy the enemy." He took a deep breath, and he lunged forward. "Follow me," he cried, not even looking back to see if his troops were heeding his urgings.

He ran forward, ignoring the enemy fire, leveling his pistol and taking careful, aimed shots. Then he reached the top of the ridge, and he drew his survival knife with the other hand. There was a cluster of Confeds right in front of him. He fired the pistol, even as he lunged forward, slashing with the knife.

His eyes darted to the side, toward groups of his soldiers, some fighting fiercely…but others…

It was inconceivable. He couldn't accept what his eyes told him. His troopers were running, fleeing from the battle. Alliance stormtroopers routing. Under his command.

Even in victory, he knew there would be disgrace now. And from the looks of things, victory was quickly slipping from his grasp. But there was another possibility, one that offered its own mercies.

He took a deep breath…then he threw himself deeper into the Confeds, shoving his knife hard under the armor of the man nearest to him, feeling the hot blood pouring out over his hand, his arm. He saw another moving behind him, and he angled his pistol and fired three times, dropping the attacker. But there were more, all around. He felt himself being dragged down, loud cracks from enemy rifles…and pain, bullets piercing his legs, his sides. But he kept fighting, swinging his blade when his pistol ran out of ammo…even as more shots pierced his body.

Finally, he fell into the snow, feeling the wet, coldness on his back. And then silence, the pain gone, a gauzy, airy feeling.

He lay still, eyes gazing up at the ice blue dawn sky.

Chapter Thirty-Two

CFS Dauntless
Krillus Asteroid Belt
39,000,000 kilometers from Santis, Krillus IV
Year 58 (307 AC)

"The enemy is stationary, Commander. They're just sitting there. Waiting."

"Very well."

The display was telling Kat the same story Wentus had just reported. But that wasn't right. She just *knew* there was something in the data she wasn't seeing. The enemy captain was a smart one, and she was sure his ship had taken major hits to its weapons systems, damage that couldn't have been repaired in a few days.

Why would he sit and wait for us? Why not run? If the Confeds are as we've been told, they should have withdrawn. He had all the time in the world to escape.

He's up to something…

"Commander, we're getting intense radiation readings throughout the asteroid field. Nothing dangerous, but it's making our scans difficult."

Is that it? Are you using the radiation to try and mislead me somehow? Or do you think I won't follow you in there?

Wentus continued, "We're also picking up a high density of

dust and particulates around the enemy vessel, Commander. It's almost as if…"

"As if what, Optiomagis?"

"As if several large asteroids impacted and destroyed each other."

Kat looked at the data on her screen, confirming what her first officer had just told her.

Perhaps they sought out a particulate-dense area to make their stand. Do they think this will interfere with our targeting?

She knew it would indeed affect targeting. But only at longer ranges. If she closed to point blank range, even the radioactive dust would be insufficient to throw off her firing locks.

Is that it? Or is it something else?

"Optiomagis, I want all fighters prepared for an immediate launch. Gold Dagger, Red Banner, and Gleaming Shield squadrons are to be armed for anti-shipping strikes. Black Fist, Darkwind, and Hydra for interception and escort operations."

"Yes, Commander."

She leaned back in her chair. Her squadrons had suffered badly so far in the engagement, and now she was sending them on another mission. She'd seen the Confed fighters in action, and she knew her people would suffer badly. But she was concerned about what the enemy was planning. If her fighters could get through and launch a damaging strike, she would feel more comfortable about closing and finishing things.

She stared straight ahead. The tactical situation seemed clear, at least in some ways. She had every reason to believe *Invictus* was in superior condition, that a straight out fight to the finish would end with her victory. Alliance doctrine offered no choices in such a situation. A crippled enemy was to be destroyed.

But what about those primaries…could they have repaired them? Is that what they want? For me to advance to close range so they can fire their main guns again?

No, that wasn't the answer, at least not solely. The enemy primaries were powerful, but there was no doubt many of its secondary batteries had been virtually destroyed. Even with the main guns it was doubtful the enemy could defeat *Invictus*.

The enemy captain is no fool. Indeed, do not underestimate him. There must be more, something I'm not considering…

Despite her concerns, Kat knew she had no choice. If her fighters failed to get through and cripple the enemy vessel, she had no choice but to advance with *Invictus* and begin the final exchange.

"Commander, squadrons report ready to launch."

She nodded, sighing softly, allowing herself a moment's hope the fighters would spare her from what she feared. But her people would have a hell of a fight on their hands to break through and reach the enemy ship. They might succeed—she had the best pilots in the Alliance with her. But doubts crept in from all sides, and cold thoughts about moving forward toward the enemy. She realized she'd allowed the enemy commander to get inside her head, and she wondered if that was insecurity on her part…or perceptiveness.

She pushed it all out of her mind. There was no point worrying about things she couldn't change. If her fighters didn't finish the job, she would have to. There was no option there, whatever risks might exist in the shadows of her mind.

"Commence launch now."

* * *

"Here they come." Stockton watched the wall of incoming dots on the small screen of his scanner. "Remember, we fight the interceptors, but the primary mission is to get the bombers. We don't let them through, regardless of the risk." His words were grim, not at all the lighthearted cockiness his pilots had come to expect. But "Raptor" Stockton knew the gravity of the situation. If his pilots let those bombers through, everyone on *Dauntless* would die. It was that simple.

"Looks like they've got the interceptors up front, Raptor. I've got fifty that says they'll try to pull us off to the side, open up a lane for the bombers."

"No bet, Condor. That's exactly what they're going to try. But we're not going for it. Blast them if you can, but don't let them pull you off station." Stockton knew his orders would be difficult ones to follow. Restricting the maneuver of his pilots put them at a disadvantage in a dogfight. But the bombers were the priority.

"Alright, Blue…pilots…" Stockton realized he had a hodgepodge of *Dauntless*'s surviving fighters with him, not just his own Blues. "…right wing, you're with me. Left wing, with Ice."

Stockton would never acknowledge that Tillis Krill was his equal in the cockpit, but he had to grudgingly admit—to himself at least—that the Yellow squadron commander was number two in the roster. And the Blue and Yellow squadron pilots with them were the best *Dauntless* had. There were two lines positioned to the rear, but Stockton knew his people had to hit the enemy attack hard. They were the biggest force, and if they let too many ships by, the reserves simply wouldn't have enough strength to stop them.

He watched as the symbols on the screen moved closer… closer. Then: "Now!"

He angled the throttle, turning his fighter and blasting the thrust nearly up to full power. He could feel the g-forces slamming into him, despite the best efforts of his ship's dampeners to counteract them. His course took him right through the enemy interceptors…toward the bombers lined up behind.

He could see the enemy birds changing course, moving to hit him before he could get into firing range of the bombers. He thought about just blasting his engines at full, making a mad dash for the bombers. But he sighed and pulled back on the thrust. Even if he could outrun the enemy interceptors, his velocity would be too high. His fighter would zip right through the enemy bombers, and by the time he could decelerate and return, the attack force would be halfway to *Dauntless*. No, his people had to focus on the interceptors first. If they could get enough of them, the second and third lines could hit the bombers.

He tugged at the controls, bringing his fighter around almost completely, and he hit the thrust again, decelerating this time. His eyes dropped to the screen, and he reached out, flipping two small levers on the control panel.

"Missiles armed," the AI announced.

He'd intended to try to save his missiles for the bombers, hoping the enemy might be careless and position the unwieldy torpedo-armed ships too far forward. But the enemy formation was textbook, and that meant his people had one job right now. Destroy the interceptors.

"Forget the bombers for now," he said into his com unit. "Clear the interceptors…leave the bombers to Lynx and the Reds behind us."

He stared straight down at the screen, adjusting his controls, moving one of the small icons into the tiny crosshairs of his scope. He waited, staring intently, making minor adjustments. Then he fired and he felt the kick as his bird lurched and his left wing missile blasted forward.

He angled the fighter hard almost immediately, hot on the heels of target number two. He was focused on the second enemy fighter when the AI announced that the first shot had hit. Another kill.

It won't be the last one today, not if we're going to keep these bastards away from Dauntless…

He fired the second missile. And then he brought his ship around again, flipping a series of switches to activate his laser cannons. It was time for close work now.

"Enemy missile lock."

The AI's voice was disconcertingly calm, considering what it had just reported.

Stockton pulled back hard on the throttle, blasting at full thrust, even as he moved his vector wildly. He could feel the sweat, his hair wet, droplets beginning to roll slowly down his neck, his back. He was focused, with every shred of intensity he could muster.

But the missile was still on his tail…

* * *

This one is good. Damned good…

Junus's hand was tight on his controls as he watched his target trying to evade the missile he'd fired. He'd had the enemy dead to rights, caught him napping, too focused on the target he'd been chasing to notice Junus sneaking up on him. Overconfidence was the bane of fighter pilots, a flaw that took down even the best. But this pilot was *good.*

His evasive maneuvers were wild, unpredictable. He'd broken the missile's lock twice, only to have the weapon reacquire. But now Junus realized the enemy was going to outlast the missile. The weapon had only a few seconds of fuel left, not enough.

His hand moved, angling the throttle, bringing his ship right toward the enemy. He had the advantage. His prey had no choice but to continue to evade the missile…and that meant Junus could get behind him.

He brought his ship around, matching the target's moves, keeping his vector aligned with the ship a few thousand kilometers ahead of him. His finger rested on the firing control. His lasers were charged and ready. This was someone important, or at least one of the enemy's top aces. Taking him down would remove a massive threat to the rest of his fighters…including the anti-ship strike moving forward behind the interceptors.

He fired, but the shot went wide, thrown off by the target's sudden change in thrust. He countered, maintaining his position and fired again. Another miss.

He took a deep breath. The pilot in front of him was the most skilled he'd ever faced…and he knew if he made any mistakes, his adversary could turn things around on him in an instant. He tapped the throttle, increasing acceleration, closing slowly as he kept firing.

* * *

"Raptor, you've got one on your tail!" "Ice" Krill looked down at the screen, watching as Stockton tried to evade the enemy fighter pursuing him. Stockton was one of the best—in truth, Krill knew, *the* best—pilot on *Dauntless.* But he was in trouble now.

"I can't shake him, Ice." Krill couldn't remember ever hearing Stockton sound so tense, but the strain, the fear, was clear now.

"I'm on my way, Raptor. Just hold on. A few more seconds."

Krill pushed his thrust to the limit, moving his vector toward a direct line to the enemy. Clearly it was a gifted pilot on Raptor's tail, an ace. But Krill knew a pilot was most vulnerable when pursuing an enemy, and chasing down Raptor would take all any pilot had to offer. It was a chance…if he could get there in time.

He saw the flashes on the scanner, the enemy firing at Raptor's ship. It was too close…he couldn't count on the enemy missing much longer. His eyes dropped to the display. He was too far away. There was no way he'd make it to close range.

Krill stared grimly at his scanner. He was focused, maintaining his eerie calm even as he recognized the gravity of the situation. Ice. The call sign had been his since the Academy, one his classmates had unanimously agreed was a perfect fit. And now he put it to the test.

He wasn't going to get close, not in time. That left one choice. He had to score a hit from long range. He stared hard at the screen. The enemy was too close to Raptor. There was no time.

He moved his hand, adjusting the firing solution. Then he fired…and missed.

Again. Another miss.

He could feel the heat on his neck, even his own unflappable demeanor beginning to fail. He and Stockton weren't friends, not exactly. But they were comrades. And they were the best, members of an elite group. He couldn't fail. He just couldn't.

He leaned forward, moving the stick slowly, lining up another shot.

His finger closed slowly, even as he was still adjusting his line. He heard the sound of the lasers firing, again and again as he held his finger on the trigger.

His eyes were locked on the targeting display when the enemy ship vanished. He leaned back, let his hand fall away from the throttle, felt the tightness drain from his muscles. He'd done it, a one in a hundred shot.

He'd saved Raptor.

*   *   *

"Thanks for the assist, Ice." There would have been a time when Stockton couldn't have imagined a worse fate than thanking his rival for saving his life. But he'd experienced total war now, and he knew it had changed him. Petty rivalries seemed pointless.

"Any time, Raptor, now let's…" Krill's voice trailed off. Stockton saw it too. An enemy fighter coming up right behind Krill.

"Ice, you've…"

"I see him, Raptor."

Stockton could hear the tension in Krill's normally even voice. He was the one in trouble now, and he knew it.

"On my way, Ice."

Stockton pulled back hard on the throttle, pushing it to the side, trying to bring his bird back toward Krill's ship. But his vector and velocity were still taking him farther from his comrade's ship. His eyes dropped to the display, looking for any other friendlies close enough to intervene. Nothing.

"Fuck!" He banged his free hand against the console as he watched what was happening on the display. Ice was maneuvering wildly, trying to shake his pursuer. But his attacker was right on his tail…and closing.

Stockton reached down, opened a small panel under his control panel. His fingers reached around, finding a small lever. He pulled.

"Deactivate safety mechanisms?" The AI's voice was dispassionate, professional.

"Yes," Stockton answered. "Increase reactor output to one twenty."

Stockton knew he was being reckless, that he was pushing his ship to the edge of its capabilities, but he didn't care. He had to get to Ice before…

He looked at the display again. Krill was trying to break free, and the enemy fighter was still hot on his tail. Stockton could see small flashes on the display, laser blasts. The attacker was shooting now.

"Damn!"

His fighter was moving toward the enemy, but he was still far out, too far for a laser shot. Still, he armed his guns. A hit at this range was improbable to the point of impossibility. But that didn't stop his finger from closing around the firing stud.

He heard the whine of his lasers as he fired. He didn't even know if a hit at this range would be powerful enough to damage the enemy. But he kept shooting anyway. He couldn't just do nothing.

He watched on the scanner as the enemy ship closed, his eyes following as Krill's ship zigzagged wildly, avoiding his pursuer's fire, but failing to break the deadly pursuit.

I've got to get there...

He felt the helplessness growing, mocking him. For all his vaunted skills as a pilot, he was watching helplessly, unable to prevent the tragedy he saw unfolding before his eyes.

He stared at the screen, even as he continued to fire. Then he saw it. Another flash on the display. A laser blast from the enemy fighter. Stockton felt his stomach heave as he saw Krill's fighter vanish from the screen.

He sat for a second, unmoving, stunned, absorbing the reality of what his scanner showed. Then the rage came, an overwhelming need for vengeance. His eyes locked on the display, on the symbol representing the enemy fighter. He hadn't been able to get there in time to save Krill...but he was damned if he'd let the bastard who killed his comrade escape.

The enemy ship changed course, thrusting hard to alter its vector. But the enemy pilot had accelerated hard to catch Krill, and now he was trapped by his own vector. Stockton came on, relentless. He was focused, obsessed. Nothing but the death of this enemy could satiate his need for revenge.

He fired, his blasts getting closer as the range fell. He saw that his enemy recognized the danger. The pilot moved his ship as erratically as it could, but its existing vector limited his options.

Stockton stared at the symbol on his screen. It was the only thing on his mind, all he lived for at that moment. He was a predator, an avenger…he was death itself.

He squeezed the firing stud, then again. And again. His eyes narrowed, he shut out everything, no thought in his head save his fighter's lasers. The screen displayed an icon, impersonal, no more than a speck of light. But he saw his enemy there, the metal of the ship, the fear in the eyes of his victim as he brought death upon him.

He tried to relax, to let his instincts take control, to put intuition as well as math into his targeting. He stared, his finger ready. Then he fired, half a dozen shots. And with the last one, the enemy fighter's symbol vanished from his scanner.

He didn't cheer as he usually did. He didn't pump his fist. He sat silently, not moving.

That was for you, Ice.

He'd avenged his comrade, but there was no satisfaction. He just felt cold, empty.

Chapter Thirty-Three

"Third wave moving up, Captain. Commander Jamison reports his people will be engaged in seconds." Darrow's voice was calm, cool. Barron was proud of his people, of how they had stood up under the pressure. Some of them might not have analyzed the situation quite as extensively as he had, but they had to know the odds were against them.

"Very well, Lieutenant." Barron toggled his own com. "Good luck, Thunder...to you and all your pilots. Our thoughts and best wishes fly with you."

"Thank you, sir. We'll get the job done."

Barron cut the line. The last thing Kyle Jamison needed now was his commanding officer distracting him.

Barron had watched his first two lines of fighters engaged the enemy strike. He'd sat silently, his eyes locked on the display as his fighters fought a savage battle with the enemy, as "Ice" Krill died. Jake Stockton had gone mad after his rival was destroyed, and he'd plunged into the enemy formations with utter disregard for danger. He'd burned through his fuel reserves, ignoring every warning to break off and return to *Dauntless*. And the pilots with him—the survivors of Blue squadron and part of Ice's Yellows—had followed his lead, extracting a gruesome price for Krill's death.

Stockton fought like some demon unleashed, and he took down no fewer than six enemies before his guns fell silent from lack of power. He was out there now, moving through space along his final vector, no fuel remaining to decelerate. And the rest of his pilots, and Krill's, the six who had survived, were in the same situation. They would be rescued if *Dauntless* won the battle. And if the enemy prevailed they would be captured… or they would suffocate in their cockpits as their life support dwindled.

Of course, we'll all be dead by then…

Barron leaned back in his chair, his eyes moving toward Darrow. "Let's get the display centered on Commander Jamison's force, Lieutenant."

"Yes, sir," Darrow snapped back. A few seconds later the holographic display morphed slowly, showing a region of empty space…and a line of small blue dots. *Dauntless*'s last line of fighters.

Darrow was covering Atara Travis's station. *Dauntless*'s first officer was down in engineering, monitoring the status of repairs.

Driving Fritzie crazy, that's what she's doing.

Fritz was a fine engineer, and one of the hardest workers he'd ever seen. But Travis was smart, probably the most intelligent officer Barron had ever met…and he included himself and his famous grandfather in that calculation. His first officer somehow kept track of every detail, every reading on every device. And she could make the snap decisions that might be the difference between life and death for them all.

Barron had a trick or two up his sleeve, stratagems he hoped might pull victory from the jaws of defeat, but he knew the battle would still be won—if it was won—as much in the engineering spaces and access tubes of his ship as on the bridge.

The primaries…if we can get the primaries back online we still have a chance.

Barron didn't know if that was possible. But with Travis and Fritzie on the job, he believed there was at least some hope. He wanted to believe it, at least.

Barron's com buzzed.

"Captain, we're all set down here." Stu Weldon was one of Barron's oldest friends. He was also *Dauntless*'s chief medical officer.

"Did you set up the aid stations?" *Dauntless* was a big ship, and men and women could die before they made it to sickbay, especially if systems like the turbolifts and intraship cars stopped functioning. Setting up aid stations in remote locations was something he remembered from his grandfather, one of the things the great admiral had done during his battles. It would almost certainly help save lives. But there was a colder, more mercenary take as well. It was a way to show the captain's concern for his crew, to squeeze that last bit of fanatical loyalty from the men and women in *Dauntless*'s compartments and at its stations.

"We're all ready, sir. Six remote locations…that's all we could staff without crippling sickbay itself."

"That's good. Hopefully they'll save some lives." Barron's voice was somber. The risk of losses was bad enough, but he knew even in the best case scenario, a lot of his people were about to die.

There was a long pause. Then: "Tyler…how many stims have you taken?"

"Stu…not now…"

"You may be captain of this ship, but you're still just a man. There's only so much your body can take. Have you gotten any sleep at all?"

"Yeah, sure. Not a lot, but enough." He was lying to his friend. It had been days since he'd gotten even a moment of sleep.

"Bullshit." It was a breach of protocol and regulations to call bullshit on your commander, but Barron knew Weldon had always fit uncomfortably in the military structure. And they had been friends since they were teenagers, sneaking out of school on crisp fall days to go hiking in the mountains.

"Here's a deal, Doc, and it's the best you're going to get. Get off my back—and keep me awake and alert, no matter what you have to pump into me—and when this is over, I'm all yours. I'll sleep, eat right, come down for you to poke and prod me to your heart's content. After the battle is over."

"Do you think you can just keep going like this endlessly?"

"What would you have me do? C'mon, Stu…you know the situation. It'll be a damned miracle if we live long enough for any of this to matter." His eyes darted around the bridge. He'd only meant that last part for Stu's ears, but he'd blurted it out anyway.

"All right, Skipper. You know best."

"Just focus on the wounded, Stu. I'm afraid we'll have more coming your way.

"Ty…you didn't cause this fight. The crew we've lost, the ones we still might lose…it's not your fault."

"I'm up here in the captain's chair, Stu, so I'll be damned if I know who else's fault it is."

Barron was staring at the display as he spoke, watching the last of his fighters engaging the incoming enemy strike. Jamison's people were doing well, chasing down the less maneuverable bombers. But he could see some were going to get through. The strike force was too well led, its ships coming in on different vectors, from multiple directions. It wasn't pilot skill that dictated some of the bombers would get through. It was pure physics.

"Gotta go, Stu. Good luck down there, my friend."

"And to you, Ty. Godspeed."

Barron turned back toward Darrow. He had a lot of confidence in his communications officer, but he missed Travis's presence on the bridge. The two of them worked effortlessly together. She even had a way of communicating to him she thought he was wrong without letting the others know.

I need her down in engineering…she can do more to win this fight down there…

"Activate defensive batteries."

"Yes, sir." A few seconds later: "All batteries report armed and ready."

The anti-fighter lasers were *Dauntless*'s tertiary batteries, smaller and less powerful than the big primaries and secondaries. They were located all over the ship's exterior, and they were designed to target incoming fighters. They were far less effective than interceptors at taking down attackers—it was hard to target something as small as a bomber with a fixed gun—but they were a hell of a lot better than nothing.

Barron stared at the display. Three bombers, maybe four. That was what was going to get through. The squadrons had performed brilliantly, virtually wiping out the enemy escorts, and tearing into the bombing force. But even one or two attackers could hurt *Dauntless* badly if they planted their torpedoes in the right place.

He sat still, silent, watching the red dots, the four craft that remained from a strike force of thirty-seven the enemy battleship had launched. His fighters had won a great victory…and now he would see if it was enough.

"All batteries, commence firing at will."

"Yes, Captain." Darrow leaned over his borrowed workstation. "All batteries, commence firing, fire at will."

Barron sat, listening for the sounds of the point defense lasers. The primaries shook *Dauntless* hard when they fired, and the secondaries had a telltale whining sound that could be heard all the way to the bridge. But the smaller anti-fighter weapons were harder to hear. There was a cracking sound when each fired, almost like a gunshot, but it required paying close attention to hear it.

He sat and waited. There was nothing else to do. Jamison and the rest of *Dauntless*'s fighters were on the way back. Whatever the attacking ships managed to do, Barron knew none of them would get home. They'd try, but enough of *Dauntless*'s birds had the fuel remaining to take them down. He wanted to feel some sort of satisfaction about that, but he didn't. He'd watched, astonished, as the enemy squadrons advanced, heedless of losses. It was hard not to respect such steadfastness, even

in a bad cause, and it only reinforced the importance of somehow winning this battle. It was more than just his own survival,
his crew's. The suicidal bravery of the Alliance forces gave him
a glimpse of what war with them would be.

He felt anger, of course, rage at the losses his people had
suffered. But the pilots in those fighters hadn't decided to come
here, they hadn't made some devil's bargain with the Union.
Their leaders had done that. He found it hard to despise warriors who were doing their duty so magnificently.

"Yes!"

Barron snapped his head around toward Darrow then back
to the display. One of the batteries had taken out an enemy
bomber.

Three left…

But they're in range now…

Barron wondered if the enemy ships would launch at long
range, or if they'd risk running the gauntlet of *Dauntless's* defensive fire to fire point blank shots.

His question was answered almost immediately. He saw three
small dots move from the larger symbols representing the enemy
bombers. Plasma torpedoes, heading straight for *Dauntless.*

His eyes stayed fixed, waiting for the enemy ships to change
their thrust vectors, to pull off…but they didn't. They just kept
coming right at *Dauntless.*

"Incoming. All hands on alert."

"Incoming. All hands on alert." Darrow repeated the order
into the shipwide com.

Barron watched the trajectories of the torpedoes. The
defensive fire had hit one, leaving only two. But both of those
had converted to plasma now, and they were heading right for
Dauntless. There wasn't time for evasive maneuvers, not now.

The massive ship shook once…then again few seconds later.
Barron had his com unit in his hand even before the vibrations
stopped. "Atara," he snapped into the microphone. "Damage
report…how bad?"

"Not too bad, Captain. It looks like we lost hull integrity in a
big section of the cargo hold."

Barron let out a loud exhale. If his ship had to get hit somewhere, that was where he wanted it.

"The other torpedo hit farther forward, but no damage to the reactors or power transmission systems…and none to primary or secondary weapons either."

"That's good news, Atara." He let out a long sigh. If that's all the enemy fighter attack accomplished, maybe his people *did* have a chance. "You and Fritzie…" His voice trailed off ominously, his eyes fixing on the main display. The enemy fighters still hadn't pulled away…and now they were accelerating. Straight toward *Dauntless*.

Barron stared right at the display, his calm expression giving way to one of absolute horror.

"Captain?" There was concern in Travis' voice. "Ty?"

Barron flipped his com to the shipwide channel. "All gunners…target those incoming fighters. At all costs."

He saw the three fighters coming on, accelerating as they did. They were firing their lasers, but Barron wasn't worried about that. It was the realization that these fighters were making suicide runs, that they were heading toward his ship at over a thousand kilometers a second, that made his blood run cold.

He saw one of them disappear, and he felt his hand clench, a silent salute to whichever of his gunnery teams had scored the hit. But the other two were still coming on.

"All stations, brace for impact!"

He felt his body tense, and then he saw another of the ships disappear. A second passed, perhaps two, time moving slowly, eerily. Then *Dauntless* shook. His gunners had taken the second fighter out too close. The debris smashed into the battleship, ripping through its armor and tearing great holes in the hull.

But Barron knew the worst wasn't over. Not yet. The last fighter was five seconds behind the first, a brief snippet of time, but for Tyler Barron it seemed to stretch to a small eternity. He knew his guns weren't going to get this one.

He felt the impact—*Dauntless* vibrated hard, and then tumbled end over end from the force of impact. He could hear a series of sickening shrieks as his ship's innards groaned under the stress, and terrible cracks as structural supports snapped. He slammed forward into his harness, and barely held back a shout from the pain. The stabilizers were out, at least temporarily, his vessel's simulated gravity out of control. The lights on the bridge blinked twice and then went out, leaving nothing but the soft glow of the battery powered emergency lamps…and the sounds of alarm bells from deep within the ship.

Chapter Thirty-Four

"Full thrust Optiomagis. Directly toward the enemy." Kat's words came from the training, from the relentless automaton a life as the scion one of the Alliance's premier Patrician families had made her. But inside, in the part of her mind where the essence of Katrine Rigellus clung to it tenuous existence, she was troubled.

"Full thrust, Commander." Wentus's response was sharp, crisp. It was clear the officer knew *Invictus* had the advantage in the fight, that it was time to deliver the final blow. Victory, the mantra of the Alliance. Her people had been somber, watching as the last of *Invictus*'s fighters were destroyed in the relentless assault on the enemy ship. They had been subdued as their ship had careened away from the enemy, trapped on a vector their disabled engines couldn't reverse. But now they were on the verge of destroying their foe. Years of education, of propaganda had taught them what to think.

Victory. In the Alliance it was the highest of all things. It made any sacrifice worth the cost. Kat saw seventy dead pilots, faces of respected subordinates...even a few she might have called friends if they hadn't been serving under her. But she knew her people saw heroes, men and women who had achieved the highest honor, death in the cause of victory.

Junus...gone...

She had watched as her fighter corps commander died. Ellian Junus had been the most gifted pilot she'd ever known, a master tactician. Yet, he'd met his match in a one on one contest against a Confederation pilot. Her people weren't supposed to accord the Confeds any real respect as warriors, but even after she destroyed the enemy ship, she knew she would always think differently about them. She was about to do what she'd been sent to do, and her success would be the start of a new war. Part of her wanted to withdraw, to pull back to Alliance space. It would mean disgrace, the end of her career. Perhaps even a firing squad if she was found guilty of cowardice in battle. Was that too great a price to save millions of lives?

Uncle Taks...he saw some of this, and he tried to tell me...

Still, she knew that her mentor would be disgraced too if she withdrew. And for all she ached for the losses her people had suffered, for all the questions she'd begun to ask herself about the codes she'd followed blindly since childhood, she knew she didn't have it in her to rebel. She was what they had made her, and if there had been another road, the branch to it was long behind her.

"All stations...prepare for battle."

"All stations report ready, Commander."

"Arm all batteries...prepare to fire."

"Yes, Commander."

Here I go, Uncle Taks. One more victory, a new round of medals, a promotion. More glory for the Regulli. And my gift to the Alliance. Another war.

She felt the force from the thrust pushing her into her chair. *Invictus* was damaged, but most of her batteries were operational, and the reactors were at almost ninety percent. They were fragile, held together by makeshift repairs, but the enemy was in far worse shape.

She'd watched her fighters attacking, braving the danger to

fire their torpedoes. They had been trapped by the pursuing enemy interceptors. There had been no chance of escape. But it was one thing to acknowledge they were as good as dead…and another to order them to make suicide runs at the enemy vessel.

It was a testament to Alliance culture and training that she'd been able to give that order…and even more of one that the pilots had accepted it without question. She'd fought all her adult life, and she'd lost many subordinates, ordered them into desperate situations. But this was the first time she'd explicitly commanded her people to die for her. She knew she would carry the weight of it all her life, that she would never forget those few terrible moments.

"Firing range in three minutes, Commander."

"Very well."

She felt a momentary flash of anger, a reaction to Wentus's strident tone. Her exec was a gifted tactician, an accomplished warrior. She respected him, and she had some vestigial affections for him too. She considered herself fortunate to have him on *Invictus*. But now she saw him differently, and she found herself repelled at the herdlike behavior he displayed. That all of her crew did.

She knew she was as much a product of Alliance culture as they were, but as she looked around the bridge, she saw no doubt, no hesitation. Just mindless adherence to the propaganda they'd been fed their entire lives.

They are what they are. It's not their fault. And are you better, superior in some way because you question things…and then follow the same doctrine they do? Or are you worse?

"Two minutes to firing range."

"Active scanners on full. I want the damage assessments updated every thirty seconds." Her scanners had picked up the torpedo hits, and the last fighter impacting into the enemy vessel. The energy readings were massive, and the damage had to be too. But that was all conjecture. And she wasn't going to underestimate her enemy.

Not this enemy…

"All batteries are to open fire immediately upon entering

range."

"Yes, Commander."

"All damage control parties to their stations." Her crew expected to move into range and dispatch a crippled enemy. But Kat wasn't so complacent.

Even a mortally wounded animal is dangerous. More dangerous…

"Yes, Commander Rigellus."

She stared straight ahead. Kat had gone into battle many times, but she was edgy now in a way she'd never been before. She could feel it in her gut. But her devotion to duty was in control.

"Launch a spread of probes, Optiomagis. I want an intensive scan of the enemy vessel and the space in front of us."

"Yes, Commander."

Kat could tell Wentus thought her caution was excessive. But right now, she didn't give a shit what he thought.

* * *

"We had to handle it manually, sir, but we got it done. All units are away, and we got close to the deployment plan. At least, I think we did."

Barron had his hand on the earpiece of his headset. "I don't know how you did it, Atara, but it's just one more reason I'm fortunate to have you as my exec."

"I wouldn't trade it for any posting in the fleet, sir." A short pause. "We did suffer two casualties, Captain. Specialists Linmore and Halston. The bulkheads down here are badly stressed, and one of them gave out. They were both blown into space before we could get to them." He could hear the pain in Travis's voice. He knew she blamed herself for the dead crewmen.

"Atara…" He wanted to comfort her, but he didn't know what to say. She wasn't at fault, not by any reasonable measure. But she would take the responsibility no matter what he said to her. "You did well," he finally added, wishing he had something better to say.

"Thank you, sir." She sighed softly. "With your permission, I'll go check on Commander Fritz. She's working on the reactors."

"I don't need to tell you how critical her success is, Atara. Whatever Fritzie needs, give it to her. Our survival is in her hands now."

"Yes, Captain. Travis out."

The last fighter had hit *Dauntless* hard, slamming into the ship's hull at enormous velocity. Much of the kinetic energy transformed into heat, melting and buckling whole sections of the hull. Chunks of shattered debris drove deeply into *Dauntless*'s guts, ripping through deck after deck, crushing systems and equipment...killing crew.

Barron knew that could have been the end, that it still could be. But as bad as the damage was, it could have been far worse. Hundreds of kilometers of cable, piping, conduits, and cooling lines had been severed, chopped up into half-melted scrap. But the reactor cores themselves were intact, and the accelerator tubes for the primaries were unaffected. *Dauntless* was out of action, dead in space with both reactors scragged. But they were repairable. If there was time.

"Captain, we're picking up energy readings from the enemy ship." Darrow turned to look over at the captain's station, and Barron could see the horror in his eyes. "They're accelerating, sir. Directly toward us."

Damn...if we had an hour. Even half an hour...

"Projected time until enemy enters firing range?"

"Four minutes, Captain."

Barron reached up and tapped the side of his headset, toggling up Fritz's direct line. "Fritzie, I need reactor power in two minutes or we're all dead." It was blunt, brutally so, but there wasn't time for anything else.

"I might be able to get one of the reactions started, but there are bound to be leaks everywhere. We'll most likely flood half the ship with radiation."

"Do it."

"Sir, a cold start like that has a lot of risks. It could scrag the reactor permanently. It could blow us up."

"Fritzie…do it." Barron's voice was firm, dripping with confidence. But he suspected Fritz saw right through him, that she knew it was all pure bullshit.

"Yes, sir."

He heard her shouting orders over the still-open channel. Then he flipped to the shipwide line. "Attention all personnel. We are about to do an emergency reactor restart. We are likely to experience radiation leakage in multiple locations. Pay attention to your rad detectors. Abandon and seal off all non-essential compartments that are affected." He paused for a moment then added, "It is my honor to be your commander. I won't lie to you. We're in a tough spot. But if we pull together, if every man and woman does his best, I have no doubt we will prevail. Now, I need everything each of you has to give."

He cut the line, slumping back in his chair. He didn't like lying to his crew, but he knew that was what they needed from him now. And much of what he said was the truth. He did believe his crew was the best in the Confederation. But he still had doubts about the outcome of the battle. He could rally his crew, but he couldn't fool himself. The odds were long. Still, none of that mattered. He was a Barron…and no matter what he was facing, he was determined to make that mean something.

Are you with me, Granddad? Because I sure could use your help now…

"Two minutes, thirty seconds to firing range."

Barron took a deep breath. "Fritzie…now…we're out of time."

"Just a few more seconds, sir."

Barron sat motionless. The bridge was silent. It seemed as though no one even drew a breath.

The seconds passed, slowly, torturously. Then: "Restarting reactor A."

Barron sucked in a deep breath. In a few seconds his ship would have power. Or he would know the battle was truly over.

He stared around the bridge, waiting. And then the main bridge lights came on. His eyes darted to his screen, to the power level monitors. Reactor A showed as operational, producing power at eighty-eight percent.

"Fritzie, you're a sorcerer, do you know that?" His eyes were still on the display, watching as the radiation reports scrolled down the screen. There were leaks, a lot of them. In the compartments of his ship, from engineering to weapons control to the AI core, his people were at their posts, ignoring nearly lethal concentrations of radiation. He was overwhelmed, with pride in the men and women he commanded, and with sadness, bitterness that such fine officers and spacers of the Confederation were slowly dying, even as they executed his commands.

Just win the fight…Stu and his people can treat the radiation cases…

"Two minutes to firing range, sir."

"All available power to engines, Lieutenant. Maximum thrust, directly away from the enemy."

"Maximum thrust, Captain…now."

Dauntless shook wildly, and Barron felt the pressure of the acceleration pushing him back into his chair for a few seconds before the partially-functioning dampeners kicked in and brought some relief.

He stared down at the display, his eyes darting back and forth between the enemy ship and *Dauntless*. There was nothing in between, no icons, no symbols. His scanners weren't picking up a thing. But he knew they were there. Ninety-four fusion mines, every one of them launched into space by his first officer and a crew of spacers. By hand. And every one of them equipped with stealth technology.

Chapter Thirty-Five

CFS Dauntless
Krillus Asteroid Belt
40,000,000 kilometers from Santis, Krillus IV
Year 58 (307 AC)

"They're running, Commander." Wentus said, his voice taking on a feral tone. "They're accelerating directly away from us."

"Very well, Commander." Kat sat still, devoid of the excitement that seemed to be taking her crew. They viewed an attempt at escape as cowardice, as a sign the enemy was beaten. She wasn't so sure. Her gut was screaming, telling her to let her adversary go, that she could hold Santis without destroying the battered enemy battleship. But her orders were clear.

Still, this enemy commander was no coward. He was no fool either. If he'd wanted to run, he'd had plenty of time to do it.

What is he up to?

"Status of probes?"

"Scanning data unchanged, Commander. Significant outer hull damage to enemy vessel. No other contacts."

Kat paused for a few seconds. Something was wrong, she could feel it. But her orders left her no choice.

"All power to the reactors, Optiomagis." Her engines were still badly damaged. She had no more than half *Invictus*'s normal thrust available. But the enemy ship was damaged also, its own acceleration far below normal. She had enough thrust to close, if she moved now. She couldn't let her prey get a head start. It was time to finish this.

"Advise engineering we need the maximum thrust they can give us." She paused. "Suspend all safeties. Full power to the engines."

"Full power to the engines, Commander."

Kat tried to keep the frown from her face as she caught Wentus's tone, his arrogant of approval at her aggressive command. She wondered if the easy victory her first officer expected would materialize. Or if, as her instincts were telling her, *Invictus* still faced a serious fight.

She leaned back as she felt the force of the acceleration. One way or another, soon she would know…

* * *

"The enemy vessel is accelerating, sir. They are matching out vector and pursuing."

Barron sat in the center of *Dauntless*'s bridge, bolt upright, unmoving. He'd tried to appear relaxed, calm for his crew, the model of the unflappable captain…but it had proven to be too much of a deception to maintain. His crew needed to see him focused and in control. But none of them were stupid enough to think he was calm.

"Very well, Lieutenant. Continue course and thrust levels."

Barron's com unit buzzed. It was Fritz.

"What is it, Fritzie?"

"I've got reactor B ready to restart. I doubt I can get it much past fifty percent output, at least at first. But it's enough to give you more thrust than the enemy has now."

Escape. Fritz was offering him a chance to get his battered ship away from the enemy. He shook his head. Running wasn't an option. But looking like he was running…

"Negative, Fritzie." He didn't want to risk his energy readings spiking, scaring off the enemy. He needed them to pursue. "Get everything ready…but don't restart. Not until I give the order."

"Yes, sir." Fritz's voice was non-committal. Like many ship's engineers, she tended not to see things beyond the confines of her engines and reactors. Tactics was the province of the captain, and hers was to see he had the technology and equipment he needed ready.

"How about the primaries?" Any fix to *Dauntless*'s main guns was likely to be fragile and short-lived. But if things went according to plan, even one good shot could be the difference between victory and defeat.

"Lieutenant Carson's team is working on them now, sir. Commander Travis is there too. They're replacing power conduits, but the accelerators themselves appear intact. We should be able to get them online in the next twenty minutes, sir. Though I can't promise how long the repairs will hold."

"Thanks, Fritzie. And good job getting the reactor ready so quickly." He was genuinely surprised at how speedily her people had finished the repairs. He suspected it was a patchwork of temporary fixes, but if Fritzie said the reactor would restart, Barron had no doubt that it would restart.

"Thank you, sir."

"Very well…carry on. Barron ou…wait, Fritzie…" Barron was deep in thought. He'd been trying to put himself in his enemy's head, wondering what he would do if the roles were reversed.

Alliance culture is aggressive, warlike, so they won't retreat. Probably not at all, but certainly not when they think they have the edge…

"Fritzie, I want you to eject some reaction mass…and some radioactives too."

"Sir?"

"I want you to release some fuel into space. Not a lot, maybe ten percent of what we've got left. And I want some wastes from the reactor ejected too. And push reactor A a little harder. Get me five percent more thrust."

"Ah…yes, sir." A short pause then understanding dawned. "Yes, sir! I'll have it done immediately."

"Carry on. Barron out."

He turned and looked at the display, his eyes focusing on the small red oval moving steadily closer to *Dauntless*.

It's you and me…a game of chess for the lives of our crew. No, not chess. Poker. And I'm raising you now. Am I bluffing? Or do I have a hand after all? It's your move…

Barron sat stone still, his eyes unmoving, locked on the enemy ship. He realized he didn't have the answer to his own question. Was he bluffing? Or would he have what he needed to win?

He wouldn't know, not until the very end.

* * *

"More readings, Commander. The enemy ship is leaking reaction mass. We're also getting clouds of radioactive materials." Wentus sounded like a predator, hot on the heels of its wounded and bleeding prey.

"Very well, Commander." The readings suggested the Confederation ship was crippled, bleeding air and fluids. That should have made her feel more confident, but it didn't. She didn't trust her adversary. He was smart, she was sure of that, in many ways, a match for her. Was he really trapped, on the verge of destruction? Or…"

"Commander, we're getting strange data from the probes… intermittent readings, almost like shadows…"

"Cut forward thrust!" Then, half a second later, "Now! Bring us around one hundred eighty degrees and decelerate at full."

Wentus looked stunned, but the officer knew how to obey orders, and Kat's tone had been deadly serious. "Cutting thrust, Commander."

Kat felt the weightlessness of free-fall for an instant before the ship's compensators reacted to the change and restored some semblance of artificial gravity to the bridge.

"Re-orienting now, Commander. Commencing full deceleration."

Kat leaned back as she again felt the pressure of maximum thrust. It forced the breath from her lungs before, once again, her ship's dampeners intervened, absorbing much of the direct force.

"Probe data directly to my screen."

"Yes, Commander."

Kat watched as the reports came streaming in. It was just as Wentus had reported. Vague contacts slipping in and out. No real data, just a series of intermittent presences.

Stealth tech…something out there is cloaked.

The Alliance was behind the Confederation in such technologies, there was little question of that. She'd run into stealth tech before, fighting against the Unaligned Systems. It was expensive and complex, and…

What would they be trying to hide out there?

"Optiomagis, I want more thrust, now. Increase reactor output, regardless of risk."

"Y…yes, Commander." Wentus repeated her commands, clearly unnerved by her obvious concern.

"And I want those probes on maximum power. Burn them out, but get me a better look at what's out there."

"Yes, Commander."

Kat watched on the screen as the shadowy images stabilized…and more appeared. Dozens, perhaps a hundred. She felt a cold feeling in her gut, and she fought back a wave of fear.

Mines.

"Activate all defensive batteries! Target those objects. Now!"

"Yes, Commander."

"Evasive maneuvers. Steer us clear."

But she knew *Invictus's* velocity was too great. She'd accelerated at full power to close with the enemy, and now her momentum was taking her right into the minefield ahead.

She nodded slowly as she watched her vessel moving on the display, getting closer to the mines with each passing second. And she knew now she was facing a commander who was her true match, a captain who could defeat her. Who might very well be on the verge of defeating her right now.

* * *

Barron watched the display, along with everyone else on *Dauntless*'s bridge. The enemy ship was moving right into the spread of mines Commander Travis and her people had positioned along the line of retreat. Now Barron would see if his tactics had worked, or if the enemy would manage to escape from the trap he'd set.

"They're decelerating, sir. From the energy readings, I'd guess they're pouring everything they can into it."

It won't be enough...

Barron's eyes darted to his own screen, confirming the enemy velocity readings. The Alliance ship would have been hard pressed to escape the minefield with full thrust, but with its damaged engines, there was no chance.

"Picking up laser fire, sir."

Of course, they can't escape, so they'll try to pick off the nearby mines. It's what I'd do.

Barron felt the tension building in his gut. It wasn't easy to target mines, but it wasn't impossible. The enemy had walked into his trap, but they could still get out unscathed. A hundred mines was all he'd had, and his makeshift minefield was far less dense than he'd have liked.

Still, it will be hard for them to get them all...

He pushed the concern from his mind. If the enemy got through unscathed, the battle was over. His ship was simply too damaged relative to its adversary. If he couldn't even the odds, his people would still fight like hell, but they would lose.

"Commander Travis..." He tapped his headset, opening the line to his first officer. "Status report?"

"We're on it, Captain. It's a mess of half-assed fixes and patchwork, but I think it will work." The first officer paused for a few seconds. Then she added, "At least I hope it will."

"Very reassuring, Atara."

"I don't lie to you, sir. We're looking at a coin toss...and that's the truth."

"Atara..." He was about to urge her to do anything she

could, but of all the people he knew who didn't need to be told that, Atara Travis was at the head of the list. "Very well… understood."

He cut the line and stared straight ahead, watching the enemy ship enter the minefield, and reminding himself to breathe every so often.

* * *

"Another hit, Commander." Wentus was staring down at his scope, reporting every time *Invictus's* defensive batteries destroyed one of the mines. Kat's gunners had picked off a dozen of the closest contacts, more than she'd dared to hope for. But she was far from sure it would be enough.

"Very well, Optiomagis. All batteries are to maintain maximum fire."

She glanced down at the scanning reports on her screen. The mines were big, probably multiple warhead devices that would send out short-ranged sprint missiles when a target ship moved close enough to trigger them. And *Invictus* was heading right into a thick cluster of them. Her ship was decelerating, trying to pull back, but Kat had already done the calculations. Her engine output just wasn't enough to bring the giant vessel to a halt. Not before it plunged through the heart of the minefield.

"Energy readings, Commander…from multiple contacts."

"Prepare for evasive maneuvers." There was no way to meaningfully change *Invictus's* vector, but even a slight blast of thrust to the side could evade an incoming missile.

"Evasive maneuvers."

Time passed, feeling like an eternity, though Kat realized it had just been a few seconds. Her eyes were on the display, watching *Invictus* move through a cluster of small red circles… watching as half a dozen of the icons disappeared, each of them replaced by eight small dots. All moving toward her ship.

"Mines activating, Commander." Wentus was just reporting what she already knew. "Multiple objects inbound."

Warheads.

Damn.

"Cut forward thrust now! Prepare to implement full evasive maneuvers!"

"Yes, Commander." All of the earlier arrogance was gone from Wentus's voice. "Scanners confirm approximately thirty-eight sprint-mode missiles incoming. Gunnery stations transferring targeting to approaching warheads."

Kat just sat at her station, watching as her crew went about their duties. She was proud of them, of their efficiency and courage. They were scared now, all the more so because just a few moments before they'd expected certain victory, not a fight for their lives. Now the only question was a stark one: could they shoot down enough of the enemy mines to prevent *Invictus* from being crippled or destroyed?

Even if they did, she wasn't ready to discount this Confederation captain. He was out there, waiting. He'd baited her into the minefield, and now she wondered if his ship was as crippled as her scanners led her to believe.

Her eyes settled on the display, watching as her gunners desperately targeted the incoming missiles. They'd taken down ten so far, which was outstanding performance, but far from enough.

"Evasive maneuvers…now."

"Initiating evasive maneuvers, Commander."

Invictus lurched hard as it swung around on its positioning jets, angling the main engines and blasting hard at a sharp angle from its current vector. She could see the ship's course shift, almost imperceptibly, and as it did, clusters of missiles zipped past. The warheads were sprint missiles. They aimed right at their target and accelerated hard. But once they went past the target, they were expended. They weren't guided units like the missiles the fighter used. There was both advantage and disadvantage in that. The sprint units were able to attain velocities far beyond those available to their guided cousins.

"Bring us to 320-111-012…full thrust." Kat was barking out orders, thrust angles as she stared at the screen, watching the missiles coming at her ship. She suspected the enemy weapons were hyper-nukes, which meant they didn't need to score a direct hit to damage *Invictus*. The weapons were designed to get as close as possible and detonate, blasting the target with heat and radiation.

Kat could feel wetness on her back. Sweat. Fear. She had done well, avoided perhaps half the incoming warheads. But now she was bracketed, clouds of missiles coming in from three directions.

"Bring us about! 233/210/045…now!"

But she was too late this time. She saw the dots on the scanner moving closer, even before Wentus could confirm her order. And then the alarms went off.

"Multiple nuclear explosions, Commander. Massive radiation levels in all outer compartments. Hull breaches in sections Green-7 though Red-9."

The bridge lights dimmed, and then they went out, leaving nothing but the emergency lamps illuminating her ship's control center.

"More detonations, Commander. Overloads on all power transmission lines. Engineering reports significant damage to reactors. Engines down to twenty-four percent output. Crew casualties severe in all affected areas…"

Kat sat and listened to the seemingly unending damage report. She'd walked into a trap, and she'd paid the price…and her people with her.

"Scanners?" she snapped.

"Still operational, Commander."

"Concentrate an active scan on the enemy vessel. Any aspect change?" She could already feel the answer in her gut.

"Yes, Commander. They are decelerating…" He turned and looked back at Kat. "Commander, their thrust is approximately fifty percent higher than previously."

Kat stared at Wentus, not a hint of surprise on her face. "I need power transmission back online, Optiomagis. And weapons. All other repairs are zero priority now. We need as many guns online as we can get, and the power to fire them."

She stared off across the bridge as her first officer confirmed and relayed her orders.

You tricked me…as I tricked you earlier at the transwarp link. Now, we're even, more or less. But the fight isn't over. Not yet, it isn't…

Chapter Thirty-Six

CFS Dauntless
Krillus Asteroid Belt
40, 500,000 kilometers from Santis, Krillus IV
307 AC

"Cut all thrust. Divert power to gunnery stations." Barron stared forward, snapping out commands. This was the final struggle. The minefield had given his people a chance, equalized the field. But they still faced a dangerous enemy. And there was no room for error now. Not if any of them wanted to live.

"Thrust at zero, Captain. All weapons stations report ready to go."

"Very well, Lieutenant. Active scanners on full...feed all targeting data directly to the gunnery stations." There was no reason not to pound away with active scanners now. Stealth no longer had a role in this battle. It was a knife fight now...brutal, close-ranged, to the death.

"All scanners on full, sir. The enemy vessel's vector is directly toward us. No thrust detected."

Barron nodded. His opponent was acting just as he would have done. Just as he was doing. The two battleships were crawling toward each other, their velocities low, their thrust zero. There was no elegance here, no fancy maneuvering. Both ships were too battered for that. This would be an exchange of gunnery, pure and simple. A pounding match until one combatant gave out.

Barron had sat on *Dauntless's* almost silent bridge, watching along with his officers as their enemy approached the spread of fusion mines they had left behind. The mines had outdated stealth systems, but with no hard data on Alliance scanning capabilities, neither Barron nor any of his crew had known what to expect. Would they detect the mines in time?

The bridge had erupted into cheers when the first of mines had gotten close enough to detonate. Over the next few minutes, Barron's people had watched as six sprint missiles closed to detonation range. None actually struck the enemy ship—a direct hit was an extremely rare event that might have vaporized even a massive battleship. But several had gotten close enough to do serious damage.

Enough, hopefully, to put us on equal playing fields...

Barron wasn't sure, but his gut told him the fight had become a match of equals.

He flipped his com unit to the shipwide channel. "This is the captain. We are about to enter combat range. I won't sugarcoat this. We're in a fight for our lives, a battle to the death. We must stop this enemy. Defeat is not an option. I've already told you how proud I am to lead a group of men and women like you, and there are no spacers anywhere I would rather have at my side during this fiery trial. Let us face battle again, my friends, and together and united, we will prevail."

He leaned back, looking around the bridge. *Dauntless* had a better chance than before, thanks to the minefield...but the cold reality was still there. His fate—the fates of all his people, and perhaps the Confederation as well—rested on the tenacity and skills of his chief engineer and her band of gifted technicians.

"Fritzie," he said, after tapping the com unit. "What's the status down there?"

"We got two more secondaries functional, sir. Don't ask me how. Try to use the port broadside. You've got fifty percent more firepower there."

Barron felt a rush of surprise. He'd thought most of the

damaged secondaries were melted rubble, unrepairable this side
of a major base. He wasn't sure what kind of wizardry his engineer had managed, but he was grateful for it. And two guns on
the same side, no less.

But that wasn't what he most wanted to know.

"Nice work, Fritzie, but what about…"

"The primaries are online too."

Barron almost shouted out with joy. "Fritzie, you are a wonder!" But his excitement was somewhat contained. He'd heard
that tone before. There was a giant 'but' there.

"Captain, they're hanging by a thread. And I can't promise
you more than one shot. With the shape the things are in and the
power levels that go though there…"

"One shot is a lot better than none, Fritzie. Maybe we'll get
lucky."

"I wouldn't count on it, sir. Which means you've got a choice.
Take a shot—possibly the only one—at long range, before their
lasers can fire on us…or hold for a crippling blow at close range,
and risk taking damage and maybe losing the guns again before
you shoot."

Barron sighed softly. He knew his engineer was right. He
had a choice to make, and no more than a few minutes to make
it. A close range hit from the accelerators could be decisive. It
could—probably would—be the battle. A longer ranged shot
would be helpful, but far less decisive. But if he held fire and the
guns were damaged again…

"All right, Fritzie…you and your people did your jobs. Now
it's time for me to do mine."

He cut the com line. He had no idea what he was going to
do.

* * *

"Primary batteries, open fire." Kat's voice was stone cold.
She was nervous, worried about her opponent, about what he
might do. But she was the matriarch of the Regulli, and she
knew what she had to do.

"Primary batteries, open fire."

Wentus repeated her command, relaying it to the gunnery teams.

Kat thought of her gun crews, located throughout the ship. Alliance designs tended to place gunners in or near their turrets. It reduced the possibility that damaged circuits or communications lines would silence otherwise functional batteries. It also ramped up casualties among gunnery crew, who were located right at the surface of the ship instead of in some well-protected control center. But losses weren't an issue, at least not those suffered in victory. Palatians who died in the cause of a battle won were revered, their families honored and cared for. And the Alliance had seen little else but victory in it sixty years of conquest.

Kat listened to the familiar sounds of her main guns firing, ignoring the flickering of the lights as the guns greedily drew every watt *Invictus's* reactor could feed them. She had considered different stratagems, trickery and deceit to lure her enemy into making a mistake. But she'd developed too much respect for this Confederation captain to assume he'd fall for any ploy she might attempt. She realized this was a struggle between two veterans, too strong warriors. It seemed counterintuitive, but she realized there was nothing for two such capable commanders to do now but close to point blank range and blast away at each other. The hardness of their armored hulls, the toughness of their crews, the industry of their engineers and damage control teams… those would be the deciding factors here.

"Scanners report two hits, Commander." A few seconds passed. "A third hit!"

"Very well, Optiomagis…all stations continue maximum rate of fire." Kat was grateful for the early hits—the enemy hadn't even opened fire yet— but she knew the range was still long, that her beams were hitting with less than fifteen percent of the power they would have at fifty thousand kilometers.

Fifty thousand klicks. Where this battle will be decided…

* * *

"We've got wounded backed up out into the corridors, Ty. The aid stations are overloaded too. We're taking a hell of a pounding. I sure hope you know what you're doing up there."

"Just keep it together down there, Stu. You worry about your job, and I'll worry about mine." Barron felt a flash of anger at his friend's choice of words. He knew *Dauntless's* chief surgeon hadn't meant anything by his comments, save for his doctor's hatred of anything that tended to tear up men and women and leave them wrecked and bleeding.

Barron hated thinking of his people going through that too, but he understood well enough, this was war. He didn't like it any more than Weldon, but he'd been raised his whole life to serve a warrior's posting.

"How are you holding it together, Ty? You're just a man, remember…whoever your grandfather was. You keep taking those stims and pushing yourself, you'll drop dead right on the bridge."

"I'll keep that in mind, Stu, but there's not much alternative now. I've…" His eyes caught Darrow's hand, waving to him. "Gotta go, Stu. Do your best down there."

He cut the line and looked over at the communications officer.

"Secondaries will be in range in thirty seconds, sir."

"All batteries open fire as soon as we're within the envelope. Fire at will, maximum intensity."

"Yes, sir…max…"

Dauntless shook hard, another hit from the enemy primaries. Barron looked down at his screen, his eyes skimming the damage reports coming in. It had been surprisingly light, considering the quality of the enemy's gunnery, but Barron knew his ship was fragile now, dozens of systems patched together in chaotic fashion. Any hit could be the one that crippled something vital. That lost the battle.

"Maximum fire, all batteries," Darrow repeated the command. A few seconds later, Barron felt the vibrations under his feet, heard the telltale whine of *Dauntless's* lasers.

Now, at least, it was a two-way fight. And he'd stack his gunners up against any that drew breath, vaunted Alliance warriors or not.

* * *

"Another hit, Commander. Battery seven is out of action." A short pause. "It appears the entire crew was killed."

Kat knew she wasn't supposed to worry about casualties, only victory. But whoever had come up with that mantra either hadn't led men and women into battle…or was a monster. The gunners in battery seven had been veterans from *Vindictus*, and they'd served with her for years. Now they were dead, probably blown to unrecognizable bits, if they hadn't been outright incinerated.

"Carry on, Optiomagis." It seemed like a lame response, but what else was there to say? The gunners of battery seven weren't the last of her people who would die in this fight. The enemy's lasers had opened fire, and half a dozen direct hits had slammed into *Invictus*. Her people had repaid the enemy in kind…no, they'd given more than they'd gotten. But the enemy gunners knew their business too, and with each hit, *Invictus* lost more power, more crew. She longed for a better strategy, something more elegant, less brutal and damaging. But there was nothing. Nothing but to continue to close.

"I want updated damage assessments. Full power to the scanners."

"Yes, Commander." Wentus leaned over the controls for a few seconds. "Commander, the scanner suite is badly damaged. Thirty percent is the best we can manage."

"Then get me thirty percent…and do it now!"

She scolded herself for letting her tension show in her tone. She did want to know what damage the enemy ship had sustained from *Invictus*'s fire, but there was one thing in particular she was concerned about. The enemy's main guns. Her engineers had assured her it was exceedingly unlikely the particle accelerators could be repaired so quickly in the field…or at all. But she wasn't going to underestimate the ship and crew facing

her. And the unintended consequence of the Alliance's culture
of superiority was doing just that. She'd learned that the hard
way, but she doubted many of her people had. Not yet.

*You would have fired those guns already if you had them, wouldn't you?
Or are you holding back, waiting until we're in point blank range?*

She knew what Alliance protocol demanded. What her crew
expected. But she was wary of this enemy…

"Reverse thrust now."

"Commander, repeat?"

"I said reverse thrust now. Bring us to a dead stop."

Wentus hesitated. "Commander, we have them…"

"I said reverse thrust, Optiomagis. Now obey my orders!"

"Yes, Commander."

She could hear the disapproval in Wentus's voice. But she
didn't give a shit.

She felt the force of deceleration slam into her, watched on
her screen as *Invictus*'s already slow velocity dropped steadily.

She had to be sure.

* * *

"What?"

"They're decelerating, sir. It looks like they're coming to a
dead halt."

Barron felt his hand clench into a fist. He caught himself just
before he slammed it down on the armrest of his chair.

Who the hell are you? How do you read my mind?

He'd known the enemy commander was good, since the
moment he'd fallen into the trap set for him at the transwarp
link. But there was only one reason for the enemy ship to stop
before closing. Fear of his main guns.

Damn.

It was his last ploy, the one tactic he could devise that offered
hope of victory…but if his enemy was too suspicious to close…

He slapped his hand on the com unit. "Fritzie, are the primaries still online?"

"Yes, Captain…but they're on the brink. The next hit could

be the one that knocks them out."

Barron felt the frustration building. He had to do something. He had to pull his enemy into short range.

Accelerate? Close with them?

No, that will only make it look more likely I'm trying to get close for a shot with the primaries. This captain will be looking for that…they'll only pull back, and they have the edge in a longer-ranged exchange.

He sat quietly for a few seconds, deep in thought. He couldn't chase the enemy. He needed them to close.

From what little intel he had on the Alliance, this seemed unlike one of their tactics. They were aggressive, wildly, desperately so.

So why the caution now?

"Fritzie, what shape is beta bay in now?"

"Beta bay? It's a wreck, sir. We got the fires out and capped the fuel line leaks, but then we just sealed it off. Alpha bay's rough too, but it's an order of magnitude better. And it's more than enough to retrieve the fighters we've got left out there, if…"

"Can you reopen some of those leaks, Fritzie…get some fires going again?"

"What? Captain, I don't…"

"Just trust me, Fritzie…and answer my question. Can we blow out the bay and control the spread of the damage to vital systems?"

"You want a small series of fires? A controlled blowout?"

"I want a massive explosion, Fritzie…one that will make anyone watching think *Dauntless* is critical."

"She's damned near critical as it is, sir…" There was a pause, and then her tone changed. "But I think I understand what you want now, sir."

"Can you do it?"

"Yes, Captain. I can do it."

"In six minutes…because that's all we've got."

There was a momentary silence. Then: "Yes, sir. Six minutes."

Barron stared at the display, at the symbol representing the enemy ship.

You won't be easily fooled...

"Fritzie, I'm going to need you to shut down both reactors when you blow out the bay." Barron paused again. "And then I'm going to need crash restarts of both of them."

"You're asking for miracles, Captain."

"It's a good thing I've got a miracle worker down there, then...isn't it? Can you manage it?"

Fritz sighed hard, but then she said, "Probably...but you're taking a hell of a risk, sir. A hundred things could go wrong."

"It's a terrible risk just being here, Fritzie. Get ready...you've only got a little over five and a half minutes left..."

Chapter Thirty-Seven

"Let's go. Move it!" Fritz was standing next to a heavy bulkhead, waving to Sam Carson and Walt billings. The two engineers were running down the corridor, carrying heavy sacks of tools.

"Drop the kits…just run!"

Carson let go of the sack, and it hit the ground with a loud crash. He pushed harder, trying to move his legs faster, his eyes on the tiny hatch ahead. He and Billings were the last of the team to evacuate the bay. They'd set the thing to blow, hopefully a controlled explosion that would look a hell of a lot worse outside than it was inside. But they'd only had a couple minutes, not nearly enough to do the job right. Any number of thinks could go wrong. The blast could fail to occur…or it could rip through the containment they'd set up, bring massive damage to *Dauntless*'s other sections, doing the enemy's job for them.

Either way, we'll know in twenty seconds…

He pushed even harder. He didn't think Captain Barron would blow the bay with his engineers still in there, but he knew Commander Fritz would slam the hatch shut and do just that if

321

the captain ordered it. He suspected she'd hate herself for it…
but she'd do it.

Carson was a combat spacer, and he'd always known he could
face the danger of battle. But now, running for that hatch, he
thought of Lise, of never seeing his newborn son. He'd always
managed his fear before, keeping it in its place. But he could
feel his heart pounding in his ears now. Images of his wife's
face when they told her he was dead. His son, a toddler, a child,
growing to adulthood, all without him there.

He lunged forward, putting the last of his strength into one
great burst. "C'mon, Walt. Move your ass." Billings was on his
tail, clearly just as motivated.

Carson dove forward through the hatch, his comrade right
on his heels. His knees hit the hard metal floor hard, pain radiat-
ing up his leg. Then he fell the rest of the way, throwing his arms
out to cushion the blow. But he was through. And he heard the
hatch slam shut…and a few second later, a loud blast.

Dauntless shook wildly, and Carson was slammed into the
wall, his already sore wrist getting pinned under his body, twisted
hard. There was pain, and fear the hatch wouldn't hold, that it—
or one of the dozen other spots that could give way— would fail
and spread devastation through *Dauntless*.

He turned over on his side, holding up his savaged wrist,
looking up at Fritz. She was on the com, ordering the reactor
shutdown. He knew she was thinking the same thing he was,
hoping the bulkheads around the bay would hold.

And hoping Captain Barron's insane plan would work…

* * *

"Massive explosions, Commander," Wentus reported. "We're
picking up large volumes of gas and fluids blasted into space."

Everyone on *Invictus's* bridge was excited. Everyone except
the battleship's commander. She was guarded, cautiously optimistic, perhaps, but no more. She was still reluctant to close,
though she knew the scanner readings would make that more
difficult. Certainly, doctrine was clear. Any failure to close now

would be viewed as gross dereliction of duty, of cowardice.

"Continue scans, Optiomagis. And maintain fire."

"Commander, we…yes, Commander."

Not yet…

The enemy ship was still moving forward, but its engines appeared to be offline. There was no thrust, just a continuing vector, modified now by the force from the explosion. The Confederation ship looked dead in space.

And if it is…

Kat knew her duty, she knew she had no choice. But she was delaying, continuing the medium range gunnery duel. Except it wasn't a duel anymore. The enemy fire had ceased entirely. She could stay where she was, even accelerate away from the enemy, maintain her range and slowly blow her target apart. But that would take longer, perhaps long enough for the enemy to manage some last ditch repairs.

"Commander, scanners report zero energy readings. The enemy's reactors are all down."

She felt what little choice she had driven away by Wentus's words. The way was the way. She was an Alliance officer…and that came before everything.

"Very well, Optiomagis. Initiate one-quarter thrust, directly toward the enemy." One-quarter was the best *Invictus* could manage while firing its batteries at full strength. And she wasn't going to stop firing, not for an instant. Not until that ship was nothing but superheated plasma.

"One-quarter thrust, Commander. Toward the enemy."

Kat sat in her chair, looking forward. She felt the imperative she'd been bred and raised to feel. The need for victory. But part of her hated to destroy such a worthy foe, and she remembered her earlier thoughts, and Commander Vennius's words…of the Confederation as an ally and not an enemy.

But that was not the way fate had chosen for things, and it wasn't for her to question orders. She could feel regret, wonder what might have been…but no more than that. The way was the way.

"All weapons, continue maximum fire."

* * *

Barron sat in the dim light of the bridge, the only illumination coming from the battery-powered emergency lights. The reactors were both down, though not because of battle damage, as it appeared to anyone watching. *Dauntless* was playing dead, floating powerless in space, her guns silent. It was a gamble, a desperate one. But it was their best chance at victory.

The ship shook again, the sounds of tortured structural elements twisting and groaning in the depths of the vessel. Barron knew *Dauntless* couldn't take much more pounding. Any hit could knock out the carefully, but tenuously repaired primary guns. That would be the end. The silence of Barron's secondaries sacrificed any other chances the Confederation vessel had of winning the fight, however remote they might have been. If Fritz and her people couldn't flash restart the reactors, they would all die. If the primaries were damaged again, they would die. Barron had bet all their lives on one desperate gamble.

"Enemy is accelerating again, Captain. Directly toward us."

Barron inhaled deeply, feeling like he hadn't taken a breath in hours. The enemy had just sat there for what had seemed like an eternity, though he knew it had been no more than a minute. He'd almost resigned himself to despair, believing his adversary had refused to take the bait. But now the enemy was coming. Just as he'd planned…and his stomach shriveled into a knot.

"Primary crews stand by."

"Primary crews ready, Captain."

He tapped the com. "Ready, Fritzie?"

"We're ready, sir." The voice on the com sounded anything but.

"Lieutenant Darrow, range."

"Ninety thousand kilometers. Velocity, two hundred kilometers per second."

"Fritzie, how long to start up the reactors?"

"A minute, Captain. If we get lucky."

I should wait…I'd love to get the shot off at fifty thousand…but I can't cut it that close…

"All right, Fritzie. Begin restart procedure. All power directly to the primaries."

"Yes, sir."

The big guns would take about forty seconds to charge up. That meant *Dauntless* had to endure almost two minutes more pounding before he could fire.

C'mon, old girl…you can do it…

"Fuck!" Barron heard Fritzie's voice through the headset. She wasn't talking to him, but she was upset. He'd heard the engineer swear before—when provoked she had a vocabulary that would shame a career crew chief. But he'd never heard her like this. "Fuck, fuck, fuck…get up there, try the main bypass." A pause. "Fuck, fuck, fuck…"

"Fritzie!" Barron raised his voice, not in anger but to get his engineer's attention.

"Sir, we've got some kind of burnout in reactor A's control system…and I've got the two units slaved together for rapid restart. If we can't get A going, it will take at least twenty minutes to disconnect the controls and fire up B alone."

Damn…you knew something could go wrong. Probably would go wrong…

"Do what you can, Fritzie."

"On it, sir."

Barron stared at the display, a rough 2D image replacing the power-hungry 3D holographic projection. The enemy ship was coming straight for them, and *Dauntless* was helpless, her tortured hill absorbing hit after hit.

"Fritzie…"

* * *

"Billings, I want a dozen more bots in there, right now!"

Fritz was standing outside the reaction chamber, shouting orders to the cluster of engineers around her. Everyone there was well aware they had to get the reactor fixed and online within minutes. Or they would all die. Everyone on *Dauntless* would die.

"The bots aren't going to get it done, Commander." Billings was staring across the engineering space, his eyes locked on Fritz's. "It's a level two overload, and there's no time to fix it. We need to work a quick bypass. It's the only way." Walt Billings was a jovial sort in less stressful moments, a jokester not above the occasional prank on one of his comrades. His reputation as a bit of a clown tended to obscure his considerable skill as an engineer. But now, in the middle of the crisis, he was focused, serious. And Fritz knew he was right.

"Get me a rad suit," she shouted to one of the aides standing next to her. "Now!"

"You can't go in there, Commander." Sam Carson was standing behind Fritz. He had been working at a panel along one of the walls, but now he turned toward the chief engineer. "The radiation level in there is off the charts. The suit's not going to be enough."

"There's no choice, Sam." Fritz turned and took the silver radiation suit her aide was handing her. "If we don't get these reactors back online, we're all dead anyway.

"I'll go, Commander." It was Walt Billings.

Carson watched in amazement. Billings was his comrade, and his friend, but he'd never thought of the engineer as a hero before.

You never know what is inside someone until something brings it out…

"No, Lieutenant," Fritz snapped back. "I'll go. You two stay out here and reroute the power supply as soon as I get the connection back online."

"Commander…"

"That's an order, Lieutenant." Fritz moved her hand down to close up the front of the rad suit…and then *Dauntless* gyrated wildly. Showers of sparks rained down from the electrical panels along the wall, and Fritz was thrown across the room.

Carson's eyes darted up, and he saw a heavy steel support, snapped in half and ready to give way. Then, another explosion ripped through the ship, and shards of shattered metal went flying around the room like shrapnel.

Carson fell hard to the ground, landing on his injured arm.

He shouted in pain, but as soon as he looked around the room, he bit back on it. Three of the technicians, at least, were dead, crushed by falling debris. Billings was down, trapped under a girder, but still alive.

"Ooooph…"

Carson heard the moan, and he knew immediately it was Fritz. The engineering chief was struggling to get back to her feet. She had a large bruise across the side of her face, and one eye was rapidly swelling shut. Then he saw it, a shard of metal, maybe forty centimeters in length, protruding from Fritz's shoulder.

She managed to get back to her feet, though she looked like she would fall any moment. Carson could see now how bad the wound was. Fritz's uniform was covered in blood.

"Help me…to the hatch, Sam," she said, clearly struggling with every word.

"Commander, you can't…"

"No choice, Sam…have to get…reactor back online…"

Carson turned his head, staring at the clear barrier between the engineering space and the reaction chamber. It looked harmless enough, no different than where he was kneeling now. But he knew invisible death waited inside that chamber…radiation a hundred times the lethal level. Even more.

"I'll go, Commander…"

"No…Sam…it's too dangerous."

"You'll never make it, Commander. I'm the only one who can do it now."

Fritz stumbled, dropping slowly to her knees.

"No…I can…" She gasped for breath.

"You know there's no choice, Commander. Give me the rad suit…" Miraculously, the shard of metal hadn't hit the open rad suit.

Fritz hesitated, but then she nodded slowly. She moved her arm, wincing in pain as she slid out of the suit. Carson reached over, helping her pull the metallic fabric off. He tried to be as gentle as possible, but it tugged against the chunk of steel in her shoulder, and she let out a loud cry.

"I'm sorry, Commander."

Fritz looked back up at him with teary eyes.

"No, Sam...I'm sorry..."

*   *   *

"All guns concentrate on the midsection...let's pound that ship right at the source of the explosion." Kat hadn't abandoned her caution, not entirely, but she was beginning to believe she had the victory. The enemy ship was still sitting dead in space, no fire, not even any power generation her scanners could detect. It certainly looked like the massive explosion had been some kind of critical hit, and every second the enemy just sat there seemed to confirm that. But she wasn't taking any chances, not with this enemy commander. The area of the explosion had to be the weak point, and she wanted every gun she could bring to bear blasting away at it.

"Yes, Commander." The arrogance was back in Wentus's voice. Kat had always served her people, and despite any private concerns she might have had, she'd always believed in the cult of Palatian strength and superiority. Her people were brave, devoted to duty, and they had prevailed in every war they had faced since they'd broken free of servitude. But now she wondered how they would handle defeat. She'd watched her first officer and the rest of her bridge crew, noting the changes in their moods and tones as the battle ebbed and flowed.

The Alliance had never faced an enemy that could defeat it, not really. The best its smaller foes had managed was to make victory costly. But even on the verge of victory, Kat recognized that this enemy could have prevailed. And she was fairly certain her people realized that too. How would it affect them? Would they push it aside, rewrite the history in their own minds, removing any recollection of potential defeat? That was likely, the solution that was most in line with the Alliance's dogmatic principles. But she knew she would never forget. And she worried what the war with the Confederation would be like...the war her victory was about to bring to her people.

She stared down at her workstation, watching on the screen as her gunnery stations fired. Her crews were racing against each other, she knew, striving to fire the kill shot, the one that destroyed the enemy vessel. But there wouldn't be one, not if the enemy's reactors were down. Not unless there was some kind of magazine full of explosives or something similar. There was no containment to breach on a scragged reactor, no "quick kill" shot that would turn a vessel into a miniature sun. The enemy was helpless, but there were still emergency systems, batteries, scattered pockets of life support. Her people would literally have to slice the enemy vessel to bits…and it was a *big* ship.

"All guns, increase to one hundred ten percent output." It was a strange order, she knew, considering the enemy's apparent status. But there was still something nagging at her, a vague concern that seemed to make no sense. She wanted her adversary blasted to atoms as quickly as possible.

"Yes, Commander…all guns to one hundred ten percent."

* * *

"Fritzie, what's going on down there?

No response. Fritz was *Dauntless*'s last hope…Barron knew that for sure. And if his engineer wasn't responding, something was terribly wrong.

Barron's eyes moved around the bridge, watching his people at their stations. They were pretending to work, though he knew without power there was little any of them could do. But there was no panic.

He was proud, more so than he could adequately describe, and he mourned for them. They were all going to die. They'd put their faith in him, followed his every command to the bitter end. And their reward would be death.

Barron thought of his grandfather, of the talks they'd had about service. They had been few. No doubt Rance Barron had thought there would be time when his young heir was older. But war had come again, and with it this time, the elder Barron's death. Talks postponed became talks that never were, and much of the old man's knowledge had died with him.

You taught me some things, grandfather...but not how to die. And not how to bear the guilt, to watch others die because they followed you. How did you do it? So many terrible battles, so many thousands dead. All of them there because they followed you. How did you endure it?

But he wasn't ready to give up. Not yet. He tapped the com unit.

"Atara?"

"Yes, sir." Travis was down in the main gunnery control center, ready to fire the primaries when the reactors restarted.

"Something's wrong down at the reactor...Fritzie's not answering my com. Get down there as quickly as you can."

"Yes, Captain. I'll report as soon as I'm there. Travis out."

Barron sat in the middle of *Dauntless*'s bridge, the nerve center of one of the Confederation's massive battleships...and he felt utterly helpless. He wanted to run to engineering himself, to see with his own eyes what was happening down there. But that would do no good. His place was here, sitting stern and unflappable...even as he felt himself falling to his doom.

* * *

Sam Carson shoved his legs into the bulky rad suit one at a time. Then he pulled it up, sliding his arms through as well.

"Sam, are you sure?" Fritz was leaning against a nearby wall. There was blood covering the front of her uniform, and a large chunk of jagged steel was still wedged in her shoulder. Her voice had become a scratchy rasp, the pain from her wounds apparent with every word.

"What choice is there, Commander?" Carson looked around the room, his eyes finally landing on the spot where the suit's head covering had landed. If I don't go, we all die." Carson hoped he sounded brave, but inside he was struggling to fight the urge to run for the door. He'd never felt fear like this, and the idea of stepping into that chamber terrified him like nothing he'd ever experienced. But there was no choice.

"You know what to do, right?"

"Yes, Commander. I know."

And if you do it fast enough…if you get out of there in a few minutes, just maybe this suit will be enough to save your life…

"You are a good man, Sam…one of the best I've ever served with…"

"Thank you, Commander." His voice cracked a little as he spoke, but he managed to cling to his fragile control. He knew Fritz meant well, but the last thing he needed now was emotion, to think about what he was about to do. This was an engineering fix and nothing more. At least that was what he told himself… that was what he needed to believe to step into that chamber.

He slid the head piece down over the suit, running his hand over the connecting strip. The rad suit was the best protection Confederation science had developed, but that chamber was full of high energy gamma rays. The suit would offer considerable protection, but it wouldn't block everything.

He stood in front of the airlock for a moment, taking a few deep breaths. The AI control system was down with the ship's main power, so he reached out and opened the emergency panel. There was a handle inside, and he placed his hand around it and pulled.

The door slid open and he stepped in. Then he turned and repeated the process with the interior panel, closing the door behind him.

There was a similar control on the inner door. He opened the panel and stared at it for a moment. When he opened it, the airlock would be flooded with radiation. He didn't know how long he had, what number of minutes and seconds his suit would keep the deadly threat at bay, or at least enough at bay that regen treatments could save his life. But he knew it wasn't long. He didn't have time to waste. *Dauntless* didn't have time to waste.

He reached out, putting his gloved hand on the control. Then his fears burst out from every corner of his mind, images of Lise, of his child…of him doubled over in sickbay, vomiting blood as his body surrendered to radiation sickness. He found himself wishing Billings or Fritz had been able to do this…and then he hated himself for those thoughts. He felt the urge to turn, to run. But he knew that wouldn't save him. If he didn't get the reactor online, he would die anyway. And everyone else on *Dauntless* would die with him.

He felt a sudden burst of determination, and he pulled on the latch. The door slid to the side, and Carson stepped out into the reaction chamber.

Okay, you're in…now do this as quickly as possible, and get the hell out of here.

* * *

Atara Travis raced down the corridor. She'd taken an intra-ship car from the gunnery station, using her command over-rides to divert battery power to the otherwise shut down system. *Dauntless* was a big ship, and the gunnery was almost a kilometer away from main engineering. Right now, seconds counted.

They were fighting for their lives, for the lives of everyone aboard *Dauntless*. And she'd be damned if she was going to let him down. But for the first time, her self-assurance was gone, and she didn't know what to do. She'd been waiting to fire the primaries, to put everything she had into making a single shot count. But now she was racing through the ship's gloomy, par-tially-lit corridors, headed to engineering to see what had hap-pened to Commander Fritz…and if there was any chance at all of getting the reactors back online before *Dauntless* was blown to atoms.

She sucked in a deep breath, pushing her legs harder as she saw the open doors to the section ahead. She raced through… and stopped abruptly. There were bodies everywhere, and wounded men and women. And lying against one of the bulk-heads was Anya Fritz, covered in blood, a huge chunk of metal sunken in her shoulder.

"Anya, what is…" She froze, her eyes fixed on the clear shielding between the engineering deck and the control room of the reaction chamber. The radiation markers were flashing red…and inside the contaminated control room she saw a single figure, clad in a bulky rad suit moving slowly toward the columns of tubes and circuits on the far wall.

"My God," she whispered to herself. Then she looked at Fritz. "Anya, who is that?"

*   *   *

Sam turned his head back and forth, scanning the conduits and control panels in front of him. There was a break, somewhere in the system. It would be an easy fix, he knew, which seemed odd considering the tremendous importance of his task. But first he had to find the malfunction.

He was moving quickly. If he wanted to get out alive, he knew time was his enemy. He could feel the frustration building. The engineering team had been able to isolate the problem, to a certain degree. But he still had to find the damaged connection, and the only way to do that was to check each one in turn.

He could feel his uniform below the metallic fabric, wet, soaked with sweat. The rad suit was hot, like an oven inside, and it was cumbersome, slowing his movements. He was tense, knowing each second that passed might be the last one, the final chance to save *Dauntless*. And he was scared to death, struggling to keep his body from shaking as he worked his way down the line of pipes and wires and conduits that made the reactor function.

Then he saw something. Not the damaged section, but a clue where to find it. It was an alarm, one that had been tripped when the damage occurred. But it was also damaged, its wiring charred.

That's why we didn't get anything on the main panel…

He reached out, holding an instrument he'd pulled from his bag. It was a battery-powered spectrographic scanner. It would pulse energy through the reactor's circuits, not enough to do anything except identify the location of the break. Carson knew it had to be close. The tripped alarm was part of a limited series of connections.

His eyes moved down to the small display on the device, and he felt a wave of excitement. There it was. But his satisfaction was short-lived. He walked about two meters, and he looked up at a bank of equipment ten meters high. And the damage was almost at the top.

He sighed, trying to ignore the clock in his head counting down the minutes until enough radiation would penetrate his suit to build up a lethal dose. He was thankful he didn't have an exact figure on how long he could survive.

Maybe I'm dead already...

There was a small access ladder next to the tower. It was an easy enough climb...for a man who wasn't wearing a baggy, ill-fitting rad suit. But there was no choice.

He reached up, grabbed the highest rung he could reach, stepping up with one foot, then the other. His sweaty hands slid around inside of his gloves, making his grip tenuous as he moved slowly upward. His injured hand ached terribly, and he tried to put most of his weight on the other hand, and his legs.

It felt like hours were passing, but he knew it had just been seconds. Still, he didn't have even seconds to waste, and he pushed harder, climbed more quickly.

Then his eyes locked on one of the panels. He could see the blackened steel around it, and he knew immediately he'd found it. Anya Fritz was the most gifted engineer he'd ever known, and she had scanned and searched every system in *Dauntless*'s reactor. Carson and his comrades had fixed and replaced dozens of components, and Fritz had declared with all the confidence she'd been able to muster that the problem he was now staring at was the last one.

Carson knew that had been a guess when she'd made it, and *Dauntless* had been pounded repeatedly since then. He could repair the severed connection and the reactor could still remain dead, damaged in a five other places, ten. But he couldn't do anything about that.

He pulled the panel off, fumbling with it in the heavy gloves. It finally came free, and slipped from his grasp, clattering loudly on the deck below.

"Damn."

He reached inside the small opening, struggling to pull out

the burnt sections of the connection. He had replacement parts with him. They weren't going to be a perfect fit, but they would do the job. Assuming he could get them in place.

He worked feverishly, the tension and fear making it hard to concentrate. He was rushing, moving too quickly for such fine work. But somehow he was getting it done. The replacement part didn't fit, but he managed to come up with a workaround. It wasn't pretty. In fact, it looked like some mad scientist's wild creation. But it should work…

He pushed the final connection in place, and he tapped the com controls on the side of his suit's headcover. "Commander, I think it's in place. The reactor should be good to go."

"Well done, Sam…now get the hell out of there."

Carson started to scrambled down the ladder, letting the toolkit drop. It hit the deck below with a crash. He felt a burst of hope. He was going to get out…and maybe, just maybe, his fix would do the trick. Captain Barron would have his power…and a chance to win the fight. A chance for all of them to survive.

Then the ship shook. Another hit.

Carson felt himself jerked hard, and he tightened his grip, struggling to hold onto the ladder. He held firm, for a few seconds. Then *Dauntless* shook again, and he felt his hand slip off the rung. He held for a second, perhaps two or three, nothing but his injured hand gripping the ladder. The pain was intense, fire shooting up from his arm, through his chest.

He felt the shattered arm giving way, his body slipping off the ladder. Then falling…and landing on the deck, hard, his face mask slamming into the solid metal floor.

His body was wracked with pain, his arm, his chest. He'd broken several ribs, he could feel that for sure. And the clear inside of his mask was splattered with blood.

The cracked, shattered mask, with a gaping hole in the center…

There was a strange sensation, a tingling feeling he'd never experienced before. He remembered his training, the classes at the Academy. Radiation was a silent killer, unnoticeable, invisible.

Except at massive levels…when it could actually be *felt*.

He felt himself beginning to lose consciousness.

"Lise, I'm sorry…"

Chapter Thirty-Eight

"Commander, we're picking up energy readings from the enemy vessel." There was surprise in Wentus's voice. And confusion.

Kat didn't answer. She looked down at her screen, staring at the numbers. The scanners were imperfect, inexact. But the power spike was massive. This was no set of batteries kicking in, no emergency power source. It was the enemy's main reactor. It couldn't be anything else.

And that means...

She felt a coldness inside her, a realization.

"All engines, reverse thrust." But even as she gave the command she knew it was too late.

"Commander..."

"Now! Full power, reverse thrust."

"Yes, Commander."

Her eyes were on her own screen, reading the incoming scanner data. The numbers didn't lie—the enemy had managed to restart their reactors. Was it a desperate repair job, an attempt to ward off imminent destruction? Or...

Or was I lured in? Was their reactor failure feigned?

She tried to imagine the raw courage and grit it would take to willingly shut down a ship's reactors, to sit and endure a pounding without answer, all to lure your enemy forward. It seemed too fantastic to believe...but then she thought about the enemy commander, about the concern she had felt all through this encounter. If this was deliberate, he'd have to have a plan to make it work, to make the risk worthwhile...and that could only mean one thing.

Those primaries...

Is it possible? That a captain would take that kind of chance to gain surprise?

"Evasive maneuvers...now!" Kat shouted out the orders, even as she realized it was too late. *Invictus* was less than sixty-thousand kilometers from the Confed ship, and even decelerating at maximum thrust, the existing momentum would take her ship to within fifty thousand kilometers before it halted.

"Yes, Commander...initiating evasive maneuvers." She could tell from the confusion in Wentus's voice her first officer hadn't yet come to the conclusion she had. She hoped he was right, that her fears were ungrounded. But she didn't believe that, not for a second.

She stared at the symbol on her display representing the enemy ship, and she wondered who was in command, what kind of man or woman she had faced in this death match over the past ten days.

Who are you?

* * *

"Maximum power to the primaries. I want those guns charged now!" Barron was leaning forward in his chair. He hadn't heard anything from engineering. Then the bridge lights came on, and the main display rebooted. One glance down at the power monitors told him Fritzie had gotten it done. *Dauntless*'s reactors were back online.

"Yes, Captain." Darrow's voice was haggard, the pressure

and strain clearly beginning to take its toll. But there was excitement too, crackling in his words as it was all across *Dauntless's* bridge. They weren't out of the fight yet. They still had a chance.

"Captain…" Travis's voice came through on his headset. She sounded exhausted, and there was something wrong, he could tell. But her words were music to his ears. "Both reactors restarted and operating. Power flow to primaries operating on full."

"Well done, Atara. My congratulations to everyone down there." He paused, then asked: "Fritzie?"

"She's wounded, sir, but I think she'll make it. There are a lot of casualties down here…" It sounded like she was going to add something, but she remained silent.

Barron swung his head toward Darrow. "Time until full charge?"

"Forty-five seconds, sir."

"Captain, there's no way I can get to a firing station, not in less than a minute." Travis's words were loud in his ears.

"Call gunnery, Atara. You would know who's…"

"There's no one there, sir. The gun crews have suffered heavy losses, and all reserves are in the outer turrets. There's nobody in main fire control now."

Barron felt his stomach clench. His wild gamble, the heroism of his people in pulling it off…and now there was no one available to fire the guns.

The ship's AI…

"Captain…the enemy is decelerating. And they are beginning evasive maneuvers."

How could they have reacted so quickly? What kind of mind reader am I up against here?

Barron opened his mouth to order the ship's AI to fire the primaries. The computer did most of the work on any shot, but the touch of an experienced gunner often made the difference between a near miss and a devastating hit, especially when the target was trying to evade. Barron wasn't sure if he believed completely in intuition, but the stats backed him up. Gunner-assisted shots had a much higher hit probability than unaided computer targeting. It defied explanation, but it was a documented fact.

But I don't have anybody to fire…

"Captain, you have to do it." Travis's words floated in the air around him, seeming unreal at first. But then he realized she was serious.

"I'm not the gunner you are, Atara."

"You learned gunnery at the Academy, just as I did…and there's no one I'd rather have at the controls than you."

Barron was about to argue again, but Darrow's voice interrupted him. "Fifteen seconds to full charge, sir."

As if to emphasize the point, *Dauntless* shook again, another hit slamming into her. Barron took a deep breath. There was no choice.

He jumped up from his seat, rushing toward Travis's station, waving Darrow away as he did. He landed hard in the chair, his hands on the controls, bringing up the targeting screen. The AI was already calculating firing solutions, displaying them on the scanner.

He was tense, his muscles twisted into rigid knots. He knew he needed to relax, to watch the target's attempts to evade, to let his mind run free, to sync with the enemy.

What will you do? Which way will you go?

The enemy's positioning jets could only minimally affect its vector…but even a move of a ship length was enough to evade a shot.

"Primaries charged, sir."

Barron stared right at the screen, shutting out the world. He pushed aside his thoughts—memories of his grandfather, concerns about his crew, his own fears—banishing them all. There was nothing, nothing save the enemy ship, and *Dauntless's* deadly primaries.

He reached out, stretched his fingers, and closed them on the firing control. He moved the lever, too much at first and then back, more gently. His gaze was focused, his hand tight, ready.

He moved his wrist again, just a small tap. And he pressed

his finger, firing.

His eyes darted up to the display, watching for a scanning report. And then it came. He'd missed clean.

He felt despair rising up from inside. He'd let them down, all of them. His people would die, and the Confederation would face a two front war...all because his aim had been off.

"Captain." It was Travis. "The primaries are still online. We're recharging them now for another shot."

Barron felt his spirits rise again, and the tension in his gut worsen. He stared at the targeting display, waiting. Thirty seconds to full charge.

Dauntless gyrated again, yet another hit. The enemy was targeting the savaged launch bay. It was an unexpected benefit of Barron's ruse. He'd wanted the enemy to believe his ship was crippled...but it hadn't occurred to him they would target the area they believed was vulnerable.

They weren't wrong—the bay was destroyed, and the inner compartments exposed, unprotected. But there was nothing there, nothing important, at least. Just Bulkhead Eight, the entrance to the quarters of the fighter wing. And his pilots weren't there. They were floating around the system in their exhausted craft, waiting to be picked up. Or they were dead. Either way, their quarters were about the least vital spot on *Dauntless* right now.

He was impressed with the enemy captain's insight and attention to detail. But this time it had served his purposes instead, bought him time. Time for a second shot.

He stared intently at the scope, tapping one way, then the other. He could see the countdown clock...*five...four...*

He gripped the firing control and sucked in a deep breath. *Two...one...*

He tapped the control again. Then once more, just a tiny adjustment. The bridge was silent, and he knew his officers were staring at him, watching to see if he would hit the enemy, and do enough damage to give them a chance in the fight. Or if their hopes would vanish with another missed shot.

Barron closed everything out of his mind. There was nothing but the enemy ship, and his guns. He felt his finger moving, slowly, deliberately. Almost there. Then, at the last instant, he moved the controls over, adjusting the shot one last time and firing. He felt the vibration under his feet as the big guns fired, and his eyes caught the flashing red light, the overload warning. He'd gotten two shots from his tortured main guns, but there wouldn't be a third. Not this side of a space dock.

He leaned back, his body aching, exhausted, drained. And then he heard the cheers.

His turned and looked back at the main display. The enemy ship's icon was flashing. He'd scored a direct hit with both primaries. It was too early for significant damage assessments, but he could see the enemy power levels dropping. Hard. Their fire stopped too—much of it, at least. There were three batteries left firing. All the rest were silent now.

He felt a rush of excitement, but he bit down on it. The battle wasn't over. Not yet.

"I want full thrust toward the enemy, Lieutenant. Immediately. All functional secondaries…open fire."

It was time to end this.

Chapter Thirty-Nine

CFS Dauntless
Krillus Asteroid Belt
40, 500,000 kilometers from Santis, Krillus IV
307 AC

Barron stared at the main display, at the woman standing amid the smoke and wreckage of her ship's shattered bridge. She wore a uniform that looked as if it had once been spotless and perfectly-tailored. But it was torn now, half a dozen rips cutting across at different spots. It was filthy too, covered with all sorts of soot and debris…and if Barron wasn't mistaken, some blood too.

He'd called off his gunners when the scanning reports showed the enemy's reactors were down, the last of its guns silenced. Confederation ships did not destroy helpless opponents. The navy adhered to a strict code of honor, the precepts of which had been laid down by none other than his grandfather. And apart from honor, he felt something for this mysterious enemy captain. Anger, of course, rage at the losses his people had suffered. But more than that. Respect.

"This is Captain Tyler Barron, commanding CFS *Dauntless*. Identify yourself."

The woman stood at something that resembled attention, though Barron could see that her leg was badly injured.

"I am Commander-Princeps Katrine Rigellus. I am…I am acting under my own authority as commander of my ship, *Invictus*."

Barron frowned. She was hiding something…or, more accurately, she was holding back.

"We know your ship is an Alliance vessel, Captain. Why attempt subterfuge?" He could see that she was uncomfortable, and she paused before answering.

"It is not subterfuge, Captain. We all obey our orders, do we not?"

"Then you do not deny that you are from the Alliance?"

"I neither confirm nor deny anything, Captain, save to say duty compels me to remain silent."

"Then why did you attack Santis, why did you attack my ship?"

"I accepted your communication request because I have come to respect your ability, Captain. But duty is my master, as I suspect it is yours. And mine now demands silence."

"There is no reason for hostilities between our people, Commander. Your attack was without cause or provocation. We have both paid a great price for this pointless conflict."

"You know little about us, Captain. And we know just as little of your Confederation. My superiors' analysis of your people was inaccurate. I am afraid they allowed themselves to be misled by others, and they have done your people a disservice." Katrine paused for a few seconds. "You are clearly a strong warrior, Captain, a capable leader. Your people are fortunate to have you."

Barron stared at the image on the screen, finding himself strangely affected by this enemy officer. Her actions had killed his people, almost killed him. The attack had been unwarranted. Still, he could sense a nobility in the woman on the screen in front of him. "As are you, Commander. But the battle is over, your ship disabled. If you surrender now…"

"That is not our way, Captain." Barron could see the sadness in her eyes, but also determination. He felt a coldness in his stomach, a fear for what this officer intended to do.

"There is no need for more of your people to die, Commander. I am sure that after appropriate diplomatic contacts are initiated, we will be able to allow you to return home."

She smiled. It was weak, tentative, but it was a smile nevertheless. "We are different, Captain, your people and mine. Our ways are not yours. Yet, you would be a fitting ally, and I regret that we met as enemies and not friends. Still, there is hope that some good may come from all of this. My people value strength above all things. When *Invictus* fails to return, the Council will suspend all planned operations against the Confederation. Your victory has proven your people to be warriors, to be respected. You will be spared the burdens of a two-front war." She paused, clearly in pain, shifting her weight. "Perhaps all is for the best here, for my victory could only have brought war and death down upon both my people and yours. Now, perhaps mine can enjoy peace, at least for a time. And yours can concentrate on defeating your longtime enemy." She paused. "If my death offers a future as neighbors, perhaps even as allies, then it will not have been in vain."

"I say again, Commander, there is no reason for you to die. The Union no doubt deceived your people. I will stand with you, urge for your survivors to be released as quickly as possible."

"No. I thank you for your words, and I know you speak from your conception of honor. But there is no route back for us. We have a saying among my people, Captain. *The way is the way.* We do not surrender. We do not return home in defeat. For us, there is only one alternative to victory. And one last duty for me to perform."

Barron stood in front of his chair, watching the woman on the screen, so recently his enemy…and now, what? He didn't know her, but for reasons he couldn't fully explain, he felt himself mourning her imminent death. He blamed her for the losses he'd suffered, but now all he could feel was regret that he'd been compelled to destroy her.

He'd felt rage during the battle, but as he listened to her words, he began to understand. She had been created even as he had, destined from birth to fill a role. The culture that had molded her was different from the one that had formed his views. But he suspected they had much in common. She'd never had a choice. In her own way, she was doing her duty, even as he had been. He could think of a hundred reasons to hate her, but in spite of them all, he realized he respected her. Given time, he even believed he could even grow to like her. To call her friend.

"Commander…" He'd intended to try one last time to persuade her, but even as he'd begun, she started to shake her head, and he realized she was as bound to what she was as much as he.

"Farewell, Captain Tyler Barron. My regards, and my respect to a fellow warrior. Join your people, and fight the war that is like to come upon you. I ask but one thing of you. If, in the fullness of time, our people do become allies…know that my spirit rides to battle with you. For it would be an honor to serve at your side and not against you. Good fortune to you, and to all who serve you."

With that the screen went dark, and Tyler Barron sat long, staring at the blackness where his enemy had been moments before.

* * *

Kat had stood while she addressed Captain Barron. He'd been a worthy adversary, an opponent a true warrior could only respect, and she had treated him as such. But now she sat down. *Invictus*'s bridge was a smoke-filled wreck, most of her officers dead. Wentus was still alive, though he was mortally wounded and barely conscious. She wasn't sure how many of her people were still alive in other sections of the ship. A significant number, no doubt, though she was sure hundreds were already dead.

Now that she'd cut the com line, she sat down. It was odd that amid the destruction and defeat, the disgrace and the shadow of death upon her, she should still have a fleeting thought once again about how comfortable her chair was. She almost laughed.

She reached down and pulled up the mini tablet she kept in the compartment next to her seat. She flicked her finger across it, and it lit up, displaying a photo. A young boy and girl. Her children. She ran her fingers over their images, and she felt strange, her eyes moist, wet with tears.

Alliance warriors don't cry...

But for all the forcefulness of her thought, all the decades of training and indoctrination, the discipline bred into her soul, she could feel the tears streaming down her cheeks. She didn't cry over her imminent death, nor even the realization that she would never see her children again, though that tore at her like knives slicing through her heart.

No, it was none of those things that had broken her. It was the realization that her children would follow her example. They would be raised as the next generation of the Regulli, as heirs to the family tradition of service and unswerving devotion to duty. They would be just as she had been. Even if they had questions, doubts, they would bury them and follow their orders. They would fight...and they would likely win glory. Until one day each came to the pass she had, the final defeat. The thought of her children staring into the same abyss yawning before her was the final blow.

She heard the com unit buzz. Captain Barron again, she knew, probably intent on making one more appeal for her to surrender. She knew the enemy commander meant well...but all the buzzing did was torment her, to tease her with glimpses of survival she knew could never be.

The children were still there in her mind, amid scenes of darkness. She tried to push the bleak thoughts aside, but they were there, clear and resolute despite all her attempts to ignore them. Each of her children, years from now, grown, blood-covered and battered, driven on by rage, by the thought of their mother, dead so many years before. They would fight, and they would find their end, death's bitter harvest in some battle years from now.

Just as I at this moment...

She felt sadness for her crew, and guilt at having failed them. Yet there was a spark of light too, gladness that at least the deaths of her people might avert war with the Confeds. Indeed, it almost certainly would. Her fall, at the hands of a single enemy vessel, shameful as it was to her legacy, would force the high command to rethink Confederation capabilities. She had no doubt they would cancel the proposed invasion, and that would save thousands of lives. Millions.

She stared back at the image of her children, seeing them now, for just a moment, not as they would look in the future, but as they appeared in the image. The Ordeal, their lives as warriors…all of it was far away from today, in the future. There would be good years at Litora Montis…hunts and fishing expeditions, and long hikes in the mountains. They would be well cared for, she knew, as the inheritors of the Rigellus estates and wealth. And Tarkus would protect them, care for them. They would be happy, she hoped, at least for many years, though she felt a twinge of pain to think of them joyous without her.

Live well, my children. Enjoy the days and the nights before duty claims you…and remember, your mother loves you always…

She took a deep breath, staring down at the tablet image as a single tear dropped from her face and hit the screen. Then, a moment later, she set it down and reached over to her control panel. "Ship control, this is Commander-Princeps Katrine Rigellus."

"Commander-Princeps Katrine Rigellus, officer in command, AS *Invictus*. Recognized."

"On my authority, initiate sequence Omega-0."

"Sequence Omega-0 initiated. Ten second countdown begun."

She closed her eyes. She had done all that was required of her, all that duty demanded. She would die now as she had lived.

Seven…

She thought back, to the births of her children, to her days as a child herself. Now she would find her end far from home and leave her children to grow up without her, just as her own father had done.

Five…

She tried hard to cling to her faith, to hold on, even as the seconds counted down, to all she had believed during her life.

Three.

"The way is the way…"

There was doubt there now as she repeated the mantra, questions she could no longer suppress. But she didn't have to. Not anymore. For her, duty was over.

One...zero.

Deep within *Invictus*, a cache of hydrogen bombs detonated, and in a fraction of a second, the Alliance's largest and proudest ship ceased to exist, vaporized in the fury of nuclear fusion. For a few seconds, the remnants of Katrine Rigellus and *Invictus* remained, a miniature sun, expanding briefly and then contracting, fading away and leaving nothing behind but the emptiness of space.

Chapter Forty

The battle was over, a victory, if anything so costly could be thus characterized. *Dauntless*'s crew had suffered terribly, but none worse than its ravaged fighter wing. The losses they had suffered were devastating. The training manuals stated that any combat unit taking casualties at such a level was effectively destroyed. But the fighter pilots were cut from tough cloth, and they accepted that they flew each mission with death as a wingman. And as a group, they'd be damned if they were destroyed, or anything like it. Each and every one of them was ready to respond if the claxons rang again, even now, to move grimly down to the bays and launch once again into combat.

But there was no call to arms now, no battlestations lamps glowing red or alarms ripping through the air. The survivors were gathered, as was their tradition, to sit up long into the night, to drink, to be there for each other…and to send off those they had lost.

"To Ice." Jake Stockton raised the silver mug above his head. His usually confident voice was tentative, shaken. He looked at the others, eleven men and seven women…all that remained of *Dauntless*'s fighter wing.

"To Ice," Kyle Jamison said, raising his own mug. "And to the others we lost here. Courageous warriors all. Heroes of the Confederation."

"Heroes of the Confederation!" The others repeated the toast in something that came close to unison.

The pilots in the room knew they were lucky to be alive. They had survived more than the battle itself, nightmare that it had been. Most of them had also been low on life support by the time the wounded *Dauntless* had managed to track them all down and tow them aboard. It had been a slow process, towing each fighter aboard the wounded mothership, and by the time Stockton had been brought in he was unconscious, moments from suffocation.

Stockton looked around the room. It wasn't the pilots' usual officer's club. Indeed, they weren't even behind Bulkhead Eight, the traditional partition of a Confederation fighter wing's territory on a mother ship. Their quarters had been destroyed, everything behind Eight a total loss. Possessions, uniforms, personal items...all gone, incinerated or blown into space. But Stockton didn't care, not even about the year's salary worth of poker chips that had been vaporized...or were floating around the Krillus system somewhere. His thoughts were with dead pilots, and one in particular, a man who had been his rival, and who had saved his life.

"The last thing Ice would have wanted would be for you to brood over his death, Jake." Jamison leaned in, putting his hand on his friend's shoulder. "We're pilots...we drink and send off our dead, and then we move on to the next battle."

They all knew there would be a next battle. Whatever had happened at Santis—and there were all kinds of rumors flying around—there was little doubt that even if the prospect of full scale war with the Alliance had receded, the Union threat remained. War was still imminent, if not here, then on the distant border, where *Dauntless* had spent ten months patrolling. It would take some time before the ship's extensive damage could be repaired, but there was little doubt they would find themselves in the middle of the fight again.

Stockton looked at his friend, his expression somber. "You're right, of course, Kyle, but…"

"No buts, Raptor. The Confederation needs you, it needs all of us. And if Ice were here, he'd be the first one to tell you that. Mourn the dead…but look to the future, to the fight to come."

Stockton sat still for a moment. Then he nodded gently and raised his mug. "The fight to come."

* * *

"You're going to make it, Sam…you just have to hang on." Walt Billings sat in a powered chair at his friend's side, leaning forward, his hand on Carson's arm. Billings' legs were gone at the knee. A regeneration procedure would return the injured engineer to duty, but that would have to wait. *Dauntless*'s sickbay was as battered as the rest of the vessel, and Billings would have to endure the confines of his chair until they reached Archellia, and the facilities needed to grow him a new pair of legs.

"You're…good…liar…" Sam Carson's voice was a barely audible rasp. The engineer had spent the last day doubled over, vomiting incessantly. Doctor Weldon had done everything he could, given Carson every drug available, both to treat his radiation sickness and to alleviate his symptoms.

Barron stood just inside the door, next to Dr. Weldon. He'd watched as Billings spoke to his friend, trying vainly to cheer up the dying man.

"Is there anything else you can do, Stu?"

Weldon sighed softly. "I'm sorry, Ty. He was too far gone by the time they got him out of that chamber. There was never anything I could do but try to make him comfortable."

"How long?" Sam Carson had been one of the most popular members of the crew, with the ship's captain no less than with his peers. And he had saved all their lives. If Carson hadn't gotten the reactors back online, Barron knew none of his people would have survived.

"He'll die today. A couple hours. Maybe three or four."

Barron just nodded. Then he walked forward, nodding again

to Billings before he knelt beside the stricken officer. "Hello, Sam." He paused, then he realized Carson couldn't see him from that angle. He leaned forward. "It's Tyler Barron."

"Captain…" Carson tried to move his head, and Barron could see from his lack of success just how weak the man was. "Sorry, sir…can't…move…much…"

"Don't apologize, Sam. You're a hero. You saved us all. Commander Fritz told me what you did. I just wanted to say…thank you." Barron paused. It wouldn't do Carson any good if he lost it. But his words alone sounded so pointless, so inadequate.

"Did…my…duty…"

"Yes, Sam…you did your duty. And more."

"Fritz?"

"She'll be okay, Sam. She's in surgery now or I'm sure she'd be here."

"How…long?"

"How long?"

"Do…I…have…"

Barron felt a lump in his throat. He struggled to force out the words, to keep his voice even. He thought about lying, about insisting Carson still had a chance. But it seemed beneath the dignity of the courageous engineer, less than he deserved, however well meaning the attempt at deceit might be. "Dr. Weldon says a few hours, Sam." A pause. "At most."

Carson exhaled softly.

"Tablet?"

Barron shook his head. "I don't know what you…"

"He wants this, sir." Billings extended his arm toward the captain. He held a small tablet in his hand.

Barron took the device and looked down at it, moving his finger across to activate it. A small image appeared on the small screen, a woman, attractive but looking exhausted…and in her arms, a baby.

Barron felt his emotions surging up inside him—guilt, anger. Sadness.

He reached down, taking Carson's arm, putting the tablet in his hand. The device fell, the dying man's hands too weak to hold it. Barron picked it up, moving it in front of Carson's eyes. He stood for a moment, and then he felt Billings reaching over, taking the tablet. "I can hold it for him, sir…I know you're busy."

Barron felt another pang. He *was* busy. *Dauntless* was a wreck, half its engineering staff in sickbay. For that matter, half its crew dead or wounded. And, while he believed what Commander Rigellus had told him, he had no proof that there weren't other Alliance forces on the way even now. Still, the idea of not having time for a dying man, one who had saved all their lives…it made him feel small, cold.

"Really, Captain…he's in and out. I don't even think he's still here, not really."

"You're a good man, Walt." Barron looked down at the lieutenant. "Stay with him, will you? Until…the end."

"I will, sir. You have my word."

Barron just nodded. Then he took one last look at Carson, and he turned and walked toward the door.

Chapter Forty-One

From the Log of Captain Tyler Barron

War. It is feared, glorified. A last resort or a cold-blooded way to achieve governmental ends. An ancient quote, its origins long lost in pre-cataclysmic history, called it the 'final argument of kings.'

I have experienced it now, in all its unsavory horror. I have watched those who served with me die, some quickly, vaporized in a fraction of a second. Others, slowly, lingering in fear and agony as their lives slipped away. I have even come to mourn for an enemy, one I also hate for the death she brought upon my people.

I always wondered why my grandfather spent so little time telling me about the great battles fought. I couldn't understand why he always turned the topic to fishing or the family estate... or any topic far from the travails of the battlefield. Now, I think, I understand him far better. I can perceive, at least in a small way, the demons that must have haunted his sleep and preyed on his mind.

I am a good son of the navy, and I serve the Confederation and its duly-constituted government. Yet, I question now the justice of men and women casting a nation into war when they have not themselves experienced it, or paid its terrible price. I do not long for a military dictatorship—far from it. We are surrounded by brutal regimes where freedom is a forgotten ideal. Yet, it sickens me to think of politicians who have never heard a shot fired making a decision that will send thousands of good men and women to hideous deaths.

I know war with the Union beckons, that my crew's respite will be but a short one before the trumpet again calls us. And we will answer, as those before us did, as my grandfather did. And in this war to come, as in those that preceded it, there will be a Barron on the front lines.

CFS Dauntless
In Space Dock
Archellia, Cassiopolis III
308 AC

Tyler Barron stood on the platform, watching solemnly as canister after canister rolled slowly from *Dauntless*'s main cargo hatch, to the accompaniment of the Confederation's anthem. Each of those two meter tubes carried one of his crew, the physical manifestation of the cost of his great "victory." He knew their sacrifices hadn't been in vain, that defeating the enemy battleship had likely averted war with the Alliance, and spared the Confederation the nightmare of a two-front battle. But standing there watching the seemingly endless procession, listening to the poor quality recording blaring through the speakers, he couldn't help but think his people deserved better.

There was an honor guard, of sorts, though it had been cobbled together from base security instead of the Marines who normally would have filled the role. Half of Archellia's Marines were on the way to Santis, and the other half were on full alert, manning their defensive positions.

He thought of his own Marines, at least the few that remained. He'd read the reports of their final battle, of another victory that seemed bitter because of its cost. His ground forces had lost no less than seventy percent of their number, and the Marines originally posted to the planet had four survivors out of forty. But, miraculously, they had defeated the enemy, in a fight that had gone on to the death.

He had hated to leave his battered troops behind, but there

had been no choice. He couldn't leave the planet unguarded, and even thirty-seven exhausted Marines could put up a fight if necessary…as the original garrison had proven. The reinforcements bound for Santis would garrison the tritium facilities and retake the battered space station, and the ships carrying them to the Rim would return with *Dauntless*'s survivors. That esteemed group included four hardy souls from the original force, including Sergeant Clete Hargraves and the officer that worthy noncom had saved beyond all hope, Lieutenant Luke Plunkett. Barron had been sorry there hadn't been time for him to meet those Marines, and he hoped he'd have the chance one day.

He was confident the Alliance threat had evaporated, that Commander Rigellus's words had been truthful and accurate. But he couldn't argue against taking precautions. Any Alliance invasion would depend on taking and holding Santis, and after what the outnumbered Marines had accomplished there, he had little doubt the five hundred now en route could hold the place indefinitely against any attack the Alliance mounted over such a distance.

His eyes panned around the cavernous room. Many of the crew were there, silently paying their respects to fallen comrades. But there were no crowds of families, no groups of mourning friends. None of his crew had been from Archellia, save one. And in all the great vastness of the bay, there was only one person not part of *Dauntless*'s crew and not on duty. No, two people.

Barron looked across the bay at Sam Carson's widow. Lise Varov was a naval officer too, and she was clad in her dress blues, standing silent, motionless, an infant cradled in her arms. She stood almost at attention, clearly struggling to keep herself together. Barron knew he would only shatter her tenuous control if he went over and spoke with her, but he also knew he had no choice. He owed it to Sam.

He walked across the room, conscious of the sound his boots made on the metal floor. Varov saw him coming about halfway there, and she turned to face him.

"Lieutenant Varov…I just wanted to express my deepest regrets for your loss." Barron could see the tears welling up in her eyes, her efforts to hold them back.

"Thank you, Captain, but please, call me Lise." Her voice was soft, tentative. "You're very kind."

"Sam was an extraordinary officer, Lise. You should know he was truly a hero. He died saving his comrades—everyone on *Dauntless*. Our survival likely averted a war with the Alliance, which means he died to protect Archellia as well. To protect you, and his son."

Varov gasped a breath, losing her struggle to hold back the tears. "He will never see his son, Captain. And my child will never know his father."

Barron was fishing for words, knowing nothing he said would be adequate. "I can't imagine your pain, Lise. And please call me Tyler...none of this captain foolishness." He hesitated, again unsure what else to say. "I considered Sam my friend, Lise, as well as one of my crew. Whatever you need...if there is ever anything I can do for you, now or ten years from now, all you have to do is ask."

She looked back at Barron, tears streaming down her cheeks now. "Thank you, Ca...Tyler. You are a good man. I can see why Sam felt he needed to go with you."

Barron felt her words like daggers. He knew she meant them as a compliment, but they only reminded him that he had led his people to Santis. They had followed him there, and nearly a quarter of them had come back in sleek, metallic coffins. Including Sam Carson.

Words failed him, and he stood silently for a moment, finally saying simply, "Remember, if there's ever anything you need..."

Lise nodded and swiped at the tears on her cheeks. "Thank you, Tyler."

Barron returned the nod...and he stood quietly for a moment. Then he turned and walked slowly toward the exit. He'd never been the kind of officer to crave battle, to seek glory. But he felt empty now, desolate.

Can this be what you felt, grandfather? Amid the parades, the celebrations, the endless honors, were you as hollowed out inside as I am now?

He wanted to flee, to resign his commission and retire to

his family estates…anyplace where no more men and women would die because they followed his orders. But he knew he couldn't, and now another person was there in this thoughts, one he hardly knew but also one he was realizing had a great impact on him.

There would be no resignation, no retreat to the family manor. Barron was a creature of duty, as fixed on his path as Katrine Rigellus had been. She'd been a noble warrior trapped in bad cause, an example of the cost such devotion extracted… and he knew in her words he had seen his own future.

Epilogue

Tyler Barron sat at the small desk in his quarters. It was quiet, peaceful—at least when the repair crews weren't in some nearby compartment, repairing one bit of battle damage after another.

His workstation's screen displayed repair reports, requisitions, supply manifests…all the things that made command of a battleship seem like drudgery. But his eyes had glazed over, drifted to the tablet in his hands. The small display held text, the final chapter of the history volume *Dauntless*'s captain had been carrying around for over a year now. He'd finally gotten through it, almost, and he was determined that nothing would stop him from finishing. Not this close to the end.

He was glad, at least, to be back onboard *Dauntless*. His battleship had been a wreck when he'd gotten her back to Archellia base, it's corridors and compartments shattered wastelands, as often as not stained red with the blood of those who had died at their stations. Barron had been relieved at first to get off *Dauntless*, to flee from the haunting of those whom he had led to death. But four months in the Starfire Suite had been more than he could take. The Archellians had fawned over his as the descendant of the great Rance Barron, but now he was the man who had saved them from Alliance invasion. At least that's the way they'd insisted on seeing it. The steady stream of dinners and other festivities grew to a veritable avalanche, one which had begun to threaten his sanity. It had been nothing but a relief when Fritzie had told him *Dauntless*'s officers' and crews' quarters were again habitable.

Barron had executed a hasty retreat, thanking the local authorities for the luxurious accommodations and assuring them he would have stayed longer had the vital repairs to his ship not called. In truth, Barron was just about useless amid the crowd of engineers and technicians gradually rebuilding *Dauntless*. But it was a good excuse, and he jumped on it.

He glanced down at the tablet, leaning back in his chair, his eyes finding the last spot he'd read. He'd gotten through perhaps fifty words when the com unit buzzed.

"Yes?" He tried, with limited success, to keep the annoyance from his voice.

"Captain, it's Atara."

He knew immediately something was wrong. Atara Travis was the steadiest officer he'd ever known, as cool as a block of ice, even under fire. But he could hear the tension in her voice.

"What is it, Atara?" But he knew already.

"The base just received a Priority One flash com, sir." She paused, and he could hear her swallowing hard. "The war…it's begun. Union forces have invaded Confederation space all along the border."

Barron put the tablet down on the desk, carelessly. It slid off a stack of reports and fell to the floor, shattering.

"Get the word to the crew, Atara. All leaves are canceled. And find Fritzie. I think she's somewhere on alpha bay. The two of you get up here. We just ran out of time. We've got to figure out how quickly we can get *Dauntless* underway, repairs finished or not.

"Yes, sir. I agree." There was a short pause. Then: "Travis out."

Barron took a deep breath and looked down at the floor, at the shards of glass that had been his tablet.

I'm never going to finish that book…

Call to Arms (Blood on the Stars II)
Available Now for Preorder
(Release January 27, 2017)

Also By Jay Allan

Marines (Crimson Worlds I)
The Cost of Victory (Crimson Worlds II)
A Little Rebellion (Crimson Worlds III)
The First Imperium (Crimson Worlds IV)
The Line Must Hold (Crimson Worlds V)
To Hell's Heart (Crimson Worlds VI)
The Shadow Legions(Crimson Worlds VII)
Even Legends Die (Crimson Worlds VIII)
The Fall (Crimson Worlds IX)
War Stories (Crimson World Prequels)
MERCS (Successors I)
The Prisoner of Eldaron (Successors II)
Into the Darkness (Refugees I)
Shadows of the Gods (Refugees II)
Revenge of the Ancients (Refugees III)
Winds of Vengeance (Refugees IV)
Shadow of Empire (Far Stars I)
Enemy in the Dark (Far Stars II)
Funeral Games (Far Stars III)
Blackhawk (Far Stars Legends I)
The Dragon's Banner
Gehenna Dawn (Portal Wars I)
The Ten Thousand (Portal Wars II)
Homefront (Portal Wars III)

www.jayallanbooks.com
www.bloodonthestars.com
www.wolfsclaw.com
www.crimsonworlds.com